DUNGEON ETERNIUM

THE DIVINE DUNGEON
BOOK 5

DAKOTA KROUT

MOUNTAINDALE
PRESS

ACKNOWLEDGMENTS

There are many people who have made this book possible. As always, the first among them is my *amazing* wife, who always encourages me to do the best at any task I set my mind to. She keeps me motivated and makes every issue seem trivial.

A thank you to my daughter, who reminds me why I am working so hard. You are a great kid.

A special thank you to all of my patrons, who supply me with an endless stream of coffee, but especially to: Nicholas Schmidt, Justin Williams, Samuel Landrie, Blas Agosto, William Merrick, Brayden Wallach, John Grover, Zachary Meyers, Dominic Q Roddan, Noel Stoios, and Keifer Gibbs!

Last of all, thank you. You made it all the way to the end of the series! It is a bittersweet moment for me, but a part of the journey is the end. Once more, thank you for being the best fans and friends I could ask for.

PROLOGUE

"This is the most amazing thing I have ever seen. The *best* feeling in the world. Abyss, everything even *sounds* different," Dale marveled, looking around with shining eyes. "I am faster, stronger, and my senses…! The B-ranks… I never imagined I could feel this *powerful*."

The Master stared at Dale with a troubled expression. "You… you are in the *B-Ranks*. You, a Mage! I… I don't understand *how*."

Dale moved his hand through the air, marveling at the incredible power he could feel. The Mana wasn't moving *through* his body, his body *was* Mana! His flesh had been transformed into something more than human; no previous increase in rank had hinted that achieving the B-ranks would be so drastically different.

He spoke in a nearly dreamy tone, hardly able to believe that this powerful voice was coming out of his mouth, "It was the water. When I created a coating of disenchanting water on myself and maintained it for long enough, I cut off all external sources of Essence. Then with my body drained of power, a hint of Spiritual power got through and grazed me ever so slightly. Instead of destroying me as I had expected, the energy flowed along and empowered the bond between myself and the dungeon."

The Master's eyes widened as he comprehended the next steps that must have occurred. "You *share a soul*! Since Cal is already bonded to a **Law**, the Spiritual energy must have sparked a preemptive ascension! *Tell me*! Did you need to climb the tower?"

<He couldn't have made it to the top of the tower on his own.> I scoffed at The Master even though I knew he couldn't hear me. Conversely, Dale could. Heh.

"I didn't," Dale admitted easily, his face shining with purest excitement. "All I did was interact with the **Law**, **Acme**."

"Bypassing the restrictions of the soul? Maybe there *is* a chance," The Master muttered softly. The eyes of the powerful cultivator went vacant as he pondered the implications, "Maybe I *could*–"

<Hey! Dale! Nice work!> I cheered for my human, and I knew he appreciated it no matter how much he pretended to dislike me. <Now, sorry to drag down the mood here, but you mentioned that I was killing the world? There was also something about how you were going to stop me? Are you planning to try to destroy me? I'm pretty hard to kill, I fight back.>

"Nothing so *dramatic*, you overrated chunk of quartz." Dale's lip curled at the interruption.

<Rude!> I called off the Goblin Bob hit squad, and they reluctantly released their prepared spells. I guess Dale gets to enjoy his first day of being a Mage.

"No, we need to find a way to rescue everyone from three things: the impact of the falling moon, the age of darkness and ice that will follow, and the deprivation of Essence caused by *Cal*." Dale closed his eyes and did something that he had been loath to do in the past. He focused on the bond between himself and the dungeon, sending the memory of his interaction with **Acme**.

I reeled from the massive revelation. My ritual, my ley lines… they were going to transform this world into a dead planet? *I* did that? The best outcome was the survival of a single race unless we somehow—what—saved people and locked them away in time?

<Seriously, Dale?> The Master was still lost in his own thoughts, but I knew he would want to rejoin the conversation soon. <Why is your news never fun? I see you coming and think, 'Oh look, it's Dale. I sure hope he's just coming in here to kill things. Otherwise, something ridiculous or sad is going to happen'.>

Dale ignored the jab, snapping his fingers to get The Master's attention. He was still unused to the power his body now contained, so his snapping fingers made a shockwave that ruffled The Master's robe. "The Master? I need to know how much time you think we have before the moon arrives."

"Time?" The Master blinked a few times, then seemed to remember where he was. "The moon. Yes. Without the Rune-script that Xenocide created actively pulling the celestial body toward us, all we need to worry about is the momentum it built up, and the pull of the Earth as it approaches. I'd say… being as conservative as possible, that we have three weeks before the first fragments begin to impact. Maybe, *maybe* a month before the majority of the mass makes landfall."

<Less than a month to save the world, hmm? Good luck, I guess.> I wasn't concerned for my own safety. I was already reinforcing my worst-case-scenario escape zone. Runes for absorbing kinetic impact, heat, cold, and anything else I could think of. It helped that I also don't eat, drink, or breathe. In general, I felt good about my prospects of survival. <Sounds like a real pain.>

"We need a plan." The Master nodded at Dale's words, and they started jogging to the surface. Dale's movement speed had increased to *far* above human levels, but The Master still had to move slowly to keep from leaving him behind. Perks of being one of the most powerful people on the planet.

<Must be nice to have legs,> I grumbled as they left me alone with my Silverwood tree and Wisp. Dale snickered at me as they erupted on to the surface of my flying island. Heh. I knew he couldn't ignore me for long. Dale loved me.

CHAPTER ONE

Dale opened the door to the council chambers just in time for a spray of blood to splatter on his face, the first blood drawn in a rapidly escalating conflict. While he knew that the delegates of the various races hadn't exactly been on good terms, walking in on a full-on brawl wasn't what he had been expecting. Dale stood in shock for a long moment, but The Master stepped in authoritatively and bellowed, "*Hold*, you fools! What is happening here?"

"Master!" A black-robed necromancer limped over, grimacing from both pain and anger. "Our undead have been constantly under assault, being attacked or destroyed! These people are killing us!"

"So you found and confronted the person or group responsible for doing this?" The Master looked around the now-silent room menacingly. "Who was it?"

The necromancer seemed pained. "Not… *quite*. A few of us came in seeking information, but they are all *denying* that they–"

"None of us are attacking your *disgusting* meat puppets!" An Amazonian woman kicked over a table and stalked over. "We don't care about them or you at *all*! We have our own issues to deal with, and you weaklings that hide behind the *corpses* of our friends–"

"The issue is not one of us attacking you. This issue is, in fact, far *more* dire than you are all thinking." Another man strode forward, his quartz-lens spectacles gleaming. "There has been a *shift* in the world's energies recently, and as far as I have been able to determine… all of this began with the fall of Valhalla. I think that Ragnarök is upon us."

Dale grew concerned; this story sounded familiar. The unknown scholar continued speaking, denying him the chance to ask questions, "I'm uncertain what exactly happened there, but as soon as the Seat of Power was destroyed… the energies of the world began to change. This is what I have been trying to tell all of you."

"Oh, *stop* it already! We have heard your insane conspiracy theories, we have *discussed* them, and we have *dismissed* them. A single city could not have been the key to the *entire world's* supply of Essence." This time, it was an Elven man who spoke, his scathing tone forcing the unknown scholar to wilt and slink away. "When someone knows what is actually happening or has a theory that is not impossible, we will discuss again. Until then we have more pressing issues."

This time it was a Dwarf who took the reins of the conversation, glaring at the necromancers and gripping a double-bladed axe, "Like the fact that these filthy dark Mages attacked us without provocation? I feel that we need to remind them of their *place*."

"I said *enough* of this." The Master's empowered voice caused people to stumble backward. He looked at the person who had been struck as he and Dale were entering the room, noting that their wound was already healed. "No lasting harm has been done, and this *will not* happen again! Now, as for what we are going to do about the fragments falling to the earth–"

"Not our issue." The Dwarven delegation stood as one and began moving toward the door. "My people have already begun our retreat to the deeps. So long as the planet itself is not cracked in half, we will have nothing to fear."

He paused, hesitating at the door. "We are not uncaring of the plight the surface dwellers face; we will accept any who wish to flee the rain of destruction… We will take them in as… *servants*. Unfortunately, we cannot allow the secrets of our people to see the light of day, and this is a rule that we must enforce. The doors to Centrum in Domum Suam will be open for one week, after that… we hope your ancestors will accept your soul with honor."

Dale looked over at The Master, confusion written large on his face. "Are you just going to let them go without saying anything?"

The Master wore a pained expression but simply nodded. "As powerful as I am, right now I cannot devote the power that would be required to press this issue. If I am correct, we have less than a month to save as many as possible. We do not have the time to save those who don't *want* to be saved. In fact, as we do not know how we are going to save *ourselves*, their plan may turn out be the only viable one."

"It won't help," Dale's prophetic words rang into the suddenly silent room. "At best, it will only prolong their deaths as the world dies around them."

"Bah." The Dwarf looked back and shook his head before slamming the door with a ringing *slam*.

Silence reigned for a few stretched heartbeats, but then Queen Brianna of the Dark Elf nation added her voice, "Dale… what are you talking about?"

Put on the spot, Dale told the gathered people what he knew about the recent shift in the world's Essence. To be on the safe side, he left out the parts about it being the dungeon's fault. This worked against him; to the gathered group, not having information about the *source* of the issue only lent credence to his ideas as being a wild conspiracy theory. A majority of them ignored his words, but Brianna seemed troubled and approached him, asking for a private conversation.

“Dale, my people are far more sensitive to the fluctuations of Essence than even others within our own species. We have trained our bodies and our constitutions to feel the slightest difference, always in the mindset of finding a new home or finding a scrap of Energy-rich Silverwood pollen. Some time ago, we felt that dense zones of Essence were being directed to flow along new channels.” Brianna paused, watching Dale’s reaction carefully. “It was far too sudden to be a natural occurrence. What do you know of this?”

“More than I want to.” Dale weakly smiled and began to explain.

CAL

“Cal, can I make a request?” Dani’s tone, more than the words, worried me.

<What’s up?>

“So, you know that there are things that I keep from you—things like the training that Grace has to go through.” Dani trailed off uncertainly. “You know I don't *like* keeping things from you, right?”

<Well, now I’m really interested in seeing where you’re going with this.> I chuckled at her wry groan.

“I just needed to mention… if there isn’t a way to divert this disaster, I might need to ask that we go to…”

<Ye~e~es?> I drew the word out but stopped trying to make jokes when I saw how uncomfortable she was. <Dani, what is it?>

“If the world is going to die from Essence reduction, I need to ask you to bring us to the Will-of-the-Wisp origin and save anyone that might be there,” Dani finished her thoughts in a rush. “I don't know *why* I’m having this feeling, but I can’t seem to get it out of my mind no matter what I do about it.

<Wait… hold on a moment.> I tried to mentally adjust. <I thought there was no information on your origins. I thought that anything you knew was passed down from previous genera-

tions. Any time we came *close* to anything that gave you a clue, you about lost your mind!>

"I know, I know." Dani let out a long sigh and bobbed in place for a few long seconds. I wisely gave her the space she needed. I didn't mind waiting so long as I got to hear about what she was hiding. "So… Wisps are typically bound to a single location. We can't generate our own Essence, and we can't really grasp at what is around us. We need a partner that can devote power to empowering us. This means… it almost certainly means that my race is a *created* race. We are not natural creatures. Even symbiotes in nature have *some* self-sustainability."

<Right, I've figured that much out.> I was glared at for my 'interruption', even though she had stopped speaking for multiple seconds.

"This is information known to us, but over the centuries… other aspects became hazy. No history can be perfectly described and passed down thousands of times, but we think that there is more to it than the simple passage of time. Something *made* us forget, but one thing that we all know… is that if there ever comes a time where our species would be wiped out… we need to do everything within our power to return home."

Dani would be hyperventilating if she had lungs. "Whatever the secret is, all I know for sure is that there is a powerful guardian protecting it, powerful enough that there has never been a Wisp that violated the taboo of making the journey, but even knowing it is forbidden, I *know* I need to go there. It pulls at me, and it is a sensation that comes from within."

<So… let me know if I am getting this correct. You want us to make a trip to your extended family as the world is ending, find a way to get past 'something' that no one has ever survived—since the very beginning—and… what? Save something that *might* be there? Figure out your history and preserve it when no one else can?> I loved the mystique, but I had a Runecrafted, multi-alloy bunker I had already made plans to visit for a few

millennia. <Can I interest you in a 'not a chance in the Abyss' during this trying time?>

"I understand that it seems like a bad plan, but I think it is something I might have to do." Dani stopped me from speaking, finishing her thought, "Not something we need to worry about right now, just something you need to be aware of. But… *keep* it in mind."

<Alright, I guess.> I cast about for something to focus my efforts on. <I'm going to go tweak my Elementals. I think I found a way to increase their Mana generation and maybe give them passive abilities, and I want to see if it works.>

"It's good to stay busy with *important* things," Dani announced breezily. I tried to determine if she was teasing me, but after eyeing her suspiciously for a few moments, I let my attention move to other projects.

CHAPTER TWO

An unexpected explosion knocked one of the Mages off his feet, and he slipped over the edge of the pit on the seventh floor. His screams were cut off quickly as the gravity distorted and compacted his body. The infernal spider Elemental Boss at the bottom finished him off as soon as his ruined body slammed into the floor.

"Corey! No! It got *Corey*!" Those remaining in the party of Mages were hard-pressed, pushing upward along the sloping ramps toward a hopeful escape. "*How*? He survived going through the haunted living room in the Tigress Queendom! If they could take him down, the rest of us don't stand a chance! We're all going to die! We're *dead*!"

"Don't invite misfortune, you *fool*!" Of the three surviving members of this expedition, this was the most powerful Mage. His control over pheromones and various biological skills had made moving through the higher floors *laughable*, but as they reached the deeper levels where such things didn't matter, his authority over the others had waned. He had been especially stymied for a small while when fighting Golems, as they were artificial constructs, but had believed that he would have more success on the lower level. The party leader had been dead wrong—heh—and now his team was paying the price for his pride.

<Well, that was a wasted effort.> Perhaps I needed to refine that Elemental, or perhaps this was just an area of growth that was going to end here for that combination. The Elemental that had knocked the Mage off the edge was planned as a type of combustion or explosion Mob, but it turned itself into a self-sacrificing trap instead. <Actually… I think those are going to become a little more prevalent.>

"Great Spirit?" Etiquette Bob looked over at me in my Core room. "Were you speaking to me?"

<No, no. Just watching a fight going on in the pit.> I turned my attention back to the danger zone, slightly embarrassed over my habit of thinking aloud.

Why hadn't I considered turning the explosive Elementals into traps before? I was going to turn this section of the pit into the single most deadly portion of the entire dungeon! I had already done all the heavy lifting involved in setting up the overcharged gravity Inscriptions, so why not start using them more fully? My mind wandered, and by the time I went back to watching the entertainment, the Mages were limping through the portal to lick their wounds. It was for the best—I needed time to implement my changes!

The simplest trap made the wall push outward, and if the target was caught by it, they would be shoved into open air to begin their deadly descent through the gravity field. When this trap was triggered, there would be sequential movement of the walls that would need to be accounted for until the area was clear once more. I was sure that I'd lose more than a few Elementals to the trap as well, but I wasn't too worried about that. The smart ones would succeed, and this would improve the overall qualities of the feral Mobs lower down the ramp.

Next, I made small cubbies in the shifting sections that would house an Elemental like the combustion version. People that had thought they were safe from the moving walls would be in for a happy little surprise if they were unable to put down the Mob before it could ignite itself.

These traps together would take down the overconfident and the unlucky; the gravity and Boss at the base would do the rest. I then speckled in a few traps that had a different effect. When these were triggered, the floor would be pulled into the wall and a short slide would send the victim off into open air—if they were surprised enough not to catch themselves in time, at least. The rock was infused with Runes and corruption, so it was unlikely that someone coming through here would be able to dig into the stone to save themselves.

<What next…?> I muttered to myself as I looked over the changed area. <I can't leave here and have the only improvement be a glorified pitfall trap…>

Was there a new Mob I could create for the area? I glanced at the rampaging war still ongoing at the top of the pit and decided against artificially selecting the best creatures. The entire theme of this floor was 'survival of the fittest', and I didn't want that to change. Plus, after they got strong enough, it was nigh impossible for me to control them.

Wind traps and various other possibilities came to mind, but the powerful people that should be coming on to this floor wouldn't be affected by a light gust of wind, and even the vanishing floor was honestly a stretch. Mages tended to be able to fly, and I was relying on surprise more than artifice to send them to their death. So, the question became—how to artifice their doom? I didn't have the answer yet, but this question demanded *research*! I left the room to its own devices for now and cackled as my attention flowed into my testing area.

The answer to my issues moving forward had to be found in Runes. Mana could create effects that I simply couldn't replicate with mechanisms or biological creatures. True, my Elementals were Mana-formed creatures, but as of yet, they were simple concentrations of pseudo-sentient energy. I started laying out Runes, trying to determine my path forward on this project. Should I work on improving the quantity and quality of the monsters or the room and the traps that it contained? Eventually, I would do both, of course, but sometimes, making that first decision would change the outcome of the second.

What would benefit me the most? Really… what would be the most fun for me to see in action? When I put it like that, I knew exactly what I wanted. I liked traps, but they didn't have the same visceral appeal to me that seeing a creature of my own design did. One of my greatest pleasures was watching Manny the Manticore do battle with a group of Mages. They almost never went in to fight him again, so it was always an impressive show to see both sides going all out. I made my choice; I would find a way to empower my Elementals!

I had mentioned to Dani that I thought I could make passive effects, and it was time to see if I was correct. I started working with an Elemental Core in my testing lab and, over the course of a few hours, started to lose my enthusiasm. This was *tough.* I could shift around the composition of the Core, I could alter the Mana type and quantity, but this only had the effect of creating a new type of Elemental. I wasn't *trying* to make a specific Elemental; I wanted something that could improve *all* of them. I did have an interesting result from my experimentation when I made a top-tier Elemental. It was half as big as even the smallest other Elemental, and it acted far differently than any other to this point.

It was a Love Elemental.

Again, not what I was going for, but I released it into the pit to see what happened. The… yeah, the result was not as I expected. When the gold-tinged, pink blob came into sensory range of the other Elementals, it acted like a massively overcharged taunt Rune. Everything near it charged and started brutally attacking… each other. The tiny blob rolled toward the edge of the pit, and I watched with fascination as the Elementals destroyed themselves trying to get at it. The little love-bubble hopped into the open air above the pit and seemingly ignored the increased gravity. It floated down, down, down… and was snatched out of the air by Imbrem Aureum.

The celestial water Elemental pulled the tiny love Core into itself and started expanding. Its golden droplets took on a pink tinge, and the B-rank-four Mob started to shrink, compressing and enhancing. When it finished absorbing the tiny love bubble, Imbrem Aureum had only reached B-rank-six, but its tier of Mana had increased significantly. As it moved, the spinning droplets that formed its body sliced through the corrupted stone floors with ease. It flowed down the ramp, finally making its move against the current floor Boss—Aranea.

<Alright… *not* what I was going for, but I can take a few minutes to see how this plays out.> As the two got closer, I thought about Dani. <Dani! Big awesome fight coming up! Get over here quick!>

She arrived just in time to see the two unbelievably powerful titans of elemental Mana exchanging their first blows. They were diametrically opposed Mana types—Aranea being mostly infernal fire and now a smattering of earth, while Imbrem Aureum was celestial, water, wind, and now something… more.

The spider-style Elemental wasted no time in attempting to shatter the Core of Imbrem Aureum, but its bladed legs were knocked off course and sliced into by the spinning droplets. Imbrem Aureum started flowing up the mangled leg, but Aranea simply sliced off its own appendage and rolled away. A *dense* concentration of black fire appeared in a small orb near Aranea's Core, and it turned that orb into a cone.

Imbrem Aureum dodged, and all the droplets that were caught by the beam fell to the floor and evaporated. The black cone of power continued uninhibited through the rock of the dungeon, melting the stone less like fire and more like potent acid. It tore out into open air and out of my vision range. <Yup, I think it's time to add some more defensive Inscriptions around myself and Mr. Tree here.>

"You think?" Dani muttered softly, enraptured by the ability of semi-sentient Mana to control itself. "I wonder if we can control this enough to make it happen how and when we want it…?"

Imbrem Aureum made a move, directing its constantly shifting motion into a directed stream. The Elemental swam through the air in a perfect laminar stream, piercing the exterior of the 'spider' and plucking out its Core. I watched in fascination as the Aranea's body dissipated into motes of black energy and was reabsorbed by my influence.

<That was exciting.>

"I don't think it's over!" Dani excitedly drew my attention back to the glowing water, which had started to twitch and shake erratically. I looked closer, expecting to see the black-and-red Core being dissolved and eaten. Instead, I saw a pink light wrapping around *both* Cores. Then a tiny pink Core became visible, and the two larger Cores began orbiting it.

The fiery body of Aranea regrew around the three Cores, and soon, a smaller version of the original Boss stood on the floor with golden water swarming around it like a regal Aura. Dani was as stunned as I was but managed to find her voice first, "Did they just combine into a *super* Elemental, or am I dreaming?"

<Oh, that was *neat*!> I inspected the creature and found that it was sitting right on the upper edge of B-rank nine. <New floor Boss, Aranea Imbrem.>

"Spider shower?" Dani scoffed at my naming convention.

<And now I have a new trap idea as well!>

"Now *that* is pure evil." Dani laughed along with me. I hoped she realized I was serious; I was already in the process of making a spider-loaded trap.

CHAPTER THREE

While it had been interesting to see the effect of a top tier Mana type interacting with lower types, it was a *huge* power investment. I couldn't make those and still expect to have enough strength to work on other issues. So, once again, I was banging my metaphorical head against a wall trying to think of something I could use to enhance all future Elementals. <Think, Cal! Think! Something in there… the solution is on the tip of my Core!>

I decided to review what I had already tested. Superpowered Mana types created powerful creatures, and in fact, the Love Elemental had been able to impact the others, drawing them in and making them fight like a… taunt Rune? …*no*. Would it be that easy? It couldn't be. I created a Core that would be used to contain some form of nature Elemental that should be mostly stone. Before I poured in Mana, I dug in and Inscribed a spider web of linked taunt Runes on the surface of the Core. *Then* I poured in Mana and let the Elemental form, releasing it into the main pit area.

There didn't seem to be much happening, but as the new Elemental joined in the war to get stronger, it naturally released a wave of Mana to empower its self-formed body. The stone cracked, and some form of a shockwave rolled off of it. Any being within range of the force turned and assaulted the new creation. They had been *taunted*! I watched raptly as the taunting Elemental defended itself, and the creatures it fought were attacked from behind by non-taunted versions. This melee was a thing of beauty!

The original Elemental was brought down, its taunt Rune along with it. I watched, wondering if the Rune would somehow transfer to the Elemental that had eaten it. The Rune didn't appear on its Core, but since Runes were so difficult to damage, it *did* appear on its body! Soon after that, the Rune reactivated, and the process started all over again.

Finally, a path forward for these creatures! I got to work, enhancing new iterations of Elemental with various Runes and testing the effects. I tried to be creative with what I gave them, as the results were fun to watch, but I needed to balance this with my other projects. Sure, I had lots to do, but I decided I needed a fun break like this. I'd get back to being serious another time.

DALE

After moving away from the council hall—full of frustration over being mostly ignored—Dale decided that it was time to see what all had changed within himself. Case in point, he was *walking* along, but every tent he passed was collapsing in the sudden, hurricane-force wind his movements created. He went over to the training area in the Academy to test his capabilities and try to learn how to control or eliminate the issues he was creating.

Dale stood in the earth-focused area, staring at his target dummy a few dozen feet away. He focused on his earth-shattering technique and released a line of Mana. The target—and the ground between Dale and the target—detonated into a curtain of slowly falling dust. Dale himself had been thrown away from his position by the concussive blast, finding himself embedded in the wall that surrounded this training area. "Well. That didn't work at all. It didn't *hurt* though...?"

"Yoo-hoo. Hello there, young man!" Headmaster Artorian awkwardly strolled up to Dale, offering him a hand. As Dale waited a moment for his head to clear, a rush of wind made Dale's damaged clothes flap. Only then did Dale realize that Artorian had been moving at breakneck speeds and that this was the first time he had been able to track a Mage traveling at that velocity. Not only that, but it hadn't *seemed* fast or irregular in the slightest. "How about a hand? We can learn to be proper Mages together!"

"That would be a huge help." Dale took the proffered hand and pulled himself out of the wall. "Why is this so *hard*? It's my *body*!" The old man nodded in agreement, having gone through similar adaptation issues.

"Mmm. There are likely a couple of things you haven't realized about yourself." Artorian took a cleansing breath and beamed a bright smile as he presented a harsh concept, "You aren't *really* human anymore, now are you?"

"W-what?" Dale took a step backward out of pure shock. The force sent him reeling into the wall again and caused more of it to fall on him.

"You've left your human flesh behind when you ascended to Magehood." Artorian sat down cross-legged on the stone floor and motioned for Dale to do the same—so he would stop running into things. "You still have a body, obviously, and although Mages have been through extensive tests in the past to show that *everything* functions the same, a human just can't do what we can."

The Headmaster let that sink in for a long moment. "A Mage is someone that has higher energetic tissue. Everything is there, but your flesh is now made of *Mana* instead of *meat*. First, we infused our existing bodies with Essence. Then as we progressed to the Mage ranks, we have replaced them altogether with Mana. You will find that essence techniques meant to empower oneself don't quite *function* anymore. Using Mana is necessary to affect ourselves."

Artorian motioned toward the still crumbling area Dale had launched an attack into. "As you recently found out, you also have considerably greater power than you are used to having. Even when one infused their entire body to the utmost with their essence, it compares to but a fraction of a Mage's base form. I've come to the conclusion this has more to do with our change in nature than it does concerning a change in the output of our abilities."

"As a higher-energy form of creature, the rules of how the world works impact us differently than when we were human. This does not, unfortunately, mean we are impervious to harm, regardless of how things may seem to C-rankers and below. Now, a simple question—do you know what the single greatest threat to a Mage is?"

"I don't," Dale mumbled with a downcast face, not certain how he felt about this revelation.

"Burnout." The sunlight Mage chuckled at Dale's expression, which soured further at thinking that the old man was playing with him. Artorian continued fondly and unperturbed, as this was an expression he often saw on students.

"Oh, I'm very serious. Did you *mean* to detonate the entire yard? Collapse the entire tent-housing district? Are you interested in having conversations with people at a regular speed or a leisurely walk in the afternoon with someone?"

Artorian offered the answers when Dale didn't speak, "The way we do things has been reversed. Mages don't need to learn how to *empower* things, they need to be able to *reign in* their Mana expenditure and learn control."

Artorian regarded Dale sternly, his inner 'concerned grandfather' showing itself.

"You—especially you—have access to a high-tiered Mana of a rank beyond even mine. I can feel it from here. Heavens, I can just about *see* it radiating off of you. Which, by the way, is a puzzle I intend to tackle at a later time."

Dale had a moment of concern; he hadn't told the headmaster about **Acme**. "Wait, you can *tell*? How?"

The old man tapped the side of his nose while he scanned Dale over, being convinced that whatever **Law** Dale was bound to… It was not present on the tier his **Love Law** had been.

"My **Law** places a deep emphasis on connections, the relationship between things, and sympathies. Noticing things is my entire shtick, and many of my early forays into techniques had to do with the purest perception. Most Mages can roughly guess the rank of another, but for most, it is an imprecise estimate. It is not for me, unless one is intentionally shielding themselves."

Artorian waved that off to return to the topic at hand. He was here to give his fellow freshly ascended Mage his wisdom and aid, not an extended questionnaire. "The important piece of information that will be useful to learn is that we don't *generate* Mana, we *channel* it. If you can't control yourself, your Mana will destroy you long before an enemy will."

"You mean I'm using Mana to *move*?" Dale thought about that. It was obvious in retrospect, but ever since gaining Mana, he had slowly been becoming faster and stronger. His normal interactions were starting to suffer, and he was obviously beginning to damage things unintentionally. His real fear was that he would damage *himself* accidentally, as Artorian had so helpfully pointed out.

"Indeed!" Artorian waved at the freshly plowed yard and chuckled. "Have you had time to consider why it is so important to refine techniques? Become *precisely* skilled at them? This is because as a Mage, any flaw in the technique is patched by Mana. Where common essence users suffer either backlash or technique failure, a Mage instead has the requisite energy siphoned from them to successfully complete the intended effect."

"As a comparison, crafters that work with Runes can make nearly *anything* work as they want… given enough power investment. Our spatial bags, for example. Those are either made by people that are able to channel *so much* Mana that they *force* it to do what they want or by people that *really* know what they are doing. Guess which one is worth more?"

Dale ignored the question and asked one of his own. He had been in a few situations already where his actions had been out of the norm, and he simply hadn't realized until now. "How do I start moving at a normal speed, then?"

Artorian had gone off-topic again and righted his lesson, considering a useful answer. "That comes back to Aura control, typically learned and studied for *years* in the C-ranks. The standard method is to restrict the amount of Mana flowing through your body, particularly your nerves and muscles. Too much to your nerves, and you will try to walk faster than your muscles can react."

"Conversely, too much power invested into your muscles, and you will crash into walls and the like before you realize you're moving. It's *fun*." His tone dripped with sarcasm. "My preferred method differs, but it looks like you would like to ask something."

"So, I'm sitting at full power to both right now, I assume?" Dale's question received a nod in response. "Alright. Aura. I'm really good at Aura. I can do this."

Dale focused on his Mana and felt it permeating his body. It was perfectly balanced, and the flow was strong and consistent. It really and truly felt like a crime against his hard work to try to tone it down, but if that is what needed to happen... Dale started putting limits on himself, and when he felt that it was correct, he started walking. Correction: *trying* to walk. His foot jerked forward, and he perfectly did the splits before falling on his side and letting his head bounce off the stone floor.

"Ha!" Artorian slapped himself on the knee in amusement. "Oh, it's so hard to believe that I did the exact same thing only a few days ago! No wonder so many people were offering to help me out!"

Dale had lost control of his limiting factor, so he was easily able to get to his feet. The downside was that he was once again moving at Mage-speed. He tried to limit himself in a different way and, this time, found himself half buried in stone with a gravel-grinding *crunch*!

Artorian calmly worked to pull him out, adding a pat to Dale's back.

"Good, yes, now let's find a nice balance between those two levels!" Artorian poked and prodded at Dale for roughly an hour longer before the young Mage was able to walk around 'normally'. Artorian was proud but still made a fatherly jab, "Excellent progress! Now, keep yourself limited like that forever and in every situation that is non-combat! Try to do it without scowling or looking constipated, my boy. You are currently making quite the show alternating between the two."

Dale stared *hard* at the man teasing him, his eyebrow twitching. "Right. *Thanks*."

"Well, I *am* your mentor!" Artorian quipped cheerfully as he wrapped up the lesson. "The standard method is a mess, is it not? I find the self-imposed limits bothersome and instead prefer to operate by concentrating and being mindful of what I am doing in a very patient and slow manner. Mages process and take in information at what we call 'Mage-speed'."

"Now, this is a bit of a misnomer, as the rest of the world still progresses in the mundane frame of motion. While it is by no means a flawless method, by extensively taking my time in discerning how my actions influence myself and the world around me, one is slowly able to reach a stable average of how such movements *feel*."

Artorian raised his hand, keeping it flat and steady to show what he meant. Although the movement appeared serene at normal speed—full of control and grace—at Mage-speed perception, Dale could see the headmaster was patient as a tranquil willow, bending only in the softest wind. Movements that should take moments instead took a minute or more when viewed as a Mage. It was this calm process his tutor wished to teach.

"This is a more natural way to grasp pace, rather than one of self-imposed limits. Practice the methods and use what works for *you*, my boy. You will find that as the concentration of Mana in your being increases, the time dilation you experience between 'Mage-speed' and 'mundane' grows as well. This is in addition to something I am formulating an idea on, which is that higher tier laws may have an exponentially *stronger* dilation experience. It's why you undoubtedly saw me wobble when I first came in. Let's get to practicing!"

It took Dale some time to find a way to maintain his concentration without inhibiting his movement, but soon, the two of them walked at a normal human speed back to the church, where a meeting was scheduled to take place that evening. On their way, Dale saw Hans and Rose walking in the same direction and called out to them. Hans turned and, upon seeing Dale, ran and jumped into his arms. "Dale! You came to *rescue* me!"

Dale pushed Hans on to the ground and stepped on him on his way to give Rose a hug. He was extra careful to maintain his control, as he didn't want to accidentally crush her. "Rose, so good to see you! How is the married life, and I also would like to know *what* the *abyss* you were thinking!"

Rose blushed and laughed. "Married life. Yeah, um, surprisingly good. Turns out Hans is mostly insecurity wrapped in vanity. When you can get through to him and make him seriously talk and think, he is skilled, knowledgeable, and genuinely caring. Even I was surprised."

"I was once a feared assassin!" Hans called from the ground, where he was waving his arms and legs to make a dirt angel. "I used to command life and death for *hundreds*! Look at what I'm reduced to! I want a face tattoo."

"Get off the ground. I *just* got you those clothes!" Rose demanded with a finger snap. Hans rolled to his feet and grumbled good-naturedly, smiling lovingly at her until she looked away. Then he stuck his tongue out and winked at Dale as Rose continued speaking, "Do you know how disgusting his leathers had gotten? I honestly think he may not have taken them off since you commissioned them for the group."

"They're lined with *Mithril*!" Hans protested heatedly, though in a hushed tone. "I'd rather not take a bath than take an arrow!"

"And we *compromised*, didn't we?" Rose responded archly. "You took a bath in a locked stone room, and now you're wearing normal clothes while those others are cleaned and get a cleaning enchantment added on to them."

"I feel naked," Hans grumbled as they continued walking.

"Be *good*, and maybe that can happen later." Rose's words shifted Hans' attitude dramatically, making both Dale and Artorian heartily laugh. "Dale, in all seriousness, I think that we really do make a good couple. We have complementary strengths, and we have different interests but enough in common that we enjoy being together and always have something to talk about. We both found someone who is completely different than we are, but we work well together. It's *surprisingly* good."

"We *get* it, you're shocked." Hans sniffed with his nose in the air. "No need to be mean about it. Really twisting the knife over there."

Before the banter could continue, they opened the door to the church and found that the open meeting everyone was able to attend was already in full swing. The Master was standing in front of the crowd and nodded at Dale as he and the people with him took their seats. "As I was saying, I think that we have determined a solution to the issue at hand. I'm sure there is a conversation that we are going to need to have, but I really think that this is the option most likely to allow us to survive."

"Spit it out already, Dark One," an Amazon called from the crowd, making The Master frown and Queen Brianna lock eyes with the offending person.

"There is an option that we have been overlooking. If you can think back two entire days, you'll recall that our societies worked together to create a portal that would be capable of redirecting the Runes that had been pulling at the moon. I have had multiple discussions with the Portal Mages, and there is an ancient design that could be repurposed. We have enough time, *perhaps*, to link the portal to a being. If we could find a Soul Space large enough, we could fit our entire populations into a safe location. Then so long as that being survived, we could return when the world has stabilized."

"Impossible!" a Spotter called from the front of the room, his contemporaries nodding along at his words. "There is no one with a Soul Space so large, and the age of darkness and ice that will occur—if the planet is not outright destroyed—will last potentially *millennia*!"

"We already have the person with a large enough Soul Space all sorted out," The Master informed them, bringing stunned silence to the area once more.

"We just need to ask permission."

CHAPTER FOUR

<I feel like something bad is about to happen.> I was getting odd chills, and talking to Dani *usually* helped. This wasn't one of those times.

"How many did you make, and are they loose in the dungeon?" She zipped around and tried to pretend she was panicking. Her laughter made me glare at her.

<Ugh, that joke's getting old! It was *one*, wait, *two* times!> I tried to think. It was only twice, right? The Madness Mushrooms and the original Distortion Cat. Yeah. Pretty sure just the twice. <No, I'm not sure *what* this is. But! Check this out. I upgraded the Elementals. I made what I'm calling 'Rune-forged Cores'!>

We watched the Elemental war playing out and the new abilities they now activated passively. It was fun! There was something about having an army of powerful beings between *you* and things that could *hurt you* that really made you feel secure. I showcased a few examples of my favorite versions, especially one that would convert Mana passing through it into an attack of whatever Mana type the Elemental was using. The Converted Mana—only what was naturally released—would create a nova of power around the Mob. This made for random explosions, a really fun deterrent for invaders.

"Dungeon, we need to talk." I screamed a *tiny* amount as The Master came out of *nowhere* and started speaking. A series of Bob Squads started running toward us, but I called them off. I really needed to find a way to prevent this intrusion from happening. "Is your Wisp nearby to translate?"

Dani flew into the open, cautiously remaining near the exit for a moment before seeming to remember that The Master is *way* faster than us. Especially me. No legs. "Hello *again*. As always, so *wonderful* to see you in person. I really love that you just show up. I'll have to remember to return the favor when the people around you sleep."

"Ah yes, the whole capturing you… unpleasantness. Now, don't bother with the empty threats. You know as well as I do that there are no people I care for that still need to sleep." The Master rubbed at his neck, obviously thinking about something. "I'll try to do something especially nice for you as an apology. For now, though, dungeon… that is, *Cal*, I have a request."

<Nothing I can do but listen,> I told him coldly. Dani spoke aloud for his benefit, and I decided right then that I would keep someone around me in the future for translation purposes. Dani was usually *really* busy.

"You reached the A-ranks. I know you have, and I know that you have an extremely high tier of Mana. Your Soul Space. How large is it?" The Master didn't bother to wait on getting to the point, it seemed. Maybe he should be bringing me bribes instead of nasty surprises like he usually does?

<Why do you want to know?> I really wanted him out of here, but it was hard for me to make that happen, and I felt that hostility would be the wrong choice for me to make.

"There is a *chance* that we might be able to modify and link the portal we had been designing to the soul of a being. Now, unfortunately, the standard size of a Soul Space would at best house one or two people. Not to mention that they'd likely suffocate before long." The Master held out his hands and made a gesture. "The *average* Soul Space is about this big, just enough to hold a single object.":

I looked into my soul, watching as my sketched-out world slowly became more and more solid. Right now, I had been working on creating air. There was little chance of suffocation thanks to this process, but the amount of available ground would hold—at *best*—a thousand bodies. <I have other plans for my soul. To be frank, the idea of having a bunch of people walking around in there isn't exactly *appealing*. Hard pass.>

"But!" The Master's veins bulged on his forehead, and he needed to take a few deep breaths to calm himself. "But you *do* have the space that would be required? If we could make an offer that was enticing enough, you would at least consider it? It wouldn't be terrible to have the entire world owe you a favor."

<Listen, The Master, I'm not saying 'no', but I kinda am. I just don't think that there would be enough benefit to me. I don't know enough about the capabilities of my Soul Space. What if someone could directly impact my *soul* while in there? Someone, say with a whole slew of *necromancers* or a type of energy far more potent than what I am able to contain or control?> I hoped I was getting my point across. <Actually, what rank *are* you right now? What Mana did you originally align with?>

The Master went silent, contemplating his options and ignoring my questions. "Will you *help* us, at least? We need to make this happen, and there are going to be things we need."

<Supply a list of things that you need, and I will make them available as rewards in the dungeon. I think that you are all most likely going to die in the near future, so I need to conserve my energy. I can't just be giving away potent artifacts and giant chunks of Mithril.> I tried to keep the glee out of my voice, but then I remembered I didn't need to. Dani was translating everything in a monotone already since she didn't want to be here. I was just pleased to be working as a dungeon again instead of as slave labor for Barry.

"That… it will be done." The Master sighed in frustration and vanished once more.

<We really need to figure out how he is doing that and come up with a way to counter it,> I informed Dani halfheartedly. She nodded, knowing just as well as I did that it was unlikely to happen.

DALE

"Hang on, you just *left*?" Dale groaned and rubbed his head. He didn't think that headaches were a thing he could get anymore, but old habits die hard. "He was obviously being greedy and looking for a way to leverage the situation to get a better deal!"

"I really don't think that's the case in this situation, Dale. He was adamantly against it." The Master was sitting in a chair, obviously having given up on survival. "I think this is the end for all of us. We should all just visit the Dwarves."

"Stop being such a prima donna!" Chandra stepped forward and lightly smacked The Master across the face. Light for her; it was hard enough to cause a glass to shatter from the reverb. "I *know* that you have higher willpower than this! You organized the world *three* times that I know of! You have a mindset that never gave up in the past, and I don't want to see you give up now!"

The Master looked up at her in shock. It had been generations since someone had acted thusly toward him. "You and I should find some time… to talk."

"*Abyss yes* we should!" Chandra crossed her arms. "I want your full story from start to finish!"

"Maybe I'll even get a chance to tell it to you." He smiled faintly at her, and they both fell silent with their eyes locked. "I'd like that a lot."

Ahem. Dale cleared his throat and brought them out of their moment. "Right, so. Can we try again with Cal? I'm pretty certain we can get through to him. Oh! *No one* threaten him, no matter how much of a pain he is being. It would end badly. Most likely it will just make him say no and *mean* it."

"Do what you will, Dale." Queen Brianna shrugged and waved her hand. "You have my blessing to do whatever you need to save my people, so long as we do not end as slaves. We are never going back to that life."

"There aren't enough of my people remaining to fight me on this, so you have the support of the Amazons." The Amazonian delegation leader shrugged and flopped into her seat. "I honestly don't think we'll survive either way."

Henry and Marie both nodded as well, even though they were now only Royals by blood. Father Richard agreed as well, speaking for the Church. The Master nodded, the final leader of a large group in the area beyond Barry, who represented the Guild. He hadn't been invited to this meeting.

"Here we go then. Cal!" Dale called into the open air.

<I. Have. Been. *Summoned*!> Dale rolled his eyes at the theatrics.

"Right. Listen, we think that you aren't thinking through the benefits of working with us. Consider this for a moment—you'd be saving untold thousands of lives and therefore becoming a hugely respected being." Dale paused to take a breath.

<That sounds *so* fun, Dale, it really does, but 'respect' won't–>

Dale interrupted in a rush, "*Then* think about how everyone will owe you a huge favor, be constantly generating Essence and Mana, and are trapped in your Soul Space until you let them out. Anyone tampering with things they shouldn't would lead to their demise, right? Especially if they swore an oath *not* to do harm. You would be able to make the rules, for *everyone*. We would just need to make a deal."

There was silence for a few long, *long* moments.

<Well… you have my attention.>

CHAPTER FIVE

Hours of negotiation had finally concluded. Luckily for me, I had Dani and Legal Bob to help me think things through, else I would have been steamrolled and shafted by this deal. As it stood, I gained more than I offered, which is all I really needed to be on board with this process.

<So, here is the final proposal from my end. Everyone that enters my Soul Space needs to offer a large donation of their Mana. I will need it in order to create everything properly. As much as I can get, for *your* benefit. I know that this means that Mages are going to be entering as weak as kittens, but that is a sacrifice I am willing to make.> I let Dale catch up to me, speaking to the others in the room. <Mages can always rest a bit and return to full strength, so I don't see this as unreasonable. That should also keep the fighting to a minimum at the start.>

<I will also want everyone to pay tribute in the form of everything they own. Until the point where I open the portal, I'm going to be offering token rewards in my dungeon that will let people get ahead in my inner world. If they want a house, they are going to need to have that token ready or build it when

they get there.> I paused to let the gathered people keep up with Dale's translation. <I will absorb *anything* that is brought into my soul—I don't want any surprises.>

<The more tokens you enter with, the better the options you are going to have. You want to build a Kingdom? Get your current power back? Have basic tools or food and water? Either get the tokens, have a deal in place already, or start from zero.> Here I got really serious, but the effect was ruined by Dale's voice. <Let me be very clear in this little recap: every bit of material, knowledge, tools, curios, everything *anyone* has… it has to be given to me. There is no taking it with you.>

When people grumbled about my heavy-handedness, I pointed out, <There's no point in leaving it here. It'll just be destroyed or lost to time. I'll give some basic tokens for this stuff in return, so they can re-accumulate wealth. Make no mistake though, it's going to be tough times for people for a long time. I haven't had enough time to make a huge amount of land or *stuff* in my world. My rules will need to be followed, or the offenders will be punished.>

By the time Dale caught up with what I was saying, the majority of people looked somewhat sick. Yikes, sure seemed hard for them to give up things that were meaningless in the long run. <Now, as for your requests. I will give you a place where you can live and thrive. I will do my best to let you continue to grow, and as people bound to me; you will never permanently die while you are in my care. Not unless you want to do so. When the world is safe, and I am able, I will return you here if you want.>

The perks I was able to offer weren't insubstantial. They knew it, and it was the only reason that a deal was struck. The conversation dragged on, and all of the topics were refined. They got a slightly better deal, refusing to have Mages pay a steep Mana cost, and seemed pleased with the results. Once everything had been discussed, the group broke up, and the various groups dispersed.

They were off to tell their people about this possibility for survival and to convince them that it was the most likely option to succeed. That said, I had no doubts that there would be a lot of casualties from the incoming moonfall because of stubbornness… and the unwillingness to let go of material goods. Hmm. Maybe they would turn to ash near a ley line and I'll be able to get their otherwise-wasted Essence and Mana?

Still, I could see that I had rekindled hope in a good amount of people. Frankly, I knew that they were desperate, and I used that information to get better terms on the agreement than I probably should have. As I was thinking about this, I watched as Tom walked over to Dale and pulled him out of the conversation he was having.

"Dale, I need to ask for your advice and help." Tom took a deep breath and stood straight. "My people don't have anyone here. There is no delegation from the Northmen, and I doubt that many people would be willing to go out of their way to attempt to rescue them."

"Whatever I can do for you, Tom, you know I will do my best." Dale thoughtlessly slapped the massive man on the shoulder, sending him tumbling away like a rock being skipped over a large lake.

A *fuff* sound popped in the space occupying the Northman's trajectory. A mote of light blazed into the shape of a person as Tom was caught by a light-blurred Artorian. The impact-force made the old man drop with a *baph* right on his skidding back, but he raised his thumb to the sky once they were at a standstill, indicating they were unharmed regardless of the dust-cloud they had just kicked up.

Dale bolted over to the Northman and pulled him and the headmaster upright. "I am *so* sorry."

Artorian shook his head at Dale with a smirk he couldn't *quite* contain as he dusted off his robes, attention turning to the living non-Mage projectile's well-being. Dale, after all, was making good progress.

Tom stood on his own as soon as the dizziness wore off. "No, I'm… I'm fine. *Hurk.* I'm fine. Listen, my brethren will be preparing for this in their own, *flawed* way. They will likely see this as some form of 'ultimate battle against nature' and attempt to attack the moon as it 'attacks' us. Even in death, they will find satisfaction. But… they *will* die. I would prefer to prevent that."

"What would you like us to do?"

Dale raised a brow as Tom once more straightened to his full height and spoke in a near-regal manner, "The portals into the North are sealed. The Wards are in place, and winter has blocked foot travel over the great barrier mountains. I doubt that there is anyone willing to fly me there, as everyone has their own issues to solve in order for their own people to be saved. Since this is the case, I formally request your assistance in convincing the dungeon to bring me to my homeland."

<Well, that wasn't what I expected to hear.> To his credit, Dale no longer flinched when I spoke. Perhaps he had gotten perceptive enough to know when my mind was present? <Ask him why I should bother to alter my flight path.>

"Tom, why would the dungeon agree to do that?" Dale quietly asked his friend and teammate, not bothering to mention that I was the one who was *really* asking. "The dungeon is already fairly begrudging about this whole 'saving others' process."

"That's a simple question to answer, Dale." Tom looked around, and then realized the futility of keeping his voice low around Mages. "The Northmen have progressed further in Rune magic than any other race. Inscriptions, Wards, Ritual magics. We have it, others don't. Dwarves have better material and physical defenses, Elves have potent techniques and abilities, Humans and Gnomes have innovations, Amazonians have total pigheadedness… but the Northmen… the Northmen have the most advanced Rune magic."

<Well, I'm sold. When do we leave? Oh right. *I* get to choose. What direction? It's… North. We're going North. Shocker, there. Oh, wait a minute…I need to seal the deal first.>

Dale ignored me. "Tom, are you sure they would even be receptive to this? At all? Would they listen to you? Would they pay the debt that you would be incurring?"

"They…" Tom swallowed deeply, and a sheen of sweat appeared on his forehead. "I would need to do a… a few things. I'd need to have my banishment revoked. Then I would need to fight for my inheritance… and then I would need to challenge my brother for the position as the leader of our people. Any *one* of those steps… well… it will not be easy."

"*How* not easy?" Dale questioned, a dark certainty appearing in his mind without Tom needing to speak at all.

"Each one of the steps is more likely to result in my death than in my success," Tom reluctantly explained with a sigh. "Getting my banishment revoked—this means that I need to *prove* that I am no longer a bloodfire Berserker. That means I will need to fight against an unknown number of enemies that are strong enough to defeat me for an unknown amount of time. I will *also* need to sustain enough damage, *lethal* damage, so I can prove my claim."

"If I manage to survive that, I may then need to fight someone that has a claim to my inheritance, if they choose to fight against me. As my position would be an enviable one, I have no doubt that the fight will be… extreme. Unless I can find a way to…" Tom paused and looked around, noting that he had the attention of everyone in the area. He hung his head. "*Ahem.* I would also need to either fight my brother, the Warlord, or convince him that my plan is the best for our people. As he is at *least* at the peak of the C-ranks by now, I truly hope that he will listen to my words."

Dale looked at his friend, a man who planned to *knowingly* go into an area that would probably kill him. A man who would risk himself for his people when they would *not* thank him for it. Dale found nothing but respect for the barbarian as he looked at him. "How quickly would your win be known, and what sort of timeline would you have from that point forward?"

Tom waved his hand back and forth in a 'who knows'

motion. “When last I was there, I would need at least a week for my people to be assembled. I know they had been working on increasing the efficiency of communication before I left. As for the actual trials… I am uncertain. I do know that everyone would know the outcome immediately, as everyone in our nation is invited to watch as these things happen.”

<Yup, I’m in. I'll transport us, but no admittance to his people without payment!> I turned to Dani and grinned savagely. <End of world entertainment is the *best* entertainment!>

CHAPTER SIX

"Cal, I'm so proud of your negotiation!" Dani was zipping around the Silverwood tree with Grace, playing a game of touch and go while talking. "Not only did you secure a huge supply of free Essence and Mana generators, but they are going to *pay* you for the privilege! I'm really impressed that you included us in your negotiation this time around. I think that really helped"

<Mm. To be fair, they are getting out of being squished by the moon, so it's not a terrible deal for them, either. Legal Bob is really working out surprisingly well. I thought it was a waste of time to teach a Goblin contract law, but you win again.> I was tinkering with various weapons and traps in the dungeon and had just upgraded the final pitfall on the first floor. Now, instead of thin stone, there was an illusion of the floor that matched the Essence type and density of the stone around it. <I set a course for the location Tom provided. Has Navigator Bob said anything about that?>

"You alright? It isn't like you to abstain from gloating." Dani flew closer to me, putting her game on hold for a moment. "Are you sick? Can you *get* sick?"

<I want to say 'no'? I'm a powerful and pretty rock.> I finished what I was doing and focused on her. <I'm... actually kind of having a crisis. I'm pretty sure that this is the first time in my existence where I am moving toward an end goal that I *chose*. Everything else was either an accident, the work of an outside party, or coercion. It feels strange that the first thing I really *chose* would be what amounts to a rescue mission.>

"That makes sense." Dani bobbed in the air. "Your life has always been a series of things that *happened* to you. What you are feeling right now is yourself grabbing hold of your future and actively working to make it happen. You are free, you are stable, and frankly, there is likely very little danger to you from the upcoming crisis. You need time to get used to your new reality and feel comfortable in it. I'm told that happens to everyone when they reach a new stage in their life."

I thought about her words. It was difficult to swallow, but I'm pretty sure she was right. I was just waiting for the moment it all fell apart, the spot where things were going well enough to *really* beat me down when the good times ended, but I *couldn't* continue thinking that way! I needed to be comfortable with who I was and where I was going. <Thanks, Dani. I needed that. Now I can focus on eating a few people.>

"There ya go!" Dani cheerfully went back to her game with Grace, laughing as the tiny Wisp escaped by dodging through the floor and created a spike as she exited.

Good stuff all around. I turned my attention inward, reaching for my Soul Space. As I entered my pseudo-world, I felt the familiar *thrill* of simultaneously *looking* at everything at once and *knowing* it on a deep and personal level. I had switched the Essence I was gathering, moving over to making habitable land after meeting with Dale. I was here now to see how it was going. I inspected one of the sketched-out continents, pleased with the progress I was seeing. A layer of bedrock to support the framework, followed by multiple layers of various soils, mulch, loam, and then grasses and plants to hold it steady.

I was cheating a tiny little bit, but who was going to call me out on it? The bedrock was a tenth as thick as it should have been, but it was still fine as I was using corrupted stone to form the layer. Otherwise I would have needed to devote a truly *massive* amount of time to forming all that rock. The other place I was cheating-but-not-cheating? There weren't any bacteria, mold, or insects in the layers that I made. I would need to add those in, else nothing on the ground would be… broken… down.

Wait. Scratch that. I could treat this entire world as one, single, *massive* dungeon. It was *me* after all. *I* would be the one to take all of that stuff in! Once I had the configuration I wanted, I could keep it that way by absorbing, regrowing, and respawning all the flora and fauna! In fact, I could even potentially add dangers and treasures, especially if I was going to have… guests.

Yes. *Yes.* I liked that. I should go and… wait, my main point, what was I doing? Right! The third and final way I was cheating? I didn't yet have a heat and light source for the planet. That's right, no sun. All the plants were sustained by the potent Essence in the air and literally *didn't* need anything else. I had an inkling that the people that were going to come here would want light, even if only to boost their mood. I'd have to figure something out. As it stood… I had nowhere *near* enough Essence or Mana to create something that could even *act* as a sun.

Until I could figure out a permanent solution, I created powerful lights that cost very little energy to create and maintain. I didn't need these *everywhere* since I currently had only a small stretch of land fully formed. A normal human could cross it with a half-hour walk. The light I came up with was pale and cast everything into high contrast, but it could be used to see; that would have to do for now. I looked at the ground, noting that with my current Essence collection, it was growing at the rate of about a square foot per second. Not as impressive as what I could now do when making air and various gasses, but this was still pretty good in my opinion.

Looking at the average size of people that I had interacted with, if everyone that came here stood really closely together… I could fit nearly ten *million* people in a single square kilometer of land. Sadly, based on how territorial even *humans* are, I highly doubted they would be fine with only that much space to wait around in for an untold amount of time.

Then again… I was *pretty* sure that I wouldn't get *that* many people joining me… No! No, keep building up land and area. Better to have it and not need it. I *did* need to create it anyway to keep my rank increasing—I think—and that *may* have swayed my decision-making process. I set it up to run automatically and moved back to the real world as my internal instructions took hold.

<Ugh. I always get such nasty vertigo when I go from having fun playing with myself to looking at that window to the outside.> I was feeling ill. Going from watching a whole *world* at once to a flat representation of area I had never seen before and didn't control… bleh. <Navigation Bob, how are we doing? How long until we reach the Northmen's lands?>

"Great Spirit." Navigation Bob nodded lightly, focused on his tasks as always. "We should arrive within a day. Having several Mages in the A and B ranks helping to push us along was an *inspired* idea. As always, I am impressed by your forethought. Our speed has increased by at least half."

<I'm sorry, what now?> I looked out at the edges of my perception, and sure enough, there was a cadre of Mages talking with each other, laughing, and *pushing my dungeon*! Alright, I needed an explanation. <Who did this? How? I mean… I see the benefit, but…>

Dani chimed in privately to keep up my image in Bob's eyes, "I'm fairly certain it was arranged by–"

<Minya.>

"–Minya. Oh, you *did* know?" Dani drifted away from the screen and began to roam around the room. "Grace is playing with some kittens, so we are alone for a little while."

<I didn't know, but this has her fingerprints all over it.> I

chuckled and shook the head of a statue. Didn't have one of my own. <I really hope she isn't promising them too much.>

I listened in on a conversation I could 'hear' from the Mages outside. "Wealth, land, and a path advancement once we go through the portal!"

"She'd better come through; she was pretty convincing, but that seems a high price for a week of work."

"She *did* swear to make it happen, so…"

I had no idea who was talking, but still, I groaned. Typical Minya. I think I needed a break, and I hadn't been watching the myriad battles going on in my dungeon. That'd calm me down.

CHAPTER SEVEN

Manny the Manticore growled a deep, satisfied purr that didn't at all match his gruesome and gory visage. He looked at his paw, where a C-ranked adventurer was weakly struggling to push himself off of the foot-long claws that were impaling him. Manny shook him back and forth as the man's friends tried their best to distract him. With a flick and a claw retraction, the man was airborne. Manny snapped his jaws around the small snack, swallowing the human and letting his powerful digestive system convert the body and equipment directly into Essence.

"What a *purr*fect treat." Manny snapped his wings open as the other people went red with rage. He launched himself into the air, spinning in place until he reached a good height, then allowed his wings to angle downward. Mana-laced wind propelled him forward far faster than should have been possible, and in an instant, his glide turned into a *pounce.* As Manny landed on his victim, yet another foolish C-ranker, the only Mage in the group raced forward and slashed a bright line into Manny's flank.

Though it hurt, Manny only laughed lightly through the

pain. The Mage screamed as poisonous and *acidic* blood instantly welted his skin and started creating black lines that crept along his veins. The huge Boss grabbed the C-ranker with both front paws, reared back, and used his amazing, *opposable thumbs* to keep a grip while tearing the man in half.

"Alex!" the Mage cried out. "No! Everyone, escape! He's too powerful! I'll hold him off!"

"We aren't going to just leave you!"

"You *must!* I'm already done for!" The Mage hopped back and erected a barrier between the exit and the Manticore. He began channeling his Mana into the most powerful Invocation he knew. To his consternation, Manny simply sat down and watched the Mage as he channeled his power. Bright lines of power formed in the air and twisted into Runic formations that swirled around him. When he finished, he fell to his knees, gasping for air. This spell formation was half barrier… and half potent weapon.

Whoever interrupted the lines would have hostile Mana rampage through them until the power source was spent. There were few things of the same rank that could survive such a blow, but it had a heavy cost. If the Mage wasn't already aware he was dying, this particular Invocation would have never been used, or if it *were* used, it should have been a *very* careful consideration. He was now too weak to walk more than a few halting steps; every resource he had was utterly spent. The most infuriating thing was that the Manticore was still just *sitting* there, simply studying the spinning formation. Ah, well. At least the others had escaped.

He looked back toward the exit and went white wherever the black lines etched in his body allowed. His few remaining teammates were on the floor already beginning to decompose from the acidic poison in their bodies. Manny cocked his head to the side and pulled his tail out of the tunnels in the floor that had been designed expressly for that purpose.

"You… *monster*!" the Mage tried to bellow, but the words came out as a weak croak.

"In*deed*," the Manticore agreed, showing bright white teeth. "Beast, horror, monstrosity, abnormality, freak, mutant savage, titan. Most specifically, *territorial guardian*."

The Mage's eyes rolled into his head, and he collapsed to the floor. The poison had taken him. I started working on the raw Mana that was in the air, siphoning it off while studying the formations. Very interesting, but it could be further refined; it was *very* wasteful. <Hey, Manny! Nice work. Question though—should I have named you a 'thesaurus-icore'? Whenever you aren't in a serious situation, you tend to monologue synonyms. I worry that'll come back to bite you.>

"It is *fun*," Manny informed me simply. "Confusion and despair in them add a flavor that I simply cannot achieve by only frightening them."

After saying this and allowing me to remove the *highly* unstable spell work still drifting in the air, he popped the Mage into his mouth and chewed, apparently savoring his 'special seasoning'. Alrighty then. Of course, now I wondered what things taste like. Maybe I should go over a few memory Cores?

I checked on my other traps and—as I had hoped—the upgrades were playing havoc with the adventurers. Dozens had died, falling through 'solid' stone or being trapped by the new cage-style areas. A few were screaming as they were showered with spiders of all sizes. It was glorious and beautiful!

There were already people spreading the information, which meant people were moving more cautiously, rolling rocks or tapping the floor ahead of them with a long pole. I laughed slightly at their antics; it was funny to see a man wearing heavy armor and weighing hundreds of pounds poking the ground with a stick. I had done *way* more than that though. In fact, I upgraded most of the simple mechanical traps into a Runic version.

Even an area where there used to be a pillar trap that would crush someone into the ceiling had been replaced by an interlocked series of gravity Runes that would all activate at once. It had the same effect, but was far more spectacular to see in action. A person would walk into the trap and suddenly be smashed on the floor like rotten fruit. This had the added benefit of making the less perceptive among them panic about 'invisible Mobs'. I was starting to feel all sorts of better; senseless violence always calmed me down.

Let's see… violence, cultivation, upgrades. I watched some fighting for the rest of the day as I tinkered with various things, but all too soon, our flight was reaching its conclusion. This was unfortunate because as we approached, we were able to notice a strange distortion in the air. Casual inspection revealed what appeared to be a thin dome of light that covered a crater of some kind. *Closer* inspection told me that this was some kind of Runework that was suspended in midair.

I was entranced by what I saw… was this the *Wards* Tom had spoken about? How did they keep this in place without binding the Runes to something? What would happen if we touched it? <…I'm gonna touch it.>

DALE

"The Wards of Fek'koff are active! They've seen us arriving!" Tom's bellow echoed around the area. "*Dale*! We *mustn't touch* the Wards! Warn the dungeon!"

"What's happening?" Dale shouted back even as he noticed a strange distortion in the air… in the direction they were traveling. Uh-oh. "Cal! *Cal*! Don't touch the Wards! Tom says something bad will happen!"

<Dale. They're *so* pretty.> Dale had never heard the voice in his head sound so *sleepy*. <I just want to get a *little* closer…>

"Why are we still moving?" Tom looked on in horror as they got ever closer to the Wards. "No! The *lure*! It must also be active… they must be trying for rare and powerful resources if they would risk the lure… Dale! The dungeon! You need to find a way to have it look away from the Wards! Break its line of sight! If it can somehow see them, it will be drawn in, and the Wards will destroy this place!"

Dale started running toward the entrance to the dungeon, the world around him seeming to move in slow motion. Even so, the Wards were creeping ever closer and starting to resolve into squiggles in the air, Runes that were unreadable at this distance. Dale stopped short, knowing that there was no way to make it to the Core of the dungeon in time. Instead, he started focusing on his connection, then *flooded* it with as much Mana as he could.

He was blasted off his feet as the ground under him swirled and scattered at high speeds. A pulse of raw Mana traveled straight to the dungeon's Core, guided only by their connected soul.

<*Ow*!> Dale had never been so happy to hear pain in another being's voice. <How the *abyss* did absorbing Mana *hurt*? That shouldn't be– *Dale*! What did you just do to me?>

"Cal! Listen! The Wards have a powerful lure written into them! If you look at the light, you, as *technically* a monster, will be drawn to them! You need to stop our travel! Cal, we are going to hit the Wards!" Dale was shouting, uncaring of the people looking at him strangely.

<What in the world are you… talking… about…?> Dale sent another pulse of Mana, burning the soles of his feet and scorching the leather of his shoes. <*Ow*! Will you *stop* that? … oh. I see. Navigation Bob, pull back, *pull back*!>

Dale couldn't see what *exactly* was happening down there, but he knew that they were too close—and moving too fast—to avoid the Wards. They *were* going to hit them. it was only a matter of how hard and how directly. He turned and *ran* back to his teammates. They had all been shopping together, so he knew roughly the area they all had been in. He moved over to them at Mage-speed, then collected them into a bearhug as gently as possible and jumped straight upward.

Dale had a good view of the area underneath of him, his empowered jump taking them nearly a hundred feet in the air before they began to slow. The party clung to him like a huddle of confused koalas, but it only took a glance downwards for them to keep their silence.

Parts of the flying island had already passed through the glowing barrier, with no apparent ill effects. The dungeon was trying to course-correct, that much was obvious. The land was lifting toward him, and the mountain was tilting back to arrest their momentum.

Then something changed.

As far as Dale could tell, the area of the dungeon that was directly infused with the dungeon's influence came in contact with the Ward. There was a thunderous cracking sound and a croaking tremor that shuddered through the dungeon as it rebounded. The Ward wasn't safe either, shown by the quickly spreading cracks that ran along the entire dome of light. Several tons of stone and earth ran off the dungeon's island, raining into the vast crater below.

Momentum caused the island to tip the other direction, screeching and vibrating where it came in contact with the highly energetic wall. It made an absolute mess for both dungeon and surface dwellers as the few non-Runed structures not locked to the ground literally shook to pieces. Comparing the constant rumblings to an earthquake was a kindness, as a simple earthquake would have done far less damage to Mountaindale.

Several other Mages made it up in the air along with Dale, having had similar ideas, each with their own Koala-huddle of people important to them latched on with significant awkwardness. Guild Mages had entire ropes of people lifted. Church Mages had more finesse and used a kind of flotation bubble to keep their flock from harm. Elves had complicated nets of woven mana keeping groups aloft, and even the Headmaster was visible in the distance, keeping entire classes of students elevated on platforms of stationary hard-light.

Slowly, the metal-grinding-metal sounds quieted, and the dungeon came to a stop, resting a few hundred feet above the

Wards which were slowly but visibly repairing themselves. Dale returned to the ground and got an earful.

<Hey, Dale! We're here! You think *they* know we're here? I could knock again!>

CHAPTER EIGHT

"You *dare* to not only return but to bring unvetted *outsiders* and a *linked portal* to our capital?" Dale had thought that Tom was huge, but next to *this* man… Tom seemed almost normal-sized. "You smash into our Wards, you are riding a *dungeon*, and how could you *possibly* bring *Amazonians*?"

Tom was remaining remarkably calm for someone so massively outclassed. This brute, this *giant* of a man was shouting at Tom so hard that his hair was waving in the artificial breeze. Tom had an air of *regality* as he responded, so different from the man Dale knew. "*Stand down.* I have returned to reclaim my position in our society, and I will not stand here and be shouted at like a simple *serf* getting smoked by a *squire.* I know our rules, our laws, and I will take responsibility for them in front of the *Warlord.*"

"*Our* laws. *Our* rules. *My* Warlord." The man nodded slightly. "Yes, you *will* take responsibility, but not as a contender to the ranks! As a *trai–*"

Tom moved so fast that Dale would have thought he was a Mage if he hadn't known the difference. His warhammer appeared in his hands, and he hit the huge man with the

Inscribed weapon hard enough to send the remains of his corpse raining to the ground far below them. "Would anyone *else* like to break the law in my presence? On that note, would anyone else like to call me a *traitor*?"

Toms last words had been roared, and his face was red with rage, but his hammer had once more vanished into his interspatial bag. A new man walked forward, his eyes locked on Tom. "Hello, Tommulus. Honestly, I cannot tell if you passed or failed this first trial. He went too far, and *I* would have killed him if he had been acting as such toward me. Only the fact that you put away your weapon immediately gives me hope that you are sincere. Why did you *really* come back?"

"Brother, I wish to save our people. I have information and a plan of action." Tom nodded to his older brother, knowing that his harsh tone might not reflect his true feelings. "I *also* know that my words will not be heard unless I regain the favor of our Warlord. It is good to see you once more, Aidan."

"I had never expected that would happen either, Tom. You were the lost, fallen soldier in my mind; sent away, never to return." Aidan shook his head sadly. "I cannot call you 'brother', no matter how I wish I could. You know the law. In fact, remember not to call those of your blood 'brother' unless you have retaken your rightful place. Otherwise, they will likely use your exile to kill you, citing that you are illegally claiming Royal status. The rivalry still runs deeply."

Tom winced, taking a step back. "Ah. My thanks for not taking offense, General. I have been away… too long."

Aidan nodded regally. "Many things have changed. I hope you survive the unfortunate changes long enough to see the positive ones."

Without another word, the man turned and walked away. The majority of the others went with him, but a few of the barbarians waited to take Tom away to an undisclosed location. Dale looked at the marvelous Ward that had already repaired itself, thinking that perhaps the generalized term 'barbarian' for this people was… erroneous. They were obviously highly developed in many areas and were known masters of combat. Right then and there, he decided to do his best to keep his mouth shut unless Tom asked him to speak.

"Do you have a cadre that will follow and work on your behalf, Outsider Tom?" one of the Northman stood forward and impatiently questioned.

"I think so." Tom looked back at Dale, who nodded in agreement. He glanced over at Hans, who also showed that he would come, as did Rose. Tom walked forward, and his three comrades walked into the unknown with him.

There was faint amusement on Tom's face as he looked at the others. "You know, you are going to be the first outsiders to walk the streets of our capital in several hundred years. You will see sights that I think only The Master has seen and is still alive to speak of. Prepare yourself to witness true strength. And beauty. Beauty beyond compare."

Dale was still working out how to fly and so needed to be lowered to the edge of the huge crater along with the rest of the group on a mobile platform. As they approached the Ward, it peeled away and allowed them entry, closing instantly behind them. Dale looked at the shimmering curtain and grimaced. "No easy escape, hmm?"

"Already feel the need to run away?" one of the redheaded Northman jeered at him, tightening his grip on a double-bladed war axe. "You should have brought companions with more willpower, *outsider*."

Tom didn't even bother to look at the man, speaking gently to no one in particular, "Some would do well to realize that within a few days, this *outsider* may once more be a General of The People. I'm sure that there are areas still in need of latrine workers."

The Northman who had spoken simply grunted and spat over the edge of the platform but remained quiet afterward. The platform stopped a dozen feet above the ground, and all the Northman hopped off, which made the platform raise even higher. Rose looked down, then at the others with her with an arched brow. "You're joking."

"If you fear heights or cannot handle the minor jarring a jump from here will inflict, you might want to leave now," Tom sincerely informed her. "I will not hold it against you."

Rose scoffed and did a backflip off the edge, landing with an easy roll and hopping to her feet. Hans laughed and followed, doing several twists and flips before landing gently on his feet. Tom went next, landing with slightly bent knees. Dale went last, deciding to have some fun with it. He hopped off, spreading his arms and legs, belly-flopping on the ground and leaving a small indentation.

"I love being a Mage." Dale laughed as he pushed himself off the ground. "I barely even felt that!"

"Dale." Tom had a hand against his brow. "Please do not act the fool in a situation where it could cost me my position and therefore the lives of my people."

"Right." Dale stood up and shook lightly, removing the dust from his outfit. The Mithril equipment he was wearing was obviously undamaged, and in only a short moment, he was fully presentable once more. As they walked, Dale looked around the area with barely contained excitement. The crater they were over was so deep that the base of it was lost to darkness now that the day was starting to creep to evening, but even so, the view was breathtaking.

They were walking on a bridge that spanned the entirety of the crater without any discernible supports. There were two other long bridges that connected to this one at nearly the exact center, creating an 'X' across the entire area. The exact center seemed to be their destination, and Dale was excited to see *why*. As they got closer, they could see that there was a circular round-about created by the bridges surrounding a hexagonal hole in the bridge. Closer, *closer* they walked. One of the guards nodded at Tom, who used that cue to step off and into the open air.

"Tom!" Rose gasped, lurching forward. Two swords

appearing at her throat stopped her movement, but the huge men didn't move any further, finding that Hans had a wetly glistening dagger pressed to their jugulars.

"Stand. Down," Hans hissed at them. They slowly stood back, then spat at his feet when they were clear.

"So, he consorts with *assassins*," one of the men sneered. "This is good to know. I go ahead to warn the Warlord."

"So, he *'consorts'*. That's what *you* sound like," Hans mocked the man, eying him critically. "How about *this*? *You* threatened my wife and lived. *Once*. How about you pass *that* on, as the next person to try a similar action *will not*."

Both of the Northmen glared at them before stepping off the edge of the bridge into the open air, leaving the small party alone. Dale looked at the couple, then at the drop-off. "He did warn us that a fear of heights would be a bad idea. Hey, if I splatter on the ground, just go ahead and head back up."

"Will do!" Hans saluted sarcastically.

After rolling his eyes slowly so Hans could see it, Dale stepped into the open air and plummeted toward the ground thousands of feet below. He had plenty of time to look around, noticing that the sides of the crater were intricately carved with mosaics and… ah-ha! There were Runes hidden among the artwork! He didn't have long to study them, but he was nearly positive that they were what created the Warded dome around this area. He made a mental note to mention that to Cal since he was pretty sure the dungeon would study that while it waited around.

In fact, he mentally reached out along his connection, "*Cal. There are Runes carved along the walls of the crater.*"

<That's great, but I still can't look at the pretty lights without something bad happening, *Dale*.> The scathing reply came nigh-instantaneously. <Thanks for rubbing it in, meanie.>

"Whoops." Dale chuckled at the thought that he got to experience this and the dungeon didn't. He wouldn't let a *location* stop him from enjoying himself. Not today. Something else he noticed was that he fell straight down. He had fallen so many times that he knew that this was unnatural.

Typically, falling like this would cause you to drift around or something, but Dale instinctively understood that there was something *pulling* on him. Ninety feet off the ground, he started to slow down. At ten feet, he was barely moving. Then whatever force had been holding him gave out, and he flopped unceremoniously to the carved stone ground. "That was awesome!"

CHAPTER NINE

Hans and Rose landed at the base of the crater just after Dale was standing again, and the assassin was clutching the nonplussed archer for dear life. They were on their feet in moments and chose not to speak about the screams they had been issuing moments ago. The entire group started walking. At a normal human walking speed, the walk would have taken half a day, which meant that *they* reached a keep within a few hours.

"We have arrived." Tom turned to speak to his friends. "Do your best to speak always to the rank of the person you are talking to, and be respectful without being deferential. We speak in terms of 'King' and such in outsider lands for your convenience, but we have no *King*. We have a *Warlord*. We don't have *Princes*; we have *Generals* of various ranks. Our nobility are our Officers, and powerful individuals are various ranks of Sergeant. All of these positions are subject to rapid—and what you would consider *brutal*—turnover. Positions are won and held by blood and competency."

"Wait, so how will you have *any* say?" Dale piped up. "Your Ki– *Warlord* must be at least in the A-ranks by now, right? No, wait, you said something about this earlier..."

Tom shook his head. "Anyone B-rank seven or above is given a different classification and serves as an Elder or Champion of The People. They are dismissed from service when it is not a time of war, to improve themselves in whatever way they deem fit. Being Warlord is demanding and leaves little time for rank advancement. It is not a position people typically seek and actually has the slowest turnover of all Officer positions."

"But aren't you trying to take that position?" Rose questioned him directly, and heads all around them snapped to them to listen to the answer.

Tom's eyes went wide. "Rose! Don't talk like that! You'll have your tongue removed! Of *course* not, I only seek to gain an audience with the Warlord where he will listen to my words and consider them!"

When nothing else happened, Tom took a few deep, calming breaths. Dale wasn't sure if he should ask questions but decided it was best to do so before entering the keep. "Why is the Warlord out here, at what must be the edge of your city?"

At this, Tom swelled with pride. "Unlike *Kings*, my people know that the duty of the leader of The People is to protect and nurture their charges. The Warlord is at the head of any confrontation and is almost always the first to join combat. They protect their people; they are not protected *by* them!"

The Northmen surrounding them slammed a fist into their metal chest piece, barking a '*Huh*' at the same time. Hans looked around with a cocked eyebrow. "So there is a society-wide sign of approval? And it's *choreographed*! Oh, my goodness, this is adorable! Why have I never been here before?"

"Hans... please..." Tom squeaked out around his embarrassment. They arrived at the gates of the keep, which rumbled open grudgingly to allow admittance. A hairless, shirtless man covered in countless tattoos stepped out, glaring at the newcomers.

"Here we go again," the tattooed man grumbled, coming to a halt before them. "Who among you vouches for the others?"

"I do," Tom responded instantly before anyone could talk or Hans could make a snide comment.

"You place these others in your honor?"

"I do," Tom responded again.

"Know then, if they speak of the secrets of our people without proper authorization, your honor is forfeit." The tattooed man locked eyes with Tom, giving a slight head shake.

"I so acknowledge and swear." Tom's words made the other man sigh softly and shake his head. Several tattoos lit up and vanished from the man, leaving bare skin behind.

"You always were too trusting, Tommulus," the man stated with deep concern in his voice. "I truly hope you are right about them."

They were ushered into the keep, and the doors slowly closed behind them. Hans looked concerned and prodded Tom with a non-poisoned dagger. "What was that all about? Did you just marry us? Did he have *Runes* tattooed on his body? That doesn't work. Why did that work?"

"That was me guaranteeing that the three of you wouldn't tell other outsiders what happens in this domicile from now on. If you do, I will be honorless, and all The People will know it." Tom swallowed deeply. "*Please* watch your words carefully."

Rose stopped in her tracks. "Tom… in the past I've heard you say 'my honor is my life'. Did you mean that *literally*?"

"Yes. Just like a Mage, if I gave my word and it was broken, then I will suffer. In this case, I'll die. *Please* keep what you see here to yourselves." Tom looked at a thunderstruck Hans. "As for the markings on his skin… our people have followed the path of Runescript further than any other. I told you, when it comes to Runes, there are none better than the Northmen."

"I thought you were being braggadocious!" Hans threw his hands into the air. "I had no idea you had a way to make Runed *people*! Can they actually use their Essence or Mana still, or are they hobbled by the tattoos?"

"No, they are fully functioning warriors." Tom puffed up his chest, obviously proud of his home nation and having fun with the response he was getting. "We can talk about it later, but only *here* and only if there is no one else listening. Or I die. Are we clear on that?"

"Yes!" Hans was nearly shouting in frustration. "Now *talk*!"

"The Warlord is ready for you." The guard opened a door.

"Whatever you do, do not speak," Tom ordered the others seriously just before they walked through the doorway, some more happy about arriving than others. Hans was nearly having a fit, and his face was twisting as he tried to hold in his questions.

Dale narrowed his eyes leerily when he saw the man awaiting them in full armor. This was easily the largest person that could still *technically* qualify as a human that he had ever seen. His armor likely weighed half a ton but didn't seem to impede his movement at all. Not only was the armor thick and dense, but it was also coated in so many Runes that the surface might as well have been a page torn from a book.

"Hello. I would say 'welcome', but you are *not*. An exile and outsiders, along with many others, a *portal to our capital*, and a flying dungeon. Not to mention, *Amazonians*?" The Warlord stood and stalked toward them, his movement eerily silent. "The orders were to destroy you all. Why are you standing in front of me?"

"Sir!" Tom barked, slamming his arms together. "This unranked individual has returned to prove his worth. I request to be tested for combat fitness!"

"You want to be *reinstated*?" the Warlord sneered, his eyes cold and calculating.

"No, *sir!* I ask only for the chance to prove that any reason for my exile is void!" Tom's eyes stayed locked straight ahead, not following the Warlord as he paced in front of him.

"Breaking your exile, hmm?" The Warlord stopped, face inches from Tom's. "Then I suppose you'll want your old position back, and you'll try coming to me to whine about something? I want to say no; I *really* want to say no. But what use are regulations if they are not followed? For anyone else, I would follow them. I can't kill you outright just because you are the blood of my blood. Oh, Tom. How I *want* to ignore regulation."

"Doesn't nepotism normally work the other way around?" Dale hadn't meant to say the words aloud, and he only realized he had when the back of his head hit the wall.

"Insubordination, speaking out of turn to a commanding officer," the Warlord coldly stated. "Ten lashes. The punishment has been assigned and delivered."

Dale stepped forward and coughed. He looked down, seeing that his clothes were slightly brighter in ten spots. Almost like metal that had been hit by a hammer. Dale looked around in confusion. He hadn't even seen the strikes, and he was a *Mage*. He should have at least *seen* them coming.

The Warlord's attention lingered almost *approvingly* on Dale's clothing for a moment as well before returning to Tom. "As I said before, I will give you the *chance* required by law. When would you like to begin?"

Tom took a knee, bowing his head. "I formally request to rejoin The People as soon as possible."

"Then we shall see if you are a force multiplier or detractor within a few hours, won't we?" The Warlord smiled, but the expression held no joy. "Bring him to the Berserker cells, and place the proper schema. Our nation will watch you rise or fall, as is the law. Your... *tagalongs* will have guest rights. We will prepare the extractors in preparation of your failure."

The man swept out of the room, and the group was shoved toward the door. Hans locked eyes with Tom. "Extractors? That doesn't sound nice."

"If I fail the examination, I will have proved that I 'lied'. I will lose all honor. Then there is nothing keeping you all from speaking to others about national secrets." Tom ran a hand through his hair. "They'll take your memories of everything that happened since passing the Wards. It won't come to that, though. I'll pass. Please have faith in me."

"Warn us before we agree to things like that by accident!"

Hans chided him, his knuckles white from gripping his fist so hard.

"You should have guessed by now that he *couldn't*," Dale inferred, getting a nod from Tom. "A geas, yes? Where a Mage swears something and his own power ensures he follows through? That… can't be safe."

"Got it in one." Tom sighed deeply as the smell of blood began to permeate the air. They were getting close to their destination. "The weight of a promise made by a Mage but in Runic form and applied to a willing non-Mage. Our life, the basis of our society, our *honor*."

"How *barbaric*," Rose whispered as she clutched Hans' arm. "How many die… just *getting* the geas?"

Tom half-grinned and winked at her. "Starting to come together, isn't it? Our moniker comes from people who knew *some* things but couldn't explain them to the general populace. 'Barbarians' indeed."

CHAPTER TEN

<Let's see…> I looked over the analytics provided by Data Bob and found that there were currently more people throwing themselves against my defenses than ever before. Not only were the cultivators in the area working hard to gain the new Soul Space tokens I was offering, but the portal to Mountaindale was running constantly. People from multiple nations were cycling in and out night and day, supplying me with fresh victims every single minute.

The Guild's attempts at regulating when people were allowed into the dungeon had broken down completely. They had been caught denying access to necromancers, and soon after that incident, people were coming and going as they pleased no matter the threat. Barry had vanished, going across the world in an attempt to rally the remainder of the Guild and bring them to safety, luckily for me. The downside to all of this activity was that I had no time to respawn creatures, reset traps, or get personally involved in many of the fights.

So, I increased the difficulty. I had Dregs managing the first four floors pretty well, and all it cost me was feeding that Wisp-Core team a fraction of the energies collected. That worked for me perfectly. Not only did I get to focus on floors that were more *fun*, but Dregs' style of doing things was different enough that people didn't expect the change when they got down to my more personalized floors. Dregs mainly used fire. *Lots* of fire.

Her style of doing things was fine, and as a bonus, it led to a lot of new people expecting that fire was the theme of the *entire* dungeon. They would get gear, potions, and weapons built around countering the fiery floors, then suddenly find that all their gear would be useless. Merchants were having a great time collecting tokens, which were now the only useful currency in the area. Gold had become worthless here with the knowledge that they couldn't use it for long.

In fact, Mountaindale had begun flooding the world at large with gold, silver, and platinum, knowing that one way or another, the currency would soon be just shiny metal. They bought artifacts, knowledge, rare materials, animals, and anything else they could think of to tempt me into granting them tokens for things they could *actually* take with them. The number of patterns I was gaining *daily* had increased to the point that I was having trouble keeping track of it all. I had a perfect memory—of course I did, everything was *crystal* clear. Heh. Still, when a list is in the multiple thousands and growing, it can become difficult to think of what you want or need.

In short… it was glorious. I was getting *bloated* with power, or I would have been if I weren't already devoting everything to my inner world. I was going to work on that later, but I was still caught up with watching everything going on in the real world. Most importantly for me right now, I was following a group of Mages as they pushed through the final challenges the golems offered to reach The Mage's Recluse. I watched the wonder appear in their eyes and knew that this was the start of a great couple of weeks for me.

This wasn't the first group of Mages to reach this level, but the Dark Elves hadn't spread the word, nor had Madame Chandra, nor The Master, nor for some reason the group that had lost a few members a few days ago. It was *less* important that everyone know about it because I knew that there was a portal being built that would give me *way* more Essence and Mana, but I still wanted my work to be appreciated. This place had been my first real attempt to make an area beautiful and *not* deadly. I had trained Attendants; I had made housing and food. Abyss take it, I wanted people to literally *fight* over the honor of living here! Maybe someday.

After the group slowly calmed down and accepted that this was a non-combat zone, they meandered until they found the stairs down to the next level. They didn't descend; instead, I watched as they claimed homes and got to some serious relaxing. Each of them had a small 'welcome basket', which, among other things, included a keygem for the portal to the surface and back. I watched as the rogue of the group snuck off, popped through the portal, and sold the information to the Guild, then to as many other people as he could before it started becoming public. He returned to the dungeon with a satchel full of tokens and got back to his new manor just before the others decided to regroup.

Heh. They were going to be surprised when they got back and found that their new discovery was already almost common knowledge. What a sneaky-sneak. I approved. They decided to take a look at the next floor but were forced to retreat before they got a proper estimation of the floor's value. The lower they went, the more the suffocating presence of my Mana impacted them. Until they had increased in ranking more, they simply wouldn't survive whatever was waiting for them; they knew it at a deep and visceral level.

Then again, it may have been the 'fear' Runes I had lightly interspersed on the stairwell, but who knew for sure? The screaming rocks might have done it, too. Really could have been anything. The Pit—as I had decided to call it—was designed for groups of Mages from B-rank-six to A-rank-zero. If you were fighting something at your own level *alone*, it would be a hard fight, but in the Pit, there were *swarms* of Elementals. You needed teamwork, the ability to adjust as you went, lots of trust, and a not-insignificant amount of *luck*. This group had the teamwork down, but if the rogue were an example of the trust between them… I would have enjoyed the snack.

I switched my view over to some C-rankers that were fighting Cats in the labyrinth. They had caught my attention a few days back, and I was trying to work out *why*. They were certainly skilled enough, but something about them felt strange. Not *bad*, just *strange*. A Flesh Cat swiped at their front liner's midsection, but he evaded the attack and returned a blow that left a shallow line of red in the Beast. Odd… he had hit pretty hard there. That should have easily taken the Cat apart.

The battle with this Cat raged on with the creature eventually trying to escape when it finally became seriously injured. The group pursued, catching and eventually felling the mutated Mob. The sheer amount of time it took for them to succeed was really tickling at my senses. I mentally reviewed the combat, looking for flaws in their fighting style, watching their muscles to see if they were holding back… *There* it was.

They weren't holding back, and they were even *more* skilled than I had originally thought. Now when I looked at the weapons and armor they were wearing, I looked at the *quality*. These people were *poor*. I mean, who uses a weighted iron longsword to fight C-ranked Beasts? Abyssal *professionals*, apparently. I was in awe, serious *awe* at their ability. I couldn't figure out *how* they didn't have better equipment; being in the C-ranks was not an easy or fast process for anyone except Dale.

I could only come up with a few answers. Either they were poor because they were funneling coins to someone else, or they were working to perfect their skills by using substandard equipment. I looked into them, noting that they had only the most basic of cultivation techniques. These were people who worked with what they had, and I was flat out impressed. I decided to test the waters and see what sort of situation they were actually in. I worked to create a treasure chest a few rooms away, one that would be hard to miss.

To maintain fairness, I directed a few of the stronger Cats in the area to guard the room, and I watched closely to see how everything played out. There was a Wither, a Cloud, and a Coiled Cat standing guard together. The tactics my Cats used now varied greatly from when they had first been created. When the adventurers appeared, the Coiled Cat sprang at them with the Cloud Cat on its back. The Cloud Cat jumped off of that Beast, then the wall, and came at the group from a different angle and above. The Wither Cat prowled around, waiting for a chance to strike.

The battle took for-*freaking*-ever. I had seen entire *floors* cleared in the amount of time it took for the outcome of this battle to be decided. Between the more advanced defenses of the Coiled Cat, who took almost no damage from any single attack; the agile Cloud Cat, who could avoid the heavy and relatively slow iron weapons; and the Wither Cat staying out of combat unless it was convenient… ugh. The people were skilled and had massive endurance. They took very few direct hits, and any grazing blows were absorbed even by the shoddy armor they wore.

Not to say that they ended the fight without any injuries, but they did well enough that they would still be able to press forward. Then they saw the treasure chest, the shining golden light it emitted strong enough to catch anyone's eye. The five men walked over and tossed open the chest, staring at the contents in shock. The leader of the group looked at one of the weapons in the chest, then at his own hand. "Is that my sword?"

"It looks the same?" his second-in-command piped up. "How is that possible? I even see the same dent on that side!"

The leader picked up the weapon, turning it over and over in confusion. He gave it an exploratory swing, and his eyes lit up. "It's the same… but better! So much better! It is light, and I can *feel* the power it contains!"

"Hey, my bow is in here!" the archer of their group exclaimed. "A quiver of my arrows, too!"

"My knives!"

"My shield!"

I laughed quietly to myself as they traded out their weapons. I was feeling pretty good about myself; my good deed of the day being finished and all. Then I heard them start talking to each other.

"This alone justifies paying for the portal to get here, but I can't believe that this dungeon only gives out wooden coins or potions usually. It's a good thing we found that merchant who likes to collect curios from the dungeon, or we wouldn't even be able to get home at the end of all of this," the archer was grumbling, but the others took it in stride.

"I guess the wild claims of incredible wealth were a little exaggerated." The leader sighed. "It's too bad. I could have really used the money."

"Same all around, boss man." Their tanker stood and swung his shield around with practiced ease. "At least we were warned about those traps at the end of each floor. Can you imagine going up to something, thinking you were about to get a reward, and then being dropped into a trap? Pretty sneaky of this place to make those."

"I'm still confused about that," the knife-user stated boldly. "I want to see what happens for myself. The odd cube almost looks like it is *asking* for the wooden coins this place gives us. How do we know that–"

"We *already* agreed not to tempt fate," the leader calmly informed him. "We have too many people relying on us to return home."

<Ugh. Just *ugh.*> I looked around until I found Minya, who was at a small shrine on the surface trying to convert people into Dungeon Born. Not many people listened after it had gotten around that none of the people she led down were seen again. Though, now that Mages would be in the Recluse, that might change. <Minya, can I ask a favor, please? A group of people in the dungeon are being scammed out of a huge fortune by a merchant up here. Can you find and punish him for me?>

"It'd be my pleasure." I filled her in on the details, and her scowl turned into a mask of rage. "I cannot stand that there is someone out there taking advantage of people when they need help the most. Consider it done, Cal."

<Thanks, Minya. You know I'm all about the fair chance. Succeed on your own merit and whatnot.> I was trying to calm down. <Abyss, *I'm* giving people a better chance to succeed and survive than this scammer is!>

"You sure are, you mass-murdering people eater."

<You say the sweetest things.>

CHAPTER ELEVEN

I had just been given an interesting plant as a gift from the first Wood Elf I had ever seen. I *really* wanted to eat her to see what the difference was between the subsets of Elves, but she didn't stick around. Next time for sure. The plant was a complicated herb that had some seriously potent medicinal properties, but that wasn't even why I was so excited about it.

The leaves of the plant could absorb corruption from the air, cleaning and purifying it. Its roots had structures on them that allowed the plant to release the earth corruption it was taking out of the air, and the rest of the corruption was used to boost its growth and medicinal properties. This sounded similar to standard plants, but this one was *way* more effective. I'd say it produced clean air at least fifty times as efficiently as another plant its own size.

Of course, the first thing that I did with this miraculous plant was to freshen up my dungeon. There's only so much that regular ferns can accomplish when you get deep enough into the dungeon. Within hours, the monsters roaming around were breathing deeper, actually physically strengthened by the clean and fresh air. Their blood had been starved of air for so long that they had adapted to it, so this boost made them *way* more energetic. I *was* worried that anyone throwing a fireball around could be up to twice as strong as usual, but I think that the trade-off was worth it.

Next, I pulled a sample of the plant into my Soul Space and started planting it in unobtrusive locations. Not only would this help to generate new air, but when people *did* start arriving, I assumed that the quality of air would drop precipitously. This would help to mitigate that factor, and it was a timely addition to my collection. I took some time to roam around, inspecting the area and watching as the earth seemed to slowly creep upward on the horizon. It was very fun to watch, *very* pretty, and if it had been anything or anywhere else, it would have been *very* disturbing to see this happen.

A thought crossed my mind, and if I had a brow, it would have furrowed. I just realized that I had not increased in rank, even with the massive gains of Essence, Mana, and the rapid expansion of my Soul Space. I was doing everything I had been instructed was needed. I had more energy than any other being at my level; I was *positive* of this fact. So, why was I not increasing in ranking? I thought back over conversations and my personal studies. I knew that higher tiers of power required greater amounts of understanding and energy to advance… Was the difference truly this drastic?

I looked at the sheer amounts of energy I was taking in. A whole lot of it. But no matter how I looked at it, I could not yet be taking in enough energy to keep up with even a fraction of what the world produced. While my ley lines had certainly changed and regulated the flow of power in the world, it was not like I was taking all of that in at once! Was there a better way to collect the power? As powerful as I was, I was still taking in nearly as much energy as I could handle at once, every second of every day. Even still, I was always able to take in refined energies from anyone who had fallen within my influence.

Perhaps that was the key to this. Currently, I was taking in as much *raw* energy as my Core could handle. Was there a way to process, to refine, to make better in any way my raw consumption? This led me to a chilling thought—dungeons were absolutely stuffed with refined Essence and Mana. I had very little issues with any dungeon core that I had been fed, but what if I was not the first to realize this? What if dungeons, *as a race,* were created for that express purpose—to feed some greater being?

If that were the case... Well, even if it were, what would change for me? I would want to grow stronger? Find a better place to hide? I had all of that, and all of my contingency plans already set. The question became—how could I use this information to my own advantage? Every Core that I encountered in the past I had already either befriended or eaten. The only thing that really concerned me was that everything I had encountered so far was always lower rank than I was.

It could be that the world had hundreds or thousands of dungeons and that they were simply deeper than my effects could reach. If I had the time, I would *eventually* find them. Most likely, it would either end up as a fight or an uneasy coexistence. Or! Or, similar to Kantor, there could be stronger dungeons that simply were not on the surface of the planet or even below it; like me... they could be flying. *There* was a scary thought. Should I make some air combat creatures?

I shook myself mentally, getting out of that tangent of thought. This planet had roughly three weeks remaining of non-destruction. Frankly, the reality was that I would likely never have to worry about encountering a stronger dungeon or dungeon-munching being. What I did need to consider and work on was passing through the A-ranks and achieving S-rank. Unfortunately... I felt my cultivation one more time before sighing. That was going to be a long way off unless something drastically changed.

DALE

Tom grunted in pain as the whip came down on his side. It was moving oddly, nearly slowly, and seemed to caress his body like a lover as it tore open a fresh line for blood to pour out of. Tom had been moving between grunting, silence, and screaming for hours at this point. The only interlude from the beatings he was taking was when a new implement was chosen to use on him or when he was force-fed his own dripping blood.

"All you need to do to make this stop is admit that you cannot *actually* control yourself," the whip wielder told Tom for the umpteenth time. "Just let your base instincts take over. Show us the animal that we all know is in there. Show us the *Blood Berserker* waiting inside of you."

Dale was nearly sick again as he looked around the antechamber at the approving nods of the people who had gathered to watch. Apparently, there was some form of Runic system in place that allowed others far distant to observe what was happening as well. Dale could not reconcile the terrible things being done in this room with the absolute stark beauty and advanced magical systems he had seen since he had arrived.

He had no idea how this people had been so mislabeled. To call them barbarians, to scoff at their lack of advancement and militaristic society… it was obvious that their methods of hiding information were effective. Then watching Tom being beaten, whipped, and healed slightly just so they could restart the process again and again? The dichotomy of this nation was making his head spin. Dale looked down at his friend who was doing his best to hold himself up proudly even though his arms were tied to posts far above him. There had been several times where Tom had fallen and been forced to rely on the bindings to keep him upright, but he always got back to his feet under his own power.

"I say once again; I have defeated the affliction." Tom somehow managed to say this calmly, even if his words were broken by his gasping breaths. "Outside of our own nation, this is such a common affliction that the treatment for it can be found with any who teach their students how to control fire. It is seen simply as a common risk of those with affinity for the flame. It is treated as such, just as a burn on the skin would be, with just as easy of a solution."

For the first time since he had started this process, he got an actual response to his small speech. The man whipping him stepped forward and said, "So you say. How thoroughly is this tested? We know the weak ways of *Outsiders*, how they coddle their children, how they do not temper themselves. Can you tell me that they have dug as deep as we have? Can you point at any of them who would test for the madness as thoroughly as we? If so, swear it upon your honor, and we will be done with this. If not, stop trying to sway us with the words of a coward."

"How is he being cowardly?" Rose whispered, burying her face into Han's shirt.

The man with the whip waited a moment, watching Tom's face. When the young man did not respond, he simply nodded and resumed his position. A moment later, the whip landed on yielding flesh once more. This continued for hours longer, deep into the night, before Tom's arms were suddenly released from their binding. He fell to the floor, unable to support his own weight. The hairiest healer Dale had ever seen stepped forward and closed any wounds that were life-threatening.

"All we have determined from this is that you have a high pain tolerance now. Possibly that you have somehow been able to find a way to resist the taste of your own blood tearing at your mind." A man nearly as large as the warlord had stepped on to the stage and approached Tom. "Now, we are going to take a look at you and determine if you have been bound by another. If so, if you have not actually come this far under your own power–"

"Sir, I have no fear. I have nothing to hide. Please commence the process." Tom was slapped across the face hard enough to send him reeling. Interrupting an officer was always a bad idea, but Tom knew that the lecture the man was giving typically took a full ten minutes. It alternated between threats, bribes, compromises, all in an attempt to force the person on trial to give in to their baser instincts.

"Your impertinence knows no bounds," the huge man stated coldly. "You have picked up the bad habits of the weak, of the lazy, of the undisciplined. It may be better for you and for us all, if you simply give in and allow us to put your name on the list of those that died with their honor intact. That is the deal I have been authorized to offer. Your exile will be posthumously revoked, and your body will be placed in the halls of the honored dead. What say you?"

Tom was silent far too long for Dale's comfort. It was obvious that he was seriously considering the deal. Finally, he shook his head. "No. As much as I do not fear dying for my people, I have made it my purpose in life to live for my people and to help them live on as well. I feel that I will not be able to–"

A second slap across the face cut off Tom's impromptu speech, hard enough to send a tooth flying. "Maggot, you will answer in the future with a simple yes or no! Binders, begin the process!"

CHAPTER TWELVE

"You know that this entire system is designed so that we should never need to take in an exile. The law exists so that we *can*, but less than ten have ever returned." Tom was strapped down to a table and fully stripped to a loincloth. His shirt had been taken off previously to prepare for the whipping. Five men stood around him, each of them carrying mystical implements used for purposes Dale could not divine. "What we are doing is not torture, I *swear* it, Tommulus. This is the *only* method that has ever been proven to force a Berserker to show themselves."

The eldest among them looked at Tom and made one final offer, "As always, there is a one in ten chance that inspection of your honor will cause your life to end. As you have gone through this process once before, you have better odds than most. Still, I urge you to take the offer that has been given to you."

When Tom did not respond, the Elder simply sighed and nodded. One by one, the five men plunged small daggers into Tom's limbs, the final one piercing his chest. There was a swell of Mana that battered the senses of everyone present, and an incredibly intricate Rune appeared in the air above Tom's face for a brief moment. Then all of the knives were taken out, and the men stepped away.

The Elder cleared his throat gently and softly called, "Medic!"

The extraordinarily hairy healer bounded forward once more and laid his hands on Tom's chest. Slowly, almost *too* slowly, the wound in his chest closed, and Tom took a deep shuddering breath. The Elder nodded and looked around the room. "His honor is intact and is his own. This man has taken no permanent mate, nor has he bound himself to another beyond seeking knowledge and personal growth. He has a teacher but no *master*. This man has not disregarded the terms of his exile and, by honor alone, is fit to return to service."

"Binders, thank you for your time and expertise," the huge man that seemed to be running this trial spoke respectfully. He then turned to look at the crowd once more. "His *honor* is intact. Unfortunately, we all know that is not enough for someone to be allowed to serve The People. The next test will begin shortly."

"There is *more* to this?" Hans was livid. Knives kept appearing in his hands and disappearing into unknown folds of his outfit. "This is a *farce*. This is a way for them to discourage people from returning when they have been sent away in disgrace. The cure for Berserker rage is well-documented and available everywhere!"

"Do you think they just refuse to use methods they have not created or discovered themselves?" Rose looked at the two of them, hoping that they would have some answers.

"It sounds plausible," Dale thoughtfully replied. "They seem to have extreme hatred for anyone outside of their own nation. I've talked to Tom about this before, and they might have good reason for it. Also, I believe the next part of this process is combat, to show that in a stressful situation, he is able to maintain himself."

Tom was pulled to his feet by the healer, handed a warhammer, and pointed toward a door. He was barely standing, but it seemed that the people assigned to his trial were not going to wait for him to be in tip-top form. At least a dozen people walked out of the door and on to the stage, all manner of weaponry showing in their hands. Each of them wore shining armor and grim expressions. The man in charge of the trial looked at Tom—who was once more wearing only his normal clothing—and began to speak.

"If you give in to your Berserker instincts, if you kill *any* of my men or if you die, you will have failed." He stepped back and off of the stage, signaling for combat to begin.

CAL

I needed to get a hold of some of the Warding schema I knew was below me. I was *positive* that it would be beneficial to my plans. In fact, it seemed almost tailor-made for dungeons and other stationary entities. Runescripts could make certain effects but needed to be powered with what amounted to a single-use charge. The ritual I had designed to carve ley lines into the world and make energy begin flowing was potent and powerful but still essentially was a constant drain of power while only having a very specific effect.

From what I understood... Wards were fundamentally different. All I knew was from the rumors floating around on my island, but if they were even a *quarter* as useful as people were saying, I needed them. Wards were—allegedly—ways to make shielding or other permanent phenomena and tie them to a power source. This power source could even be something as simple as ambient Essence, which would be consumed as needed. From what I could tell, Wards were the little brother of Runescripting and followed very similar principles.

I had been able to make things that were *similar* to Wards, such as creating areas of enhanced gravity. This had actually been the application of physical forces and not an energetic barrier that would stop people, projectiles, or techniques. I really hoped that Dale's team was successful and they convinced the Northmen to hand all of that sweet information over.

Otherwise, I would need to learn how to do it with trial and error or stage an assault against an entire nation and scoop up all the information before they destroyed it. Or… perhaps there was a third option. A *dastardly* option. Mu-hu-*ha-ha*!

I started carefully navigating the island toward the ground, using the resistance of the Wards to settle as closely as possible to the rim of the huge crater. Then—*hee-hee*—I began extending my influence and adding the wall of the crater to my 'dungeon'. Eventually, I would reach something that was connected to the Wards, and at that point, I could outright steal it! I was betting that it would be placed in a central location—likely the midpoint and bottom of this entire depression—but depending on how long I'd be staying here, I might get at it.

Stone, water, dirt. I had been losing huge amounts from my Island, thousands of tons of material. I had the space; I knew that my enchantments and Runescripts were up to the task of transporting anything extra that I took on. Because of this, I *really* did not hold back. When I left here, one way or another, I would be taking a big chunk of this land. Of course, the majority of my efforts went toward sending a line of influence deeper and deeper, following the wall of the cliff.

I set my influence to flow along without my full attention, which turned out to be a very good idea. After only a few hours, I found something. Something beautiful. Now it was mine. *Mine*! I caressed this beautiful symbol, this Masterwork of swirls and loops, the most perfect conduits for energy that… oops. I accidentally ate it.

I couldn't help myself! It was so good that I'd simply *needed* to try it! Luckily, or unfortunately, or some combination of both… as I studied what I had just absorbed, I realized that it had to be part of the Ward that made the 'lure'. It was a self-contained symbol, which meant that, most likely, it was etched all over the entire crater. Destroying this one single portion of it should not damage the integrity of the Ward at large.

I was glad that I had kept my influence moving because every other active process I needed had come to a halt when I had started looking over the lure. I got back to work, then started processing the information I had gained. The lure was incredibly intriguing beyond its function to make it interesting. If this was an example of what Wards would look like, how they would function, how they were made… yeah, I was going to need a lot more examples.

Normally, I could extrapolate from incomplete data. I did not think that was going to be the case here until I had a much larger repository of knowledge. Frankly, I had no idea how fleshy brains had been able to create this work of art. In fact, it would not surprise me at all to learn that the Northmen had a captive or friendly dungeon that did the hard work for them.

As far as I could understand it, and using this lure as proof of concept, a Ward was a Runescript that contained a *pattern*. Then whatever pattern had been affixed to the Runes would have the intrinsic ability of the creature, usable as the creator saw fit. Seeing as how a pattern was used to create a creature an object from pure energy—such as a dungeon monster—it was highly unlikely that simple creatures like the humans below me could have unlocked the secrets needed to create this. This made my theory of a dungeon working with them far more plausible. What really scared me… as I studied the lure and chewed thoughtfully on the pattern… I realized why it was so effective.

This Ward was created using the energy pattern of a demonic creature, namely a succubus. The only reason I knew this was because I could now create a succubus—if I wanted to—with this information. There was only *one* reason I could think of that a dungeon would have access to this sort of information.

Somewhere below me was an infernal dungeon.

CHAPTER THIRTEEN

As I continued to take more of the crater wall as my own property, I decided more and more that I didn't care if the Northmen were acting of their own free will. So, a dungeon gets control of a nation or two? Good for the dungeon! That's an *inspiration*, not a detriment! Yeah! If I ever met this dungeon in person, I'd congratulate it as I tried to eat or take control of its area. Maybe I would even get my chance if I dug deep enough.

There was another benefit to getting this Ward. Now that I had the Runes that powered and directed the power of a succubus as well as the demon's pattern, I could create a defense against it. I decided to slow down my influence spread and take a short while to design the needed protections. If I hit another lure as I was, I would once again eat it. Eventually, this would be noticed, and I would likely have a fight on my hands as the Northmen tried to stop me. I started to build my defense, selecting Runes that should specifically counter the lure. This was harder than it should have been since I needed to go through every single Rune I had and determine which would be the most effective.

This is one of the real issues that I faced with using Runes. Right then and there, I decided to start classifying all of them by type and give them a name. As it stood, Runes only had an effect listed. For instance, if I were to put a Runecrafted weapon with a fire effect out into my dungeon, it would be called a 'flaming sword' or some such nonsense. From now on, every new Rune combination would get a specific name, and I would save that for future use! Otherwise, I had to do everything by memory or remake it entirely.

Creating a new Runescript wasn't a huge issue, as I did have perfect memory. It was simply time-consuming and inefficient. Calling everything 'Rune', 'Runescript', or 'series of Runes' was also getting confusing. I put my new plan into action immediately, completing my anti-lure setup and keeping it in my mind as 'demonic attraction filter'. It was an excessively complicated schema, so I didn't feel too bad about the long-though-concise name. Besides, no one would be seeing it except for me. Actually implementing it was trickier, as it required me to filter my perception through a somewhat small circle. On the plus side, once I did get the hang of using it, I was far more confident about allowing my power to eat away at the crater wall.

Over the course of the next few hours, I was able to find three more of the Ward-shapes. I wasn't sure what the proper designation for them was, but Ward-shape seemed to fit fairly well. Each time I found one, I absorbed then replaced it. Within a few moments, it would be reactivated by the energy circling the crater. As far as I could tell, this was a minor drain on the Ward and should not be noticed. Using my new classification system, the Wards that I took were 'Allow Essence', 'Block Mana', and 'Repel Flesh'.

I was still looking for the protections against my flying dungeon. I needed to find and be able to disable them just in case I wanted to stage an invasion at some point. Another positive, since I had a defense against the lure—my Bobs and I were able to look directly at the Wards and plot a course that should maximize our efficiency. I had given Bob a task, and now my influence was flowing along the cliff face in a pattern I would not have expected. It was only thanks to his directions that we had found the three Wards that we had, and at our current pace, we should be able to collect a few extras before making it to the bottom of the crater.

Of course, though my attention was mostly on this, my mind was not as limited as a human such as Dale. I was also working on refining my monsters, traps, and rewards. Another part of my mind was working on classifying all of my Runes and putting existing setups into a different part of my mind. If this weren't enough, I was also begrudgingly working with The Master on his 'Masterpiece'. Personally, I thought it was quite narcissistic to name a contraption after yourself like that. Even though other people assured me 'Masterpiece' was common terminology, *I* knew he was calling it that for his own ego. He couldn't sneak one past me!

Now, in my own mind, I really wasn't doing too much with that project. The Master would submit a list of materials or various Runescripting that was necessary for his project. Diplomat Bob would take the list, get my attention, and take the Inscribed materials back to The Master when I had finished. Even without devoting my entire attention to that project, I was still able to complete it a million times faster than would have been possible without me. I should give myself more credit. I should actually call that non-inconsequential assistance.

After all, I ensured that my work was of the highest possible quality since I would eventually be directly benefiting from the possibly hundreds of thousands of people who would use the finished portal. That was worth more than considering myself as a minor assistant on this project! Still, I had better things to do and concerns that were more directly and immediately important to me.

For example, now that I had a lure Ward, I could work on fully reverse-engineering it and turning it into a zone of 'someone else's problem'. The Elvish Embassy on my surface achieved this by Inscribing every single chunk of building material with a series of linked Runes. So wasteful. I had no idea how they were able to power that all day, every day, without some form of internal power source. Did that building house a dungeon…? No… *probably* not?

I eventually came up with a system of inverted taunt Runes linked by the connecting Runes of the original lure. It sounds simple, but making the connections sync up was the work of a master artist, carver, and philosopher all rolled into one. They did *not* want to play nice. The next step was *testing* it. A single Ward like this should project a bubble of power only a few feet in diameter, and since I did not have the massive linkages that must have been used in this crater, I was going to need to figure out a system on my own. Or I could steal the one that was currently in place down below, but I didn't think I had that kind of time.

I put a shining gold treasure chest on the first floor in a highly traversed area with the Ward placed on its lid. I supplied the initial power requirements, but I had upgraded the original Ward system with 'essence collection' Runes on the outer edge. They would only supply a trickle of power, but there would be almost no impact on the ambient Essence. There were only thirty seconds where people were not in the area, and in that time, I lifted the treasure chest out of the floor and into the selected spot. Then it was time to wait.

Dozens of parties walked past the brilliantly shining treasure chest, some of them even tripping and falling over it; I had placed it in the center of the room. This test run only continued until a Mage-led party entered the room. The cold, bored eyes of the Mage lit up when he saw the treasure chest. When no one else with him seemed to be excited, he grew confused and became worried that he was looking at an illusion. He went over and touched the treasure chest, throwing it open and destroying the Ward in the process.

The people with him were all students, and though they were excited to see the chest, they knew that they would not get anything out of it. The rules were you had to participate in *gaining* the loot to *get* any of it. For me, this highlighted the fact that Mages were far from simple creatures; it would take a greater amount of effort to trick them.

I replicated the setup of the chest on a lower level, this time using my powerful Mana to create the Ward. As soon as I applied this to the treasure chest, it exploded into a ball of fire and chaotic energy. Well. Ah. Hmm. *Well.* It seemed that I needed to upgrade the materials I was working with if I wanted them to handle the stress of the magical forces moving through them.

That was easy enough. I didn't need to alter the design of the chest too much, simply adding a small disk of diamond about the size of a person's hand to the lid. I placed the 'ignore me' Warding schema on the disk and tried again. This time, the setup was stable—even if only just barely.

If I tried to use my full power to create the Ward, it was likely that I would need to use more varied materials and likely a Core that could contain and distribute the power. Somehow, I was also going to need to find a way to enhance this to the point that people above my own rank would be impacted. This would require quite a bit of trial and error, research, and dangerous experimentation. At the same time, it was good to have hobbies to work on in the future.

CHAPTER FOURTEEN

I continued the expenditure of my influence deep into the night. The undamaged Moon—and the shattered Moon fragments—were all glowing brightly with reflected light, halfway through the night sky by the time I reached the bottom of the crater. I directed my mind along the path and began worming my Essence through the created path. I was straining to control all of the newly acquired land by the time I reached the center of the crater, thousands of feet down and across. Having so much land so far from my core without other factors in play made it difficult to keep everything stable.

I had expected to find some form of control mechanism where I had just touched. Instead, I found a Runescript that I immediately named 'Kinetic Dampener'. Apparently, it would create a force about one hundred feet above its activation that would slow things down gradually as they approached. Though interesting, it was not what I had been hoping for. I was starting to get frustrated; practically speaking, this crater was far too large for me to explore every bit of it with my influence. I didn't have the sort of forces needed to explore it in person with creatures… I decided instead to consolidate my control and decide from there.

As an outlet for my frustration, I disabled the kinetic dampener before moving on. Someone should *splatter* for this inconvenience, and I didn't particularly care who at this point. I moved my mind along the path of influence created overnight, following it to the first point where it began to get shaky. Then I dug my influence a little bit deeper into the stone, hollowed out a section, and installed a totem. This totem was a simple amplifier, similar to what I had used to destroy another dungeon back in the Amazonians' capital but far more refined. Which meant smaller, more compact, and harder to detect.

With a totem in place, my shaky control strengthened and solidified. I repeated this process as necessary, even boldly placing a totem a few feet underneath the center of the crater. Then since I had no way to explore the crater at large, I decided to go straight down and see what I found. Dig, dig, dig. Dirt, rock… empty space? I absorbed a section of the surface of the stone and created a tiny viewing Rune at the start of the empty area. When it was complete, I linked it to the viewing portal in the navigation room. What in the…?

There was a city down there! Did I find a Dwarven stronghold? What was this place? Under a layer of… let me see, one hundred and eight feet of stone, there was a *city*! I placed a totem just above the stone and decided to start extending my influence through the air. This was much more difficult than stone, as I needed to also spend an equal amount of Essence in order to maintain the influence in a bubble, but it would still be easier and more cost-effective than trying to get to a wall.

Ow. My influence rebounded painfully as I began moving downwards. Here it was—the dungeon I had been expecting to find. This place was not Dwarven made, nor was it made by hand. I had found the true secret of the Northmen, the fact that their entire society lived in a single, *massive*, dungeon. I couldn't wait to tell *everyone*! Wait, perhaps there was a better way. I 'tasted' the air, and just as expected, this was an infernal dungeon. There were hints of other forms of Essence, Mana, even an unquantifiable energy that must be Spiritual power. But the dungeon itself? It was in the Mage ranks. As far as I could tell, the lower A-ranks.

How? How did a dungeon that must have survived for so long and housed an entire nation, end up staying in the A-ranks? Then again, perhaps it was for the simple fact of the matter that it only had access to a single type of Essence. This would have been mitigated somewhat as it ascended into the Mage ranks, but it was extremely normal for even Mages who could move around to take hundreds or even thousands of years to ascend again. I did not exactly have it *easy*, but I had a great head start over most other beings. Even so, my speed of advancement had slowed to a crawl, and this dungeon outranked me. Drat.

Theoretically, I could fight against this place. It was possible that my maximum-tier Mana would allow me to fight above my rank. It was *also* possible that this place could crush me with overwhelming waves of Mana if I tried. I needed to take the middle ground and not in a 'territory claiming' way. This meant that I needed to get this dungeon's attention.

I sent a burst of Mana along my stream of influence and slammed it against the dungeon's territory three times, like someone knocking on a door. On the third knock, the power in the air for twenty feet around the 'knock' collapsed like a soap bubble and created a sound like thunder. Whoops.

DALE

"Get *up*, Tom," Dale whispered into the suddenly-silent amphitheater. Tom had taken another body blow and was losing too much blood. He had fallen to the ground and was barely moving anymore. Tom must have found his thirtieth wind because he pushed against the floor and staggered upright. Flames danced across his open wounds, sealing the blood in his body and forming thick scar tissue. Normally, this was begging for infection and a slow death by sepsis, but if Tom survived this 'trial', he would be given healing by powerful clerics and healers.

The trial was 'fair', in that Tom's opponents were only a *little* more powerful than he was. Only a rank or two, which meant that if there were *ten* of Tom against one of them, it might have been in his favor. Instead, there were ten people arrayed against Tom, and the only thing keeping him alive was his skill and his opponent's hesitation to go all out against someone at a lower rank.

This was the only time Northman culture had been in Tom's favor since they arrived, and Tom was making sure to capitalize on it by calling out challenges to an individual. The others would pause and step back while Tom battled. He had defeated two opponents this way over the course of the night, but now, he was barely able to hold himself together. The redhead stood as tall as he could and bellowed a pained war cry into the air. He raised his hammer, knowing that this was likely as far as his attempts to save his people would bring him.

As Tom took a step forward, the echoes of his shout still resounding in the area, all of his opponents—and indeed the entire population of Northmen—visibly cringed and clutched at their chests. Moments later, the sound of far-off thunder reached their ears. When the Northmen regained their bearings and glanced at the stage, sounds of shock and rage filled the room.

Tom was standing over the crumpled forms of the dozen men he had been facing and was now holding a hammer in each hand. His chest was heaving, and many of his wounds had reopened across his body. Tom coughed, and a spray of bright blood flecked his lips. "I… claim… victory."

The proctor of the trial stepped forward, red-faced. "You can't claim *victory*, you *che*–"

An explosion of fire and air knocked the proctor off his feet and sent him sprawling to the floor. He looked up to see Hans' eyes glittering nearly as dangerously as the knives at his jugulars.

Hans spoke softly, but his words were audible to the entire room and anyone viewing from afar.

"Oh, *please* inform me how my *student* cheated. I would love to hear how using the environment to your advantage in warfare against a *much stronger* group of enemies is cheating. It's just, I *really* hope I like your answer." Hans was wearing a faint smile, and no one dared to move. The proctor's throat was bobbing furiously as he alternated between rage and caution.

A door slammed open, nearly causing Hans to flinch and open the throat held hostage under his daggers. The Warlord stalked into the room, taking in the scene and dismissing it. "Tom. Did you have anything to do with that thunder?"

"Sir. No, sir." Tom was swaying on his feet.

The Warlord stared at him for a few more moments, then glanced at the fallen people, finally rolling his eyes at the scene Hans was making. "Tom, you are cleared for duty, having proven that your instincts do not control you. You are to report for basic training at three bells. Any questions?"

"No. Sir." Tom took a deep breath. "But I do have a request, sir."

The room went deadly still, and the air seemed to thicken. The Warlord narrowed his eyes. "Is. That. So?"

"Yes, sir."

"Oh, by *all* means, make your request."

"I would like to issue a challenge to General Beinn for his position. My old position." Tom could no longer remain standing and collapsed to the floor.

"I offer a duel. Uno Ictu."

CHAPTER FIFTEEN

"By one stroke, eh?" The Warlord shook his head firmly. "You realize that as the challenged, Beinn strikes first?"

"Yes, sir." Tom's voice was fading.

"Medic! Keep him awake." The Warlord strode closer and leaned down even as the healer started working on Tom. "When?"

"As soon as he can get here and I am functional enough for combat," Tom spoke slightly more firmly, the color beginning to return to his cheeks as the magic replaced his leaking blood.

"Hmph." The Warlord stood tall and looked at a Rune on the wall. "You heard him, Beinn. Get down here. A challenge in front of the nation cannot stand unresolved. *Foolish* little brother."

The last words had been directed at Tom, who simply smiled slightly at the massive warrior. "Sir… it's good to be part of The People again. I thank you for the chance."

"It was the *law*." The Warlord shook his head. "You know as well as I did that you were supposed to die in this challenge. I also know that the Binders weren't especially *gentle*."

"Life isn't gentle." Tom coughed a ball of phlegm and blood

out. "It is good to be one of The People. It is good to face the world. It is good to see the truth."

"Private, reign in your tongue," the Warlord chided more gently than he had spoken to Tom in the last day. "I will call this blood-loss rambling, but any more will be insubordination. Just sit there, *shut your mouth*, and be healed. And *you*, get off my soldier."

Hans plastered an innocent expression on his face and vanished in a flash of heat. Dale was able to track his movements, but anyone under the Mage ranks lost sight of him completely. In a moment, he was back in his seat with an arm around Rose. "Yes, sir!"

The Warlord rolled his eyes and started impatiently tapping his foot. Another door opened, and Tom's belongings were unceremoniously dropped by his side. The courier saluted the Warlord, gave an almost imperceptible shake of his head, and ran off. The massive Northman sighed and leaned in to talk to Tom, but Dale's sharp ears could hear the whispers nonetheless.

"Fool, the only magic in your armor is a cleaning spell. If *I* know that, Beinn knows that by now. He's going to cut you in half with contemptuous ease. Apologize to him as he arrives, kowtow if needed. I'll blame the strikes to your head and blood loss, and you might live to see the rising sun." The Warlord's words were an order, but one that Tom couldn't follow.

The main stone door slammed open, cracking into the wall with a sharp *snap*. "I am here to accept the challenge and welcome the opportunity to finish what was once between us, *private*."

"General Beinn." Tom stood under his own power and began to put on his leather armor. "Do you accept the terms of the duel and swear on your honor to abide by the outcome?"

"If the terms are a single attack each, with the Warlord determining the victor if both survive, then yes." Beinn walked slowly down the main aisle, smiling as he drew a long katana out of an interspatial bag. Beinn looked to be in his late twenties, similar to Tom, but was far more muscular and obviously well trained and equipped. He had long, black hair pulled into a tight bun, and his severe hairstyle accentuated his cold, brown eyes.

Unlike the bulky armor others were wearing, Beinn was wearing almost *thin* armor. Tom recognized it as the base armor that Northman War armor would fit on to and realized that Beinn wasn't taking this duel seriously. Beinn must have had an informant tell him about the results of Tom's leather armor being scanned for magic as the Warlord had warned him.

Cough.

The two duelists tore their burning glares away from each other and looked at the Warlord. "Tom. Do you have anything to *say*?"

"No, sir."

"Oh, you little–" The Warlord snarled and shook his head sadly. "Stand apart. This is Uno Ictu, and as such, only one blow will be exchanged. This is a test of your weapons and ability, not collateral damage. If either of you are hit hard enough that you will impact a wall, you will be caught *gently*. As the challenged… Beinn is allowed to strike first. Live by your honor… "

"Die by your honor," the rest of the room, except for Hans, echoed with the saying. Hans made a rude gesture at Beinn.

The duelists faced each other, both in a ready stance. Beinn allowed his lips to curl upward, and his malice-filled eyes took in Tom's much smaller form. "So much *less* than you used to be, *private* Tom. It took a few years, but I finally have a chance to *earn* my position instead of getting *promoted* to it. Even if you are lesser, I am glad to finally have this worry behind me."

"We'll have time to catch up later, *General*." Tom's lips barely moved as he braced himself.

"Oh… but we *won't*, will we?" Beinn gripped his sword handle in one hand and its sheath in the other. For a tense moment, they simply stared at each other… and then a crescent of silver flashed through the air. Dale watched almost in slow-motion as the blade was drawn, slashed Tom across his midsection, and was resheathed. Beinn stood tall as the force of the attack seemed to transfer to Tom, and his smug face slowly registered shock as Tom began *flying* away.

The Warlord was suddenly behind Tom, and the young man was pulled out of the air and returned to his starting position. He coughed a painful, chest-wracking cough. Three of his ribs were broken on his right side, and his lung was punctured by one of the fragments. Still, terrified confusion was the only emotion present on Beinn's face. In the entire room, there were only four people unsurprised by Tom still being alive.

"B-but... *how*?" Beinn's sword appeared in his hand, and he inspected the edge to see if he had been sabotaged. "You aren't wearing magical protections, and my sword is intact... Are you disguising your cultivation?"

Tom's massive warhammer came out of his bag and broke the stone where it landed. "My turn."

He gripped the handle of his warhammer with both hands and swung as hard as his critically-injured body could manage... and Beinn *dodged*. Tom couldn't fully control his swing anymore, and his warhammer continued on and struck a stone protrusion, reducing it to powder. Tom looked at his opponent in confusion. "...What?"

The Warlord had Beinn in an iron grip and was holding him in the air by his neck. "Did you just *dodge* a blow during Uno Ictu? A blow by a *lower-ranked cultivator*? A *private*?"

"He couldn't have *possibly* survived my attack!" Beinn choked out, trying to pry the thick fingers from his windpipe. "Someone... *saved*... him."

Tom stepped forward and pulled apart the flap in his armor that the super sharp katana had created. Gleaming, silver-purple metal shone through. "Mithril weave. My own preparations are what saved me."

"*Cowardice* is what saved *you*, Beinn." The Warlord threw the man to the ground. "That blow would have killed you, and you knew it. Someone told you all the capabilities of General Tom's armor and weapons, or they *thought* they did. You came here full of arrogance, not even bothering to wear your full *armor*. Report to basic training at three bells, private. Dismissed."

Tom's face was a rictus of conflicting emotions. "Sir… did you call me *General Tom*?"

"I did, and speak freely." The Warlord allowed a grin to play over his face. "Generals are able to converse with the Warlord without issue, after all."

Dale was watching Beinn, expecting foul play when the man didn't get to his feet right away. To his surprise, Beinn stood and marched out with a depressed but resigned look. What was going *on* with this society?

"I suppose you didn't come here without a plan of action. Something drove you here." The Warlord tapped the armor on his hip. "Is this more of a *private* conversation or something to announce to the nation."

"I… both. Sir." Tom looked down, then up, face full of determination. "Sir, I must speak to you first."

"Then let us speak." The Warlord put a hand on Tom's shoulder and directed him away from the room. "Privately, then we will return what was taken from you. Then we will address The People once more. We have missed you… Brother."

CHAPTER SIXTEEN

Well, no one panicked, and there didn't appear to be people swarming out to fight me. Maybe the dungeon recognized that I wasn't trying to be hostile? I extended a tendril of influence once more, just to see what would happen. Would I be attacked? Would we be able to chat? I was *not* expecting the influence in the area to *flinch* and run away.

<Hey! I'm just trying to talk to you!> I mentally shouted into the area so far below me. I had a moment of deja vu, and I wondered if Kantor had ever been frustrated in his attempts to reach out and discuss with others of his kind. Perhaps he had, but I kind of assumed that he would have destroyed anyone who ignored him. Maybe that is what this dungeon was worried about; maybe it knew that being an infernal dungeon was a death sentence from the outside world.

Seconds ticked by, and finally, a reply came. The voice was smooth, charismatic, reminding me of oily politicians and the now-devoured merchant that had been scamming people on my surface. <Why, hello there! I can't say I have ever had the pleasure of speaking with a friendly being such as yourself! All I

have ever seen of our kind is raving animals or some form of weaponized, overly judgmental crusader.>

<That is unsurprising. Everything I have learned points toward our type not gaining intelligence until they are truly ancient.> Small talk! I was making *small talk* with another dungeon! The Dungeon Core, Dregs—who I had captured and placed in charge of my first few levels—and I spoke a little, but holding a conversation was beyond the magma Core.

I quickly put my excitement aside and got down to business. <Listen, we are here because one of the moons that circles our planet was destroyed and is falling to the Earth. We are trying to save as many people as we can, and to me, that means *any* intelligent being. Do you have an exit strategy or a way to survive the oncoming calamity? I can take you with me if you like.>

<I *have* heard about this. Sounds terrible. Well, my plan is to ride it out and absorb all of the death energy that I'm certain will be permeating the planet at that point.> The dungeon quieted at that point, obviously expecting me to say something chiding, or maybe it was just feeling out my reaction for the *next* thing it said. <If I gain enough power, I may even be able to create a stable portal to the abyss!>

<And… what about all of the Northmen living in your depths? Are they dungeon born, and you can raise them after they are wiped out?> Please say yes, please say yes…

<None of them! They all have a simple binding that makes them malleable to my will, but I found that simply letting them control their own fate brought me a higher return on Essence and Mana than if I had been trying to use them directly. My experiment on them was coming to an end either way. At this point, they have become too stable, and I would have needed to clean the rats out of my tunnels.> The dungeon seemed very pleased that I was seemingly unconcerned. <The fragments of the Moon will simply help me to make that happen with minimal risk to myself!>

I did not think it would be so easy, and frankly, I did not think this place would survive the moonfall. Even if it did, there would be so much disruption to the ambient Essence that this place would probably starve to death. I had originally planned on offering asylum, but its goal of opening a stable portal to the abyss was a deal-breaker for me. Still, perhaps it would be a good idea to offer a negotiation.

<Best of luck to you!> I replied as winningly as possible. <I'm going to be moving away from this area shortly, and I was wondering if you would be interested in an exchange of knowledge before I went?>

The dungeon seemed to relax; apparently, it thought that it would have an edge in making deals. Actually, I decided to be extra careful. This was a being that was likely used to making extremely complicated deals with entities that would destroy it. <I suppose we can arrange a little something. What do you have to trade?>

<First let's talk about what I'm hoping to gain!> If I could sweat, I would be right now. I flipped its opening tactic against it, trying to avoid giving away information for free and decided to be as direct as possible. <I've gained access to a few of your Ward designs, and I really like what I see. Seeing as how I am building up as many defenses for myself as possible, I would be remiss in not attempting to supplement them with these ingenious creations.>

<Ah, direct flattery!> The Infernal dungeon chuckled. <I can see why the rodents infesting my area like it so much! As I'm sure you can understand, my Warding system is the work of several hundred years. Truly, it is my greatest achievement! How could I possibly allow myself to trade it away?>

I groaned internally; he was obviously trying to artificially increase his price. That was the point where negotiations began in earnest. Tiny bit by tiny bit, we created a deal. The dungeon would give me a significant amount of Ward schemas, and I would supplement its knowledge of Runes. My knowledge of Runes was only as extensive as it was because the town where Runes had been researched, collected, and stored had been demolished and its people had moved to live on me. A deal had given me the full collection of the Spotter's work in book form, and I was making full use of this knowledge now.

Of course, the Northmen and dungeon in conjunction had a vast repository of Runes as well. This meant that I had to supplement my offer. I eventually added samples of plants, traps, some experiments I had been working on, knowledge of Elementals and how to make them, and each of the most efficient materials for various basic elements.

I knew that I was being taken for a ride, but I had a few more things I was planning on getting out of this infernal negotiator. Before we finalized our deal, I put my plan into play. <Now, before I hand any of this over, let us both swear on our Mana that we will act in good faith during this exchange. I will give you everything I promised; you will give me everything you promised. I will leave and take no action against you. You will not send anything—or anyone—to attack or work against me.>

My trading partner was silent long enough that I was very glad I included this addendum. Then it pretended that it had not had any malicious intent whatsoever and joyfully agreed, <Of course! I so swear, on the condition that you will as well.>

I also made the oath and could feel the tightening in my Core that signified a binding oath. We exchanged all of our promised knowledge and goods, and I casually slipped a little *more* into the conversation, <Before I go, I just wanted to mention that I have an interest in taking the barbarians infesting your depths when I go. I know that you mentioned that they were not yours to control perfectly, but if you were to swear that you would push them my direction if they were considering it… I might have *one* more thing you would be interested in.>

Distraction was evident in its voice, as it must have been perusing what I had given it. <Is that so? So far, I am not disappointed, but what else could you have that would–>

I sent along a few images of Manny the Manticore. A few of it fighting adventurers and a few where it was using the spikes on its body to banish demons. I assumed that this was a dungeon driven primarily by fear, and it would be open to the idea of having a Boss monster protecting it against the things it summoned getting out of control. <This is a creature that I made, an amalgamation of multiple patterns, talents, and oh-so-much trial and error. There is nothing natural like it on the planet, and it is currently absolutely unique.>

The bait was presented, so I silently waited for it to be taken. It didn't take long. <All you want in return is a promise that I will nudge the Northman into your depths if they are on the fence about it? I suppose I could do that…>

The dungeon made its oath to me, and it took everything I had to hide my glee. I sent along the detailed instructions on how to create a Manticore, exchanged a few more pleasantries, then followed my oath and started retracting my influence. I giggled to myself. <Goodbye forever, sucker.>

Devoting only a small fraction of myself to reeling in my power, I sent the majority of my attention to parsing and cataloging all of the new magical effects I now had access to. As much as it seemed that I had been scammed, it was obvious that over the years, the infernal dungeon had forgotten what was at the center of all of its Warding schema. Namely, the full pattern for whatever creature ability was powering the Ward.

I *love* two for one specials, and now, I had a *lot* of research to complete.

CHAPTER SEVENTEEN

The Warlord stood stock-still, staring at his supposedly subservient sibling. He shook his head back and forth slowly, unable to believe the words that were about to come out of his mouth. "Tom, moments ago I had planned to rebuke you. I had planned to have you returned to your position and prepare for the greatest Glory along with our entire nation."

Tom sharply inhaled and made as if to speak. Only the Warlord holding up a hand stopped him. "Something has changed. In my mind, I knew that you were correct. Your way forward is valid. Still, our traditions and laws are in place for a reason, and I was going to deny you. But now, now… I feel the will of The People pressing me to accept your words. I do not know why it favors you so highly, so much as to even intervene when you should have died during your trials, but it is clear what we must do."

"But, before we address the nation…" the Warlord opened his desk and pulled out a single, shining Core, "you have returned, and you have earned your place amongst us once more. It is my duty and my *pleasure* to return to you what was taken upon your exile."

Tom stared at the red-tinged Core on the desk and, with trembling fingers, reached forward and reverently grasped it. He wiped a manly tear from his eye, removed his upper-body armor, then tore his borrowed shirt off as he moved the object toward his chest. The trace work of a Rune began to appear, shining on his chest. Tom pressed the Core into the only open space of the luminescent tattoo and stiffened as energy began to course through him.

More than the flood of Essence, greater than the return of the Northman Royal cultivation techniques, Tom basked in the details of his childhood returning. When he had been exiled, all information not pertaining to his direct chain of command had been stripped away. Many of the events *remained* in his mind, but all of the fine details, all of the emotions, and *especially* all of the joy had been taken. Only certain key memories, such as his mother, had been left to preserve his mind. With their return, Tom began to undergo a radical shift.

The previously well-muscled and impressive figure began to swell. His muscles bulged outwards, his bones lengthened and became denser, and it was obvious by the new clarity in his gaze that his intelligence had been increased. Tom's body was now on par for size and musculature to match the Warlord himself.

Tom's cultivation spiral was shattered and used as fuel to rebuild a *better* version in an instant—his long-ago original. More and more Essence began to flow into him and was bound by the spiral. Just under ten minutes later, Tom was restored to his previous glory—body, mind, and cultivation.

"Looks like I'll need to get my armor adjusted." Tom looked down at the previously-baggy leather pants that were now straining to contain his thick legs. It looked like he was wearing children's leggings. Then his fiery gaze snapped up to the Warlord. "Sir. It's good to be back."

"Welcome, General." The Warlord's tone had shifted, and respect now suffused his voice. "The People have missed you."

"As I have missed The People." Tom moved his arm, marveling at the motion. His cultivation had been fully absorbed, and he was currently at C-rank-five. "I feel like Beinn has let the D-ranked armies rest on their laurels while I've been away. How bad is it?"

"The quality of our weakest army has suffered somewhat," the Warlord admitted freely. "You were the best trainer in two-handed weapons that we had seen in generations. For abyss-sake, even *without* that memory, you came back here with a weapon practically *humming* with power and perfectly suited to your old style. It is a part of you that we could not seem to take."

Tom smiled viciously. "I do wonder what it will be like to wield 'Thud', now that I remember the *proper* way to do it."

"You always did have a terrible naming sense." The Warlord chuckled, slapping an arm around his brother and guiding him toward the exit. "Let's go address the nation."

They walked back to the amphitheater at a pace easily double their first trip. Tom kept his eyes on the space he expected to see his team and allowed a wide grin to run across his face when he saw their reactions. There was delight and interest showing on Dale's face, surprise and sizing up from Rose, and finally, shock and outrage from Hans.

"Are you *kidding* me?" Hans stood and shouted into the silent room. "Is *everyone* I know able to jump ranks like this? Have I just been held in the dark and there's an easy way to ascend? Am I a *joke* to you?"

Dale grabbed Hans and pulled him down into his seat, fixing Tom with a penetrating stare. "Easy, Hans. I'm *sure* we'll all hear the reason for this later."

"My *People*!" The Warlord was standing on the blood-soaked stage and bellowing into the air. "A new path forward has been exposed! A new hope for our survival and continued prosperity. We are going to throw our might—and our magic—behind the creation of a portal to a new land!"

Silence filled the room, only the reverberations of the Warlord's voice still being heard. Then another man stepped on to the stage. The Warlord glared at him, his hands falling to his sides. "General Aiden, what is the meaning of this?"

"Sir, I am concerned that you are suggesting that we *flee*," Aiden spoke the last words bitterly. "By law, we cannot run from our nation's issues."

"Feel for the will of The People, Aiden," the Warlord stated calmly. He looked around at everyone gathered. "*All* of you, feel for the will of The People. This is the correct course for all of us, and it *is* going to be the path we tread."

Aiden saluted and stepped off the stage. The Warlord had an annoyed expression on now, but he continued explaining the plans he had made. Finally, he began issuing orders to be carried out at once. When he was finished, he came to talk with Tom and the Outsiders. "You four, can you secure a portal from your floating base for our use? If we have to follow you across the world, we will not be of much use."

"It should be manageable." Dale nodded at the Warlord, and they were given permission to go back up and begin working to accommodate the Northmen.

Turning toward Tom, the Warlord harrumphed. "I know that you have only just returned, but would you be willing to work as our go-between? It would be helpful for the people above to see a familiar face, and you can resume your duties after we survive this… inconvenience."

Tom paused only for a moment but relaxed when he saw that he wasn't being set aside and this was a true issue. "I see. Would I have permission to bring my war armor along?"

"Everything that isn't attached to the ground by indelible magic is going, Tom. Bring whatever you want." The Warlord stopped and turned away. "Since… since we are going to be donating everything to the dungeon in return for a new home, I lift the restriction on all of you. You will be able to explain whatever you need in order to secure a powerful position for us."

"I will do my best." Tom slumped a little; he had been looking forward to seeing old friends and visiting family.

Hans reached over, patting the huge man on his upper back even though he practically needed to jump to do so. "Don't worry, Tom. You'll have plenty of time to visit, make new friends, and tell *me* how the *abyss* you jumped in *rank*!"

The people around him laughed, and Hans started to twitch. "I *knew* it! There's a conspiracy to make me the world's slowest cultivator! I'm–"

Hans had his knives in his hands and took a menacing step toward Tom, but Dale had decided to intervene and whacked the assassin in the back of the head. Dale lifted the unconscious man and started walking back the way they had entered. "So, how do we get back up?"

"I can bring us to the surface, and all Outsiders can take the lift from there." Tom started walking away, leaving his friends to follow. Now that he had his memories back, he was starting to return to the mentality of his previous life. There was an air of command about him, and he seemed to expect that the others would listen without question. As they walked, Tom stopped a squire and ordered him to meet them at the lifts with his armor. In fact, several times through their journey he stopped other people and ordered them to bring him goods.

"Going a little power-mad, Tom ol' buddy?" Hans poked Tom with a finger from his princess-carry position in Dale's arms. When that didn't get a reaction, he did it with his dagger.

Tom winced and flinched away, then turned and glared at his mentor. "Weren't you supposed to be unconscious?"

Hans held up a hand. "Seems like you're getting back to old habits. I'm just gonna go ahead and remind you that your old habits got you exiled. Your *new* habits and friends got you back into a certain position you are already apparently abusing."

Tom's mouth clicked shut, and he could only nod wearily. "Fair point, Hans. It's just… I have decades of conflicting information in my head now. For abyss sake! I didn't even know that I was in my late sixties. I thought I was in my mid-to-late *twenties* at most."

"Wait, what?" Hans' grin lit up the room. It must have been a trick of fire Essence. "You're *older* than me? *Yes*!"

CHAPTER EIGHTEEN

I was losing my *mind* over all the new effects I could create with Wards. In fact, I was planning on designing an entirely new floor based around the Wards. Essentially, I was going to make a series of connected rooms that were a *skills* test. Normally, this was not something that would be dangerous; after all, a skills test is a way to improve yourself! Not *my* skills tests, though. If the person trying to get to me were unskilled, they would likely explode.

I had been debating on where to place this new trial. After all, it would be easy enough to put it between different areas that already existed. After careful experimentation, I decided that while I might use some of my new Warding schema throughout the dungeon, an effect overlooked by the infernal dungeon. I thought it was deserving of its own floor.

It was a simple concept; whenever a Mage entered the room, they would need to destroy an object in an area they could not physically access. I was thinking the target might be through a small tunnel or something. They would also need to put Mana into a Core the same distance away. It did not have to happen simultaneously, but I assumed a lot of people would think that it *would* need to happen that way.

The reason this would be difficult would be the style of Warding in the rooms. I would make five rooms on this floor, and to progress to the next in the series, you would have to complete them in order. The Wards would be designed to increase the flow of Mana and Essence in an area. If a technique was executed flawlessly, there would be no leakage of Mana or Essence. Unfortunately for most Mages, they did not bother to perfect their techniques, focusing on learning to push out *more* power rather than getting *good* at what they did. Typically, they would simply flood the spell form they were attempting with power, knowing that it would do what they wanted it to do in the end.

I planned to take advantage of their laziness by doing nothing except making the power draw increase by double in each room. Since there were only five rooms, the maximum I could get away with was increasing the cost of a technique or incantation by thirty-two. Even so, I could increase the strength and power requirements of the object they needed to destroy as well as the object they needed to fill with Mana.

I started designing the rooms, and my hopes to create a new floor entirely were dashed. I could only make the rooms so big before the Wards would not affect them entirely. If I wanted to concentrate the power requirements, the largest I could make the room was a perfect square about ten feet wide. I was not going to waste an *entire floor* on five tiny rooms! Instead, the rooms were added to the bottom of the Elemental Pit.

People who made it to the base of the pit could exit the dungeon immediately or go into the skill rooms. Of course, I moved myself and the Silverwood tree to the end of the rooms, so now anyone who wanted to get to me needed to not only be vastly powerful but extraordinary skilled! Or simply powerful enough to make up for their lack of skill. Or an S-ranker who could essentially ignore my setup. Or… yeah, there were potentially a lot of people that could just come to see me. I *really* needed to find a way to defend against the S-ranks.

I shook off the morose thought, returning to the fun I was having creating this next trap. I mean… skill room. Heh. I was fairly certain that these five rooms would account for more Mages dying than any other portion of the entire dungeon combined. When they tried to shatter the target I was going to make, the Wards would siphon off any Mana that was not perfectly controlled, causing the Mages to increase the amount of power flowing through them, which would be siphoned off… *pop* goes the Magous!

Conversely, this would be an excellent place for a Mage to perfect their abilities. If they could make it through all five rooms, whatever ability they were using to make it happen should be completely mastered. This would allow for incredible power and personal growth. Or they would be hasty, and I would see if they were *tasty*. Was that a poem? Can I call that a poem? Whatever, I am the *dungeon Core*! I can call it a poem if I want, and no one but Dani can stop me! Since she's been busy training Grace, I have free reign! Mwa-ha-hah!

I had created the five rooms, but I had only completed the Warding in the first two before I felt my control fluctuate. Drat, there must be adventurers stepping on to this floor. Creating anything permanently magical—such as Runes or Wards—was a task that demanded perfection. I had learned my lesson on this long ago, so I stopped what I was doing and waited for the challengers to make themselves known. I took a look at the adventuring group and found myself slightly shocked. The lowest ranked person in this group was in the upper B-ranks. There were even two people in the early A-ranks, and all of them seem to be taking this floor extremely seriously.

The group waded through the Elementals, their movements efficient and refined. Not every strike was a deathblow since the condensed Mana bodies of the Elementals allowed them to be extremely resilient. Still, this group of people outclassed the Mobs by a large degree. Luckily for me, their progress slowed greatly when they came across the first of the Runeforged Elementals.

This one was an Elemental that had taken to defeating opponents and attaching their Cores to itself. It looked like a series of balls that were barely touching each other, and all of the Cores could be launched to allow the original Elemental to create itself once more. I called this a Hive Elemental, and I had Runeforged the controlling Elemental upon the principles I had learned watching the Love Elemental take over the Boss at the bottom of the pit. When this creature was in control of all of the Cores, its power was boosted by a varied percentage.

It could sacrifice that bonus to create a small—if uncontrollable—army to do battle. If these adventurers had not appeared, I had fully expected that this would soon be the floor Boss. It had collected a large amount of power and Cores, and it began using them to great effect. Three Rune-enhanced effects began: a powerful taunt, a swirl of crystalline shards, and an insidious Aura of *rot*.

The Mages who were able to resist the taunt did their best to assess the greatest threat that was coming from the Elemental and started throwing Mana around. They were targeting the spheres that seemed to be creating the potent effects, but the Elemental used the rotational motion it followed to swing the spheres out of the way and to dodge at angles that were entirely unnatural.

A saw blade of crystals cut into a Mage as he lashed out at close range, but the Mage only took a shallow cut. He tried to ignore it, but the Aura of rot set in instantly and the wound began to fester. Since this was an unnatural occurrence, and the rot wasn't a weak variation of tiny creatures, black lines started to race up his arm. His teammate noticed the issue even if the taunted Mage didn't and tossed his partner behind him

The A-ranker swept forward, crossing the distance in a series of forty-five-degree angled movements. Her elbow came down on the orb controlling the taunt effect, and the Elemental connected to the hive-mind popped as if it were a soap bubble.

Another orb came around, revealing itself to be an explosive Elemental by detonating in her face and sending her flipping toward the edge of the chasm. She got herself under control and forced her feet to the floor only a few feet from the edge. She flipped her singed hair out of her face and glared at the creature blocking their path. "Alrighty, *now* you're more than just an obstacle. Die."

One of the other Mages appeared behind the hive mind, holding up his hands and starting an incantation, "*Omae wa Mou Shindeiru.*"

Just as his Mana started to churn out of him, the hive mind proved that being able to see in only one direction at a time was a poor evolutionary decision. A cone of corrupted water slammed into the Mage and bound him to the wall with an unbelievably sticky solution. It raced toward the struggling Mage but was intercepted by a massive plane of force slamming it to the ground as the second A-ranker finally used one of his more potent abilities.

Since it was held in place, the female A-ranker dove at it and started smashing the Cores until she finally found the controller, and the others all tried to escape. It seemed that my Hive Elemental was too young to survive such a competent group, and I was really beating myself up about not giving this one more time to mature. Next time for sure.

CHAPTER NINETEEN

The female A-ranker stepped forward and picked up the Core of the hive-mind, seeming to be shocked at what she saw. "This has a *mind* Rune Inscribed on it! Do you think that was how it was controlling the others? Or is there something more *sinister* at play?"

"We already know that the dungeon has near-human intelligence. Why is it so surprising that it can come up with new, more powerful monsters?" her opposite drawled. I *suppose* he was correct if by 'near-human intelligence' he meant far, *far* smarter than a human. "This does not change our goal at all, and we should be able to secure the necessary resources with a few passes through this floor. Let's get back to work."

They collected every Core they found, everything they considered a potential resource, although they did their best to avoid large groups of Elementals. When they got to the ramp, they started descending into the pit, and I was able to watch my newest traps in action! When the first of them triggered the moving walls, the rest of them groaned in annoyance. I laughed at that; in fact, the only thing I like better than annoying someone with traps was hearing them groan from a bad pun.

That's how you knew that a pun was mature, after all—when it was full *groan*.

"Alright, looks like they are at least moving in sequence." The male A-ranker looked at his team and rolled his eyes. "Just make sure not to get knocked off. If our information was correct, even *we* would not survive the fall."

"Which is just the *weirdest* thing!" a high B-ranked, female Elf grumbled. "I haven't taken damage from falling in two hundred *years*. I just can't seem to wrap my mind around a fall being *dangerous*, you know?"

"Right?" The third person in line laughed. "I'm guessing it has something to do with all of that connected Runescript around this inverted-tornado of a pit?"

"You know as much as we do." The female A-ranker shrugged and moved ahead. "Let's get going. You never know if something is going to jump over the edge of the pit."

I stopped an Elemental just before it was going to jump over the edge of the pit at them; that would have been too cliché. Every two or three seconds, the walls would shift, and the group would be separated from each other. I kept attempting to activate traps, but this was a group of serious dungeon crawling professionals. If the floor dropped out from under them, they braced themselves against the very walls that were supposed to ensure their doom. Three times, an explosive Elemental popped out into the small area they were trapped in and was chucked into the center of the pit before it could self-detonate.

In fact, they were so efficient and effective that I did not want my newly upgraded Boss's trial run to be against them. I opened a small trap door, and the Boss sunk into the floor. To compensate, I added a slightly larger treasure chest to the room with several tokens in it that should easily distract them. They cleared the entire ramp down to the base, and though they were struggling with the increased gravity, they hadn't passed through it fast enough to cause them harm.

Seeing that there was a follow-up room, they became excited and elated instead of confused and concerned as I had hoped they would. One of the Mages spoke, giving me an 'aha' moment, "The information we had about this floor is wrong! We must be the first ones to see this change!"

As a group, they passed into the next room. The door shut behind them but did not lock, since I didn't think that would be fair. If the only way to escape was to master or at least greatly improve an ability, leaving no way to retreat would result in unfair deaths. Also, I had flat-out written instructions on how to pass to the next room, so there should be no confusion as to how to get through here.

I didn't explain that the Mana cost would be doubled in this room, but I was sure they would figure that out very quickly. One of the B-ranked Mages stepped forward and sent a vibration-based attack at the crystal sculpture they needed to break. He was successful and shattered the object on his first try. I was pleased with the outcome as well since I had been able to absorb a huge wave of siphoned Mana.

The Mage grunted and sank to one knee, breathing heavily. "Celestial *feces*, that really took it out of me! Not sure what just happened, but I couldn't stop channeling Mana into that technique. It wasn't deadly, but I sure wasn't expecting that! It took… at least triple the amount of Mana I had thought I would be investing."

"That's strange… Let me try meeting this second requirement." The male A-ranker looked over at the Core that was waiting to be charged with Mana and sent a stream of power toward it. His diffuse Mana rolled off him, and in a few seconds, his face tightened in pain and his fingers began to smoke. He squinted his eyes, tightening his Mana into a controlled thread. The Core was soon full of power, and the door to the next room popped open.

"*Abyss,* that *hurt*!" The A-ranker shook his hand, then poured a flask of water over it. The water turned to steam upon contact, and the eyes of the onlookers widened in concern. "If I didn't put a leash on my Mana and carefully control it into the Core, the room *sucked* the Mana out of me! How is this *possible*?

This is a level of sophistication I haven't seen anywhere in this dungeon before now!"

"Then it must be *new*." The female A-ranker looked into the next room and narrowed her eyes when she saw an identical setup. "Who here has the best control?"

No one said anything for a long moment. Then the lowest B-ranked man stepped forward reluctantly. "I spent ten years longer in the C-ranks than any of you, but that was because I had pretty dense corruption. I needed to develop my Essence control really well to break into the B-ranks… so I'm likely to be the choice for this task."

Any further discussion was interrupted as a treasure chest flipped out of the wall. The sudden movement of the wall opening up startled the Mages so much that they attacked it, even though the two High Magous shouted at them to stop. The room began to *hum* with power, and the stone floors were vibrating as the Mages tried to rein in their power.

Two of them managed to stop themselves, but the last one panicked. His body began to glow as more and more Mana was channeled, but before he could detonate, the A-ranked female tackled him and pulled him out of the room.

The Mage fell unconscious from pain arriving from multiple sources—the backlash of the draining Wards hitting him as well as his body over-channeling Mana and nearly burning out. The others didn't mind carrying him along, so when they felt it was safe to return to the skill area, they dragged him back into the room—mainly so an Elemental didn't get a free snack. The male A-ranker nodded at his partner and addressed the group.

"New rule: no Mana, physical attacks *only* unless necessary to face these challenges."

The treasure chest was long since melted to slag, and everything in it had been similarly destroyed. A plane of energy ran down one wall, and a one-way portal appeared. One of the Mages sighed. "Should we head out or try the next room?"

"The first one nearly got us, and if we want to come back here, we are going to need to clear the entire Pit again. We can try the next room, but we are using *extreme* caution." The female sent these orders, and I was confused about who the party leader was. Or… maybe the two top-ranked people simply shared the responsibilities? That seemed like a power struggle waiting to happen. I wonder if I could make it happen *sooner*…?

CHAPTER TWENTY

The group of powerhouses moved into the next room, and the portal in the first fizzled out. If they wanted to leave now, they would need to either complete this skill room or climb out of the Elemental Pit. This time, they started their skill test with attempting to fill the Core. The male A-ranker focused his Mana into the tip of his finger and sent it spinning as a double helix to the dull gem. In a few moments, the Core was glowing a potent and beautiful cherry-red, and the High Magous stopped.

"Whew!" He wiped imagined sweat from his brow. "That's really tough, but I actually think it's helping me control myself better. I sure wish this was somewhere easier to access, but it makes sense that the hardest challenge yet is right at the end. Filling that Core is like trying to walk through those gravity Runes but with your mind!"

I enjoyed the comparison and watched excitedly as the 'well-controlled' Mage sent an ability at the *diamond* target that needed to be destroyed. He *really* took his time, and there was hardly any Mana wasted as he threw out his assault... which bounced off the target and into the wall. "Drat, that sucker is pretty tough."

"Think you can break it with a different attack, or do we need to give it a try?" The female put a stabilizing hand on the Mage, who shook his head.

"Thanks, Anna, but I want to try again." One of them *finally* said a name out loud! I was getting sick of thinking of them as person number one, two, and so on.

Anna nodded and gestured for him to continue when ready. The Mage took a deep breath and began focusing intently. Just as he started releasing his Mana in a condensed spellform, I let a treasure chest pop out of the wall and slam on to the stone. The sudden noise from an unexpected direction distracted him *just* enough to introduce instability into his attempt.

Instead of a clean technique, his divided attention allowed a thread of Mana to remain connected to the ability, and the Wards began draining him. Anna picked him up and charged out of the room, but I didn't mind. In the next room, the draw was halved, but he continued to leak Mana like a sieve. The great part about these Wards was that they were multiplicative, *and* they were all connected together within their area of effects. There was no escape from the pull once it had latched on unless you got out of *all* the rooms.

The Mage fell unconscious from the pain as they escaped the final room, but the thread of power was cut off. Now there were two down, but the group had successfully cleared the rooms. If *only* I had been able to set up the last few rooms before they got down here! Anna returned to the room and looked over at her co-leader. "Anything good as a reward?"

"Looks like we got a farmstead package." The High Magous held up a few tokens. "Five acres of land, a farmhouse, ten of three animal types, various seeds."

Anna sighed and nodded. "Good. I think we are on the right track by coming down here. It wasn't what we were after, but if we want to set up a sect, we'll need farmers, right?"

"Right."

"Keep going into the next room, or head to the surface?" Anna seemed to be putting the question to a vote.

"Already looked at the next room." The only conscious Mage shook her head. "Exact same setup. Correct me if I'm wrong, but this room was even harder to use Mana in, right?"

"Yes," responded the male a *touch* despondently. "Looks like each room requires greater control to get through. I say we go get these guys taken care of and try another day."

"Works for me." Anna and the others left through the portal, carrying their fallen with them and arriving in the Mage's Recluse with a single step.

<Oh, thank *goodness* they didn't try the next room!> I started getting busy, frankly a little nervously. <My reputation would have been ruined.>

Finishing my thought with a low chuckle, I finished working on the remaining rooms, getting all of the Warding in place and reinforcing the walls. I hadn't considered it before, but if a Mage burnt out in here, the result would be explosive, and I needed to have a way to release the pressure. Before even *that*, I needed to make sure the blast was contained. *Celestial*, but it was getting difficult to eat people quietly.

DALE

As the group rode the levitating platform upward toward the imposing flying mountain, Dale wryly grinned and glanced at Tom. "Hey. How did this city get named Fek'koff?"

"What do you mean?" Tom blinked a few times; he had been lost in thought.

"You told us when we got here that we were about to crash into 'the Wards of Fek'koff'. How'd the city get named that?" Dale waved at the glowing, dome-covered crater.

"It didn't, this is Outpost Alpha One." Tom rolled his eyes. Dale was funny sometimes. "The *Ward* system is named Fek'koff. Every time someone *did* find this place or asked too many questions about it, the only response was 'Fek'koff'. The nickname stuck."

"What the…?" Hans grasped at his chest. "You mean to tell me that the Northmen have a sense of *humor*? This might be the most startling discovery of our entire stay here!"

"And you wonder *why* the place is named Fek'koff," Tom muttered loudly and darkly. His words made the others laugh, and he allowed a slow grin to crack his stony face. "Also, to me and mine, we aren't the 'Northmen'. We are 'The People'. It is an important distinction."

"Yeah, he just… hit the ground. Didn't even try to slow down." One of The People was talking to another who was controlling the platform. "We got his armor back, but… it's gonna need some serious cleaning."

"That's unfortunate, but I'm also glad I wasn't the one who found the issue." The platform controller shook himself.

Tom raised his voice to get their attention, "Sergeant. What was that about?"

"Ah. Sir." The guard with them flushed, then stood at attention. "The Rune work in the crater that arrests the motion of people falling has failed. No one noticed until it was… already fully inactive."

Rose turned slightly green. "That's… odd timing. I guess I'm glad it happened *after* we got here."

"Yeah…" Dale agreed slowly. Then he squinted his eyes; who did he know that had a habit of taking Runes and setting traps? Sending his thoughts along his connection to Cal, he tried to keep his mental voice cool, "*Cal, did you disable the Runes that catch people in this crater?*"

<May~y~be?>

"*Hah. That's a good one. I'd normally be pretty upset, but I'm not super happy with the Northmen. Hey, we have good news. Tell you all about it when we get back.*" Dale could feel surprise flowing back along the connection.

The voice in his head made a valid point, <Why not just tell

me now while you are stuck on that platform? Less wasted time.>

This caused Dale to pause; that was probably a better idea than making both of them wait. He described everything that had happened, including how the Northmen were going to be joining them and bringing all the magical knowledge and items they owned. Dale played back the fight that had occurred, the saving grace, and the resolution of the conflicts.

The air shook as the dungeon shifted from how hard Cal's laughter was. <Dale! Hah! This is *amazing*! Listen, I can fill in a few blank spots for you. Let me tell you what part I played in you succeeding down there. I can't believe I get everything I bargained for *and* all the stuff the other dungeon has! I bet it didn't even *think* about that!>

While the story was being told, Dale's eyes got wider and wider. At the end of the story, Dale shook his head ruefully and joined in the laughter. That scenario had worked out better than they could have possibly hoped. The part where Cal had tried to get the dungeon's attention and the infernal dungeon had sent confusion to everyone connected to it? That had saved Tom and allowed *every other* event to progress. It was likely wise not to tell Tom about it until they were alone, but frankly, his status as unconnected and exiled from 'the will of The People' was what had ultimately saved his life.

They became level with the island and stepped off the magical lift. The platform began to drop, and the returning heroes started walking toward the area the leaders usually congregated. Really, the only impediment to this plan of relaxation and debriefing was when a blurred figure slammed into Dale and sent him careening into the stone of the mountain a hundred paces away. The rock shattered, and Dale flopped bonelessly to the ground.

"You think that *just* because you reached the B-ranks, our agreement is *complete* and you no longer need to show up for your training?" Gomei was already standing next to Dale. He picked the human up off the ground by the neck, then threw him toward the training arena. "*All* it means is that I no longer need to *coddle* you!"

Gomei turned to look at the other members of the returning party. "What? Don't you have something to go report, or do you want to *participate*?"

The three people started walking away without missing a beat, staring straight ahead and allowing the suddenly pouring sweat to trickle down their faces unabated. By the time they felt safe enough to look around again, Gomei was gone and loud crunching noises were coming from the arena.

"Is it wrong that I want to know what's going on?" Hans sighed and almost started walking toward the arena. "You know, it is the dream of every assassin to learn the Moon Elf combat style. Do you think he might be serious about participating?"

Rose took his hand and pulled him along firmly. "I can nearly guarantee that when he says 'participating', he means as a target. Gonna have to let that dream go for a while, I'm afraid. Though, who knows what the future holds?"

CHAPTER TWENTY-ONE

<Hey, Dale. Question for you.>

"Yeah, Cal?" Dale whispered the words. Not in an attempt to hide himself or be stealthy, it was because currently, he could barely breathe. A strike to his chest by Gomei had driven the air from his lungs, and now, he was trying to regain his wind while holding off three 'flame-touched greater lizards'.

<So, there are a few people working on setting up a portal for the Northmen. I've been talking to my Wisp, Dani, and she's pretty adamant that we go to another hidden location.> The words paused as Dale focused on some tricky footwork to avoid a blast of flaming Mana. <Right, so, there's no more help from me in seeking out people. Just wanted to let you know. I'm not really excited about this trip, but it is really out of character for her to be this pushy. Any advice?>

"That's fine, Cal. We're in crunch time anyway." Dale landed a blow on a lizard's neck, using his Aura to simulate 'sharpness' or 'sword Aura'. With his fingers held rigidly, his hand acted as a sword and sliced open the creature from neck to groin. Dale winced; he was still getting used to using *only* as much Mana as intended. "Advice on… what? Relationships? Try Hans."

"Is this too *easy*?" Gomei shouted at him. "You can talk to your friends at the same time as working through my training? You should have just *said* so! I'm *happy* to increase the difficulty!"

Gomei pulled a few leavers, and a swarm of the lizards charged at Dale from the wide-open gates. "Let's go over today's lesson again, Dale! I'll ask a question, and you answer! What are we working on?"

"We are working on controlling my body when my Mana is at full power!" Dale shouted in reply, stomping on the foot of a lizard to bury it in the stone and give him a moment to dodge away from its follow up strike.

"*Why*?" Gomei's word physically rattled Dale.

"So that I am used to the motions, and using my body as a weapon becomes second nature!" Dale flipped in the air, grabbing a Beast as he moved and chucking it ignobly at another of its kind.

"Why doesn't *everyone* leave their full-powered Mana in their bodies at *all times*?" Gomei shouted over the meaty sound of two bodies crushing each other.

"They don't want to damage themselves and the people around them!" Dale snapped back thoughtlessly.

Gomei appeared next to Dale and slapped him across the face and into a huddle of the lizards. "*Wrong*! Try *again*!"

"Leaving the body stuffed with Mana can cause burnout!" Dale turned the slap into a corkscrew dive, drilling through the chest of a lizard and emerging coated in blood on the other side.

Once again Gomei was next to him, and this time, Dale was whacked straight into the ground. "*Wrong*! *Wrong*! *Wrong*! The *real* reason… is that most Mages don't take the time to learn how to actually *control* themselves at *all times*! They only act as a true Mage when it is *convenient* or when they are in *battle*! This. Makes. Them. *Weak*!"

Gomei was shouting in his winded trainee's face. He flickered and vanished, giving Dale a view down a lizard's open mouth as it lunged for him. Dale reached out and gripped the jaws closing in on him, tearing the mandibles off the Beast's skull.

"I don't understand."

"*Correct!*" Gomei laughed from his position by the levers. "Do you think Moon Elves leave their bodies undefended, weak, barely perceptive? What is even the *point* of being a Mage if you are going to act like a C-ranker in your normal life? Today's lesson is this: you will have your Mana flowing through you *at all times*. Control it. Control yourself. People 'burn out' because they cannot control their Mana or stop it from rampaging in *unwanted* ways. They damage things around them because they cannot control *themselves*."

Dale was so shocked over this revelation that he failed to properly execute a block and was taken to the ground by a scaly tackle. The other lizards in the arena piled on, and Dale was hidden under a sea of biting and wiggling bodies. A flash of Mana made all of them still, and Dale pushed through the pile of steaming meat and scales. "You mean that Moon Elves... *always*?"

"*Always*," Gomei confirmed, leaning forward with gleaming eyes. "This is why we are better at *everything* than a normal Mage. We don't *neuter* ourselves for *convenience*. Also, a point in your favor. I'm a trifle surprised that you grasped Sword Aura so easily. In another life, it would have likely been your ultimate ability. Here, it will be only another tool in your arsenal."

"It *does* feel natural," Dale admitted as he shifted his Aura back to a thin mesh of pure **Acme** Mana. He had found that the natural state acted to dampen any Mana coming toward him, as it would absorb a portion of any type. It wasn't suited to truly being used in combat in its raw form, much to Dale's displeasure. "But how will I get anything done in the next few weeks?"

"What have you been training with us for?" Gomei closed his eyes, remembering that Dale was a human and needed more hand-holding to reach a conclusion. "Use the martial forms for movement. You've been working to learn our habits and footwork. *Use* them. You think that the silent steps are only used for murder? Apply them to *all* your motion. They are crafted to create minimal impact on your surroundings, keeping you hidden. Moving in such a way will reduce the risk you have of blowing down the camps with a sonic boom, at the very least."

Dale coughed, trying not to blush from the less-than-subtle jab. He hopped in the air and twisted, flinging off any blood that hadn't already dried on him. "What about speaking or listening?"

"I won't lie—it's going to be boring listening to people speaking at what feels like half speed. It's going to be *hard* not accidentally hurting someone." Gomei was now inches from Dale's face, seeming to have flowed across the ground to arrive. "I cannot express how important it is to have fine control as a Mage. Even the dungeon has started to recognize this, much to our amusement and the near-death of multiple Mages."

"What?"

"Nothing for you to concern yourself with right now, Dale." Gomei looked around and confirmed that every opponent had been defeated. "I think you have a solid grasp on what we were trying to teach you today. *Ignore* societal norms. Be *better* than those around you. They are lazy; you are not. If you *are* lazy, we will fix that."

Dale swallowed deeply and nodded. "Not lazy, teacher! Not lazy at all over here."

"Alright. Looks like the sun's coming up." Gomei glared at the sky. It was throwing off his sense of time. They had been traveling east and north, and thanks to the portal system, he was familiar with the fact that the sun rose at different times during the day around the world. Still, he had wanted to keep Dale fighting until sunup, and this *technically* counted. "Get going. I have my own work to do."

Dale grimaced as the Elf vanished. He must be using some combination of invisibility and speed because Dale *still* couldn't track him using normal methods. Walking toward the mess hall of the Academy, Dale did his best to ignore the people around him. You would think that the early morning would mean people should be sleeping, but most of the students and *all* of the teachers could go without sleep for extended periods. Add that to the fact that the world as they knew it was ending, and the only way to prepare… was to fight.

It was obvious that tensions were mounting. The portal to Cal's soul was still not operational, and since that was the only escape plan, people were getting ever more nervous. The sleep deprivation and constant fighting weren't helping with that. Dale accepted his portion of food from the attendant and found a table, groaning as he sat. With a small amount of focus, he shifted his external Aura to a sunlight pattern and let the light healing take care of his bruises and irritable mood. Anyone who came near him was touched by the Mana-powered Aura and walked away with a smile.

He noticed that and shrugged. Why *not* let them gain a benefit from his presence? Dale stood from his seat and smashed into the ceiling, reducing his chair to kindling at the same time. He fell back to the ground and destroyed the table as he landed. "Ugh. I had been doing so well."

"Hey!" One of the people serving food came over and glowered at him. "You can't just smash the place up because you don't like something! Pay for this damage!"

"Sorryaboutthat." Dale's words were so fast that they were nearly unintelligible. He took a calming breath and tried again, "I. Am. Sorry. About. That."

When speaking slowly and deliberately, he was able to mimic a normal sentence to the man's ears. Dale handed over a few silver coins, and the server nodded stiffly. "Good. Didn't mean to come over so angry, just a lot of people smashing things these days. Looked like you did it intentionally 'cause you *really* wrecked that table… but you used your face to do it. Listen, I hear they have a training center for Mages now if you need help? You new at this?"

"I'm good, thank you." Dale sounded normal, and he carefully shifted his weight around in the steps needed for total body control. To those watching, Dale stood smoothly and seemed to almost *flow* out of the room. His extreme grace was actually him moving very slowly and picking where to put every footfall, but anyone under the Mage ranks simply wouldn't be able to tell. Dale rolled his eyes when he saw people watching him. "Too bad I didn't train as a dancer. I bet I wouldn't get smacked in the face so often."

CHAPTER TWENTY-TWO

"Dale." Hans grabbed Dale's hands and pulled him down into a seated position across from him. "Dale, I need…"

"Yes, Hans?" Dale was trying not to laugh out loud. "Are you finally going to confess your deep and true love for me?"

"How did you *know*?" Seeing Dale's shocked expression, Hans slapped him hard enough to make his face move slightly. Hans grumbled at the lack of reaction. "Abyss-touched Mages. No, you little blighter! I need your help. My cultivation progress is basically nonexistent. *Rose* is catching up to me in cultivation, which is great, but she's been cultivating for less than a year. I need to advance again. I want to be able to spend forever with her, and I am aging by the day. Sure, it's slow, but I don't want to look like Mr. Wrinkles—*Artorian* that is—by the time I'm a Mage. Can you help me?"

"Woof." Dale shook his head and grinned. "That's pretty rough, Hans! Have you tried this little blue potion I've been hearing abou–"

"No 'old man issue' jokes please." Hans forestalled the inevitable and his mouth formed into a hard line. "Can you do something? A technique, a–"

"Can I see your cultivation?" Dale cut him off with a direct question. Hans looked nervous at this, and for good reason. Normally, it was easy for someone to look at someone and get a *sense* of their cultivation, and below the C-ranks, it was in plain view for all. But when an Aura had been formed, the *actual* cultivation of a person was hidden, and only estimations could be made. Since this information could easily be used against Hans, Dale was essentially asking for a huge amount of trust. Hans swallowed and nodded, sending a small thread of Essence to Dale. Then he sat and tried to absorb as much Essence as possible from the surroundings.

Latching on to the thread, Dale followed it to Hans' Center and looked around. There was very little corruption, and from what Dale could tell, the Aura was well-made. The only thing… the amount of Essence trickling into his Chi spiral was absolutely *miniscule*, and Hans was currently actively cultivating. Dale's *passive* Essence collection was higher than this by a large amount. Dale opened his eyes and looked at Hans with a huge question spilling out of his mouth, "Do you have only the Guild's basic cultivation technique?"

"Yeah." Hans rubbed his head and looked down. "Noble ones have protections or… people that hunt you down if you steal or use them."

Dale started to scoff but thought back to his own experiences. Now that he thought on it, he had *never* seen a cultivation technique for sale, but then again, he had only left Mountaindale a few times. Even the *Academy* didn't teach cultivation methods, only ways to *use* the cultivation you had previously acquired. Then again, it was a *new* Academy. Truth be told, everything Dale had, he had been *gifted*. How common was this issue? "Do you *want* me to help you?"

"If you think you can," Hans calmly replied. Dale took his hand again and went to look at the Chi. The pattern wasn't *bad*, but with Cal around, there were far better methods. There! In the wall of Hans' Center… that was an affinity channel that was blocked. Dale's mind zeroed in on that, and he grunted. If only he knew how to open affinity channels, he could help his friend just by opening them. As far as he had heard, it required a specialized Mage to–

Dale brushed against the blockage and felt a spark of **Acme** Mana travel along the connection between them. Hans gagged and spewed black bile all over Dale's lap. The assassin dry-heaved rotten fluid for another long minute, then looked up at Dale with tears running down his face. "What the *abyss* did you do to me?"

"I… I'm not sure, I was only–"

"I thought you were just *looking.*" Hans coughed a few more times, spitting out black and sludgy mucous. Then he went still, his eyes half closing as he focused inward to look for damage. "Alright. Dale. What… Why do I have a perfect water affinity now? How did you? I. *What*?"

"You're kidding," Dale flatly announced.

"I'm *not.*" Hans looked at Dale in awe. "*Never* tell another person about this. Most Mages can force open affinity channels for others but usually only partly, and it isn't something that people who do it for a living will appreciate. What you did would cost someone the same amount as a *castle*, Dale. No, even more. *Perfect* affinity?"

Hans shook his head and looked like he might cry. "It's impossible."

Dale coughed and looked at Hans sidelong. "Um. So, you are happy about this? Or is this a bad thing? I know you have a fire affinity…"

"Are you joking? *Obviously*, this is the best thing ever!"

"So. Want me to do the rest of them?" Dale's words made Hans freeze momentarily, but then he started laughing like a madman. When he could finally contain himself again, he nodded vigorously.

The process took some trial and error, but within an hour, Hans had *six* perfect affinities. Looking at his Chi spiral now showed the same amount of Essence coming from each source, but now, the cumulative passive collection outpaced Hans' previous *active* collection by at least double. Hans was completely thunderstruck and nearly had tears in his eyes. "I just… I can't believe it."

"I have no idea how to give you a cultivation technique," Dale informed him sadly. "Otherwise, I totally would. You know that, right?"

Hans waved him off. "Don't worry about it. Frankly, with the world ending and… with all of these affinities… I'm thinking now might be the time to risk stealing one or two from a certain family I'm not fond of."

"Wait, *what*?" Dale rocked back on his heels, Hans's words managing what his slap had been unable to a short while back.

"Well… I *do* know where a few Noble houses keep their secrets." Hans grinned darkly. "I might be able to fool their owners for a couple weeks, and that's all we need, right?"

"What would Rose say about all this?" Dale directly questioned him. "Would she *want* you to do this?"

"Not a chance," Hans stated without concern, "but she needs a better method as well. What she got from Madame Chandra isn't suited to her. The High Magous was an *elemental* cultivator, and the trickle of celestial and infernal was all she ever needed. Unless Rose joined the church with a binding vow, they wouldn't give her what she needs. Just like with the Guild, actually. The more closely you bind yourself to them, the better the perks are but the less freedom you have."

"Why don't I just clear her affinity channels like I did for you?" Dale made the offer easily.

"Please do!" Hans stared his friend in the eyes, then winked broadly. "But I'd like to give her a gift from *me*."

"You're out of your mind." Dale watched as Hans turned and started stalking toward the portal. "Hans! If you plan to be sneaky… take a bath before you go! It really matters!"

Hans didn't stop walking, but his path changed *just* a little. Dale snorted, glad he had been able to do something great for his friend. Then he looked at the whirlwind of dirt created by snorting and had to hold back another one. Full-power-everything was really hard to get used to.

"Hey, Cal," Dale said to the open air as he barged to the front of the line and stepped into the third floor of the dungeon.

<How's it going, Dale?> There was a pause. <Are you about to go on a rampage or something?>

"Depends. When we go to your inner world, do I get nice things?" Dale stared at a small fortification in the distance. "I mean, it's my inner world too, right?"

<I… see what's about to happen, but no. You want things, you earn them like everyone else.> Dale didn't even wait to hear the entire answer, sprinting at the hexagonal fortification and clearing the wall in a long leap. The Goblins in the fort never got a chance to fight back, all of them dying to a single finger jabbed against their noggin.

<I was wondering about the whole 'you going through the portal' thing. I think that would be a paradox. I think you are not going to be able to do so, or you'd just be reabsorbed into me.> Dale grunted at me, though I could see the fear start to rise up in him. <Can I interest you in a fight against something *else* to take your mind off your concerns and get you to stop murdering Goblins? Perhaps a Manticore on the fifth floor?>

"Well," Dale started as he kicked open a chest and pulled out the tokens it contained, "if I do survive the transition, I'm looking for resources, weapons, armor, and land. I want to make an Academy, maybe put it on a mountain that *doesn't* fly all over the place and get into dangerous situations? It sounds appealing."

<It sounds *boring.*> Dale heard a groan in his mind as I considered my options. Didn't want him trying to tinker with *my* Soul Space. <*Fi~i~ine.* I'll make you a deal. You beat Manny alone, and I'll give you a mountain. Everything else you mentioned is already in chests on the lower floors—just clear them, and you'll get what you want. Stop killing my Goblins. They didn't do anything to you. Recently, at least.>

"Thanks, Cal ol' pal." Dale started walking toward the stairs, then caught himself and returned to the portal area, skipping to the end of the labyrinth by using his keygem. As he stood staring at the door to the dungeon's Manticore Boss, he had a sudden worry. "Hey. Cal. If I die in here, will you bring me back?"

<Eh.>

"*What*!" Dale shouted into the empty air. "Why *wouldn't* you?"

<I don't know. It seems like a pain?> My reply was completely unsatisfactory for Dale, it seemed. <Look, I mean, at this point, do I *need* you walking around out there? Maybe it would be nice to have control of my *entire* soul again, you know? >

Dale thought furiously for an answer and snapped his fingers when he figured out what to say. "Cal. I'm only a B-rank zero human. You're already in the A-ranks, yeah? What happens if I reconnect to you? Do I get into the A-ranks, or do you drop down to the B-ranks?"

Silence reigned for a long moment. <Fine. But if you die, you lose your gear. I can convert Mithril into a hefty amount of Essence. About seven C-ranker's worth, if you remember.>

Dale paused, debating on if he wanted to go in this room. Slowly, he nodded. "Alright. I need battle experience as a Mage. I have to control my body. I need to be comfortable with my new power. I'd also like to own a mountain again. So… deal."

The door in front of him slowly opened on its own, a sign that the dungeon was watching. Dale sighed at the theatrics and passed a bit of Mana through his armor, locking it in place at his joints. He unrolled the fabric that lay around his neck and fully covered his face and head. The Mithril weave should stop the Manticore's stinger and give Dale a fighting chance in this battle.

As he stepped into the room, the Manticore swooped down and alighted on the ground in front of him. "Chump, soft touch, sucker, mark, victim, dupe… *fool*. I know this scent. You came here once before, unprepared. Again you arrive, also unready, but this time without powerful allies. My thanks."

Dale had no idea why this creature could speak, but it gave him pause. This creature was *intelligent*; it used not only its body for combat but its mind as well. He may have made a serious mistake. An impact to his back sent him stumbling forward, and his head whipped around fast enough to see the Manticore's stinger retracting into the ground. Knowing he had only an instant to take advantage of the creature's immobile status, Dale sprinted forward and began battling in earnest.

It would have already been over for Dale if he hadn't been wearing the armor that he was, and he knew it. He threw his frustration into his attacks and punched directly into the paw coming at him. Dale's Mana was of a higher tier and purity than what flowed through Manny, and this helped mitigate the fact that Manny was at a higher ranking… but it didn't *negate* the fact.

Frankly, that was a dumb move by the human. Dale was spun around by the collision, though the blow coming at him hit his torso with far less strength behind it. Still, he was tossed across the room and into the wall.

CHAPTER TWENTY-THREE

<Hey, Dani. Want to watch Dale fight Manny?> I called over to my lovely Wisp, glad I had remembered even *if* the battle had already started. <It's already started!>

"Feces, Cal!" Dani zipped over as I connected my sight to a viewing rune that would allow the Mobs in this area to watch the entire fight. "Give a Wisp some warning!"

Dale appeared on the wall just as he was sliding under a paw swing that would have torn him in half when he was still in the C-ranks. There was a collective cheer in the area as a few Bobs clustered closer to see what was happening. Fights featuring Dale were getting rarer, and he always had a large number of my people rooting against him.

As Dale went under the paw, he punched upward into Manny's wrist and put the Manticore off balance. The sheer improbability of this happening was an interesting conundrum for me. I knew that Mana increased physical abilities, but it still astounded me to see a human punch a creature ten times his size and make the Beast stumble or go flying. Lots of cognitive dissonance tied up with Mana.

Manny was *really* hard to *keep* off balance though; the fact of the matter was that he had excellent control of his multiple limbs and body. The Boss turned the stumble into a *stab*, jabbing Dale with a thick spike from his wing. Ha! Dale would have a *nasty* bruise in the morning if he survived this. If not, oh well. I'd recreate him with a nasty bruise.

Dale had gone tumbling away, but now, he grabbed a rock in his left hand. Was he going to throw it at…? Mana surged into his hands, and he crushed the rock as he brought his hands together. Using the friction generated by his actions, Dale directed his Mana to empower the static, and a bolt of eye-searing lightning erupted from his palms. The power surged across the intervening space, hitting Manny in the wing and causing the appendage to spasm uncontrollably.

<What in the…? He figured out *lightning*? *Watt*?> I glanced sidelong at Dani. <This is a shocking development.>

Dani ignored me. Not unexpected. Back to the fight.

Manny sat down on the stone floor and glared at Dale, snarling as his wing stopped twitching. Dale caught his breath, seemed to focus, and *stomped*. The floor around him collapsed downward, trapping the Manticore tail that was moving through the tunnel beneath him. Manny screeched and pulled on his tail in an attempt to dislodge it from the floor, but it was slow going. Dale took a few more deep breaths, focusing inward and building to a crescendo of Mana usage. He stepped forward, landing a punch on Manny's neck while breathing out a *Pah*.

If I hadn't been able to see Mana, I would have had no idea what he had just done. Manny's head slipped from his body even as the mirrored ceiling above him shattered in a spectacular explosion. Dale had used a technique; he absolutely *must* have. His Mana had flowed into a pattern and captured a thin line of air. Then his movement had sent the empowered gust at Manny, where it acted as a garrote—a cutting wire of super-compressed air that had broken down after reaching the target and began rapidly expanding.

The cut it had initially made had been small and possibly

not even deadly, but as the air expanded, it had created a cavitation bubble *inside* Manny that literally tore his head off. Then the leftover energy had continued forward and rebounded off the ceiling, making it look like an explosion. Something I had seen *inside* Dale had me even more excited than the fight had been. I had never noticed what actually happened when someone activated a technique because their innards weren't visible to me. Even Dale's hadn't been until recently, but he hadn't used a technique in my depths since well before then.

<Dale… do you have any idea what you've just done?> I slowly asked the human.

"Looks like I *won*." Dale smirked even as he sat down to conserve energy. Heat was rolling off of him, a sure sign that the technique he just used wasn't even *close* to mastered yet. "So, about that mountain."

<Yeah, yeah. You'll get your token.> It can't actually be that easy… can it? <Hey, Dale? Want to try a new technique?>

"*What*?" Dale popped to his feet, excitement glowing on his face. Oh, wait. That's body heat from overuse of Mana. "Someone lost a *technique* in here?"

<Mmm,> I murmured noncommittally. Which one, which one? I've been using this a lot recently—let me quickly turn it into a memory stone, add in the constraints needed for moving through flesh, and… <Here you go!>

A memory stone dropped out of the air, quickly caught by Dale. He pressed it to his head, looking up in confusion after letting the information flow over. "That's odd."

Drat. He's on to me. <What, ah, what's the matter, Dale?>

"This must have been from a *super* amazing memory stone crafter. There aren't any emotions attached to it, no strange memories of the actual creation process. Just… pure information." Dale looked at the stone in his hand in amazement.

<Why don't you try it out? Here, I'll give you a target.> A moment later, a Basher appeared in the room. It hopped around in confusion, squeaking softly in terror from the scent of

Manticore blood in the air. <Sorry little guy, you only get to live for about thirty seconds.>

I turned my attention to Dale, who had his hand outstretched. A look of intense concentration was showing on his face, and the air began to distort around his hands. He pressed his hand *down*, and the Basher squeaked and splattered on the floor. Dale stopped using his Mana, staring at the remains of the Basher in shock. "What just happened?"

<I learned how to make *techniques* is what happened,> I informed him smugly. <All you have to do is move your Mana through your meridians in a certain pattern, then hold that pattern out in the world, right?>

"Right?"

<What you are *actually* doing is creating a Rune and converting Mana into the type of Mana or Essence needed for the Rune to work!> I shouted in excitement. <*That's* why not everyone can use every type of technique, why they need to have a certain amount of 'affinity' for it! That must also be why you can't put Runes on flesh—it distorts the natural meridian pathways below! I've just made a *massive* breakthrough, Dale! I can't wait to start experimentation on people!>

"I'm happy for you." Dale looked at his hand and then the Basher once more. "What was that? What did I do?"

<Ah. It was a gravity… spell? It's a Rune, not an inborn ability, and 'technique' sounds silly after I finally know what they actually are. Since you are 'spelling out' the Rune in your body and pushing out what you 'spell', I'm calling it a *spell* now.> I saw his confusion and realized that I was getting off on a tangent. <You made the bunny too heavy. It went *squish*. Do it again to make other things go *squish*. Add more Mana to make the squish harder and faster.>

"It took so *little* Mana though." Dale sat down and crossed his arms. "Why was this so much more effective and efficient than the other memory stone techniques I've studied?"

<*Spells*,> I corrected him, getting an eye roll in return. <If you want to know why things work correctly, use the words I

use. The *reason* it was better was that I know *exactly* what needed to be done, and this was tailored directly to your meridians. Using someone else's spell—that they created for themselves—will always be inefficient.>

"Does this mean I can master this… *spell* really easily?" Dale was excited about that prospect and for good reason. He had been able to direct his Mana more precisely than with any other tech– *spell.* Dale could also feel that this was more directly powerful than most of his other options, and mastering it would mean that he could use it nigh-instantly and with very little cost.

<It should. Gotta warn you, even though it is a high tier spell, it isn't gonna be too useful against other Mages unless you *really* outclass them. At best, you'll slow them down to a standstill. I have a floor set up with *hundreds* of this Rune interlocking and empowering each other. Even then, half the time, Mages will survive going through them. I know what you're thinking: 'why haven't I met them?' Easy. The shock of falling and getting hurt lets the Boss finish them pretty easily.> I could see that Dale had a lot to process and play with, so I figured it was time for me to do other things.

<Here's the token for a mountain.> A wooden chip dropped down and bounced off his head. <Here's a keygem for the next floor. I'd go check it out if I were you.>

Oh, hold on. The next floor was all golems. He had seen it before. Eh. Whatever, the portal was in the entryway of that floor. Dale would figure it out. Until then, I had a lot more work to do. My panic… orb… was coming along nicely. Should I call it a safe house? Safe orb? Run away sphere? Whatever, it was the place I was stocking with all sorts of goodies for myself. I had reinforced it again but this time with Wards and Cores. Even if the planet were destroyed, my little safe area *should* now keep me safe, secure, and well-fed for a few decades if I rationed properly.

All I would need to do then is secure a new source of Essence and hope for the best.

CHAPTER TWENTY-FOUR

"Well, *that* was a fun run." Dale stared at the faceless Golems waiting for him to step on their paths and fully decided against going through here alone. "Back to the surface, I guess?"

He walked toward the portal, using his newfound gravity 'spell' to hinder the movements of the huge Cats that patrolled the edges of this space. Dale grunted in dissatisfaction when he realized that he couldn't use the spell to squish the Cats, only make it nearly impossible for them to move. He had been *hoping* that he had a new and glorious weapon. Still, Dale had to smile when he realized that he had a long way to go before mastering this ability; maybe squashing Cats *was* in his future!

The silver lining was pretty clear with this spell—the Cats not being able to move *did* make it easy to end them and gain a Core. He was happily attacking another as a second one caught him by surprise. Then he realized the *real* weakness of the spell. It had a *very* small area of effect, at least compared to some of his other abilities. Dale smiled at the Coiled Cat, which was ineffectually gnawing on his leg. The C-ranked Cat was causing Dale some pain, but it was too weak to break through his

Mana-infused skin. "Thanks, little guy! I'm learning so *much* today!"

Then he punched down and siphoned off some Essence using the Runes on his gauntlet. The Cat, suddenly weakened and dizzy, stumbled away only to be met with a heavy blow that made everything go black for it. Dale swiftly added another Core to his bag and walked out of the portal. "Huh. Normally I come out and really enjoy the fresh air... What changed? Something stinks."

"Dale!" A voice Dale still flinched at broke his peaceful mood, and Minya appeared in front of him. "I *knew* if I waited around here, you would show up."

"Didn't you ask *Cal*?" the Mithril-clad Mage asked with crossed arms.

"You can't *possibly* still hold that against me!" Minya asserted while matching his hard look. "I know what you've been up to and all the benefits that you're getting from working with him. You *know* that there are a lot of people who hate *you* now, ever since your talk with The Master in *public* about sharing a soul with the dungeon. They think you are benefitting from the death of their friends and loved ones."

Dale was speechless. He hadn't thought about that at all, and he had *known* that it would be an issue. Whoops. Minya smirked and continued speaking, knowing that her point had been driven home, "So, I was wondering if you would go with me to the *Pleasure House* and we could... talk about things."

"I don't... you and I are... ah, fine. I guess that's okay." Dale sighed and started walking with her. "I *have* been avoiding you for a long while, and we really should clear a few things up. Clear the air, if you will. What is it that stinks out here, *seriously*?"

"I'm glad you see it that way." Minya softly laughed, lapsing into silence as they traveled and ignoring his question. Maybe she just didn't know. Dale was watching the people they passed and saw recognition on *far* too many faces. Whether it was happiness, excitement... or *resentment* on their faces, Dale decided that Minya had been speaking the truth, and his days of anonymity were over.

As they walked into the massive tree that had been grown as the restaurant, Madame Chandra herself was there to greet them. Dale had interacted with her a few times recently but only when they were in a group. Looking at her now, Dale nearly fell over in shock. "Chandra! What happened! Your power… your *rank*! It's like looking at the *sun*! What sort of upgrade did you get?"

"Ha!" Chandra laughed in his face. "I'm surprised and pleased with you, Dale! Most of the men who have talked to me recently never even notice something has changed. Let me look at *you*, Mr. *Mage*. That took us all by surprise, so I thought I'd let you take a peek at *my* power to see what it was like to notice a sudden massive power shift! Tables are turning in *here*!"

"In fact, you have a *lot* of Mana moving around in you right now, don't you? Hmm. Oh, I see… following Moon Elf traditions, are we?" As she spoke, Madame Chandra's voice sped up, allowing Dale to have a conversation at a normal pace. He smiled in relief as she did so; everyone being so slow had been making him grumpy. Maybe that was why Mages had always seemed so arrogant in the past? "Careful with all that power, Dale. Failure *absolutely* means death at… whatever tier you're playing around in. You have beautiful Mana, by the way, even if your Aura is doing a great job of concealing your *exact* ranking."

"Speaking of tiers, you weren't this powerful the last time I saw you—as you just stated—but what changed?" Dale looked the five-foot-tall woman over, shaking his head in wonder. Then his eyes lit up as he remembered a conversation from a few weeks back. "Is this a Path advancement? Is this what that means? What's the new one, and how did you do it?"

"*Nature*." Madame Chandra's eyes glinted in pleasure. "I'm near the pinnacle of the elements, and I'm easily able to fend off any type of attack that contains even a *drop* of elemental power. Fire, stone, water, air… I can control it *all* better than someone who is an expert in just *one* of them. I am *quite* pleased.

As for the advancement, I followed the paths laid out in the dungeon. It was quite informative."

"No kidding." Dale smiled at her, then surprised her with a hug. "Congratulations, Madame. This is exciting!"

"Yes, yes. Now, I see you've brought a lovely lady with you today. Let's get you seated." Madame Chandra winked at Dale, who turned red in an instant. He had *not* thought through how this 'meeting' would appear from an outside perspective. Did Minya *plan* this? Was this intended as... a *date*? Celestial feces. There was no way, right? He and Minya were so *very* opposite in views.

They were led to the top of the restaurant, where only the very *best* ingredients were used to create only the *finest* dishes. The branches around them opened up, allowing a spectacular view of not only the skyland but the world below them. As far as Dale could see, there was only blue. When had they gotten out over the ocean? Dale's brow furrowed, and he nearly stood up to go investigate why they were out to sea—when Minya began speaking.

"So, Dale. We finally can relate to each other, and I *really* think that we have a lot to talk about." She clasped her hands and leaned forward on the table, locking eyes with him and keeping a very serious expression on her face.

"Sure. Yeah. Let's talk." Dale sat and waited for her to begin asking questions. The silence stretched a little too long, and Minya sat back with a groan. "What's... on your mind?"

"Ugh. Let me guess, you have a *couple* of friends that you are close to and not much other social interaction at all, right?" Minya rolled her eyes at Dale's predictable defensive response. "Listen, relax, and we can just *talk* for a while. It's hard to find people that actually understand what I mean when I speak about the dungeon and the odd jobs that he gives me."

An hour later, they were still at the table, laughing over the remains of the food. Dale was trying his hardest to catch his breath and speak but was having trouble. "And—*ha*—and then Cal says 'oops. Hey, Dale, I did a thing'. I tried to ask what he meant, and by the time I was able to form the words, I was flying across the room, *bleeding* as the *rocks* around me began screaming!"

The laughter quieted, and they lapsed into companionable silence. After griping about Cal for the last hour, they were actually feeling connected and were getting on good terms. Then Minya did something Dale had *not* been expecting. She stood up, came close, and kissed him deeply.

While this was a surprise, at this point in the date—turns out, yes, a date—Dale was not opposed. Another kiss followed the first, and another... soon Minya closed her eyes and softly sighed, "Oh. *Cal.*"

Bam.

Dale was on the other side of the room—half embedded in the wooden wall—and had let Minya fall face-first to the floor as she leaned forward with closed eyes. "*What?*"

CAL

<Hey, Dani. I'm getting a little worried about what's happening in the upper layers of the dungeon.> I watched as the fight I was observing began to get more intense, growling a little as the walls began to shatter under the pressure the Mages were exuding. <There's a fight going on between a few of the factions. I think they are using my influence to hide what's going on from The Master.>

"So, what's the issue?" Dani connected with me and watched as a few necromancers fought off nearly double their number by pulling corpses out of interspatial bags and adding them to the fight. "Let them kill each other off. So what, why are you concerned?"

I changed what she was seeing, and as a Mage died, their Mana seeped away and out of the dungeon. I was able to grab a portion of it, but the vast majority vanished into the world. <See what I mean? I'm too far away from them to grab all of that, and Dregs can't take in foreign Mana without exploding. I

wouldn't care if they were fighting a few layers lower. Also, they are smashing up my walls and floor.>

"Well, get someone down here," Dani told me brusquely, and I had to hold myself back from snapping at her.

<For some reason, Dale and Minya are both outside of my influence. I could call them through our bond, but it might take too long for them to get back from wherever they are. Oh, see, the fight is already over. What a *waste*.> The Necromancers had won but had lost half their number. Their friends were shoved into bags, and the undead quickly followed. They seemed *furious*, which could have been because of the attackers that survived had run off, carrying the bodies of their fallen. No net gain for the necros, which was a frustration I understood.

<I'm not a fan of necromancers, even if I've mostly gotten over my old hatred of them. I *do* think that this is the second time this has happened down here, and I'm going to need to start setting up fail-safes for when it happens again.> I thought about that for a long moment. <I'm going to go have fun with this actually. At some point, this place is either going to cleanly work together… or erupt into open warfare. I'm betting on open warfare, so we need to prepare for that.>

I sent my mind up into the council chambers, which were as empty as they always were when not in use. I took measurements and began putting the preliminary requirements in place… time to set up some Wards. If they were going to fight, there was nothing that said that it was going to have to happen in my depths, right? Mu-hu-ha-ha.

CHAPTER TWENTY-FIVE

<All done!> My words caught Dani off guard, and she tumbled through the air in surprise. <Wards set up every ten feet in the council chamber—not as useful or dangerous as the ones down here, but still. Wards created at the mouth of the dungeon. Mana leaks in the dungeon, tries to escape, and it gets funneled to me before it can. Fighting breaks out in the council? Attacker goes *pop*, and I get the Mana. Now no one can accuse me of not caring if their race survives!>

"Why can't they accuse you of that?" Dani asked a few moments later, trying to pretend she hadn't been caught off guard by my enthusiasm. "At least one person is going to explode before they figure out you have turned against their infighting, and then they're going to think you trapped the place just to kill important people."

I stared at her, trying to make a good comeback. An explanation. A… to the abyss with it. <I tried?>

"You *sure* did, Cal."

<Listen, there's a meeting today to discuss the progress on the soul-portal thingy. As far as I can tell, they are getting close to finishing it but have no way to test it. In other words, this

should be *fun.*> I laughed lowly, knowing that there would be a fight. There was *always* a fight. <Tempers are going to go out of control, and Mana will follow. Hopefully, multiple people will attack at once. It'd be good to get rid of all the hotheads at once. Certainly don't want them in *me.*>

"Speaking of *you*, how is the world coming along?" Dani sent happy joy-joy thoughts as I did my best to create a satisfactory answer.

<It's fun! The first several miles are complete, and it's getting faster and easier as time goes on. It's as if… how best to put this… ah! My soul recognizes what I have been making. As long as I make more things that are similar, I am able to make them at a pace much faster than normal.> It was the best answer I could come up with. Soul-stuff was hard to explain. <Like how using a spell gets easier over time for people.>

"That's *excellent*, Cal!" Dani verbally applauded me. "So, you think that we'll have enough room to keep people, then?"

<Oh, easily. I'm a little surprised at how *few* people are interested in going to my soul, but that's fine by me. I bet that'll change as impending doom looms and a valid option is presented.> I looked over my little world and took the time to add a few details to one area or another. It would be important to add variety to the landscape and the plants eventually, but for now, grass and endless plains would have to do. I had placed a few trees and various herbs to test what it took to make them there and had added plenty of 'extra air' plants, but otherwise, the world was currently fairly monotonous.

But there was room, and there was air and food, and this entire place was a shelter for the races. <Water! *Abyss*! I forgot to add water!>

It was a good thing I had remembered since there were only a few things people actually needed to survive. Forgetting one of them wouldn't have gone over well, though I could have kept the people alive *by force*. I cut a few channels for water and let my soul take on the image of the water that would fill them. As the life-granting liquid appeared, I felt something *change*.

<I ranked up! I'm A-rank one now!> Dani was excited for me, and I was able to guess the answer before she asked the question. <I needed to provide the basics for life! Now that life is sustainable, I'm betting that my Soul Space has been recognized by **Acme**!>

"I hate to be a pill, but you forgot to add *water* to your world?" Dani paused for a moment, and I chose not to fill the silence. "Cal… what other basic things does your world need? Have you added *Essence* to the place yet? Free-floating Essence, that is, not just what was used to make land?"

Celestial. Fecal. Matter. <Do you really…?>

"Think that it's needed? Yes. Yes, I *really* do." Dani watched me closely as I reached into myself and started allowing a portion of the collected Essence pour into the air. Some unconscious part of me relaxed, and I could feel my world actively growing instead of remaining stagnant-yet-perfect in the state I had left it.

<I don't understand…>

"Did it help?" My silence spoke for me. "Well, it was a power-rich place. Mana rich, Essence rich, but there were no resources available to expand with. I'm betting that it was like every bit of your soul was holding its breath, waiting for something to happen. Like being paranoid at all times."

<I didn't even realize how horrible it was.> Relaxation was flowing through me, and the strange bottleneck I hadn't realized even *existed* vanished. <I feel good. What's next?>

Dani started to list off a few things that needed to be done, and I diligently worked my way through them. A few hours passed like this before one of the Bobs got my attention. "Great Spirit! You wanted to know when the next council meeting was going to be starting. You have only a few moments until they begin arriving!"

I sent a pleading emotion to Dani, who snorted and bobbed in the air. "You can go have fun, but there is still a lot to get done, so you are going to have to come back and work *afterward*!

That section where the Mages were fighting is still all messed up, and you need to fix it!"

<Let *Dregs* do it. Why do we even have them around if they don't *do* anything?> I grumbled the words even as I turned my attention to the chambers so far above me. I hadn't seen this before, and I wanted to know what went on when people didn't have anyone to impress.

"Magma Cores are lazy, and you know it! If she didn't have her Wisp pushing her to create, Dregs would have just sat in the area for millennia."

<Oh, Dani, meeting starting—gotta-go-bye!>

An Amazonian strode into the council chambers, looking absolutely *exhausted.* I actually felt bad for her for a moment. Typically, her people only showed their proud side, hiding anything that could even be thought of as weakness. Losing ninety-nine percent of their entire civilization to the attacks by The Master must have been a more serious blow to morale than I had thought it would be, at least, if this were the person I was going to base my judgment off of. Perhaps I had been too quick to judge them in the past? After all, if they were here and working with The Master, even though he had destroyed them…

The next person to enter was a High Elf who seemed to glide across the floor and sit with exceeding grace. I looked on in surprise and then started laughing. I was able to see under the robes he was wearing, and his steps had been so quick that it looked like he was bouncing in place like a hopped-up Basher. Was *that* what they did so they could look pretty when walking? *Ha*! Also, ever since the door had opened, the Amazonian had regained her haughty demeanor, but now, I at least knew it was an act.

Each of the groups that arrived had their own little ways to 'subtly' show dominance. Every time they did something 'special', it made me laugh. There was a new group that had joined —Wood Elves. They came into the room in perfect step with each other, and even more than that, they mirrored each other perfectly. When one turned to look to the left, they *all* turned left. Weird. I think it was a way to show unity?

Prince Henry and Queen Marie were the only group to walk in and have no apparent ego. They simply took their places and plopped down. I approved of this for a *few* reasons and let them know. <You're both doing great. Listen. You are representing humanity again, but you are also here for *me*. Whatever you do, don't throw *any* Mana around in here. I'll let you know why in a little while.>

They nodded, keeping their eyes flickering between the other races and peoples. Watchful. I like that. Of course, they looked like they had been dipped in metal, specifically Mithril. That meant that they didn't *look* particularly human and, in fact, could nearly be considered on the same level as my Golems in terms of features. This armor was different than Dale's and would *always* cover them when they were in the presence of other people. Only when they were alone—or with just each other—would their armor melt away, actually *into* their skin. Hope they continued to like each other long-term.

The Master was the last to arrive, and he did so by simply stepping out of nothing and sitting down in his seat. The already-quiet room went *dead* silent, and so he began to speak, "Let's discuss."

Those words were enough for the room to erupt into shouting, and powerful lungs made for painful echoes in the enclosed space.

"We were brutally *attacked*–"

"Why do we bother with these lower–"

"Hello, it's good to be included–"

"*You* were attacked? *We* were the ones–"

"Oh, stop it." The Master's words weren't as forcefully ejected as the others were, but still, he cut through the noise like a flame-enchanted sword through a Basher. There was a flare of light as a Guild member ignored him and sent a bolt of death at an unprepared necromancer. Luckily for the necromancer—and *not* so great for the attacker—my Wards latched on to the poorly-built spell structure, tearing the bolt apart and draining the man at double the rate of his Mana waste.

He dropped to his knees as power was pulled through him, and his arms began to glow. "What… what did you *do* to me, necromantic *filth*?"

Sadly, I hadn't been able to create the Wards to the same intensity as the more dangerous skill rooms in my depths, as that required a three-dimensional space. The ceiling was just too high to be effective, and the shining man wasn't near any walls. Too bad. Still, no one was moving to help the attacker, and his clothes started to smolder as Mana continued flowing out of him.

"*I* did nothing. This must be divine retribution!" the attacked necromancer replied smugly as he watched the Mage slowly burn to death. "You all saw, he attacked me for no reason!"

"I… *pant*… I don't know what's happening!" The Guild member's clothes officially burst into flame, but the small fire found no purchase on his powerful flesh. "I can't… I *don't know what's happening*!"

"Someone get him out of here before he explodes and singes my scarf." One of the High Elves made a 'shoo' motion, and a few Guild members grabbed the man and dragged him away. Of course, as soon as he got out of the room, his Mana stopped seeping away, and he came back into the chamber. Ignoring the looks and his singed shirt, he took his seat and stared at The Master stoically.

"Apparently, my words are not *enough*." The Master growled dangerously, raising the hackles of everyone in the room. "The *next* person to make an attack like that *dies. How does that sound*?"

The room shook with his fury, the table cracked, and dust rained from the ceiling. The world around him began to lose color, bleached by his power. I watched with rapt attention, waiting for him to lash out and smush these insects like I knew he could. Instead, he calmed down, and they began speaking about *logistics* and the morale loss of various populations. Then they began to talk on migration efforts, and I completely lost interest. Ah, well. It had been a fun attempt. Maybe my efforts would pay off in the future?

"I'm sorry I lost my temper." The Master was visibly restraining himself, knowing that any emotional displays could only mark him as weak. That was *not* what he needed right now, especially as he had not been able to close his wounds. The fight against Xenocide had been a tenth of a second away from ending *everything* for him, and the accounting was still coming due.

The Master waited a moment to see if anyone would speak up for him, but just like always before… it seemed he was going to have to rely on himself. "We simply do not have the time, we cannot spare the energy, and we *cannot* fight amongst ourselves. *Two weeks*. We have at most two weeks to put together a mastercraft portal that should be the work of a *generation*. If we are going to save our people… put aside your hatred at *least* until your own people are safe."

There. The Master decided *right there* that If self-serving interests wouldn't end this internal conflict… that he would just find another use for their *energy*. As a point of fact, the bodies of Mages provided rare materials for crafting.

CHAPTER TWENTY-SIX

"There he goes now. The *cheater*."

Dale whipped his head around, but enough people were looking at him that he couldn't pinpoint who had spoken. Normally, he wouldn't have associated that title with himself, but after what Minya had told him, it was starting to get under his skin. He nudged Hans *very* gently, calling attention to himself. "Hans, what was that all about? Someone just called me a cheater? What does that even *mean*?"

"Oh that?" Hans waved his hand dismissively. "They just think that you rose to power too quickly, that you achieved a high rank too young, and that the dungeon unfairly benefits you. I'm pretty sure there is only a *nebulous* plan to murder you to relieve tension. Nothing to worry about, just rank jealousy. Ha! *Rank* jealousy. Literal *and* figurative!"

Dale stopped short, took a deep breath, and slowly let it go. It was important to have a positive relationship with those around you, but right now, he had other things that were more important. Dale was having serious doubts about the quality of and reasoning *for* their relationship, but he had decided to go into the dungeon with Minya to challenge the Golems. Hans was walking with him for 'moral support', but in reality, he simply wanted to see the person that could cause Dale to become so flustered and frustrated.

Minya was getting a lot of attention, and it was obvious that they had seen her before she had seen them. There was a crowd of people around her that she was speaking—perhaps *preaching* —with. "There is an *easier* way, everyone! Instead of the need for a huge, unprotected portal, why not simply use the direct method of putting your mind into a Core and giving it to the Great Spirit below us? *Why* do you need your old bodies?"

"Because otherwise we still *die*! What's wrong with you? Of course, we want to go there in our *bodies*!" The crowd was growing restless, and this comment made the more fidgety amongst them go still before allowing their hands to drift to hidden pockets… almost as if they expected blood to soon fly.

"Minya," Dale softly called, knowing that she would be able to hear him.

She glanced over and smiled at him, sending a bright comment to the onlookers, "The option will always be there! At least for, well… you know what I mean."

Dale wasn't sure how to handle the looks that were an odd mixture of hatred and jealousy he gained simply by having Minya saunter over to him, take his hand, and pull him to the entrance of the dungeon. Hans giving him a thumbs up and salacious wink didn't help the situation. "Do you *have* to be parading me around like this?"

"Of course, I do!" Minya's expression took on a dark edge. "If you'd rather fight through the tower of ascension alone, for the *first*–"

"Alright, *alright* already!" Dale sped his steps up to Mage-speed, and they left all the wandering eyes behind them. "Plus, whatever Cal has in here, it can't actually be just like the tower."

"No. It really can't." Minya smirked at him. "Cal's version is *far* easier. You just need to fight something."

"Can we just talk like normal people, or do you toss around ominous sayings for a living?" Dale growled, still not looking directly at her. He was embarrassed by their last encounter; how could he not have understood that she was only after him for his connection to Cal? Dale held out a keygem, and a rift appeared in the air before him. Stepping through the portal, he caught a Cat by the scruff of its neck and chucked it toward the nearest Golem.

The Cat never reached the target, instead getting caught by gravity Runes and dropped into a portal that opened to the bottom of the mountain. It had a *long* way to fall before it would reach the arctic waters of the ocean far below. Minya shook her head disapprovingly. "You should know better than to put monsters outside of Cal's influence like that. What a waste of Essence!"

Dale gave her a flat stare, and she turned to the paths, full of annoyance. "Whatever, Dale. What path would you like to challenge? One of the base elements, infernal, or celestial?"

"It shouldn't matter. Fire?" Dale finally looked directly at Minya, who had her eyes closed and seemed to be counting. "Actually, I don't know your Mana type. What's your specialization? Tier?"

"Effervescence. Two."

Dale waited for more, but it seemed nothing was forthcoming. "I have *questions*..."

"You and everyone else that *ever* hears that." Minya waved him off like an extra-annoying insect. "It's tier two, wind and water. It's a *valid* Mana type."

Dale could hear the invitation to *say* something. He ignored the dare in her voice, waving at the path of fire. "Let's go on that one. What are you after, by the way? What is it that you are hoping to get out of this dungeon dive?"

"I'm trying to get a field of rare herbs," Minya responded succinctly. "I am a beast tamer, a dungeon explorer, and a researcher. Powerful herbs are useful for all of my jobs and hobbies, but all of my sway with Cal has been used up just by him keeping me alive. So, I'm going to *hunt* for what I want."

Nodding along, Dale put his other concerns out of his mind

and focused on his immediate goals. "Agreed. I want to secure a stable area for myself and the people I want to be around. I don't like the instability I've been dealing with, and want to find a way to do what *I* want in safety and comfort. Let's go fight our way to a better future."

"To a better future!" Minya shouted, charging into the flames ahead of him. Dale cursed and followed, arriving on the small island just as a torrential blast of flames ignited the air. Minya shifted her Aura to deal with the attack, deflecting the fire to either side even as the heat scorched her outfit. Dale burst through the remaining blaze, ignoring the minor pain of the Mana-infused fire that penetrated his defenses.

He hopped over Minya, reaching back and translating his momentum into power as he punched the Golem's torso. The force he exerted cracked the mineral structure, and the Golem went spinning ass over teakettle. It righted itself using a directed blast of fire, riding the momentum and catching Minya's leg as she tried to dodge. She screamed as it began superheating its body by directing pure fire Mana into its hands.

Minya had to directly pit the water Mana in her Aura against the pure flames and was quickly losing the battle. Dale arrived with a crushing blow, splintering the Mob's left elbow. It was forced to release the hold it had, and Minya gained distance by kicking off the construct's already-damaged chest. Dale followed her motion with an earth-infused attack using his knee, and the Golem's Core was broken out of the main body. It rolled nearly to the edge of the platform before Minya caught up and stored the Mana-filled object in her spatial bag.

"Whew!" She wiped her forehead though no sweat had appeared. "That was *fun.* Should that have been so difficult? That was only the first Golem in the area!"

"Don't forget that these are commonly set up for a five-person team," Dale reminded her even as he worked to decide the best path forward. "We are going to need to be careful. I have a lot of raw power and my bodily training, but I don't have a ton of experience or refined skills. You…"

"Yeah, yeah." Minya waved off his discomfort. "You assume I don't have a lot of raw power, so I need to rely on what I have learned over the years. I'm still recovering from multiple years of Mana deprivation, so trust me when I tell you I understand my limits."

Dale decided against pointing out the handprints burned into her thigh and pointed instead at the path that connected to the earthen element. "Want to run down the lava path? It would be easy for you to defend since it would be elements opposed to your own. Also, I'm pretty sure I can handle most of the low-tier Golems on my own without too much trouble."

Minya put her hands on her hips and cocked an eyebrow. "Didn't we *just* agree not to underestimate them? I've been watching these things since Cal made them. They are *dangerous*."

Dale let his head roll back while he groaned. "Can we just *go* before the moon strikes?"

"Fine, lava path it is." Minya strode away forward, though Dale soon overtook her and stormed down the path at the lava Golem. He used his earth-shattering tech—that is, his *spell*—in hopes of ending this battle as it began.

A thick barrier of Mana intercepted his spell, eroding it to the point that only a few thick flakes of stone fell from the construct. Dale was forced to dodge to the side as the Golem's retaliatory strike mimicked a small-scale eruption, flooding the space he had been standing with superheated stone. Dale's skin sizzled as empowered sparks charred his exposed flesh. "Son of the *abyss*!"

Minya burst through the heat, a gout of steam trailing behind her as the protective water coating on her body vaporized. A staff appeared in her hands, and she struck the floor just in front of the Golem. The water and air interacted with the suffocating heat and exploded upward, tossing the Tom-sized golem into the air. Seeing his chance, Dale focused his new gravity spell, and the Golem slammed back to the platform. With the Golem off balance, it was simplicity itself to smash the Core out of the prone body.

Tossing the Core into his bag, Dale looked around at the hazy air, only able to get a general understanding of where he was in relation to the center of the room. "Minya… we're gonna be here a while, huh?"

"Yup." She cracked her neck by tilting her head to the side sharply. "Once we get past a few more, the ones at the start come back, so it is also a fight to retreat."

"Alright, maybe we take a few minutes and figure out how to work together a little better?"

"I thought you'd never ask."

CHAPTER TWENTY-SEVEN

General Aiden stood still in the dungeon as the Amazonians cautiously explored the area. His squad was with him, using the cover provided by the dungeon to set up their ambush. These *oathbreakers* thought that they would just wait around? That they would let people without honor into a world where killing them meant nothing? No. No, Aiden would ensure that if any Amazonians survived... it wasn't for lack of effort on his part.

As the Amazonians walked toward the treasure chest in the center of the room, Aiden shook his head in disgust. They didn't even bother to check for traps; they didn't think anything on this level could possibly hurt them. Normally, they would even be correct. Not today. Today was the start of *vengeance*. Most people wouldn't understand how *dangerous* people who had nothing to lose could be. They wouldn't understand the terrible things these *Amazonians* had done. That they *needed* to be destroyed.

Whamp!

The strange sound of a Ward activating and suffusing the air with power sounded through the room, and the Amazonians froze. One of them had touched the chest and had keyed the trap to her power. It was vamping her, using her own Mana to power itself. Since he and his people were wearing keys to the Wards, they sauntered up to the paralyzed group and watched hope flee while despair set in.

"Oh, look what we have here." Aiden smirked at the members of the group, who were all struggling mightily.

"Maybe if you had gone to an area *appropriate* to your rank, you would–" Five swords swung out, and five heads fell to the floor. The Ward snapped and popped, fizzling out. "–have been better prepared. Maybe you would have even survived. Instead, you took the easy way out, a way with no struggle or growth. We don't need people like you in our new world."

"C-rankers killing Mages!" Aiden released a sigh of contentment as the bodies began to vanish, converted into raw power for the dungeon to use at its leisure. "A gift, a sacrifice to you, dungeon! May we bring you ever more power! May we grow in strength together, forevermore!"

The squad of Northmen cleaned their weapons with a flicker of Essence, their densely Inscribed weapons being handled with more care and respect than the lives they had just ended. Aiden glanced around at the men with him, motioning for them to walk. "Let's move out! These Amazonian oath-breakers aren't going to go extinct by themselves!"

CAL

Three *entire* days. That was how long it took me to make my way through and categorize all the information given to me by the infernal dungeon. That being had been *scary* smart, even though it had seemed that most of the info was of an unusable affinity for the being. The raw information it had dumped into my mind in return for what I now realized was a *pittance* was astounding. I took control of a Cat and made it shake its head, just so that I could visually express myself.

<Dani, I'm always amazed by how much *more* there is for me to learn. There is an ocean of amazing things, and all I have

is a bucket to hold a little in.> I was happy. Really, I was. The thought that there was nowhere else to go, that I had reached the epitome without realizing it, had been haunting me. Now… now, I at least realized how *little* I actually knew and how little of what I knew that I *understood*. <Can you imagine it? We are going to be together for eternity—learning, growing, and *eating*!>

"How do you go straight from deep philosophical and existential thinking to talking about food?" Dani laughed at me as I sent an image of a sheep back at her. "Feeling *sheepish*? Is that what that is?"

<Hey, you're getting better at understanding what I mean!>

"I just understand that I was *over*thinking what you were sending in the past," Dani retorted archly. "Taking it at face value, also known as *simply as possible*, usually gives me the correct answer."

<Ouch.> I winced, by which I mean the Cat I was controlling started making strange faces. <Anyway… um… what was I saying? Right! All of this new information has been sorted, and I have a good handle on how things are interacting. What I'm doing now is looking for patterns, repeated schematics or variables that are interchangeable on a micro or macro level. If I can find what I'm looking for, I'll be able to parse any data or use modular, formulaic options for the creation of new Runes.>

I paused, waiting for a response. There wasn't one. <How's *that* for taking my words at face value? If I explained everything I do all the time, I'd drive you insane.>

"Fine, fine. Maybe there *is* a mind somewhere in that overgrown crystal." Dani's words were a backhanded compliment, but I still smirked about the fact that I had been able to shock her into silence without making a monster appear out of thin air. "The question now becomes—what are you going to use all of your new Wards and… formulaic options *for*?"

<Well, Dani…> I paused for dramatic effect. <I'm *not* entirely sure.>

"*Ugh*! All that talk was just hot air, wasn't it?" Dani groaned and nearly fell to the ground.

<No, I'm sure an option will present itself to me. I might not have time to go around and make a whole bunch of new floors and the like, but this will all be information useful within my Soul Space, right? When other people are using it and *finding* uses for these, I will as well. All of that knowledge will be mine to use as I see fit.> I trailed off, starry-eyed. Might need to fix this poor Cat when I left. Starlight pouring out of eye-holes tended to leave them… crispy.

"So, you're going to use people to *power* yourself as well as explore ways to use their ideas? This sounds dark, Cal…" Dani's voice trailed off uncertainly.

<It isn't like *that*, Dani!> I protested my innocence. <You know as well as I do that without me, they don't stand a chance. It isn't like I'm going to keep them locked up inside me for tens of thousands of years just because I *can*. The deal was as soon as they can be released safely, I will make it happen. They are getting a lot out of this too!>

"Yeah, yeah." Dani slowly stirred the air around her, a Wisp's version of a sigh. "I get it, Cal. Just remember that when people are trapped against their will for a long time… they get resentful of whatever is keeping them there. I'd hate to see someone get out and try to smash you just because you were the instrument of their detainment."

<I will work to ensure that is something that never happens,> I promised her. <Also, *really* off topic, sorry about this. There is a group of Northmen going around and massacring Amazonians. Should I just *go* with it or…? They *are* dedicating the kills to me and taking no trophies. Lots of power tied up in some of the stuff I'm… acquiring.>

Dani took a look at the situation and grunted noncommittally. "No, they know that they have enemies. The Northmen are *technically* giving them a fighting chance. Traps… traps are a danger people are supposed to be well aware of. This is on them, and let me repeat why—the Amazonians *know* that they have enemies."

<That's kinda what I was thinking, too. Glad to have it confirmed.>

"If they did anything else, even taking some of the gear, I'd have you send a Bob Squad after them," Dani continued with her thoughts, taking me by surprise. "They have a blood feud, so I understand their logic, but if they aren't going to let people survive, we need as many resources as we can get to complete the project at hand."

<Alright.> I thought about it for a long minute. <I am *slightly* confused by your logic because they are breaking the rules and deal we had in place, but it means less work for me, so… meh.>

"There will always be time to punish them when there is no *escape*, Cal." Dani's words conjured dark images in my mind, and the Cat I was inhabiting started shivering violently. "Hundreds of years of punishment will be a better deterrent than a few simple deaths *now*."

I underlined a point on my mental checklist once more. This made eighteen lines under this particular point—Don't cross Dani.

CHAPTER TWENTY-EIGHT

Dale and Minya literally crawled out of the portal, fresh blood pasting their clothes to their bodies. Dale was gasping, directing his Aura to create the healing-light-aspect of the sun. Minya was in even worse condition, barely conscious and gasping for as much air as her lungs could take. Only the aftereffect of Dale's Aura kept her moving.

"We… *cough* how did we survive that?" Dale wheezed the question using every last drop of stamina he had.

Minya didn't answer right away, simply lying next to him in a slowly growing pool of their co-mingled blood. "Luck?"

"Must… have…. been," Dale agreed over the next few seconds. As he calmed himself, he was able to allow Mana to flow into his body once more. He had been *dangerously* close to losing control of his power when they were fighting the final golem on that floor and had been forced to cut himself off as soon as he struck the final blow.

Now, his armor siphoned a drop of his Mana and tightened in a contorting pattern on his limbs, re-aligning the serious breaks. Dale shook his head wearily; he needed to find a proper healer, but he took a moment to thank Cal for his foresight. His armor was nearly sentient and would tighten to act as a splint and cast when needed. Unfortunately, it required power from *him* to do so, and if he were Mana deprived… so was his armor.

He was able to get to his feet but couldn't really help Minya since his arms had both broken during the final fight. He nudged her with his toe, and she grunted to show that she was still alive. "C'mon, Minya, let's get to the clerics."

"Just let me bleed to death, Dale. Cal will bring me back, right?" Minya whined her words, and Dale laughed despite himself. "That's *dark*, Minya."

"Nah, just like necromancers, Cal is simply a *really* late healer." Minya got to her feet, took a single step, and turned her head to vomit. "Ugh. I think I have a concussion."

"Not surprising." Dale remembered her stepping in and saving him from taking a blow that would have broken his neck, but she had bounced off a few rocks as she tumbled away. "Thanks, by the way."

"It's what teammates do." She growled, focusing on putting one foot in front of the other. Luckily, the healing station wasn't far away from the exit of the dungeon, and they were soon surrounded by people who could restore them. After agreeing to the price, they had glowing Mana pouring into their wounds. A gentler light was entering Minya's head, and her irises slowly came to be the same size.

Dale tipped the healers a full gold coin each *after* paying the fee, and when he got a look of shock from Minya, he shrugged and walked away. When they were far enough away, he explained himself, "It might as well be *dirt* at this point. Can't take it with us into Cal, right? Why not make a few people happy, maybe build some good will?"

Minya thought on that for a short while, nodding as they continued walking. "That makes a certain kind of sense. Looks like I'm about to have a shopping spree."

"There ya go." Dale let a slow grin creep across his face. "Get it all out of your system—no shopping for a *long* time after we get into Cal."

Minya blanched, making Dale laugh long and hard at her expense. Shopping was her treat, her reward, her guilty pleasure! Maybe someday, she could convince Cal to let her set up fun shopping centers or something…? Just then, she realized that she looked like a murder victim. A wave of bubbly Mana fizzled along her body, and the blood on her clothes, hair, and skin was removed and destroyed. She turned to offer the service to Dale but then realized that he was perfectly clean.

When he was asked about that, he told her about his sunlight Aura and the huge versatility it offered. Suitably impressed, she continued making conversation until noticing that a constant stream of people was moving along the path to the Academy. "Dale, do you know what this is all about?"

"Nope, I can ask though." Dale tapped a person who didn't look as eager as all the others, asking for information.

The man was wearing students' robes, obviously a member of the Academy. "You didn't hear? The Master let it be known that he was going to be offering a lecture today and that any student or member of the Academy was welcome to attend. Since no one knows anything about him, everyone is losing their minds. I bet it'll just be some stupid motivational speech again."

Dale thanked him and glanced at Minya. She nodded, and they both joined the stream of people pouring into the stone structure. They got to the main courtyard, finding it *stuffed* with people of all walks of life. There was only standing room, and a few Mages had even begun levitating groups off the ground so more people could participate. Dale saw that and grumbled, "*Abyss*, I really need to learn how to fly."

"Just *one more* thing I could teach you, Dale." Minya was speaking into his ear to be heard, and the buzz of her lips made him shiver… not *unpleasantly*. "I hope that our time together today has made you more receptive to my *advances*."

Dale couldn't think of anything to say, overcome as he was by conflicting thoughts and emotions. Luckily for him, The Master made his appearance at that moment. Stepping out of nowhere, the dark figure soon had the attention of everyone present.

"There is more to the world than most people will ever understand," The Master launched directly into his lecture without preamble. "Today, I am going to give you a closely guarded secret of those in the S-ranks. The key to ascending into the Spiritual ranks, in fact. Feel free to write it down, to share the knowledge with anyone you'd like."

His words caused shocked muttering, which turned into aggrieved clamoring. People were trying to decide if he was being condescending or if… just maybe… he was telling the truth. If so, he was about to answer a question that had plagued the races for generations. As the first syllable left The Master's mouth, all extraneous noise ended. "Many have walked the path of Magehood, only to become foiled at the final step, and so many have never understood *why*."

"I would be doing a disservice to the Academy if I did not impart other wisdom to you beforehand." This caused groans to spill from a few undisciplined mouths, and a crooked smile to wash over The Master's. "Let us walk through the various methods of advancement."

"Firstly, there is the original step upon the road of cultivation. All people are able to absorb the Essence of the heavens and the earth. As we all know, the purity and quantity that we can bring in will determine how far we can advance on the path… for most." The Master stopped here, but only annoyance was reflected back at him. He didn't particularly care; the fundamentals were important.

"Once we have obtained a method of cultivation, a way to keep the quality and quantity high, the Chi Spiral becomes of the utmost necessity. In fact, most cultivators do not recognize anyone under the D-ranks as actual cultivators. I'm sure many of you have experienced this truth. In fact, point at anyone accepted by the Academy as an F-ranker, and I will give you a spatial bag right *now*." The Master waited, and a few people quickly exchanged whispered conversations, but no one took him up on his offer.

"Exactly. Something for you all to be careful about is that most Mages see *anyone* below the C-ranks the same way. Use caution, for in the hearts of many lie arrogance." He collected his thoughts for a moment. "From the D-ranks to the C-ranks, collecting power is of the utmost importance. Beyond large quantities of Essence, there is only one feature that defines a C-ranker—Aura—the ability to enhance every *bit* of your body and mind with Essence, create a passive shielding around yourself, and shape your power for raw usage."

People were nodding in the area, and a few D-rankers were writing the information down. Typically, information was given on a 'need-to-know' basis. "From the C-ranks to the B-ranks, becoming a Mage, advancing through the tower of ascension is needed. This binds your soul to a **Law,** an aspect of reality, a fundamental node of *pure meaning*. Now, the higher you climb in the Tower, the higher the tier of Mana you will be able to channel."

"There is a way to gain a higher tier, but it is *normally* considered too difficult to truly consider. The only *known* way to climb higher is a 'Path Advancement'. This is not only the acquisition of a large amount of information, but the new path must be a **Law** that contains the **Law** to which you have been bonded—a set of power that contains its lesser self." The Master grinned as he saw the plethora of confused faces.

"If you think that is hard to understand, you need to begin taking your studies in this Academy more seriously. Having a strong body is important, but a strong mind will always bring you further." The Master stopped his chiding and continued, "From the B-ranks to the A-ranks, you need to create a Soul Space. This is a term that many of you have heard recently. As you know, going into a Soul Space is our plan to survive the incoming *desolation*."

As he finished speaking, he pointed up at the shards of the moon that were visible even during the day now. "A strong soul, a firm understanding of your capabilities and responsibilities, and *lots* of practice will allow you to enter the S-ranks. Maybe. There can only be a *single* S-ranker of *any given **Law***. At this point, you have bonded to your **Law** to such a degree that you become the embodiment, the *Incarnation* of that **Law**."

"You may wonder why then is the S-rank called the 'Spiritual' rank? Why not the 'Incarnation' rank?" The Master let people nod along before moving on. "Do you remember me speaking of *Soul Space*? To step into the S-ranks, you must *invert* your power. What is *outside* becomes the *inner* world, what is outside becomes *made* of what had previously been solidified. When you look directly at me, you are not seeing flesh or Mana made flesh. You are seeing my soul, formed into a facsimile of my actual body. Upon obtaining the S-ranks, the body goes away. Your *mental self* shapes your being, fueled by the power you now have. It's similar to the Mage-rank body replacement, just with another—*higher*—energy. Good luck using this information to attain the rank I have."

With that final phrase, The Master vanished the same way he had arrived. For a long beat, no one made a sound. Then a Mage broke the silence and sent the crowd into a frenzy with a simple phrase, "What the *abyss*?"

CHAPTER TWENTY-NINE

<Oh, look!> I brought the Academy grounds up on a screen in the navigation room. <It *expl~o~oded.*>

Chaos filled the courtyard. People were falling out of the air as Mages forgot to levitate them, people were shouting at each other, and large swaths of the crowd were attempting to leave and *discuss* what they had just learned. I brought up Dale, who didn't even notice as someone tried to stab him in the kidneys. The dagger—with the word 'hubris' printed along its blade—broke on his armor, and he did *pause* momentarily as the sound of the metal bouncing off the ground reached his ears. Ugh, *Dale*. That's such a *Dale* thing to do. To not even *notice* an assassination attempt.

"Did any of it make sense to you?" Dani interrogated me adroitly. "Did you gain any enlightenment, make any plans for the future?"

<Well… I won't really know if the S-ranks are what he says for a long time, right? Beyond that, it seemed like he knew what he was talking about. At least none of it was *false.*> I pondered on The Master's words. <No, he was as accurate as he under-

stands how to be, but just as we have all found out, there's always another path to power.>

"You mean like what Artorian did?" Dani accurately inferred. "How he designed what seems to be an entirely unique system for cleansing his corruption while still increasing in rank?"

<*Exactly* like that,> I confirmed while steadily eyeing the situation above. <If he hadn't been desperate to advance to the B-ranks, he would have never made a deal with me. He was *that* close to being able to do it on his own.>

"I forgot to ask you, what did *you* get out of making that deal? What were the details of the offer he made to you?"

I grinned wolfishly, and the Cat I was still toying with toppled over into unconsciousness. <Whoops, too much strain on Mr. Kitty. I'll heal him up in a few minutes. He deserves a big reward. Anyway. Artorian needed power for some kind of a rescue or something. Didn't really care too much. What *I* got out of it was–>

Boom!

I cut off my comments, looking around the immediate area. <Sorry, do you hear people screaming?>

"No. What? Should I?"

<Yeah, oh, neat.> I was looking at the surface where a few Mages were being beaten down by a huge creature in articulating metal armor. <There is… something going on up there. Dani, I have *no idea* what that thing is.>

"I'll get Grace to the escape portal."

<Could you please just *look* at that thing?> Her jokes weren't even funny! I brought my 'sight' on to the creature as it fought, and Dani gasped.

"*Cal*! That's! That's one of Kantor's B-ranked *Boss Mobs*!" She was so shocked that I wasn't sure how to take this information.

<Um. How is that possible? Kantor died a *while* ago.> Her glare shut me *right* up. <I'm so sorry for your loss.>

"Uh-huh." Well, *that* would mean a fight later. I wonder if I could use my Mobs against her during an argument? ...Probably a bad idea. "We need to get her in here. I'm sure she will have information that we are going to want, if not *need*."

<I'm on it!> I promised her seriously. <Dale! Minya! Need you for a... *thing*!>

"*What kind of 'thing', Cal?*" Dale's typically paranoid mental response came.

"*Yes, Great Spirit!*" Minya's replies always cheered me up. "*Where do you want us?*"

<Rescue operation! I need you to get over to the *Pleasure House*. There's some kind of Mob that just landed and was attacked. It's holding out for now, but it is apparently one of Kantor's original Boss Mobs.> I let that sink in, even as they began moving. <We need her alive! She came here willingly!>

One of the greatest benefits of becoming a Mage was the reduction in travel time. Dale caused barely *any* damage as he ran, a sign of his improvement. He still caused *some* damage, but I fixed it on the fly since he was doing me a favor. They came into view of the massive creature and pulled up short.

"That's a *she*?" Dale muttered under his breath, getting swatted by Minya for his rudeness. They looked over the huge humanoid, and we realized at the same time that this Mob was coated in armor similar to what I had put King Henry and Queen Marie in. "Are you sure it's here with peaceful intentions?"

<Nope.>

"*Lovely*." Dale spat to the side even as he moved closer. Blades were bouncing off armor, *spells* were being redirected, and Mages went soaring whenever a hit connected. "Everybody *back off*!"

It took a few repetitions of this shout for him to be heard, but Minya played a part by stopping people from rejoining combat after they were knocked back. A simple phrase from her made them stop and think. "It is hitting only *non*-lethal areas! Back off!"

When a stalemate had been reached, Dale stepped forward

with his hands to his sides. "Boss Mob, you come from Kantor's dungeon? Why are you here?"

The metal along the huge being's body shifted, popped, and reformed. All dents and damage had been fixed, and the creature now seemed twice as imposing. "I come to place for Dani. Have final order to find and arrive. Got present from Kantyor."

Deep in the dungeon, Dani gasped and let out a shuddering gust of wind.

"I *knew* it!"

Dale looked up at the creature, deciding to just go ahead and bring it into the dungeon. "Follow me… um. I'm sorry, what is your name and, ah, race?"

"Am *Ogre*!" A fist bounced off her metal clad-chest. "Enemies weep, run in terror! Ogre have no mercy!"

"Your name? Are there more of your people?" Dale prodded as they walked slowly and carefully through the crowd.

"Just me! Am Boss!" she stated proudly, then hesitated. "Never earn name. You want give me name?"

"Um. Sure." Dale tried to play for time as he thought. "You are the only one of–"

"*Oni*!" the Ogre bellowed happily. "Me the Oni! Thank you for name, Born of the Dungeon!"

Dale sputtered as he heard what was happening, but luckily, people were laughing at him too hard to really think about what the Ogre was saying. Dale got the Ogre to the entrance and let her go ahead. He seemed like he planned to follow her, but I stopped him. <Thanks, Dale. We've got this from here.>

As soon as Oni stepped into my area, I had noticed something… off. There was a conspicuous lack of Essence or Mana wasted by the Mob, and any power that came too close simply vanished. <Hi there, Oni. Welcome.>

"Hi there, young Dungeon. You did good for only… eleven years old? Twelve? I 'member when we met you, but you were bad at talking!" Oni laughed like a proud nanny, and I seemed to have been robbed of my ability to speak coherently for a few moments.

<Erm. I'm not actually sure… I have difficulty with time.> I shook my poor Cat to clear my mind, and it fell 'asleep' again. Oops. <Listen, I need to know why you're here before I let you come all the way down here.>

"There be no *let*. Me free Mob. Oni is a free Ogre! Oni does what wants!" the Ogre bellowed excitedly. "Oni was given a sock!"

<I'm… I'm not sure what that means?> I turned to Dani. <Does that mean something to you?>

"Nope?" Dani was just as confused as I was. Good, at least that was cleared up.

<Would you please tell us why you came here?> I tried going as polite as possible.

"Can do!" Oni nodded deeply as she waded through the streams of Bashers bouncing off her armor. "Was given task by Kan-tyor when he was being… word is hard… means attacked and taken over. *Invaded*!"

Her last word was screamed with such ferocious glee that two bunnies had to flop to the ground and put their paws over their damaged ears. "I did it! I 'membered word!"

<Very good job, Oni,> I soothingly congratulated her. <What was the task?>

"Oh." Oni concentrated, and her armor began to vanish, retracting from her limbs and body and being sucked into a small backpack she had been wearing under the armor. "Easy task, hard to do. Had to bring Dani's brudda to her. Something about helping him and… nep… nepo… *nepotism*! Nepotism keeping him safe!"

"Wait. *Brother*?" Dani had no idea what was going on, and I smelled a trap.

I decided it was time for the direct approach, and I started waking up my heavy hitters. <If it is Dani's 'brother', then why are you carrying a dungeon Core in your bag?>

"Wait a second, Cal! *Mu*? Mu, is that you in there?" Her voice was strange. Was she happy or angry?

Then a voice I had never heard before reached my mind. <Hey there, lil sis! Yup, it's me! I hear you are putting together a rescue mission? Was that for me, or is something else going on? >

"Cal. Eat them," Dani ordered me. Ah. Mad. *Mad* is what her voice had been. Got it noted for future cross-checks against strange delays in responses. Filing information under 'aspects of terror, avoid at all cost'. All set, back to the conversation at hand.

<Consider it done, person who is really in charge of this operation!> Six Bob Squads should be enough for this. <Go get 'em, boys!>

CHAPTER THIRTY

<Wait! *Wait!*> the strange little backpack dungeon begged. Nope. My lovely Wisp wanted him gone, he was gone. Let's see… Next, I should work on building up my inner world. Maybe I would work on the ley lines that were crisscrossing the entire planet? I could- <Hey! Listen to me, you *crazy Wisp!*>

I was a little startled that they were still alive. Oh, right. Travel time for bipedal Mages through the dungeon still exceeded seven seconds from the lowest floors. The Bobs were moving but hadn't yet arrived. Silly me, I had just considered it such a done deal that–

"Mu, I told you that if I ever saw you again, I would make sure to kill you," Dani coldly informed him. "Instant death like Cal is promising… is the *best-case* scenario for you."

<I shattered *one* other Core! Didn't it work out? Would you *prefer* to be teaching a drooling *Dire Turkey* Dungeon Core how to speak? That's where you'd be if you weren't here! Look at this place! It's *flying!*> Mu was getting desperate, and it was showing.

<Hey. Why can't I find your influence? I should be able to crush you from here.> It didn't *really* matter to me, I'd win either way, but… still, I was curious.

<Cal, right? Cal? Listen, buddy. This bag I'm in is my entire dungeon. I have only one Mob, and it isn't even… Oni? My actual Mob is a living metal construct that can act as armor!> Mu was close to being ended, but that was still fun info. <Dani is mad because I shattered a Core she was supposed to bond with before we met *you*. I didn't think it was good enough for her, so I took it out on the sly. *That's* why she's mad at me! Help me out here! You should be my best friend right now!>

<Hmm. I'm not typically the voice of reason in our relationship…> I pondered for a bit, letting him sweat. Or… whatever the equivalent was. <Usually I'm the one to run screaming at projects with massive enthusiasm, but in this case, I'll give it a try.>

Dani was waiting for the battle to begin, but I told the Bobs to back off for a moment. <Dani, my sweet. Could you maybe, *possibly* be willing to hear him out for a little while?>

"I'm sure *Oni* will be able to tell us whatever we need." She dismissed my words coldly. "We can let *her* live. Good compromise."

<I'm sure you're right, but still… he is your… brother, right? Actually, how does that work?> I was going off topic, but she was more than happy to explain.

"Obviously, there is no way to *actually* be brother and sister. Not like humans are. We were both simply trained in the same area for a good long time. Since we knew each other for so long, we started teasing each other about being related. Now he's trying to not die by bringing up our *prior* good relationship." She stopped talking, and I knew that I was going to need to put my figurative foot down.

<I don't often do this, but I'm gonna go ahead and not kill them. I'll bring them down here, and Mu *can beg for his life really hard.*> That last part was directed at Mu, and I think he got the picture.

<You won't regret this, Cal! I have a ton of info to share with you. Kantor gave me as much raw data as he could, and I can't even use it.> Mu certainly knew how to play on my greedy

interior, but if he was lying… he would find out that I was even less forgiving than Dani. Feed the greed, happy. Otherwise, feed the dungeon. *I'm* still happy, though slightly disappointed.

"Fine! But he'd better stay away from Grace. I don't even *care* if they'd be compatible!" Dani flew off in a huff, but her words made me twitch. *Excuse* me? Abyss *right* he'd better stay away from Grace! I'd go full murder-Mage on him!

<Mu, are you here looking for a Wisp?> I voiced my question as calmly as possible.

<Do you have other Wisps here?> Mu seemed hopeful, but then his tone changed. <No… I've never found a compatible color. I'm really *average*, but I've kinda given up on it, hence—backpack dungeon.>

I laughed out loud at that—in a manner of speaking—and opened a secret panel in the wall to let them bypass a few issues. Oni entered, and they walked through the darkness for a few minutes before sliding off a ledge and into a hole that would bring them all the way down to me. Oni didn't scream in fear as was expected but laughed instead. Ah, the Mob mentality of expecting to always return to life.

From the freefall, she was taken on to a perfectly smooth rock slide that had water pouring through it. A very safe and comfortable ride… I was pretty sure. Yeah. Okay, good, she survived. This part was new, so I wasn't sure she would.

<Welcome!>

DALE

"Aiden? What are you doing here?" Tom had just met up with Dale to discuss some issues he foresaw, when his older brother walked into the area. "Aren't you supposed to be working with the troops and getting them prepared to march?"

"Tom!" Aiden walked over with a bright smile on his face. "I am here to pick up a portal to use for our people. It should be coming through the *main* portal soon, and we are going to bring it back to the outpost. Good to see you!"

"You look well!" Tom's smile could have melted the heart of a Golem. "Getting plenty of exercise?"

"You know, I've been having a *very* large amount of success in the dungeon here!" Aiden matched Tom's enthusiasm, clapping him on the back and sitting down to talk. "We were just about to head out, but I wouldn't mind–"

"*Aiden*? No, this is too surreal!" A metallic voice floated to their table followed by a huge, armored form appearing next to them.

"Henry? Is that you in that wall of metal?" Aiden shot to his feet and inspected the perfectly fitted gear. "*B-ranks*? How in the *abyss* did all of that happen to you? Is this entire suit *Mithril*?"

"Ha! I made the best deal of my life!" Henry couldn't take his eyes off of his childhood friend, even if Aiden couldn't see it. "I've missed the Northmen and you especially! Did you ever decide on a Mana recipe for yourself? We should go on a hunt sometime soon!"

"Hold on, hold *on*!" Aiden laughed in reply, his conversation with Tom forgotten. "Yes, we've missed you, too. I have plans for a Mana recipe, but I'm not entirely sold on the idea yet. Where would we hunt, and finally, what deal do you speak of?"

"Ah, I apologize! It has been a while since I have seen anyone from…" Henry trailed off, looking away.

"Oh, that's right. Your family." Aiden placed his dinner-plate-sized hand on the King's shoulder. "I heard the news, friend. My deepest condolences go with them. They are honored by my people, having stood strong even in the face of certain death."

"My thanks." Henry cleared his throat and tried again in a falsely chipper tone, "As for a hunt, why, this dungeon contains a labyrinth filled with game and creatures to test ourselves against! There is even a forest along one of the paths. As for the deal… I traded service to the dungeon for access to the power that I needed. And now, *ha*! *Everyone* and their tamed Beast has to go into the dungeon! Best deal I've ever made."

"No kidding." Aiden seemed to be considering something

and looked back at the mouth of the dungeon. "That sounds *very* interesting."

"I think that path is closed for most," Henry seemed uncomfortable, thinking that he had said too much, "but as I said, why don't we get together for a hunt soon?"

"I would like that very much." Aiden grasped Tom's bicep and gave a tight squeeze. "For now, I need to speak with my brother and resume my duties. Henry, we *will* make it happen."

Henry left with a brilliant smile that no one could see, and Aiden spent a few minutes discussing plans with Tom before heading out. Tom watched him go, disgruntled by having been ignored. "Dale, I really wanted to see respect in the eyes of my brother. I wanted to hear his congratulations and preen under the influence of a man I respect. Why do I feel so let down?"

"Oh, Tom." Minya had arrived just in time to catch his words. "You can never gain respect from your family or those who knew you as you grew into the person you are now. They will always see you as the child they once knew. Honestly, big guy, do you *want* your family to see you so drastically different than you once were? You might find that their reaction to having shattered expectations is not as *happy* as you wished."

"Got a story there?" Dale tried to tease an explanation out of her, but she simply shook her head sadly.

"Nothing I want to share." Minya glanced around and leaned in to speak to them more directly, "Dale, Cal is acting weird, and people are *losing it* over the fact that monsters are showing up to visit the dungeon. They are wondering what it means for them, how this will change things."

"While I'm worried for Cal, is there something *I* can do about all of this?" Dale showed his palms and shrugged.

Minya took a deep breath. "There's more. Barry is back, and he found out that The Master is weakening. He's staging a coup, making a bid for leadership of the area again by getting the people on his side."

"Oh, come *on*!" Dale dropped his head into his hands.

CHAPTER THIRTY-ONE

Barry and The Master stood across from each other, staring daggers back and forth. The intense pressure they were devoting to the action was *actually enough* to kill a standard human if it were directed at them. Barry took a deep, satisfied breath and then *smirked.*

"I see the rumors are true. You are leaking power like a *sieve.* I cannot believe that I missed it before, but you had hidden it so *well* when I saw you last!" Barry laughed and took a decisive step forward. "Right now, I might not be able to fight you and be guaranteed to *win*, but I bet I could force you into a stalemate at this point. If I can make *that* happen… Let's be honest with each other, *The Master*, people would side with me against you. I think that this much is obvious! Here is what I offer you now—I'll let you stay here and finish the soul portal, but otherwise, there are going to be some *changes.*"

"I could just kill you *right now* and take my chances on the rest," The Master mildly stated, also taking a smooth step forward. Barry's eyes bulged out, and his breath started coming harder. "I think that with *you* out of the way, your *minions* wouldn't be too much of an issue. You *also* seem to forget that I *too* have an army at my beck and call."

"They've been losing power!" Barry barked in a fury, losing face in front of the crowd, forcing his hand. "Their *corpses* fall to the ground, and unless the dead stay within visual range, they either go wild or falter! There simply isn't enough free power for them to maintain control!"

"Mmm." The Master's eyes were locked on Barry's heart, and the man could tell. "I wonder… how much I care at this point? Is it worth finally destroying you? Should I follow my instincts after all these years and all of our skirmishes?"

"Give me control! Don't make me fight you. Do this, and I will allow the people in your care to remain unharmed. I will punish *any* of my people who harm them, to the same extent as the harmed individual. Your dark army will be allowed into the portal and to safety. I will *personally* care for them." Barry narrowed his eyes. "Conversely, if I need to fight, and *when* you lose… I will personally *eradicate* them."

"Swear it," The Master stated softly. "Swear to me that they will be treated properly. That you will personally care for them. All of the things you just said. Especially that all of my people will be allowed access to the portal. That *I* will also be treated as such if it is within your power. Then… I care not who is the one that needs to squabble for power and make the treaties that get us through each day. *You* can be the one to deal with the minutiae and annoyances of the day-to-day."

"So long as you agree to my demands on this specific subject, I so swear," Barry solemnly announced, causing his Aura to wrap around himself and create a new bond. The ground fell apart under his feet, and the earth hovered in the air around him. The world, and his power, had accepted the deal.

"Good enough, I suppose." The Master sighed and stepped aside. "*You* deal with the politics. I'll go get this portal finished, and maybe even find a way to save those of the higher ranks. I heard a great idea—from the non-cultivator *Tyler* no less—

about shoving A-rankers in Mana-containment crates and seeing what happens. Might be fun to try."

The Master vanished with a *pop*, and Barry's face seemed to melt and reform into a malicious grin. "Excellent. First off, we have some new rules! Humans and High Elves *alone* are allowed access to the dungeon if they are not a member of the Guild. All others must *petition* the Guild for access. No more *monsters* getting in!"

"*High* Elves?" Queen Brianna stepped forward dangerously.

"Yes." Barry stared at her, not backing down a bit. "Feel free to *petition* for access or *fight* me for the right to make the rules."

Brianna took a deep breath and vanished from the area. Barry grunted and watched an empty space move away at high speed. "That's what I *thought*. There have been *many* disappearances recently, so for the *safety* of all involved, the Guild decree is that only those *proven* to be effective may enter. So, humans and High Elves only. Get moving."

Guild members began flooding out of the portal, moving to secure the dungeon opening. Any who resisted or complained were sent away with a beating at the *least*. Several shops were 'requisitioned', but when they tried this with the *Pleasure House*, anyone making demands was snared by the tree-building and thrown over the edge of Mountaindale. A different kind of power-grab in that area and not one that was going the Guild's way.

In short order, the area and Mountaindale itself was once more heavily under the control of the Guild. This didn't go over well, especially since this version of the Guild was a *regime* instead of the self-sacrificing group it *used* to be. Tensions between the races began to flare up once more. Grudges that had been put aside when there was a clear-cut goal in place were remembered and acted upon.

More than one body was dumped into the dungeon over the course of the next few hours.

CAL

<So, Mu, tell me some stories about Dani when she was younger.> I was teasing Dani, and it was working *so* well! She was bright red, shifting to green every once in a while. <I want to see her squirm!>

<Sure, Cal! So, there was this one time that she was supposed to be learning how to channel fire Essence into water so an adventuring party could boil water for a stew.> Mu started laughing, and Dani started to growl. <Well, there was a big bowl of salad next to it, and let's just say that's the story of how we learned that Dani can't and *shouldn't* cook... by her burning a salad!>

We shared a good laugh, right until Dani grabbed some Mana and chucked Mu's backpack into a treasure chest. "I'm gonna give you to a *fishy* as a *trinket*!"

<Cal, help! I don't want to be a reward!> Mu started laughing here, knowing that he could easily escape on his own. I'm *pretty* sure he could, at least. Maybe he didn't want to test Dani. Wise. Still, had to keep the joke going!

<Dani, we can't give him away! I only give out *useful* rewards!> I shouted this, which seemed to cheer Dani up. Mu was protesting loudly, and finally, Dani gave in and brought him back into the open. After we had gotten all of the fun out of the way, I decided to get down to business. <Mu, what made you seek us out?>

Silence followed my question, for long enough that I thought he wasn't going to respond. <Ehh... so I have a message from Kantor. He was old and smart enough to see that there were going to be bad things happening, especially to *him*. People kept appearing and taking Mana readings, then *more* than just readings. Still, he thought he had enough contingencies in place to survive.>

Mu continued after a few seconds of remembrance, <Obviously, he was wrong. Contingencies only work if you have time to *use* them. Now, frankly, I have nowhere to go, and I really like

my backpack. Wyvern leather. But, all of this information is going to waste, and I want you to have it. But that's not the message. Kantor told me that under *no* circumstances were we allowed to go north… where you are *currently* going. The origin.>

"Do you know what's there?" Dani instantly queried.

<I *don't.*> Mu growled at her. <You aren't *listening*. Kantor knew what was there, and he told me that when he went there… that was the closest he ever got to dying. Before… you know. *Actually* dying.>

"I have to go, Mu. It's too important, even if I don't know *why*. I *need* to go." Dani wouldn't hear any more about this and kept changing the subject whenever he tried to press the issue. "So, what would *you* like to do while you're here?"

<Fine, Dani. I just hope that you aren't making a *huge mistake*.> Mu waited, but Dani didn't speak. <Cal, we need to get an information transfer started. This is going to take a while, especially since there is a lot of it that I don't understand. I have the info but no perspective or way to relate it to myself. A lot of it is designed for a dungeon in the upper A-ranks.>

The entire dungeon started to rain. *That* was how much I was drooling about the idea of gaining this information. Mu kept speaking, but I barely heard him, <I don't want anything in return—I'm just following the last wishes of Kantor. So, are you ready?>

<I am *so* ready.> I nearly *snarled*. Extending a tendril of Essence, I connected to the backpack and was met with a wall of information, mathematical equations, genetic information, and various untapped uses for Essences. In short, it was everything I wanted it to be and *so* much more.

As the last of the raw data came into me, the entire lifelong studies of Kantor, Mana began to well up in my Core. A spiraling concussive force knocked a few leaves off the Silverwood tree, marking my advancement to A-rank-two.

CHAPTER THIRTY-TWO

Dale stood on the edge of Mountaindale with nearly every person that lived in the area—as well as a whole lot of people that didn't—watching as the first chunk of the moon came close enough to fall to earth. He had seen shooting stars before, but this was… different. No one knew what was about to happen, and the portal to the Soul Space wasn't operational. This *could* be the end. It certainly wasn't the largest chunk, maybe a few thousand feet wide, and it was only moving a little faster than gravity would normally bring it down. So, there was a *chance.*

The chunk of the moon seemed to catch on fire, making everyone gasp. Was the moon full of *fire* Essence? That explained why it was so bright at night, but… the flaming object vanished over the horizon. Nothing seemed to happen over the next few minutes. That should have landed in the ocean since the entire world was a single landmass with only a few islands dotting the rest of the sphere. Thirty minutes passed, and people began to disperse in relief when it became obvious that the world was still surviving.

"Hans, do you think we are getting scared for no good reason?" Dale asked his friend as soon as they were in a more private location. "Perhaps most of this will miss us, and we will simply get a few extra landmasses out of the deal?"

"I have no point of reference, Dale." Hans lifted his pint and drained it, smacking his lips as he finished it off. "Listen, sorry you haven't been seeing much of me lately. Been hitting the cultivation pretty hard after we worked out that… thing. I also found a Noble family that was willing to 'donate' the *other* 'thing' I needed."

Dale smiled with a hint of relief; Hans sometimes liked to mess with him to see what would happen. "No worries–"

The room they were in shook so violently that the windows fragmented and lost their glass. The shaking didn't subside right away, continuing at the same intensity for nearly a full minute. The air was roaring with *strange* sounds, like thunder mixed with a forge as the tide came in. When everything settled, Dale calmly stood up, helped Hans and Rose to their feet, then stepped outside.

One of the great benefits to building the area in the way they had was that most if not all of the structures were more than *built*, they were *Runecrafted*. Not a single building had toppled, which helped to keep any casualties to a minimum. "Anyone know what's going on?"

<Sure, Dale.> Dale jumped as the voice entered his mind directly. <As far as I can tell, there was huge destruction from that flaming moonrock. One of the reasons we survived unscathed for the most part is that not only are we *really* far away from where it landed, we are also airborne. You can't see it from where you are, but the ocean below is… is just… *borked*. Broken and churning beyond reason. All the water is flowing *toward* the impact, and that's really strange. Gonna see some strange stuff soon, I bet. Heh. Looks like the tide is really *impacted* by the moon, huh?>

"You're making jokes about the moon hitting the ocean? Now? Cal, focus. How much damage do you think we are looking at?" Dale quietly asked amongst the screaming and loud questions flying around. He kept telling himself that nothing good would happen to him if he reacted to the dungeon's jokes, but he couldn't help himself.

<*Lots*. Dale, the *ocean* is moving. Whatever happened when that chunk hit us isn't over yet.> There was a pause. <*Lo~o~ots* of damage.>

"Extra ominous, thanks." Dale tried to think of something useful he could be doing and couldn't really think of much. He shrugged and started emitting a sunlight Aura. If nothing else, this would help calm the people around him and slowly fix any injuries they had sustained. "Hans, I'm betting that this will light a fire in anyone who hadn't been all that concerned about this moonfall before."

Rose spoke up after looking at all the concerned and hard faces around them, "I think you might be on to something, Dale. Hey… if it were this bad in the *air*, do you think anyone on the ground—or underground—is happy right now?"

Dale didn't move, considering her words. "Let's go and make sure that there is room to start receiving refugees and the like. I'm… yeah, I'm not the best one to make choices for people. Can we see if we can get a higher-ranked cleric to run logistics? That way we know that people coming in will have someone that *cares* if they live or die. I don't think that the Guild is a good place to be anymore."

"I don't mind going," Rose offered, getting a nod from Dale. She turned away, but Hans reeled her in for a quick smooch.

"Be careful. When people think they have nothing to lose, they start doing *very* dumb things," Hans whispered in her ear.

"I'm a pro. Let them *try* to catch me." Rose gave him a cocky grin and a thumbs-up before darting off. In moments, she was running along rooftops and bouncing off walls to maintain momentum.

<Speaking of people you expect to do stupid things…> Dale wasn't sure what was meant by this statement at first, but then Barry appeared in the air above the Academy.

"Listen up, everyone. From this point forward, every resource is devoted to completing our escape from this dying planet." Barry was enhancing his voice, and Dale winced since he could just *imagine* the terrible plans going through the Guild leader's head. "We are going to be accepting 'donations' from *everyone*. One-tenth of everything you have, whether you have been here or are just arriving. That is how much you get to *keep*. The remaining nine-of-ten resources will be *donated* to the Guild, just in case there is something that we might be able to use to speed our escape."

Silence reigned, though the fury being directed at the S-ranker was palpable. His gaze sharpened, and his voice took on a dangerous edge. "Unless, of course, you'd rather not be *allowed* to escape with us when the portal is functioning."

His unsubtle threat made most people turn away. Not wanting to be left behind was a big motivator. People began justifying their inability to say no, telling themselves that it didn't matter, that they couldn't bring much with them into the Soul Space anyway, Barry vanished shortly thereafter, allowing everyone to breathe a little easier.

"Cal. As far as you can tell, how close are they to finishing the portal?" Dale voiced into the empty air. Hans looked over with shining eyes, *very* interested in hearing the answer to this.

<They are *close*, but they are missing something. They keep *thinking* it is done, but then they can't find whatever it is that's keeping it from activating.> The flow of words paused, then resumed in a sour tone, <The Master is having a hard time. Oh, and he's getting weaker every day. So that's fun. Real great for my mental health.>

"Thanks, Cal. If there's anything we can do to help, let us know?" Dale didn't get an answer, so he relayed the information to Hans, who was patiently waiting to hear what he had to say, "No good news, Hans."

"Well… abyss." Hans rubbed the back of his neck, looking in the direction Rose had vanished. "Do you think it is time to start looking into other options? Making a few contingency plans of our own? I finally have something I'm not willing to risk on a gamble."

"Very sweet, I'm sure." Minya appeared with a sound like a giant soap-bubble popping. Hans screeched and did a backflip, landing with knives in his hands. "Nice. Hey, Dale, I think that we are getting into a dangerous area. Something Cal has been discussing with Dani recently… We could be getting into an area that'd be worse for our health than simply finding a place to sleep for a thousand years or so."

"Do you have details?" Hans politely inquired, his weapons once more hidden somewhere on his body.

"I don't, but I think we are going to find out sooner rather than later." Her grim words were punctuated by a blaze of shifting light that filled the sky. It looked beautiful, but they could tell that there was a *huge* amount of Essence and Mana in those lines. "What in the *abyss* is that?"

"The lights of the North." A barbarian had come close enough to overhear their conversation, and he was staring at the sky with eyes full of wonder. "I thought that they were only a myth!"

"Can you… What is the myth?" Dale tossed politeness to the side and went right for the information he needed.

"The *lights of the north.*" The barbarian looked at them knowingly, but upon seeing their confused faces, he rolled his eyes and explained, "They light the way to the greatest treasure upon this earth, but only one man has ever followed their siren call and returned. It is said that whoever follows the path without the willpower to sacrifice their dreams can never return, but that there is no *need* to return. Immortality, the path *above* the S-ranks. That is what lies at the end of those lights."

"And we are flying straight at something straight out of mythology," Minya pointed out, swallowing deeply. Even myths and legends usually had a kernel of truth in them, and most likely, the truth here… was that no one returned after following the lights.

CHAPTER THIRTY-THREE

<Whoa. That's some *serious* power echoing along those lines.> I siphoned off just a little *taste*, feeling a texture I had never tried before. It contained a hint of celestial, sunlight, and *something*. <It almost feels *familiar*, but I just can't place it.>

"What feels familiar?" Dani wondered idly, watching the light sparkle above the clouds. "The energy in there? Yeah, The Master uses something similar."

<*That's* where it's from!> I excitedly exclaimed. <I *knew* it was… actually, what does he embody? What **Law** is he bound to?>

"Not a clue," Dani returned with her version of a shrug.

<What are you guys doing? Can I come see?> Mu's muffled voice called from his treasure chest. He must have been trying to make a point because a small wall like that meant nothing to our method of communication.

"No! Learn not to say dumb things, and you can come out!" Dani snarled at the box. Poor little backpack dungeon. On a tangent now, I found that I felt bad that Mu was a millionth my own size. Maybe I could donate some land to him in my Soul Space.

<Sorry, Mu! If it helps, Oni is having a great time out here.> I was watching Oni's body decompose rapidly, but I was pretty sure I could make a convincing new copy before Mu was let out of his chest.

<Oh, good! I hadn't heard her speaking in a little while. I was getting worried.> Mu's words made me grimace. It wasn't *my* fault that the Ogre insisted on testing her mettle against Manny. I actually tried to stop her out of respect to Mu, but I wasn't going to lie and say that I tried *hard*. I now had an Ogre pattern! That was pretty neat. It was a *Kantor original*, even!

"I feel like you are being silly over there," Dani whispered to me, to which I could only agree.

<Yeah… I'm feeling a little like a collector of shiny pebbles. Even if I have a superior pattern of something, I always want to get a variant or interesting version. I want a *shiny* version, you know?> I was hoping that she would simply let the conversation go, but *I* had to end it when she pestered me to explain myself. I guess she didn't see Manny take Oni down in under three seconds. *Prolly* for the best.

I had to change the subject, and the brilliant sky gave me a perfect out. <So, does this spark any of your racial memories or whatever it is that you have?>

"It… something about it does." She watched the sky a while longer. "I guess it is the fact that the patterns in the sky have a bit of a Will-of-the-Wisp to them. Not a *heavy* effect, but anyone seeing the sky wants to follow it to see what is going on."

Just like that, the slight nagging compulsion that had been nagging me broke, and I realized that I had been under an *incredibly* subtle lure effect. <Wow. I… that *had* me, Dani. How was it so easy for me to break?>

"You're bound to a pink Wisp, Cal. Mind-altering effects just have less hold on you when you realize they exist." Dani was still staring at the sky, but I was reeling from the news.

<*What*?>

"Oh, *abyss*, did I just–" Dani went into near-panic mode and started zipping away.

<*Hold* it!> I barked at her, probably the roughest I had ever been with her. <You mean to tell me that you can shield my mind from certain effects?>

"I... Cal, I shouldn't be discussing the secrets of my people."

<I don't have any secrets from *you*!>

"Cal..." She stirred the air in agitation. "It isn't *my* information to give. It's just... you know what? To the abyss with it, why *shouldn't* I tell you? Look, different colored Wisps have different abilities, which is why you need to bond with a certain color. It creates a *balance*."

<Care to offer an example?> I was feeling twitchy about this for some reason.

"I might as well." Dani came over and landed on the Silverwood tree. "You're a blue Core, and so you needed a Wisp that could more freely balance your mind. You were *supposed* to be a water Essence Core, prone to flights of fancy and extremely changeable. Luckily, that still held true."

<Hey!>

"If I'm *wrong*, tell me I'm wrong." Dani smirked at me, pausing briefly to give me a chance to speak up. "Thought so. Now, we aren't ever supposed to talk about this because it builds resentment, distrust, and animosity when it's known that someone is coming in to... guide you."

<Control you,> I responded flatly.

"*Balance* you," Dani firmly stated. "Mu over there needs a Wisp that can help control Essence so that he could build a dungeon. Otherwise, he can only inhabit preset, prebuilt areas. Or *backpacks*, apparently."

<Like a Wisp that can move through stone and shape it?> I lost some color. Mu was going to 'play' in 'his' treasure chest anytime Grace was anywhere *near* this area.

"Exactly." Dani quieted and sighed. "Someone that can get you to be doing your best *together*. A partner in all things. You and I are a really good example."

<Alright, Dani. I'll let it drop, but you know I just want to

be included in all this… secret Wisp society stuff. Just tell me, and I *promise* I'll let it go if needed, okay?> An implosion of Mana signified that I was *bound* to my words, shocking her.

"Ah… alright, Cal. I'm… thank you." Dani zipped in a tight circle around me, which I had found was her version of a hug. "It's good to know that I can tell you anything. I don't know why I had doubts."

<Hard to break the habits of a lifetime, I get it,> I consoled her, even though I was waiting for the flood of information to begin. I'd be patient. For now. <Listen, is there *anything* else you can tell me about these lights?>

"If I remember correctly, they are called the 'aurora borealis'. I don't have much information, but they are not a *natural* phenomenon. That's… really all I know about it."

<Then I guess we get to learn about this the *fun* way!> I tilted the gyroscope forward, and the Skyland sped up once more. <Let's go learn what's at the top of the world!>

"Yeah!" Dani responded enthusiastically.

We watched the terrain pass, but still, nothing came into view. Now feeling a tish silly, I laughed and delved deep into my inner world. If there was no danger, no land, and therefore nothing for me to do beyond upkeep, I needed to do everything I could to get my Soul Space up to snuff. There were three giant factors for me to consider: keeping people alive, getting as many of them as possible, and keeping them under control. Maybe I should figure out a way to keep people away from who they hated? Was that even a good idea?

Nah. Instead, why not just let them sort all that junk out for themselves? Populations can sort themselves out much more quickly and accurately than I can do it for them, right? So, I really feel like my time will be better spent on solidifying and populating the areas. It was getting to the point that I was getting bored with the repetition, so I decided to have a little fun. I am a dungeon after all, and people would be *expecting* dangers and monsters!

I built up a series of defenses around a small area, then

copied the new area a few times and remade it in multiple locations. Alright. Starting areas for people to migrate to have been set. Easy enough. The next step was to introduce creatures to the new system and let them build up naturally and over time. Once again, I was starting an ecosystem from scratch and hoping that everything would settle nicely. It was one thing to make this happen in a contained and easily controlled system like a dungeon, but across a world? Much… slower. Luckily, I had only a few miles in total created.

The bugs were just getting settled when I felt my dungeon get rocked to the side. Seeing as I tended to be moving much faster in my inner world than the actual world did, so I wasn't too worried about getting back in time to understand what was going on. Drifting out of my Soul Space, my focus fell on the Bobs just as they began reacting to whatever had hit us.

<Bob, what's happening?>

"Great Spirit!" Bob called back, not taking his eyes off the viewing screen. "It appears that we are not the only ones following this stream of power. There are creatures in the air and in the sea below! They are *powerful*, and I think we will start taking losses if we are attacked!"

<How powerful? B-ranks? A? How many, and is there any reason you can see that they're here?> I paused and would have rolled eyes if I had any available. <Beyond the potent lure of the lights, that is?>

"There seems to be very little consistency." Bob paused and looked over the screens. "In fact, they are from *all* over, as far as I can tell. As if–"

<As if they ran out of energy, especially the energy they need to survive, and started gravitating toward anything still radiating free power?> My thoughts were going down an 'uh-oh' route. <Could it be that we found the creatures that my shifting of ley lines evicted? I think this is something we should let the people upstairs know about.>

"Probably best, Great Spirit."

CHAPTER THIRTY-FOUR

<Dale, sweetheart!> Dale's eyes popped open, and his irises dilated in annoyance. <Time to wake up! We're under attack.>

"First off, I was *cultivating*, not sleeping. Next, *how* are we under attack? Did we land?" Dale's words were angry, but his tone was defeated, fully understanding that there was nothing he could do at this point to ignore the dungeon.

<Right, well, it seems that we are flying into a swarm of creatures that are hungry. Mana or Essence starved, actually. So, they are likely going to be landing and attacking the delicious sources of power on the surface, starting… now.> In the distance, Dale heard a scream of pain and terror, echoed quickly by many more.

"The Academy!" Dale was on his feet and running toward the screams in an instant. The people at the Academy were *weak*, just learning how to control their bodies and cultivation! If they were attacked—no, Cal said that the attackers were after power… Dale adjusted his charging sprint, aiming for the entrance to the dungeon. In moments, the attackers were in view. "What are…?"

Dale didn't finish the question, instead landing among the

flight-capable creatures with his fists leading the way. He winced as the first blow felt like punching a wall had when he was a fishy. <I'll keep you updated as you fight, Dale, just so I can get you their weaknesses and types.>

"You. Just. Want. Free. Monsters!" Each of Dale's words were clipped, and he was speaking at Mage speed as he punched the leathery creature below him. When blunt force trauma didn't seem to be doing the trick, Dale coated his hands in sword Aura and shifted from fists to rigid palms. Empowering his blows with Mana, Dale sunk his hands deeply into the unknown creature and grabbed on to any organs he could find, tearing the monster up from the inside. At this point, it finally noticed his existence and screeched in pain.

The screech was a potent ability, some form of sonic or wind attack, and if Dale hadn't been holding tightly to the body, he would have been blown away. Instead, he layered a drop of Mana over his ear canals and continued his grim work. He opened the creature more deeply, then released a burst of sword Aura that damaged the beast enough to bring it down entirely.

<Nice job, Dale!> There was a slight pause and a low whistle. <Looks like this is a 'young adult Wyvern'. If this were a human, it would be a nineteen-year-old farmer. If there are stronger versions of this creature, be careful. Its capacity for growth… its potential… it's off the charts.>

Water started to collect on the ground around Dale, and he snorted condescendingly. "I knew it. You're drooling, Cal."

<It was a good meal is all!> The words sounded especially defensive to Dale, but the water vanished in an instant, and a new order came in, <Feathered creature over there! Caution, it seems to be an aeromancer of some sort. If it gets you in the air, it'll tear you apart. Likely level in the mid-B-ranks, but it has a few people fighting against it currently. You might tip the scales in your side's favor.>

"Thanks, Cal." Dale dashed off, debating on how to handle the creature ahead of him. It was likely *far* stronger than him, but he had a few extra tricks up his sleeve that most people didn't. He swung his arm through the air, and a hair-thin line of sword Mana extended away from him and… bounced off the smallest feathers of the creature. "Yikes."

"You've been overusing that ability." Gomei appeared next to Dale, staring at their feathered foe. "If you use something too much, you become predictable to your enemies. Remember, Dale, you *do* have enemies. You can handle this opponent. I'm off to find more worthy prey. Consider this battle your training for the evening."

"Gomei?" Dale looked over, but the Elf was already gone. At least Dale wouldn't be punished for missing a training session. He was secretly relieved; uncontrolled monsters that didn't have an issue with him personally were a comparative relief. Dale sprinted forward, trying to think of a way to take down this huge beast. He landed on its back and started punching, but the thick feathers and downy fur underneath absorbed the blows with ease.

He flipped off of the creature as it swiveled its head around like an owl to snap at him, but his distraction was beneficial in allowing a Mage that had been under attack to dance out of the way. Slashing talons tore a deep furrow in the ground, and a gust of wind threw dirt into the faces of the attacking Mages. It wouldn't have damaged them, but the people affected still raised their arms to shield their vision as the Beast had intended. It lashed out and tore a chunk out of one of the attacking Mage's calves, downing the man and pouncing on him.

"No! All of you, punch forward in three, two, *now*!" With a synchronicity that could only be achieved by hearing, reacting, and moving at superhuman speeds, the gathered group punched straight forward. Once again, Dale had the disconcerting feeling of hitting what felt like a wall though there was nothing in his path. The creature collapsed as the back of its head exploded outward, and it collapsed on the fallen Mage. "Good! Get him to the healers. Let's get moving!"

Dale watched the group run off, wondering how they had just achieved that feat of power. <Dale, looks like you guys took

down a 'Griffin'. B-rank-*six*, nice work! Must have been an air-dungeon designed creature. *Woof* there is some shoddy systems in that beasty!>

"Can you please just direct me to the next threat that I can handle? Also, can you get some Goblins out here or something?" Dale winced as a small, stone building shattered from the pressure of a few higher-ranked Beasts fighting Mages. "We are starting to take damage."

<Sorry, Dale, can't do it. Too much chance of people attacking the Goblins instead of the monsters, and I need to be ready in case they try coming after me down here.>

Dale grunted and returned to battle, doing his best to find ways to join a group of fighters in attacking Beasts whenever he got the chance. His next few battles were relatively easy, but then he joined in against a giant toad with tiny wings. Somehow, likely Mana, the Beast was able to jump to extreme heights and remain hovering at that altitude. This allowed it to chase any Mages that were attempting to escape, or it could avoid attacks that should have taken it down.

Dale's sword Aura skittered off the creature, its skin somehow refusing to part for the incredibly sharp Mana. Like the Griffin, the toad didn't seem to be hurt by blunt attacks, so Dale was having trouble finding ways to damage the Beast. It landed on the ground to crush a student beneath it and made to jump away as a potent lightning bolt was being directed at its face. In a moment of inspiration, Dale sent out a bit of Mana and connected tendrils of air-aligned Mana to the air around it. He had used this method in the past to slow himself when falling, and now, it was far more potent. The toad tried to jump but only made it a few feet off the ground before slamming back down—just in time for a surge of power to fry its brain.

"Nice work, kid!" someone called to Dale, but the man vanished before Dale could get a good look at him.

"Thanks!" Dale called back uncertainly. There was more work to do, so he rejoined the fray. He threw himself at enemies with abandon, knowing that if he didn't take them out, someone else could very well be badly hurt. Each time a student or lower-ranked person was squashed, smothered, crushed, or torn apart, Dale felt that he was failing them. Though he was no longer legally the Noble in charge of this area, it was still important to him, and the people were supposed to have *someone* fighting for them!

"Where is *the Guild*?" Dale bellowed into the air, gaining attention more from the monsters than the people fighting against them. "Where are the High-rankers. Where is *Barry*?"

There was no answer, and the fighting raged for another hour before they seemed to pass some sort of zone that kept the monsters from following. Or, perhaps, they had simply passed through the swarming beasts and come out the other side. Either way, Dale could finally take a moment to breathe and look around the area. The Academy was missing several buildings, the ground was awash with blood, and bodies of creatures and people were strewn all over the place.

Dale closed his eyes and breathed deeply, then opened them upon hearing a noise. He saw someone lifting the bodies of the Beasts that had been slain, and a cursory glance showed that this was happening all over. What infuriated Dale was the sight of the Guild crest that each of them was wearing. "What are you doing? I killed that one."

"The Guild has claimed all the fallen for resources." The man shrugged and held up his hands as Dale's Mana started to boil into his Aura and press down on the man. "You want to go to war with Barry? Be my guest, but I'm just following orders. I won't fight you for the body, but someone *else* will just come to collect it from you."

"I am getting sick and *tired* of this… dictatorship!" Dale snarled, turning his eyes toward the location the bodies were being carried or dragged. He blanched as he saw that it wasn't *just* the Beasts being carried there. Now he understood what the man meant when he said 'the fallen were being claimed for resources'. Something needed to be done.

CHAPTER THIRTY-FIVE

While all the fighting was going on up top, there were a few developments deep in the dungeon. Certain people were not using their time wisely and were instead using the attack as a distraction to forward their own agenda.

Aiden sauntered toward a trio of Amazonians that had been caught by his most recent traps, pulling out his daggers and drawing them across the throats of his unresisting racial enemies. He smiled as the blood splatter hit his face, barely even trying to get out of the way. "There we go, three fewer foul oathbreakers for the transition. I hope that you're enjoying all this free power, dungeon!"

Almost as in response to his words, a section of the wall rumbled upward, revealing a small room with a golden treasure chest in the center. Aiden's eyes went wide, and he hastily cleaned and sheathed his blades. He walked over to the chest, being careful to watch for traps and ensuring that he had a way out if the wall started to come back down. Aiden wasn't about to be trapped by his own methods of hunting, after all!

After double and triple checking everything, he carefully directed his Mana on to the chest and used it to pry the chest open at a distance. There was a letter inside, an actual paper that had words across it! The Northman General chuckled at how *quaint* that was and brought the paper close enough to read. His eyes widened in abject greed and filled with manic glee as he read what could *only* be an offer from the dungeon.

You have proven your power over others and have clearly shown what lies in your heart! I, the dungeon Cal, hereby make you an offer! I will grant you physical strength beyond the realm of possibility for your current form in return for only a decade of continuous and dedicated service which will begin as soon as you enter into my Soul Space. If you die during this time in an area that is under my influence, I will return you to life until the end of your service. To agree, all you need to do is drop a drop of blood on to this document and press the seal to your forehead!

Aiden stared at the document, unsure if he was going to take this offer. The scent of blood washed over him, and he looked back to see that the bodies of the Amazonians were *not* decomposing, and sounds of movement and speaking were reaching his ears. He smiled darkly, knowing that he had been played by the dungeon. "Fair enough, Cal the dungeon. I have been wanting to make a deal with you anyway!"

A drop of blood touched the paper, and the crest was brought to his head. "I'm just happy to know that you understand the value of my–"

With a grunt of pain, Aiden's words cut off. His entire mind had just been copied! How? There were no memory stones that could hold so much potency! Aiden's protest fell flat as a voice entered his mind. <Oh, Aiden, Aiden, *Aiden*. This was never a *reward*. You've been a Beast the entire time that you've been here, preying on the wounded and weak. I try to balance things, to make things *fair* and understandable. Now I have your permission to show the rest of the world what kind of a creature you really are.>

The ground fell out from under the Mage, which wouldn't have been an issue if the roof above him hadn't begun dripping a rain that left him feeling weak. "Disenchanting water?"

<Very much so.> Aiden fell down and into darkness. <Let's

get started, shall we? Physical strength beyond your capabilities it is…>

A strangely spiraling bolt of lightning landed on one of the few Beasts still in the area, and as the intense light vanished, a man faded into view where the energy had impacted. A spear was in his hands, and the Beast he had stabbed fell to the ground with severe energy burns covering nearly every inch of skin.

"Good. Now that this is taken care of…" The man looked around, one eye covered by a patch of golden cloth that radiated a strange energy. "Who is the measly worm that destroyed my people?"

A huge, black raven circled down out of the sky and alighted on his shoulder, another one visible in the air far above them as daylight threatened to arrive properly. The raven warbled into the air, and the grizzled fighter whipped his head around to rest his gaze firmly upon Dale. "You? Ow? Impossible. But… just in case."

Another flash of lightning, green this time, struck from the clear sky. Dale seized up as the power washed over him, and he fell to the ground shivering. The man apparently thought that this was a sign of his death and started to stride away. The raven croaked, and the man stopped and turned to look at Dale once more. "He lives?"

Dale opened his eyes, launching to his feet and staring down the man who had just attempted to murder him on a hunch. "*Why* would you do that? Wait… you're…"

"That voice." The man dissolved and reformed inches in front of Dale. "I went on the hunt with you and my brothers before that tragedy. The Noble. The Apprentice. Dale?"

"Yeah?" Dale shook his head to clear out the static. "I never went hunting with someone as strong as… wait. You're–"

"I am now Odin." Lightning seemed to flash in his eye as he

stared into Dale's now-exposed face. "First, how did you survive? Second, how did you kill my people?"

Dale certainly wasn't about to inform the world about his Mithril clothing that seemed to redirect the Mana to go *around* him instead of *through* him. "I have no idea what you are talking about… Odin."

Better to call crazy people how they wanted to be called, in Dale's opinion. The charged man in front of him cocked his head to the side. "Yes, I am uncertain how you were involved, but Huggin hasn't been wrong yet. He tells me that your Essence signature was all over the area, that *you* somehow killed hundreds or thousands in mere seconds."

Dale snorted derisively. "If I had that kind of raw power lying around, do you think I would be hoarding it instead of trying my best to keep people alive?"

Odin looked around at the dead with dispassionate eyes, shrugging and staring at Dale once more. "I once thought that I understood human nature, that I was a good judge of character. I have been proven wrong far too often. Now, I do what I feel needs to be done."

"Quick, instant, deadly." Dale looked at the man deeply, trying to understand how a person could undergo such a drastic change over the course of… months? "You seem to embody lightning, but there is more underneath. I just can't see *exactly* what it is."

Odin's eye flicked to the birds, but he didn't answer any of Dale's following questions. Instead, he raised a hand to vaporize the young man. Dale raised a hand and waved at the forming lightning. "Oh, stop it. How about we just chat for a few minutes. See if we can't figure out what is *actually* happening here?"

In spite of his casual words, Dale was tense and preparing to defend against the attack. There was a tracing of Mana swirling around him, enough to give someone a nasty shock if they grabbed at him. If Gomei's lessons had taught him anything, he knew that using lightning to defend against lightning was a good plan. For unknown reasons, it would follow the tracing he had created in the air if he were stuck again. That coupled with his armor and Dale figured he had a good shot of surviving long enough to get somewhere... safer.

"My sect is dead, wiped out in an instant." Odin reached up and touched his golden patch. "I've given much in order to gain enough strength to avenge my people before the moon takes that last simple joy from me. If I need to destroy the entire world to make it happen, I swore I would find the killer and exact justice."

"Was that *exactly* what you swore, Thunderer?" The Master literally walked out of nowhere and put a hand on the startled Asgardian. "If so, I may be able to help you. If not, I will need to destroy you to stop you from hurting all of us."

"Those were my exact words, Dark One." Odin glowered at The Master, preparing to fight. "I warn you. Even at your rank, I may be able to destroy you if you attempt to deceive me."

"I see what you are wearing, and I understand its significance." The Master put a hand on Odin and looked him in the eye. "Possibly more than you do. Let's talk."

The two vanished, and Dale decided that it was a good time to sit down. He didn't mind the slight splash of blood as he landed in a puddle, that had been *way* too intense for him. He closed his eyes, and a thought crossed his mind that refused to be banished.

"Somehow, this is Cal's fault."

CHAPTER THIRTY-SIX

<Well, that was all exciting and fun.> As much as I really wanted to make light of the situation, I was truly shaken and out of sorts. There had been a huge number of creatures in the area, and I was hesitant to be the one to inform Dale that it was only thanks to the *really* powerful people that we were still flying in one piece.

"Can we *not* do that again?" Dani shuddered and flew over to the Silverwood tree to her usual perch. "I don't understand why you are always thrust into deadly situations so suddenly."

<Hey now, to be fair, we are only here because you forced our hand. For the first time, I can really say that us being out and about in a dangerous area is *your* fault! Ha!> I crowed my laughter to the skies, though only a few people could actually hear it.

"Yes, well, if we are being *actually* fair," Dani snapped back wryly, "then we would look at those creatures and see that they are only out and about because *you* displaced them."

<You know, because we all need to be on the same side, I think we shouldn't point fingers here,> I quickly backtracked

my statements. <Let's just focus on what we need to do *next.* Fix it forward and all that.>

"Neither of us have fingers." Dani chuckled at my expense.

<As I was *saying,*> I pushed forward, knowing that Dani had me on this one, <the ambient Essence in the air is getting stronger and stronger. We must be getting close to whatever it is that is releasing all of this power. What do you want to do here? We have already seen that there is a huge number of monsters in the area, and I doubt they'll get *weaker* as we get closer to whatever this place is. Forward… or run for it?>

"I need to go forward, Cal." Dani shook her head sadly as I remained silent. "I… if I need to go alone, I understand. This is risking a lot, and I can just–"

<You obviously know that I'd never go for that, right?> I responded drolly. <Dani, for now until forever, wherever you are is where *I* want to be. If that means we charge forward into the unknown and fail, then by the *abyss,* we will be doing it together! Forward it is.>

A few minutes passed in silence as we continued, each of us silent for our own reasons. Bob coughed uncomfortably from one of the screens to the navigation room that I kept up at all times now and started speaking, "Uhh. I really hope that I'm not interrupting too terribly, but I really need to let you know that we have spotted a landmass on the horizon, and if we continue this pace, we should arrive within an hour."

I jumped at the chance to kickstart the conversation again and sent feelings of joy and pleasure to Bob. He relaxed and continued working as I thanked him. <Alright, here is the plan, everyone! Charge forward and hope for the best, and we'll be ready to escape at any moment and restart elsewhere!>

Possibly *not* my most inspiring speech ever, but that was fine by me. Everyone here knew that their job was a permanent one —one way or another. So long as I lived, they would as well. The landmass in the distance was getting clearer with each passing second, though there was an oddity that took me too long—in my opinion—to notice. <Is the sun not shining on that? No, it has to be, right? You all couldn't see it otherwise?>

"I think that whatever sunlight is landing there is just kinda *stopping*?" Dani hypothesized leerily. "You're right though, there has to be *some* light on it!"

<We have an hour to guess, I suppose. It's way too far to know for sure since I obviously can't reach out and test it directly. Yet.> I sent a command to the Bobs, <Alrighty. People! Give me your best guesses. Think about it for a little while we fly. I'm going to take the next little bit to look around and see the changes that occurred in the aftermath of the fight here. Ready? Go!>

I followed a well-worn path up to where The Master was working on the super-intricate portal. Odin was standing near him, listening to the reasoning behind their plan, the merits and detriments, and he didn't seem all that impressed. The thundering voice of his shattered the calm of the room, causing multiple technicians to flinch away, "You are asking me to abandon my oath? You *dare*?"

"Your oath to *whom*, Odin?" The Master's voice was calm, but his words cracked like a whip. "A dead people? A city that no longer exists? Do you think I haven't visited your people in the past? Are your traditions dead as well, or do they carry on through *you*? What was the final will of your people? Death and forgetfulness of everything they held dear or was it seeking the restoration of your society? You are the only one who can accomplish that feat, are you not?"

"*I* am also the only one who can say exactly what *my* traditions are now, Dark One!" Odin stepped forward, and a static build-up discharged into the air, causing a small peal of thunder to crack the air, forcing the room's occupants to glance over in annoyance. "If I say my intentions are vengeance, then *that* is my *people's* intentions!"

"What of the transformation I see two of your people have somehow been put through?" The Master continued without a single change to his demeanor. "I feel that they should have some say as well. Do they wish you to go on an unrepentant murder spree? Will killing people weaker than you be *helpful*? Are they pleased with your actions?"

"They will follow what I say." For the first time, Odin glanced away. I was watching this with great delight. What *fascinating* things sentients would do to convince others! I needed to try this out. Appealing to morality and not even of the person in question but a larger group that *might* condemn their actions? It made sense. Everyone seemed to want to have the respect of others. I just wanted to eat them and get more powerful, but maybe I was just more honest with myself than most people were.

"What a great life *you* have chosen for them, then. To die so that you can satisfy misguided wrath." The Master shook his head. "Walk among the people here then, and tell me that all of them need to suffer the same fate as your people because you are sulking. I warn you, slaying an innocent will be the last action you are allowed to take. This place is under *my* protection."

Aww. What a big ol' softie. How did he ever get such a terrible reputation? Oh right, the giant, bone-clad demons. Beyond that though? Well, the murders. Alright, yeah, I keep forgetting about those pesky laws that people bind themselves with. This conversation seemed to be at an end, but before I left, I took a look at the portal and fixed a few small imperfections in the power flow. It wouldn't make sense to have this thing explode and undo all the work that we were doing trying to save the world.

Let's see… what else was there to do? Dale seemed to be fine, good for him… Oh, there was that one little project I had going with the Northman that had been murdering people. I looked in at him and watched for a minute as he fought against the Inscribed bars that were holding him in place. Good, the flesh grafts were taking hold. I had been worried when the blood I had been creating in his veins started to clot all over the place, but with some modifications to his liver and kidneys, the clots had soon stopped appearing.

I felt a *little* bad about all the pain he was experiencing but wasn't too worried. If his mind broke, I had a backup copy that I could put in place. I needed to see the limits of what I could do to a living person, and I needed him to be alive and aware as the process continued so that he could let me know in real time where things were going wrong. Case in point…

"Ohh… my jaw…" the words were slurred and barely recognizable, but that was an easy fix! The bone broke in a few places and lengthened. Then I generated new mandible tissue to fix everything up. Good, good. Everything was going correctly. The design for living flesh modification had been one of the many things I had been traded by the infernal dungeon. This was also the method the Northmen had been using to have Runes put into their flesh. They were not tattoos as I had originally thought; they were actually *growths* inside of them! It was utterly fascinating to me. Normally, I had to do this all directly, and now there was a method for automating it! Pure excitement, but obviously, this wasn't something I was going to be able to test on someone I *liked.*

"Great Spirit, we are only a few minutes out from the landmass!" Bob interrupted my thinking, but I liked that he only did it for important events.

<Sounds great, Bob, let me–>

A section of my influence was destroyed instantly and easily, collapsing inward and blowing a few tons of stone off the side of my mountain. I never knew that I could feel nauseous before, but, yu~u~p! I felt really bad suddenly because I knew what this was. I had even done this a few times before, and I could tell that this wasn't an attack.

There was a dungeon out there, knocking on my influence to get my attention.

CHAPTER THIRTY-SEVEN

"Sorry, Dale." Hans shrugged and scooted a little closer to Rose. "Those are *monsters*. Monsters that we can't really hope to defeat in any kind of reasonable way. Did you never wonder why teams were always comprised of a C-rank maximum? Then all Mage rank groups were *all* Mages or better? Those guys that all hung out at the Mages' Guild, did their own thing?"

"I guess I hadn't really thought of it that way." Dale sat down carefully, knowing that he was all riled up and liable to break something if he let his power or emotions run through him unchecked right now. "I really liked our team though. I don't want my advancement to keep us from being together."

"Well, you are always welcome to guard us in deeper layers of the dungeon while we cultivate as fast as possible. That is what the instructors in the Academy do, isn't it?" Rose squeezed Hans' hand and looked Dale in the eye. "On a serious note, Dale, you really should be taking this time to get stronger. We don't begrudge you that. We would be doing the same thing, and you need to work really hard to stay ahead as a Mage."

"'We', huh?" Dale sighed and leaned back, using light

currents of air to hold himself in place as he thought. "How's that going? Also, seriously, that was a really short turnaround from hatred to marriage, Rose. What was up with that? I know that we kinda touched on it a couple weeks ago, but it still seems… too much."

"Hey now, no need to delve too deeply into the underpinnings of my relationship, thank *you*!" Hans glared at Dale, only to back off as Rose poked him in the head.

"Just stop. I'm not about to change my mind!" Rose waited for the expected wink, then responded to Dale, "To be perfectly honest, Dale… we had been in a relationship since the second week of knowing each other. I insisted that we didn't tell anyone since I was worried that you would treat us differently if we were a known couple. Hans *agreed* to keep it from everyone but told me that the best way to hide it was by him acting like he *was* into me at all times. So, I was *overly* mean to him in public, and he stayed the same."

"And *you* had no faith that it would work." Hans laughed at her, getting an elbow to the ribs for his ribbing.

"Well, it worked on me." Dale showed his palms and shook his head.

"You are the *epitome* of relationship awareness," Rose dryly informed him. "You can't even tell when people are after *you*. I can't say I'm surprised that you didn't see *our* romance. *Anyway*, when Adam died, we… *decided* that it was better to be together as much as possible. Hidden romance is fun and all, but when you are afraid to accept a hug in public because you are worried about what 'they' will think? We realized it was time to put all that foolishness behind us."

"She actually almost *killed* me with an arrow when I was going in to comfort her." Hans shook his head. "I'm not often one for ultimatums, but I feel like I was justified in demanding 'stop shooting me'."

"Huh." Dale watched the two of them, then simply sat up and examined them. Now that his senses were *so* much better, it was obvious that they were together. A slight lip-dye that hadn't come off of Hans that matched Rose's lip coloration, a scent from their clothes showing they had been washed together, and a slight spray of blood on Rose's clothing that only came from close range stabbing—and she was an archer. "Well, I guess it makes sense. It just really seemed to come out of nowhere for me."

"That was the intent." Hans shrugged and looked up as the door to the place blasted inward. Tom trotted through the entryway, a look of serious concern on his face.

"Friends, I have two serious issues." Tom took a deep breath and looked between them. "First and most concerning is that it appears my brother, General Aiden, is missing. He was last seen entering the dungeon, and I fear the worst. Second…"

A huge shape loomed behind him, and a pair of arms as wide as his torso reached around the Northman. "It seems that I have attracted the ardor of the Ogre that– *hup!*"

Tom stopped speaking as the air was driven from his lungs by a tight squeeze. "T-hom! You cannot hide from Oni! I find you *anywhere*!"

"Cal? What's going on here?" Dale directed his attention downward, but this caused a headache for some reason. Was there something that was messing with their connection? Was the dungeon keeping him out for a specific reason? "Cal? Ow! What the…? Ugh, my head. Sorry, Tom. Looks like you're on your own for this one."

"How did you two *meet*?" Rose drew out the last word, a grin playing across her lips as she watched the Ogre.

"He killed me with *hammer*!" Oni proudly declared. "Was most instant and painless death I've ever had! I knew it was love, right then!"

"It seems that she really likes my weapon," Tom bitterly admitted. "As my hammer is bound to me, she seems to like me as well. I really need to find my brother, Dale. We can't afford a war right now."

"Do you think it will come to that?" Hans asked as he stood up from the table and walked towards the Ogre. With the flick of a wrist, he injected something through his daggers and into her arm. She glanced at him in a fury, then collapsed. "Don't look at me like that, all of you! It's just a *really* strong muscle relaxant, designed to impact Mages, pushed through heavily Inscribed daggers that allow you to inject poison deeply into people. She's fine, and my bet is that she can move in a few hours at the *latest*. Let's go find the brother?"

Tom looked at Oni sprawled on the floor and groaned. With Dale's help, they moved her into a corner and sat her upright, then left the area. They were walking across the courtyard of the Academy when a door was smashed off its hinges, and Odin stormed past. Dale watched him walk by warily. Hans had no such compunctions. "What does everyone have against opening doors *normally* today?"

Dale stepped forward and grounded the lightning that surged toward Hans, dispersing the offhanded assault with minimal effort. Odin grunted and vanished with a flash, taking no care to keep his passing from damaging his surroundings. Hans watched the trail of damage whilst shaking his head. "Some people have *no* manners."

"Listen here, you little–" Rose growled at her spouse, only to be cut off as someone shouted in the distance.

"We're above land again!" The group paused and looked at each other. Were they at the mysterious destination the dungeon had been taking them to? A blast shook the entire mountain, and the scream of tortured stone rang through the area.

"Something's wrong!" a new voice took up the cry, obviously aided by Mana. "We've been attacked, and the land below us… it isn't *earth*, it's… ice? And it is positively *swarming* with creatures! We need anyone who might be able to explain the situation to report to the Guild at *once*!"

"Listen, Tom," Dale prodded his friend, "when Cal starts talking again, I'll ask about your brother, but for now, we need to trust that he wouldn't put himself in a bad situation. I think we need to get a handle on whatever is going on around here. The monsters, a new land… I think we are somewhere we really shouldn't be. Can we handle this and give your brother privacy for a little longer?"

"I suppose I don't really have a *choice*, do I?" Tom growled, looking away. "I should have known better than to ask for help."

"That's unfair." Dale gestured at the panicking crowds. "How would we explore the dungeon faster than just asking it when we can? People might be hurt, and we could be under attack! I was *just* walking with you to find your brother!"

Tom looked away in shame. "Right, I am sorry. I am a little… stressed."

"It's fine, man." Dale clapped the barbarian on the side, sending him reeling. "Let's go take a look."

"That's seven hits I owe you now, Dale!" Tom called as he regained his balance.

The group walked to the edge of the mountain and peered over, something that had been far too common in recent days. Below them stretched a dark land filled with oddly shaped creatures and obvious beasts. There were no obvious monsters in the air, luckily, but it was so cold outside that any non-Mage needed protective gear or to keep an Aura of fire on themselves at all times. While the sun was peeking over the horizon, it seemed reluctant to rise any distance above the waterline.

This meant that the land remained in shadow, and the stars, moon, and falling moon were all still visible. Hans scooted closer to Rose and wrapped his arm around her. "It would be so beautiful if I wasn't so sure everything I'm seeing is ready to jump out and kill us. Or fall on us. You know. Like the moon."

"Isn't danger part of the beauty?" Rose queried with a half-smile.

"Only on you." Hans kissed her on the cheek. "Everything else can go ahead and be dangerous at a nice, safe distance."

"If that were anyone else speaking, I would throw them off the edge," Tom grumbled good-naturedly. "Sickeningly *sweet* is still sickening."

CHAPTER THIRTY-EIGHT

I extended a tendril of Essence, allowing that to reach into the air below my dungeon. I felt a *presence* connect to it for a moment before it was obliterated. If I were a human, I would be *so* pale right now. But… the feeling hadn't been malicious. It felt like someone that had a really high grip strength grabbing a delicate glass cup without being told that it was fragile. Alright. I could work with that.

Again, I extended some Essence, but this time, I used the purest Essence I could manage and packed it into a *dense* slip of power. Okay. Now, all I needed to do was wait until– *gah*! Again, the Essence shattered and dissipated, but it had *almost* survived. Time to take it up a level. Mana this time, packed and dense enough that there would be some questions if a human or other sentient saw it. As it was **Acme**, the highest tier of Mana and I had poured some serious power into it, I figured I would– *ow*!

It held… *barely*. I was *shocked* that it had been a close thing, but now, the *presence* on the other end of this connection began to communicate with me. That is, I *think* it was trying to do so. The thoughts were *mountainous*, monolithic pictographs of energy that I was fully unable to comprehend. I decided to try speaking, and I really hoped it wouldn't be seen as rude. <Hello there! I'd like to thank you right away for not killing me accidentally or intentionally.>

There was a pause in the link, and it seemed that the dungeon on the other end was thinking. I kept speaking, mainly to offer as many words as possible and complimented it on everything from the environment to the creature swarms on the ground. The aurora was of particular beauty and allure today, wasn't it? Then I felt something, a kind of… *hole* in the connection that I was feeling. I was *ecstatic* because I knew *exactly* what this was! The dungeon was requesting information from me, and I was almost certain that it wanted the language I was using. Done and done.

I sent over the information happily and waited a few moments as the dungeon digested the information and translated its own thoughts for me. <This… language is… inaccurate. It leaves… much to interpretation and context. An unparagoned sesquipedalian as myself prefers the accoutrements of language acumen which facilitates non-anomalistic vernacular.>

Well, that had escalated quickly. Going from not speaking the language to becoming beyond an expert showed an intelligence on par with my own. <Hi there, I'm Cal. I'd like to mention right off the bat that I make jokes when I am uncomfortable.>

There was a slight pause, and then the dungeon spoke again, <Would you feel more comfortable if I used language you are more familiar with? I reanalyzed the language packet you sent and found the words you use with the most frequency. I see that you are both comforted and disturbed by this choice so I will move on to the true topic of conversation. Why are you here, young dungeon? I do like visitors, so much so that they typically never leave, but I feel that in this case, you are here for a reason… *not* selfish. Very rare and worth hearing out before I obliterate everything that you are.>

It was a good thing that I was a Core and didn't have the

same panic-inducing chemicals running through me like a human brain did, else I would be shivering in a corner right now. <Yes, I… *ahem*… there is a bit of a story behind that. So, there is this guy, Xenocide, who–>

The connection between us snapped, my extended Mana being absorbed into what felt like an unending chasm. I had to forcefully cut off that extended tendril, else there was danger of this draining my Core as well! In a moment, the feeling stopped, but my mountain was slowly falling through the air, all of the ambient power having been sucked out of the area. I had to devote some of my Mana to keeping us afloat, and even still, we were spiraling down too quickly for comfort.

I regained control about one thousand two hundred fifty-six feet off the ground and slowly started to climb into the air again. It took a half hour or so before I could try again, but I *hesitantly* extended a Mana tendril again. I had a feeling that if I tried to run, I wouldn't get very far. The Mana was grasped firmly nigh-instantaneously, reaffirming my choice. <I am sorry, little one. As you know, I have not had that name given to me, as your language is so… *new*, but the physical description that you sent matches a troublesome insect that has been pestering me for centuries. I will inspect you to see if you are his creature, and if so, I will make an *example* of you.>

<Does he kill your creatures, make insulting gestures, then strip and dance around on their corpses?> I was already exhausted by this conversation. There was far too much panic involved. Just ignore the threats and move on.

<*Yes*,> The dungeon growled, making me vibrate hard enough that I felt microscopic cracks form across the entirety of my surface. <I want him *dead*.>

<Right, so this guy tried to end the world.> I paused, but there was no information flowing back to me right now, so I continued, <He set up a huge Ritual that was designed to pull the moon to the earth, ending all life. He was planning on using the accumulated madness to ascend.>

<Fool,> the response was succinct, but it got the point

across. <He may well succeed, but then what? If he stays, he would become the weakest cultivator in existence even as he became the strongest. His plan would backfire on a scale that I doubt he has the sanity to consider. Now, what of you? How did you come here?>

<I was asked to come here on account of my Wisp. Dani.> I looked at her and linked her into my thoughts. <She was the one who felt utterly compelled to come here, and I couldn't do aught but listen.>

His serious and formal speech was infecting me, it seemed. Dani sent a mental acknowledgment but didn't speak. Odd, for her. The dungeon spoke again, <Why? Did not this aberration *fail* in his plot to destroy us all? You are not here to offer me the power that you have accumulated as a tribute?>

"Yes, no, and *no*. Not sure why that last one had been mixed in. His plans were delayed, but the moon was demolished and even now is raining chunks of rock to the earth," Dani carefully explained. "The moon… we were given a vision that there would be very few survivors. We are doing everything we can to save those that it is possible to save, but we are making only slow progress."

The dungeon spoke to Cal, words that Cal had been dreading and expecting, <I suppose I could help you… for a price. I have surrounded you with my creatures, though I could swat you like a fly from here, so I have no doubt you will acquiesce.>

<What could someone like myself offer to *you*?> I was flabbergasted, honestly. Really. It was dangerous ground, but it was also a little flattering to know that this ancient being wanted me to do something for it.

<First of all, look up.> Up? What was up? I glanced upward and nearly stifled a scream. I failed, and the scream came out, though weakly.

Ah*hh*h!

Dani gave me the strangest look she could possibly manage, so I explained myself and my oddly-intimate sounding screech.

<Right, so, it looks like the main body of the moon is falling *here*. It's *huge*, and I have no idea why I didn't see it earlier.>

<My luring ability kept any truly unsettling things from being perceived. That is until I opened a space for you to look out and see what was waiting for you. Though you may not have been pulled along by my lure directly, there are simply things I can do that you cannot,> the dungeon explained easily. <As for the favor you can do for me, first, I need access to all of your memories. I need to know that you can be trusted, and this will also grant me the ability to know what it is that you need most.>

<You want into my head?>

<Your Core, actually.>

All I could think of was the fact that this dungeon was so powerful that he was smashing my most potent Mana by *twitching*. <Right, well… I don't know if that's a good idea. You seem, um, *smashy*.>

<You will come to no harm from this.> An aurora exploded outward from the sky, a signal that his power had accepted his words as fact and would destroy him if he were wrong. While it would be nice to take someone with me, I still didn't want to offer myself up to be broken like that. <Or I can decide that you are *not* trustworthy.>

Creatures faded into existence around my dungeon. Huge, flying serpents, strange amalgamations of creatures, dozen-armed humanoids in a lotus position… the list went on and on. <Oh, good. I was wondering why you didn't have air defenders. The lure thing again?>

<Correct,> came the stern response. <Choose.>

<Lovely. I suppose nothing to do but work together, huh?> I nervously opened my mind along the connection and felt a whisper of pain as unintelligible energy swept over my mind, taking a copy in an instant.

<Done.> At least it had been fast. <I see. There have been many interesting events in your life. As it currently stands, Cal, it seems that your greatest threat comes not from the falling

moon but from angry and uncontrollable cultivators that mean you personal harm.>

<As far as I know, which of course... *you* know.> I felt *really* strange about this scenario.

<Then it would only make sense for me to teach you how to defend yourself against the S-rankers that mean to harm you.> The dungeon chuckled at my incredulity.

<That's *possible*?>

<Very much so, as you shall soon see. You were on the right track with the infernal cannons you have stored and prepared.> There was a pause. <Your other plan, to drop this 'Barry' into fewmets... not as good.>

"Told you," Dani chimed in.

<And... the favor?>

<Is simple, Cal. I need you to save me.>

<You're joking,> I responded flatly.

<Cal, the *moon is falling on me*.> There was exasperation in his tone as if he really didn't want to admit weakness. <Me *specifically*. Xenocide has targeted me with this weapon, and a weapon of this magnitude will likely actually *work*. Truly, Cal, it will not be difficult to take me with you. All you need to do is finally connect to that Silverwood tree you are underutilizing and allow me access though mine. Frankly, *containing* me will be a much more taxing proposition.>

<I see that I have a lot to learn from you,> I wearily gave tacit approval. <What should I call you? Teacher? Master? Is sensei a thing?>

<Just call me by my name, Cal.> The dungeon was laughing now, a deep and terrible sound that honestly terrified me even as it caused the *entire continent* below us to shift. <I am *Dungeon Eternium*.>

CHAPTER THIRTY-NINE

"Dale!" a voice called out frantically. Dale felt a flash of irritation; why did so many conversations start like this for him? Couldn't people just say 'hello' like they were supposed to do? Then he understood as a dark cloud seemed to obscure everything. No, wait… nothing was hidden! Everything was just… empty. Then Mountaindale started to fall out of the sky, and the screaming started.

Grabbing everyone in range that wasn't a Mage, Dale tossed out streamers of Mana and connected them to the walls so they wouldn't break if the dungeon hit the ground. This, sadly, was a *bad* idea as he felt Mana *surge* out of him and into the nothingness around himself. Then as if it had never arrived, the feeling was gone. Dale was panting *hard*, and the dungeon started to slow gradually. "What was *that*?"

"I have no idea," Hans started, then looked at his hands. "It was if all the Mana and Essence was sucked out of the world. I could only see what was touched by light. There was… nothing else."

Dale agreed; that was *exactly* what it had been like. "I never want to have to go back to only seeing the surface layer of things. That's what being a cultivator is all about! Yuck."

A necromancer stumbled into the area, his face ashen and tears rolling down his cheeks. "Please… get The Master… an enslavement of my people has started."

"What?" Dale was shocked for a split second, his high-order processing skills allowing him to grasp the situation and sprinting off to The Master. By the time he got to the area where the portal frame was kept, he found that there were people waiting. Specifically, Barry had already arrived and was speaking to The Master.

"Just like that, all of the tricks and corpses that your people were using to defend themselves fell at the exact. Same. Moment." Barry laughed in The Master's haggard face. "Now, *finally*, your people will be put back in their proper place! What fortuitous timing as well, just as you were planning on announcing that the portal was complete!"

"I can still consign you to oblivion, *Barry the Devourer*." The Master threatened, his power seeping outward. "How did you bypass your oath to me?

"I think not, *trash*." Barry smiled. "I've also kept my word *perfectly*. *The* necromancers, you see, are perfectly fine and are being taken care of by *me*, *personally*. It is just that most are in holding units that *we* have been making and importing or wearing *this* handy device."

The Master paled at the ugly, Inscribed collar that the de facto leader of the Guild was holding up. "You *dare* to–"

"I see you remember your time in a slave collar. Don't you, *male*?" Barry's grin was a snarl, but though his word choice was odd, it seemed to have personal meaning to The Master. "I heard the whole story from the Amazonians. So… you then remember that if the person controlling the slave dies, *all of them* do as well? Because *I* currently control the necromancers that live. *I* am 'The Master', if you will. Now, you will hand over the gate key to this portal, or all your people will remain enslaved *forever*. Also, the portal *itself* will be destroyed. You have a choice.

Kill *everyone* that could *possibly* be saved by going through there, or let me rule them all. Choose."

"You are a twisted man, Barry." The Master held out an object which was carefully taken by Barry.

"Huh." Barry squinted at the key, then at The Master. "I honestly expected you to say some cheesy line like 'death is better than servitude' or some malarky."

The Master shook his head slowly. "As long as there is life, there is hope."

"*There* it is!" Barry shouted with false joviality, grabbing The Master and throwing him through the wall. "You're under house arrest. You'll get a beautiful, first-hand view of the world ending. In the meantime, it's time for me to consolidate my power and start the migration process!"

Barry turned and vanished, his laughter echoing in the area for a long moment longer. Dale walked forward, passing the dispersing crowd and stepping up to The Master. "Now… now what?"

"Now nothing," The Master responded flatly. "He wins. I recommend… *bowing*, I suppose?"

"You aren't actually… giving *up*?" Dale frantically demanded. "You are The Master! The herald of freedom for the oppressed! The man who never gave up even when all seemed lost! You are going to throw all that away *now*?"

"Throw away *what*? Throw away a *reputation*?" The Master scoffed. "Dale, do you understand what is like to spend *four. Hundred. Years.* As the person who fought back when all was lost? That's how long I've been fighting for the freedom and respect that we are owed, and now—in the final hour of our world—the people relying on me were collared and rendered powerless. I'm not going to do anything to hurt them anymore. Fighting back now will only *kill them*."

"Won't that be preferable to most of them?" Dale demanded with clenched fists. "What heinous acts will they be forced to participate in? What will happen to *them*? What if

Barry just orders them to stand out in the open as the moon lands on them?"

"If you want to do something about it, *Dale*, then I suppose you should," The Master snarled back, the power in his body resonating with the world around him and causing the color to be leached out of the area. He coughed, and the world snapped back to normal. His anger had fled, and he was clutching his chest and grimacing. "Ugh."

"What actually happened to you out there?" Dale demanded, feeling like the man in front of him was getting weaker by the second.

"I lost," came the bitter reply.

"I meant when Xenocide grabbed you and acted like you were a sacrifice," Dale explained more fully.

"Oh." The Master sighed and sat down. "Nothing that would normally be an issue if I had *time* to fix it. Xenocide grabbed my Center and damaged it. With everyone else, he fed it to his blood Runes, but mine was simply dispersed. Damage to an S-ranker is damage done to the soul. This typically means very little, as the soul is incredibly resilient, but what he did was damage the actual image of *me* that was imprinted on my soul. Until I am able to heal that, the image my soul has of me is a weakening and hurt person."

Dale tried to accept the explanation at face value but was having trouble wrapping his mind around it. "Your... soul image? You mentioned this before, but it is a confusing idea."

"As an S-ranker, our body is *made* of our soul," The Master explained with a heavy sigh. "While I am very *good* at soul-based attacks and defense, Xenocide *specializes* in soul attacks. Madness can infect who you are as a person, it can insidiously alter the very makeup of your soul, and I'm afraid that Xenocide had his hooks in me for a *very* long time. He was tearing out his artificial madness and using it to drag the *entirety* of the soul's power into his Runes. That was why he could handle all of the most powerful people in the world like children... He had power over us for centuries, and we never even noticed."

"What will it take for you to fix this?" Dale queried uneasily. "Can you defeat the collars? Can you heal yourself?"

"Give me about ninety years to focus on healing all the damage in myself, and sure." The Master shook his head gravely. "Sadly, we have a week—at best."

Dale turned and stalked away. He couldn't believe that the man who was supposed to be the greatest threat to life and civilized society would end up in such a state. Such a weak and pathetic state. Dale decided that even if it took his entire life, he would fight against this being that had taken the world for his own. Then when all of that was over, somehow, he would work to end Xenocide as well.

He paused, reevaluating his new choices. Dale shook his head, trying to figure out where these thoughts were coming from. This wasn't natural, was it? To dedicate yourself to defeating opponents that were so much stronger than you that it was the difference between heaven and earth? Even as he thought the words, he found that he hated that phrase. Then he had to chuckle. "Who would say that in a serious manner?"

In a more realistic sense, Dale knew that his first priority should be ensuring his survival in the new and current world order. That started with making sure that Barry had no issue with him, and he was sure that the man held grudges against him for working so closely with The Master if nothing else. What would be the next step? Going into the world Cal built? That seemed like a dangerous proposition, even *if* it would allow them to survive for a longer period of time. There was nothing that said for sure that it *would* keep them alive, after all.

Dale needed to do something active; his mind was going wild with all the various scenarios and circumstances that he could find himself in. He walked around until he saw Minya talking to a large group of people and waited patiently until she was free. To her credit, there was no more talk of joining Cal, there were only answers to the myriad questions being tossed at her.

As the small crowd went about their business, Dale walked

up to Minya and struck up a conversation, "Hey, Minya! I'm feeling pretty out of sorts, and I was really hoping that you'd be interested in coming with me to get some exercise. Interested?"

"A little stress relief?" Minya smiled at him and blushed lightly. "While I wasn't sure if we would pick things up after my faux pas, I'm really glad that you came back. I'd love to get you some stress relief. It's been a long while for me as well."

"Let's get going then!" Dale smiled at her as she took his arm. Odd, but that was fine. They started walking and soon were at the portal to the dungeon. She looked at him with confusion in her eyes, but they sparkled as he laid out his plan. "I hear that there is a Mage's area under the next level? If we can get to it, apparently there are great… benefits?"

"That sounds *lovely*." Minya's face turned predatory as she looked at the portal to the second layer of golems. She planned to have *plenty* of fun today.

CHAPTER FORTY

"Just wondering, Dale," Minya started as she looked out at the various paths leading to the center of the room, "but didn't we leave here all torn up last time? Do you have a plan to get past all the creatures in our way? Are we sneaking somehow?"

"No." Dale hesitated, then shrugged at her. "Look, to be frank... even though I know we might not make it, I know that there is little chance of either of us staying dead if we die in here. Maybe that isn't the best mentality to have, but I want to start taking serious chances. I think that's the only way for me to actually get stronger. If you want to go back, I understand."

"No, no." Minya smiled happily. "I'm just happy to see you start having some faith in Cal! Let's get to fighting!"

Dale was agitated. Was that what was happening here? He was trusting the dark half of his soul? Maybe that was good, in the grand scheme of things... but he didn't like it. Cal was base greed and hunger. Maybe not hunger in the traditional sense, but he wanted power, knowledge, and new things like the mythological dragons did. In all the old tales, there was never a case of that going *well* for the people involved. Right now though, the only thing he could do was move forward. Specifically, at that golem that was taunting him.

He opened his assault by throwing a brick at the construct and using his earth-shattering technique on it midair. The brick exploded and sent shrapnel flying at the golem, and Dale was *certain* he would get a reaction from it. Somehow, the golem *dodged* even the smallest speck of the stone and then returned to its original taunting posture. Dale tore through the air as fast as he could move, swiping with his fists to land blows. Each time his fists came close, the golem slipped away. Dale was getting more and more frustrated with each attempt. He had no fear of getting tired out, but he wanted to *vent* on something, abyss *take it*!

Just as he was about to unleash a torrent of Mana blades at it, the Golem shivered and vanished into motes of light. Dale landed and looked around in confusion. "What?"

Minya got his attention by holding up a small Core. "Looks like this was a rainbow golem. Illusions, no actual substance except the Core and a little armor on it."

"That's a *thing*?" Dale shook his head and glowered at the Core that had been fooling him into attacking the air. "How did you find it?"

"When I saw it dodge a *cloud* of debris, I figured something was up." Minya gestured with her hand, and a wave of water swept over the floor. "I did this, and the spot that broke the water turned out to have an illusion Core sitting and patiently waiting."

"Huh. Smart thinking."

"Well, I have all this mental acuity from becoming a Mage, it just felt like such a waste not to use it." Minya flipped her hair dramatically, and Dale could only laugh at her antics.

"Fair enough, but let's keep going." Dale started walking deeper on to the floor. "I really want to hit something."

"I get that. I *also* want to hit something," Minya commented, checking out Dale's butt as he walked ahead of her. "What, ah, do you think this next opponent will be?"

"If this is the water and celestial path, that one will likely connect with..." Dale squinted at the shifting curtain of Essence that impaired his view of other platforms and tried to see what kind of golems were on them. "Either fire or wind? Not sure. It shouldn't matter too much."

"Let's do it," Minya said, eyes locked with Dale.

"Alright, great! Here we go!" Dale charged at the next platform while Minya sighed. Dale decided to go for the blunt attack out of the gates and filled his body with the 'spell' Cal had granted him. He released it on the golem and smirked as it stumbled. It had tried to jump, making Dale lean toward the idea that this was a wind-enhanced version. "Careful, I think I'm keeping it on the ground!"

"Got it, Dale!" Minya ran forward with foaming water covering her arms. She swung a fist at the golem, and the water extended into a bubbling blade that seemed to *vibrate* as it tore into the mineral body. The Core exploded as her attack sliced into it, and even Dale was surprised by the brutality that she was able to bring to bear. "Whoo! That was grizzly."

Dale shook his head as her words unconsciously mimicked his thoughts. He smirked at the joke in his head and nodded at her. "Nice work! I hope they are all this easy."

He stepped on to the path for the next area, and as he took a few steps, the path below him vanished. He yelled in shock, but thanks to his higher processing speed, he was able to catch himself in midair. He was now *slowly* falling to the open chasm that would drop him off of Mountaindale, but with relief, he felt a tendril of water latch on to him and yank him to safety.

"Still haven't figured out flight?" Minya commented as they looked at the other available paths.

"Not so much," Dale admitted as she pointed at a series of Runes that had been creating a walkway.

"Look at that!" She traced a few of the Runes and shook her head in wonder. "The path *was* there, but it was made out of solidified light! After a certain number of footfalls, this was designed to vanish! If you had sprinted down the path, it would have dropped you right about halfway between the platforms! Brilliant!"

"Also, kinda rude." Dale shook his head. Then his eyes went wide as he made a realization. "Sheesh, that is one of the few traps that could have killed me permanently! Drat, Cal! If you had tossed me outside and I died down there, what would you have done?"

No answer came back to him, so Dale was forced to just stand there and steam. Once all the water had boiled off of him from Minya's rescue, they took a few cautious steps along the next path and attacked the next platform. This time, things weren't as easy. The golem in question seemed to be using some form of oscillating sound waves that created audio and visual hallucinations. Dale got punched in the face three times by Minya and twice in the head by the Golem before he was able to shift his Aura to a thick water that absorbed the sounds enough for him to track them to the source and smash the golem.

As that one fell, Dale dropped to the ground, groaning and clutching at his damaged skull. A few minutes of regeneration Aura were needed to progress any further. As he climbed to his feet, he blinked a few times and took a deep breath. "Alright, let's start taking a look at plans now. We're three in and so we need to fight two more before we reach the Boss. I'd like to not get punched in the face anymore as well, if at all possible."

"*So* sorry about that, Dale!" Minya weakly grinned.

"Eh." He let the Aura continue to heal him as he thought. "It looks like we're on a path to the finish that focuses on messing with our minds. I don't know how much more of that I can take, so I'm planning to go in absolutely *ready* this time, and I'll just detonate a sword Aura cluster in all directions."

"Sounds foolish." Minya shook her head at his expression. "Here, just let me."

She raced ahead, hitting the platform with a *fwoosh*. Water crested and swept across the platform before wrapping around the golem and starting to *squeeze*. "Got him! Finish this guy off, Dale!"

Dale was across the platform and hitting the stone body in an instant, his hand going through and yanking out the target Core, which he promptly tossed into a bag. "So… what rank are you again?"

"Hee." Minya giggled and raced to the next platform. "We're just lucky that this path doesn't seem to be focused on martial prowess, but I gotta warn you that the Boss will be really hard to fight."

Another quick and easy kill showed Dale that he had been underestimating Minya to a huge degree, especially as the path to the center area was revealed. "So, you were really letting me go all out while you were holding back?"

"You needed to hit something," she shrugged as they looked at the golden Golem Boss that was waiting patiently for them while petting a Basher, "but physical combat is my weakest area. That's why I got so torn up on the last floor. I wasn't faking weakness to let you feel strong. I'm a tamer and a researcher. It just so happens that I am better at combat than the mind-oriented golems we were fighting today. I'm going to be nowhere *near* as effective against her."

"Her?" Dale looked at the golden Golem and realized that it did have a rather distinctive shape. "Huh. That's an Elf look-alike? I bet they hate that."

"No idea!" Minya took a step forward and checked the path for traps. "All I know for sure is that she's strong, fast, and *really* good in close combat. I've died twice here!"

The cheerful way that she offered up that information startled Dale, but he was glad to have the knowledge that resurrection was something Cal could do for other people. "Any weaknesses?"

"Don't hurt the Basher," Minya responded cryptically. "Not worth it."

"Why?" Dale looked at the mutated rabbit. "Does she get stronger?"

"Kinda." Minya hummed a low growl. "The Basher forces her to fight you with one hand. If you kill it, she either goes all out on you or curls up and drops through the ground. If she leaves, there's no keygem for the area, and you have to fight through here again."

"Oh." Dale raised his fists and settled into a combat pose. It was time to start combat in a smart manner. He stepped forward cautiously but still far faster than a normal human could run. The Golem suddenly *launched* at him, and Dale coated the exterior of his arms with sword Aura to block her overhead strike. His crossed arms managed to turn the blow, but he still grunted as he pushed her back.

"I'll join in if I see you in trouble, but this could be a good time to hone your hand to hand combat!"

"*What?*" This was not something you announced *during* combat! That was something that needed to be *agreed* upon! Dale spun and slammed the side of his booted foot into the golem's shin, sending it skidding without seeming to cause harm. The golem lifted a finger and sprayed a gaseous attack at him that Dale had no chance to block.

"*Ugh!*" He clenched at his face, his sensitive nose twitching. "Only Cal would give a creature a *fart* attack!"

The distraction nearly worked on him, and at the last moment, he jumped back and took a blow to the collarbone that was meant for his neck. Dale started moving as fast as his body could handle, the Moon Elf forms blending into each other, one after another. The Golem was keeping pace with him, and he realized that she was using a similar style, but this style was more heavily focused on defense and probing attacks meant to keep her in working order while taking down multiple targets.

Dale's style was meant for single-target assassination. It featured *heavy* blows and strikes to vital areas while keeping him moving at all times. In fact, it almost seemed like these two styles had been created in conjunction as diametric opposites of each other. If Dale had to guess, he would say that this was a

High Elf fighting style, and for it to be so perfectly matched against him meant that it was likely a Royal technique. Had there ever been a High Elf Royal in here that might have dropped this combat manual?

They traded blows back and forth, but the fatal weakness of the golem was that it was also forced to defend the Basher. Dale made sure to keep away from hitting the rabbit, but he also *pretended* he was going to so that he could create openings. To conclude the fight, he feigned at the bunny with a glowing palm, then whirled around and slammed a shadow-wrapped foot into the neck of the golem. The motion caused the golem to fall, and Dale dropped on top of it and tore out its Core.

“I did it!” Dale shouted, holding the golden Core in the air like a great prize.

“Nice work, Dale!” Minya was at his side in an instant, handing him a keygem that had formed. “Let me show you the housing available on the next floor. There are beds that are so soft that you think you’re on a cloud!”

“Why would I need a bed? We don’t sleep.” Dale questioned as he was pulled along. Her mischievous smile wasn't helping his concern.

“I’ll explain soon.”

CHAPTER FORTY-ONE

<Alright.> I was staring at the Silverwood tree above me. Glaring might actually be a better word. It seemed nervous, for a tree. <Here's the deal—I know that you can hear me, and I'm hoping that the reason you haven't been responding is that you simply don't form words in the same way that other beings do.>

<Maybe you even *have* been talking to me and think that I'm rude for not responding via scent trails or something,> I allowed this explanation graciously. <*However*! Now that I *know* that there is a way to connect to you, by the *abyss*, you and I are going to become friends!>

Alrighty. The next step after making a personal connection to the tree was to make an *energetic* connection to said tree. Mmmhmmm. How had this not already happened? Was this guy just a chubby leech that had been mooching on my power for so long that I didn't even think of it anymore? Was it going to reject the connection to me because it had as much as it needed without ever having to *let* me bond? It was time to find out.

According to Eternium, what I needed to do was… strange. I needed to give Mana to the tree even as I pulled Mana *from* the tree. This would only work if the tree *wanted* it to happen, which weirded me out a little. Trees weren't supposed to want things. I'm a rock—I should know how strange it was to *want* things. I needed to make a stream of power… done. Connect it to the root system… done. 'Kay. Now, if the tree wanted a connection to me, it would take the offered power and use it to forge Mana that would come back to me. If this happened, we would create a system similar to the Meridians used while cultivating.

I waited and waited, but nothing seemed to be happening. I kept the power going, but I needed to be doing other things. I took a look at the surface and winced; things were a *mess* up there. We were slowly flying away from the territory owned by Eternium, but he wasn't going to let us go *all* the way out until he was safe from the desolation aimed at him. I thought it was strange that an SSS-ranked dungeon Core was threatened by a rock falling on him, but it made more sense from the perspective of planets colliding.

While Eternium could likely destroy the planet if it tried hard enough, it would take a lot of time and preparation. Also, it had defenses in place, but who prepared for the *moon* to fall on them? That would be madness! Oh, right, wait. That was the issue here in the first place. Oh, there was a new Mage in the Mage's Recluse? Let's take a look at who… Dale? Oh, that was good for him! I should look in on his progress and see– *Wow*! Dale! My goodness, he and Minya were certainly *enthusiastic* to have reached this level together. I'll leave them to… celebrating for now.

I thought back to the long conversation that Eternium and I had been having. There was very little gain from the deal I had been forced to make. He knew *everything* that I did, and in return, he had given me a method to potentially protect myself. I wasn't pleased that there was so much luck involved to make the protections work, but a chance was a chance. The modifications to the infernal cannons were being prepared right now since I had a feeling someone was going a little power-mad upstairs.

A strange fluctuation brought my attention to The Master, who had warped into the dungeon. Right where I used to be located, actually. He looked around, frowned, took another step, and popped into existence next to me. His voice was a bit too accusatory for my tastes, "You moved."

<I do that pretty frequently.> When there was no response, I called a Bob into the room and had him translate for me. The conversation was far easier at that point.

"I want a favor," The Master more *demanded* than asked.

<Another one?> I quipped, though Bob was too slow to state my words before The Master continued.

"I need you to save my necromancers, the people that were all relying on me. They were enslaved." The Master was staring at the Silverwood tree, which seemed to be moving in a breeze despite the lack of airflow in this area. "Surely, you understand that following the orders of another, instead of your own, is the height of despair."

<I get it, I really do, but what am I supposed to do?> I took a look at the newly enslaved people and had Bob shrug for me. <Their own Aura prevents me from absorbing the collars they are wearing right now. If they enter my Soul Space, I suppose I could eat away at them, but what sort of relationship would that leave me with Barry, who might take that opportunity to destroy me for going against him? Are *you* going to protect me from his wrath, forever?>

"Save them all, and I will destroy him myself," The Master swore to me.

I ignored the special effects this created and had Bob stare at him. <What if one of them dies? That oath suddenly becomes nullified, and I am all sorts of up poop creek without a paddle.>

"I did *everything* for this! To save us!" The Master punched a wall and filled the room with rock dust and rubble. "He *stole* it all away for a power play! He will doom us all for his *ego*!"

<For now, unless you can explain to me what I can do to help this situation, I need you not to be here.> I had Bob wave at the entrance. <If there is a way that I can think of to save them without truly risking myself, I'll do what I can. I cannot promise anything, though. I truly hope you understand.>

"Of *course*, I understand." The Master slumped against the uneven wall, somehow forming the unbelievably strong stone into a kind of chair. "*Centuries* of people putting themselves first, no matter how hard I try to keep them seeing the bigger picture and understanding the benefits that working together can actually accomplish. What could we do, what could we make, if we used the millennia of life we can attain… to lift each other *up* instead of fighting for scraps of ephemeral power."

<I like your vision, Ter.> I chuckled as he sent a bolt of *nothing* whizzing past Bob's ear and left a hole all the way through my dungeon before vanishing from my perception. Bob didn't laugh along with me. <Got it, no nicknames. Look at things from my perspective. My entire life has been a fight for survival, and I don't see that changing for a long, *long* time. Even the people I save, I need to be wary of! Since people that are too powerful could pop me from the outside *or* the inside for no reason beyond wanting to see what happens. Give me a way to protect myself or kill my foes on your own, and I'll save your people.>

"The only thing that I could give you to defeat him would be *me*, and you are too weak to create a deal with me with *you* in charge." The Master started pacing around the room, his uncontrolled power making the stone warp under him. "Could I give them all memory stones from you? Let them know that they will be resurrected if they die in the area?"

<All I know is that I couldn't bring them back at their current power.> I started thinking over the offer; it wasn't a bad deal for me. <Would they submit to that? I think that they could regain their power, but if they were to die, they would come back far weaker.>

The Master could only hold up his hands and shrug. "They

would take the deal, and if not… I feel that I could make this choice for them. It is in their best interests."

<Good, good.> I laughed, making The Master flush with fury. <Nothing says 'I care about you' like forcing someone's mind into a gem and killing them. In fact, I feel like that story is somehow… familiar…>

"I assume you are speaking on your *personal* experience?" The Master stated the words almost blandly, but I could tell that the situation was getting to him. "I had nothing to do with your other half going through a portal in time and creating you. That is… more *confusing* than it is realistic."

<I'd rather not think about it,> I told him, glad that the conversation was moving along. <The unbridled chaos mixing with that portal could have created or done *anything*. What if we had somehow connected to a potent, untamed creature? Or summoned a meteor that came through from space? It could have ended all of us in an eyeblink, and we'd have never known what happened.>

"So, you *won't* agree to attempt to meddle with time?" The Master was… joking, I think?

<Never again,> I firmly announced. <I will *never* intentionally attempt to change the past. Nothing good comes from that.>

"*Fine.*" The Master sighed, holding up a hand. "Could I get a bag of about ninety Cores, please? I have some brethren to 'liberate'."

<I am *really* looking forward to it.>

CHAPTER FORTY-TWO

While I waited for the Silverwood tree to accept me or for The Master to kill off all of his people and deliver them to me, I *did* have a few other projects in the works. While we were talking, Eternium asked me to save as many Wisps and dungeons as I could. I was really happy that he hadn't made that request a few months ago; I'm pretty sure I took down most of the dungeons that were connected to the surface of the planet, and that conversation could have gotten awkward. Obviously, he knew that I had done so, but now, there was a swarm of Wisps and Cores being delivered to me via Eternium's creatures. Apparently, he was a 'collector' of sorts. Or the origin of the species. Details were fuzzy.

<Dani, I'm confused.> My words got her attention right away, and she zipped over with Grace in tow. I had Bob toss Mu's backpack into a chest. <So, wasn't Eternium supposed to be really dangerous and murder-happy? You were so nervous coming here that I almost feel like my meeting with him was… hmm. Now that time has passed and upon further reflection, my meeting wasn't so bad. Maybe Eternium isn't that homicidal, after all.>

"I was thinking about that, too," Dani admitted, flying in slow circles. "I think that he originally didn't want to be bothered all that often. He seemed oddly happy to have company, so I think the eons of loneliness might have gotten to him. Otherwise, I think he turned off the fear that we normally should have had. He allowed us to feel fear toward things like the moon falling and a few of his monsters while we could see them, but I couldn't seem to muster fear or outrage while we were focused on him, you know?"

<Huh. Now that I think about it… all I can really remember is slight caution when he wanted to scan my memories. I would have fought that tooth and nail before.> I shuddered, thinking back over the conversation in a new light. Eternium had done some *seriously* scary things, and I had just taken it all in stride. That was so much more *terrifying* in retrospect. He could affect my mind with so much ease that I didn't and couldn't notice at the time. It made sense, I suppose. He was apparently the oldest surviving dungeon on the planet, and he had created the Wisp race that guided all the dungeons that could be found. It would be *stranger* if he *didn't* have some sort of hold on me.

"Still. Cal," Dani stopped moving for a moment and stared at me, "I found *the* secret of my race! The progenitor of my species! I can finally right misconceptions and tell others what it is that we were missing all these years! I… I don't know what to feel right now. Who all can I tell? Who will live through this?"

<Dani, we'll find anyone we can, and I'm sure Eternium has Wisps that he wants us to protect. Listen, I'm going to go check on Aiden, and we should be getting a demand from Barry pretty soon as well. Since the portal is built, I'm sure they are going to be wanting to send people into me as soon as possible.> I started to drift away, but Dani started talking, and I didn't want to be rude.

"Are you ready for that?" Dani had concern in her voice, and she was speaking in hushed tones so as not to get Grace worried. "I'm worried that an influx of people into your brand-new Soul Space might put a lot of strain on you. I don't want you getting hurt because you are trying to *help* people. It's just so… backward."

<No fear there,> I promised her. <If at any time I feel like I am in danger, I'll stop the process right away. Alright, gotta go!>

I zoomed my main focus over to Aiden, taking a look at the changes that had been wrought. He now stood about nine feet tall, was *massively* muscled, and covered in a thick coat of white fur. I had combined his body with that of a Warg, a powerful, wolf-type Beast that had been sacrificed to me. I was pleased with the result; all of his senses had been enhanced, his body had been enhanced to an amazing degree… all that remained was to see how this impacted his day-to-day life. Would he need more food than normal to keep up with nutrition requirements? How would his cultivation be impacted?

I suddenly realized that I hadn't intended to make his fur white. That was odd; what had happened there? Looking into his head, I found that his fur was white due to the massive pain and stress that had been placed on his mind and body. Drat. I had been hoping to get away from having to insert a backup, but his mind was ravaged. He was broken beyond repair, so with a sigh, I had a Core brought over and overwrote his mind with a copy from the start of this process. The General went limp and didn't stir for a few minutes. I took that time to fix a few of the issues I was noticing as well as increasing his pain resistance a good amount.

When his eyes opened, there was no Beast looking out. There was a confused intelligence that was seeking answers. <Hello there, Aiden! Congrats on your new form! I hope you like the alterations.>

"What… how long have I been out?" Aiden was gently lowered to the ground, the manacles and chains keeping him in place slipping off and clattering to the floor. "What did you do to me?"

<I made you the monster on the outside that you are on the

inside!> I cheerfully explained to him. <You know, most people really frown on hunting their own species. I made you this way so you won't feel any qualms about doing what you do! Now, you can go out and be a monster to your heart's content.>

"You are punishing me?" The ex-Northman realized with horror. "I was killing Amazonians to satisfy your hunger!"

<No, no you weren't.> My voice took on a hard edge. <I pride myself on fairness and a way to succeed, *always*. You were placing people in traps that there was no escape from, then killing them slowly. The only *chance* for fairness in that scenario would be if they noticed the trap ahead of time. You made sure that didn't happen, and let's not pretend you weren't doing this for your own personal vendetta. Now. Run along, and do try to enjoy your new body. I think you will actually like it more than you think once you get a feel for it.>

Aiden held up a massive paw-hand, looking at the thick claws that tipped his fingers. He scratched the razor-sharp edge over a stone, an eyebrow quirking in surprise as the stone gained a deep gouge. He stood up and up… at his full height, he looked around the small room and flexed, feeling incomparably powerful. He looked to the doorway and dashed out of it to test his speed. "Ah-wooo!"

The Wolfman ran along the path, headed for the surface. With each pounding step, he found greater joy in the motion and speed he was able to achieve. By the time he reached the surface, all thoughts of this form being a punishment had vanished… though not naturally.

I watched as the Wolfman ran from my depths, and I worked in real time to alter his emotions and memories. He would soon love me and be incredibly thankful for his new body, no matter what his thoughts originally would have been. All that remained to be seen at this point was the reactions of other people as he– He just died. Who…? Looks like Odin hit him with lightning as he tried to leave. Alright, let's try this again…

The Wolfman was spawned into the small room, we had a similar conversation, he tried out his claws and body, and raced off to the surface. Alright… this time, he made sure to call out and speak to people before fully showing his body to the population. Good. He took my advice. Let's see how long he lasts this time.

I was chuckling about this development all the way until he vanished from my senses along with Dale's friend Tom. They stepped through the portal, and… from there, I was uncertain. Likely they went to the Northman homeland? I supposed that I could create him again if needed, but right now, it was more important to focus in on–

"*Dungeon*!" Barry shouted into my depths, causing dust to fall from the first *and* second floor ceiling as they reverberated. "It's time to begin the process! We are going to activate the new portal. Get yourself ready, and send along someone that can translate for you!"

I thought about it, then looked at my small escape portal below me. Should I just leave all this behind? It would be the work of an instant to save myself, Dani, and Grace. Perhaps a few minutes longer to grab all the things that I wanted to come along with me. Should I just make a run for it and leave all these things to their fates?

Should I leave the races, the S-rankers, the dungeon capable of swallowing the world… and run for it? Perhaps if Barry gets too uppity. If he tries anything or attempts to enslave me, I would be *out* of here, and they could all suffer the consequences. To prepare for that…

<Bob, start bringing along the memory Cores. I think it is time to get everything ready for our miraculous escape.> I looked at everything else going on and decided that, yup, it was time to get moving. Contingency plans didn't work unless you had time to use them, after all!

"Yes, Great Spirit."

CHAPTER FORTY-THREE

"My people! It is time to gather ourselves for the exodus!" Barry was speaking into the air, and even though he didn't seem to be shouting, he was clearly heard by the entire population of Mountaindale. "As we speak, we are activating the legendary Soul Gate! With a single step, each person will be able to enter a new realm! The realm of the dungeon's soul! Fear not, my people! We have removed the teeth of this dungeon, and created a set of rules that it is bound by! Please gather to witness history in the making!"

Wow. That was sure a special speech, wasn't it? Barry was preening like a peacock, and I made a note to make an actual bird with his face. Not many people would understand the reference; they would just think that they were ugly peacocks... but this is one of those things I planned to do for me, not for *understanding.* There was a team of Mages standing around the gate, and after a nod from Barry, they started feeding Mana into the intricate structure. It began to slowly shift through multiple colorations, going from a jewel-encrusted pure white to a *hot* red in mere moments.

I looked on for a few seconds, waiting until the time was

right. As the color shifted from red to blue-tinged yellow, I focused my willpower on the gate. As I did so, the color changes faltered, and the entire structure rapidly became a dark charcoal color. I also felt a change within myself as *something* began to happen. A point of light appeared in my Soul Space which began to rapidly stretch and wiggle. It. Abyssal. *Hurt*!

<Ow, feces! What in the abyss is this garbage? I wasn't told that this would hurt. What is this farce of a magical gate?> I vented my pain and rage on anyone that could hear me, and with the corner of my attention, I could see Barry smile a vicious smile. He *knew* this would hurt! Had The Master known? I'd eat them all!

"It seems that the dungeon is actually following through on this process!" Barry announced as the gate shifted to a darker and darker coloration. No… it wasn't changing color anymore; it was simply absorbing all the light that reached its surface! I can't really explain the difference, but it was a strange thing to see a brightly-colored masterpiece turn into a pit of utter darkness. The entire time, a tunnel was being *carved* into my interior. That was the only way I could describe what was happening. A *chunk* of my soul was being torn open and fed into the gate to power it.

For some reason, I had kinda been expecting that I would lose a chunk of my soul to this thing, but I had honestly been expecting that Dale would need to be sacrificed to it to power the portal. Obviously, I hadn't been intending on informing him of that fact, but good for him that he wouldn't need to be fed to something to save a bunch of people he didn't know. He *would* have done it, too. I'm just *sure* of it; he is that much of an altruist. Bleh. Good, making fun of Dale was having the intended effect of making me feel better about what was going on.

"Inform our allies," the monster in Elven skin announced. "It is time for them to begin the march. Ensure that they bring plenty of tribute as they arrive as well."

I perked up when I heard the word *tribute*. Ah yes, that would make my wounds hurt less. Getting fed some shiny and new objects and knowledge. I would *glut* myself on all of the things coming into me; I would take it all and use it to make sure that I could build powerful defenses throughout my soul. Never again would I allow such a miserable thing to happen to me, this much I swore to myself in a non-magically binding way. Frankly, I didn't know what I had been expecting, and it made sense that this process hurt. I sighed as I resigned myself to the pain; there was a *hole* in me from an outside source. This was no different from a sword wound or a claw in the side; it was simply the location of the wound that was so grievous.

One thing that made me laugh a little was that Dale was on the floor writhing in pain. He had no idea why he was in pain suddenly and was thinking that he was poisoned or something. Silly Dale, not realizing that we were linked. Pain in my soul was pain in his as well, after all! Alright, it wasn't *funny*, but I found myself feeling better after I saw it. I assured Minya that he would be fine, even though I was still feeling like someone was pouring bees made of fire into me.

Soon, the process began to slow, though the pain remained. There was a hole in me, and I didn't really expect that it would feel pleasant anytime soon. I was sure that I either needed to last long enough to heal up around the sore spot or, preferably, just remove the portal and heal the jagged edges. While this was going on, I suddenly began to gain large amounts of infernal Essence and Mana. I looked toward the source, finding that The Master was using the distraction of the opening portal to collect his people into easily transportable Cores. The bodies were left where they fell, but my influence started working on them, their gear, and the slave collars that they wore. Now *there* was a design I had no interest in replicating.

Barry noticed that something was off but could only scowl since he noticed too late. He sent along a command to the slaves to die, but The Master had already secured their minds. I could see the nervousness on Barry's face, but I was certain that The Master wouldn't get involved in the affairs of the area anymore.

He had no personal stake in anything, and people had been letting him down far too frequently.

The Master arrived next to me, and in an instant, eighty-seven Cores were offered to me. I absorbed them all, and soon, I had the sentient inhabitants of my Soul Space. I sent along a booming voice into their area, making them flinch, <Welcome! Haven't named this area yet, but you are in my world now! Please make sure to let me know how things are, give me feedback on things like temperature and air quality… really everything. Thanks!>

Now, I could have simply created anyone who I had the mind of in my inner world, but that required a level of trust that I hadn't really seen much of. Not only did someone need to give me a copy of their most personal object—their minds—but they also needed to provide all the energy for their body to be reborn. Otherwise, I just wouldn't do it. Now, the reason this was difficult was that the person needed to die. *Most* people were really banking on the portal being opened, for some reason.

Speaking of the opening portal, *why* was it taking so long? It felt like there was someone stretching the pain out intentionally… then I noticed that it was opening in an area where time was still acting funky. Time moved a *lot* faster in this area, and the discrepancy meant that I was unintentionally dragging out my own agony. Well, that was an easy fix. I shifted the landscape around, and suddenly, the portal was in a standard time zone. In moments, the portal stabilized. I felt a cold wind blow into me as the air pressure differential caused the portal to start sucking in great gouts of fresh air from the outside.

I wasn't going to complain, but it felt a little strange to go from pure air to this mix of chemicals and what tasted like the cumulative exhalation of ten thousand people. Sighs of relief? Blch. Tasted like stale cookies. The pain leveled off to a dull throbbing, and I heard Barry start speaking.

"Let's get started!" he roared to the cheering crowd. "The

faster we get everyone in here, the faster you can become stronger and wealthy in this new land!"

"We can just… go in?" someone near the front asked in a shocked tone.

"Everyone here has been working for this moment!" Barry graciously waved at the dark stain on the world that showed a land of twilight they had never before witnessed. "Go on, find the reward you have been seeking! Those that come after will be the ones to pay tribute and tolls. Just remember, going through means that you accept the rules of the dungeon, and you will be magically bound to the agreement."

People looked up at the sky where a gigantic, white expanse could be seen looming closer. With that final assurance that this was the best hope for survival, the first refugee stepped through and into my world. I felt something odd, like waking up at night and seeing an object that looked like a nightmare visage. It shook me but didn't *impact* me. People started to pour through the air-sucking portal, and I began to think that this would be a *lot* harder than I had first imagined.

In the depths of my dungeon, I saw Dale's eyes pop open and look into Minya's concerned ones. "What just happened?"

Minya smiled at him and brushed his brown hair out of his eyes. "Progress."

CHAPTER FORTY-FOUR

"Progress?" Dale winced as he stood up. "Why does progress *hurt* so much? The worst of it is gone, but it's just kind of throbbing continuously now."

"Cal popped in and mentioned that they opened the portal up there," Minya explained with a smile. "Would you like to go check it out, or would you like to… stay here a little longer?"

"*Stay here longer*," Dale responded so fast that he nearly shouted at her. "Uh, that is…"

"Good to know that I haven't lost my touch!" Minya grabbed Dale by the arm and started pulling him to the villa they had picked, but Dale felt a sudden phantom pain and clutched at his gut.

"*Ugh*." He spat out a glob of blood and stared at the substance until it was absorbed by the dungeon. "Oh, that can't be good."

"Blood? From what?" Minya paled. "Oh no. I used too much force and–"

"*No*, no. This is from whatever Cal is doing." Dale didn't miss the look of excitement on her face and internally sighed at the thought that this lady might like his other half more than him. Oh well. "It's not *stopping* is the issue. Maybe we can run upstairs and see what's going on?"

"Hmm." Minya looked him over and smiled. "Well. I know that you wouldn't be leaving unless you felt it was *really* important at this point, so alright. I guess you'll just have to make it up to me *later*."

Dale smiled nervously. It was a fun thought, but he also knew that he needed to see what could affect him from such a distance. They walked toward the portal on this level, standing ready for combat but also physically closer than they ever had before. Leaving the dungeon, they were slightly put out over the huge line that had formed. Minya tapped on the shoulders of a man to get his attention and asked what was going on.

"What're ya even talking about? This is the line to get into the new world!" The man glared at them up and down. "No line jumpin'!"

"So… if we want to get close enough to see what's going on. We are going to have to wait in line?" Dale looked at the snaking river of people, wincing when he found that he could see neither the front or back. "At least it is moving pretty quick?"

"Dale!" Minya pinched him on the side and pointed at the air. "We're *Mages*. Come on!"

With that exclamation, she grabbed his hand and surged into the air on a geyser of frothing water. The ground dropped away from Dale, and he watched with awe as the entire landscape below him was revealed. As the last rays of light that would reach this area for the day began to fade, the aurora also appeared in the sky, and the world lit up. Dale looked around with a wide smile as they began descending to Mountaindale, and the smile slowly fell away as he took in the view.

There was a dark scar on the ground, and as they got closer, he could feel a *pull*. He thought it was in his mind at first, but when his clothes started fluttering in the *direction* of the blemish, he knew that it was an actual effect of the portal. This seemed to have a benefit and a detriment to the line of people waiting. The detriment was that people were hesitant to approach, the benefit was that as they got close, they were *pulled* through the portal. Instant mitigation of choice.

Dale and Minya landed and walked toward the portal amid an outcry from the people in line. It petered off quickly since Barry had actually encouraged the entire population to allow higher-ranked people to go through first, though he was keeping a small population to provide security and keep things running smoothly during the transition. Dale and Minya took a look at the procession, and this close, they could even see through the portal to the people within. Obviously, they were surviving the transition, which eased Dale's concern greatly. Still, each time someone stepped through, he felt a small phantom pain.

"I see…" Dale watched the next few people who walked—or were yanked—through the portal. "Their rank directly determines how much pain I feel when they step through."

"Does it hurt all the time after they are through?" Minya inquired, eyes still on the line of moving people.

Dale considered the question while a few more people made their way through. "I don't think so? It is more like they are moving through a raw wound, and the size and density of their Aura is rubbing at the sore spot. If the Mages were going through first, it makes sense that the most pain was right away."

"Sure." Minya looked over at him. "I'm looking forward to getting in there, but I can certainly wait around for a while."

Dale sent a coy smile her way. "I *like* the sound of that."

"Hey!" A Guild Mage landed next to them. "Mages are supposed to have gone in already! Get moving or find somewhere else to be! You're drawing far too much attention, and people are getting nervous. That guy in line just asked someone if you hadn't gone in because you didn't trust the process!"

"Sorry, we'll get out of the way!" Minya gripped Dale's arm before he could say anything, and in a moment, they were both airborne. "Let's go find somewhere comfy to watch the end of the world."

They landed on the top of one of the Academy spires and lay back on the slight incline to watch the moon getting ever closer. Between the colors in the night sky, the enormous shards of the moon in the sky, and the noise coming from the people and monsters in the area, the night was alive and vibrant. Minya rolled toward Dale and stared at him, after a few long moments finally asking a question, "Dale, why did you fight getting together with me for so long?"

The young Mage shifted uncomfortably on the stone surface of the building. "Listen, Minya. I have a complicated history with Cal, and you jumped right into working with him with such enthusiasm that I figured that you were going to do something to intentionally hurt all of us."

He sighed and lay as flat as possible, watching the moon loom ever closer in the sky. "Just a few… how long has it been? It feels like days… but it's been so much longer. Just *yesterday*, I was helping the Guild to build a wall to keep in the monsters that were spawning in the dungeon. I was a sheepherder who found a magical cave of wonders. I was seeing my Center for the first time. I was dodging the attacks of an abomination! All of this, all of the bad things in my life seemed to stem from interaction with a single person."

"All of the good things too, I suppose." Dale petered off, continuing only after his mind was clear. "It's just been so *much*, Minya. Every day was me waking up to see who was trying to kill me that day. Then a beautiful woman walks out of the dungeon and starts telling everyone that something we all *know* is a predator… is actually a nice and friendly creature. *Then* she comes over to me and wants to be friendly, without having ever known me or interacted with me? I was *concerned*. Do you know that Cal once made a tunnel to my clothes chest and had a Goblin with a knife pop out at me?"

"Ha!" Minya started laughing, and Dale stared at her before

suddenly joining in. They continued beyond what was reasonable, only slowly quieting. "I needed that. Thanks, Dale. Now, as to the other stuff… you know that I only wanted to know about you because Cal talks about you all the time? Whenever he is watching someone fight, it is always a comparison to your own fighting ability. When an interesting technique is used, he mutters about how he could make it better and wants you to test it for him."

"Huh."

"That's all you have to say?" Minya laughed at him. "I really hate to say it, but you guys have really similar qualities. You always seem to be thinking of the other person, and even though you both grumble about it… you always work really hard to protect each other. Such *manly* best friends."

"He's not my best friend," Dale grumbled, spurring on another laugh from Minya. "Ugh."

"Of *course,* he's not." Minya patted him on the arm, then snuggled up to him. "So… do you think that you are going to go through that portal?"

"That's the million-gold question, isn't it?" Dale waved at the moon. "Look at that thing. I don't want to be stuck out here while that lands on my head, but… when I was looking at the portal… I felt like it was *home*. Like if I went in there, I would either cease to be or become something more. I think… I think that if I go in there, I'll go back to being part of Cal."

Minya looked horrified. "Dale! No, you'll be fine! There's no way that could–"

"There's no way to tell, though. Is there?" Dale smiled at her. "I'm sorry to worry you, but I *am* kind of glad that you *are* worried."

"Well… I *do* kinda like you," Minya announced with a languorous grin. "Hey. If Cal did somehow absorb you, wouldn't he just remake you as soon as possible so that he didn't have to deal with you in his mind at all times?"

"That… is a very good question." Dale looked up at the shifting night sky and went silent while he enjoyed the body heat rolling off of Minya. Sometimes, it was nice to just *enjoy* your evening. "I just don't ever want to stop *existing*. I'm going to wait as long as I can and enjoy life as much as possible before I *need* to do this. I hope… I hope you understand."

"Of course."

CHAPTER FORTY-FIVE

Dale and Minya spent a few hours watching nearly the entire population of Mountaindale vanishing into the air, and for a short while, the sound of silence reigned supreme. Then there was a deep groan from the mountain as a few sections of stone shifted around, and there was a constantly increasing amount of ruckus from the dungeon as new monsters continued to spawn without anyone in the area to cull them. Dale listened to the noise level increase, then frowned as he realized that there *couldn't* be this much noise from the dungeon alone.

He crawled to the edge of the roof and looked over. He recoiled in shock at the rows of metal-clad warriors standing in perfect formation. They must have been moving with perfect precision and control to have only alerted them when they were this close! He watched as the men stood aside as a *much* taller… person? Walked to the front and spoke into the dungeon.

"Great Spirit!" the voice was raspy and strange. "My people, *The* People, ask to receive your blessing as we enter this new land! I have taken the place of my elder brother, and am now the Warchief of our nation!"

<You've got to be kidding me.> Dale heard the words, even

though they weren't directed at him. <You convinced everyone that your punishment is the life *they* should choose?>

"The blessing of might has proven its worth, Great Spirit." Aiden smiled, showing silvery-white incisors. "They have all decided that they would like to join me on this path to power."

<All of them?>

Aiden frowned. "There are a *few* squads that have refused to transform, but as of now, they are outcasts. They will arrive *separately*."

<Well… alright.> Dale shook his head at their eagerness in Cal's thoughts, though Aiden likely couldn't catch it. <You'll owe me for this.>

"I don't mind at all." Aiden grinned darkly.

<Alrighty then, Aiden Silverfang, progenitor of the Wolfman race.> The Warchief's smile only broadened. <Bring your people along, and welcome.>

Aiden turned to his people and shouted, "I have secured special favor with the dungeon! We will be the first race to *properly* accept the gifts it will offer, and we have earned much! Onward, to our new lands!"

There was a sound of thunder as the collective group slammed a fist into their chest and began marching forward. This procession was much larger than what had been on Mountaindale, as an entire nation of people, but still moved through faster than the unorganized rabble had managed. Dale took calming and soothing breaths constantly, doing his best to calm the ragged edges of his soul. "This is fine, I'm fine…"

<If it helps, being able to feel your soul and interact with it has increased your rank,> Cal interrupted Dale's inner monologue. <B-rank… two? The very leading edge of it?>

"When did I get B-rank *one*?" Dale was shocked by the shift.

<Not my job to monitor you all the time,> Cal grumbled and moved away. Dale smiled, seeing the interaction in a different light after the conversation with Minya.

"Aww, he *does* care!" Dale chuckled along with Minya as they watched the last of the silver-metal-clad warriors pass below. He rubbed his chest, wincing as his mind returned to the pain that he was feeling in his soul. “Feels like the worst heartburn of my life mixed with an infected claw wound.”

<Hey, Dale,> the dungeon interrupted Dale’s grumbling in a sudden reversal of situation. <Can I eat those buildings if no one is in them?>

Dale looked around at the empty structures and shrugged. “I see no reason not to do so. Go for it.”

In an instant, the buildings furthest away from the portal began to tremble, then sank into the ground over the next few minutes. The wall that had been built around the city crumbled inward, and soon, all that was left behind was open land with grass quickly growing over it. Closer and closer the destruction crept until all that remained were the Academy, a few buildings directly around the portal, and the Guild’s building that still swarmed with people. It was fun to watch ‘nature’ reclaim in an hour what should have taken hundreds of years.

The young Mage felt a pang in his heart as the city that he had played a crucial role in creating underwent such rapid destruction. He put a smile on his face and motioned for Minya to join him in another area; Cal wanted to get started on this building next. As they tumbled through the air, they saw a glimmer of gold appear from the portal area. Before they hit the ground, there was a swarm of High Elves in the area. The Elves glanced at the humans, sniffed disdainfully, and strolled to the Soul Portal.

Not a single one of them failed to bow to Barry as they passed through, though the S-ranker only acknowledged a single one of them—the Elder who paid the tribute. As the procession started, Dale’s pain levels shot up. Not a single one of these people were under the B-ranks, and the only saving grace was that there was only a few thousand total that came through. More humans started arriving then, and as the day wore on, the line to escape the incumbent doom only grew.

Barry had the Guild members who policed the area begin to force everyone to *run* through the portal, and soon, the entire sea of species began to follow suit. For the vast majority of the people, only a slight shuffling jog was needed, but as the pace continued, there was significant progress made. The moon was looming ever closer, and if they didn't make it through, they would all die. Only three days remained until the worst began to arrive, but there were smaller chunks arriving daily.

At one point, a huge detachment of Wood Elves arrived, though all that were able to go through the portal were the children and otherwise young members of their race. Each group of five was clustered around a sapling, and they transported it with utmost care. Whenever they went through, they would always ensure that the tree would fit through the portal. For reasons unknown, if the tree wouldn't fit, the group would *leave*. Dale wondered why they didn't just put the tree in a spatial storage device, but there was no response coming, and the Wood Elves he got close to would vanish like morning dew under the sun.

Dale and Minya spent the entire day watching various groups and factions pass through, and as the hour got late, the people started becoming more ragged, singed, or seemed to be injured or in shock. At one point, people coming through the main 'on to Mountaindale' portal were screaming, and moments later, a massive gout of flame raced out of the portal after them. The operator cut the link and questioned those that had made it through. It seemed a moon stone had landed near the city, and the population center had apparently been obliterated.

Nodding, the portal operator simply opened the gate to the next location and told them to hurry. Dwarves started rumbling through, carrying very little in the way of physical wealth. Barry stopped them and informed them that their toll had not been paid. They explained that they had broken from their tribes in an attempt to survive and most of their gear had been taken before they were allowed to escape. Barry stared at them, seeking any hint of deception, then noticed a few wearing Guild badges. With a sigh, he motioned for them to hurry, and the full group started coming through.

Dale stared after the group as they moved through and wondered if they had enough of a population to stay viable over time. Then again, the High Elves had only arrived with seventy-five hundred people as well, and the Dwarves numbered at *least* ten thousand. The human shrugged and wished the best for them, returning to his comfortable spot to watch everyone passing. He smirked as the Dwarves finished; Barry had stepped away to go to a meeting, and hundreds of Dark Elves chose that moment to erupt out of their embassy and through the portal, carrying everything they could possibly get their hands on.

Not only the things that they were bringing to offer, but they also made sure to rob the treasury that Barry was collecting tribute in. There was a roar that crossed the entire mountain, and the last Elf lost a leg as he dove through the portal. Barry tried to go after him but passed through the portal and into the wall of the building. Dale dropped to his knees and *wheezed* from the pain of the man *brushing* his soul, but it seemed that the S-ranker couldn't enter the portal even if he tried. The Dark Elves were safe from him—for now. A few of the Mages were set as guards to the treasury, and the constant flow continued.

CHAPTER FORTY-SIX

My soul felt swollen. I was aching and in pain, and Barry hadn't helped matters by touching the portal. The wound in my soul felt feverish and infected now, and I was thinking about closing it whether or not people were ready to see it happen. But… there was a benefit that I was seeing right away.

People had been fighting *almost* since the second person made it through the portal. When the Mages got going, throwing power every which way, I started seeing benefits from it that I hadn't even been able to achieve in the deepest layers of my dungeon. Every *bit* of the used Mana was absorbed into the surroundings or air, just like in the world, but in *here* that, meant that it was absorbed by *me*. So as more and more people joined in fighting over territory, fighting the monsters outside of the portal area, or just using their power for day-to-day things, my power would grow at the same rate as their usage.

I liked *that* enough to force myself to keep the portal open. Plus, all of the free air was really helpful in keeping everyone breathing. I had thought that I was doing well in my creation of atmosphere, but I forgot that humans breathe so *much*! And just *constantly*! Lungs. Pah. So inefficient. I had also forgotten that the plants in my world needed another catalyst in order to produce air constantly, and it came from people breathing the clean air and soiling it. Now that there was so much soil in the air from them, the air production had started to ramp up. Still, they would have been in trouble if the portal hadn't brought in a few days' worth of usable air already.

I was also getting all sorts of useful items from the people that had been entering this place. For some reason, they seemed not to understand that they weren't allowed to have things. They were only allowed to have what they had earned from *me*. So, this translated to armor falling to pieces, weapons melting out of hands, food turning to ashes, liquids vaporizing, and wealth pouring out of pockets and into the soil. By the time anyone took five steps through into my world, they were all wearing what I was calling 'starting gear'. Simple clothes, no weapons, no money. No food either, but I would do for them what I had done for my Goblins way back when. Big table of food for a few days while they got all set up.

It was a good plan, in my opinion. As time wore on, fewer and fewer people came through the portal, though it remained open for the stragglers. I looked around for familiar faces and saw that Aiden and King Henry were talking and planning on setting up in the same area. They discussed the location and ran off to scout the area together. As both of them had been altered by me, they moved quickly and started having fun, finally getting to test their bodies to the fullest.

Aiden had a body powerful beyond his ranking, and Henry had a higher tier as a Mage. They moved through their enemies, talked, and seemed to just have fun. It was nice to see my people bonding. Others were not so pleased to be in each other's company. There were dozens of assassinations, murders, brawls, and terrible injuries. I stored the minds of anyone killed, telling myself that I'd bring them back later. When things weren't so hectic, perhaps. Then I felt a *new* connection and wrenched my mind out of my Soul Space and into the real world.

There was a single flower blooming on the Silverwood tree that loomed above me. I had left open a small channel of Mana flowing into its roots, and it had seemingly accepted the connection! A root started wiggling around and eventually started extending to me along the open-air path of Mana I had created. It touched the surface of my Core and passed *through* it! I followed the ethereal root as it wound down and into my soul, and I directed it to the seventh continent that I had sketched out. I had devoted a *significant* amount of my resources to creating a small oasis, the only portion of this continent that had a physical presence.

The ghostly root touched down into the perfect soil, and a pulse of *life* raced down and into the dirt. A small seed formed and sprouted roots that reached *almost* to the edge of the oasis I had formed. A single inch of the plant appeared above ground with a tiny, silver leaf showing. Neat. Then I *felt* the tree speaking to me. Not… *words* but desires and instructions. The Soul Silverwood Tree began pulling in Mana, Mana, and more Mana. Then it *grew*. When it reached the same size as the tree in the world above, small buds began to grow. I could peek through the petals and saw small clusters of gems clutched within.

<I see that you have succeeded,> Eternium's voice flipped my entire mountain twice before I could get back into control, and I had to count to keep my fury at the—unintentional—assault. <How ripe are the Cores the tree has grown?>

<I don't even understand the question enough to formulate a response to that,> I sent back, a little of my frustration slipping through.

<It matters not. Allow me to…> I felt the invasion of a mind and power so far beyond my comprehension that it was like an ant staring at an Inscribed weapon. Pure *power* raced into my Silverwood tree, and by using that as a filter, Eternium sent Soul Energy into the tree inside of me. I was *terrified*. I had an injection of power, and now a *huge* amount of it, that would corrupt and destroy me in an instant if I came in contact with

it. The Soul Silverwood tree bloomed and grew even as the one in real life began to wither and blister.

A new blossom formed after the tree had reached ten feet tall, and a bud formed that was supported by three branches. I looked at the gem it contained and saw that it was as transparent as the finest glass, though I was sure it would be entirely unbreakable to me. <Good, my new Core has been formed.>

<What… Is this how natural Cores are *made*?> I was intrigued, horrified, and excited to have this information.

<Not normally, no,> Eternium dashed my hopes. <The World Tree can be used to form nearly any sentient creature and is entirely influenced by the one it connects with. Right now, you can allow any Core-based being into your tree, which will blossom and release them when enough power has been gathered to sustain them. I'm sure you saw how these trees in the wild drop orb-like seeds that contain other trees, yes? This is the same process. Now, instead of letting the tree grow a mind within that new Core, I will simply begin the process with my own mind.>

<And other Cores?> I questioned quickly. <How will I save them?>

<If they have a Silverwood connection, they can request aid from you and be transported via the roots of their tree into this one. Eventually, their hibernation will end and they will be reborn.> Eternium paused and seemed to consider something. <The tree will also produce Wisps, but their coloration will be based off of the Mana fed to them. Have your Wisp manage that. Now that a connection has formed, she will instinctively understand the process.>

<That's… disconcerting.> I was oddly disturbed that a tree could give birth to multiple races at once. <Oh… what about the Wisps that are currently bound to the Cores?>

<The binding will pull them as well, and they will undergo a similar process,> Eternium explained not-very-patiently. <I need to begin this, Cal. It is not a short process. As I do, I highly recommend that you leave this area at once. Everything held in

check by me will slowly begin to wander, and they will likely be *hungry.*>

<Good enough for me!> It was finally time to get out of this creepy location that I never should have come near, and frankly, it was going to take me a couple days to clear the edge of the territory Eternium had claimed. At least Dani was happy that we had done as she wished, and I gained a new ally—hopefully—in this powerful dungeon. I really liked the dungeon, and its advice might be really helpful… Maybe I would name something after it as thanks? I glanced at the new Core on the Soul Silverwood tree that was starting to glow. He had started the transfer! I was going to have a *much* more powerful soul contained in *my* soul! We did it!

…yay.

CHAPTER FORTY-SEVEN

There had been so *many* people! I felt so *swollen* and *bleh*! Ugh, was this what Hans felt like after eating cheese? Now I understood his groaning in the middle of the night after gorging upon fondue. How much more did I need to go through? I turned my attention upward, moving my mind slowly to avoid hurting myself. When I arrived, I got some *great* news.

"That's everyone," Barry announced to the group after the portal on to Mountaindale had been unused for a few hours. "The A-ranker's crates were a success, so you are truly the last that will ever cross inward! If there is anyone else out there, then they are unable to make it through the portal at this time, which means *ever*. The rest of you, get through to the new world. I'll see you all soon, and if not… celestial's speed the way for you all! Get moving!"

The Mages surrounding the area saluted with tears in their eyes, knowing that it was impossible that Barry would ever be able to fit through the portal. He was far too powerful, and they had already had an example of him failing to escape the oncoming desolation. Reluctantly, the last few guards and all of the remaining members of the Guild took their turn and marched through the portal.

Barry watched them go, nodding at each of them as they vanished. When the last had passed, he looked around carefully and examined his surroundings. Seeing and sensing no one in the immediate area, a smile began to grow on his lips. "Three hundred seventy-four thousand, four hundred seventy-three people have gone through the portal… plus or minus a few *extra* sneaky Dark Elves. I'm so glad we able to save so many."

This was a side I hadn't expected to see from Barry… was he acting? Did he think there was someone watching that was going to act against him somehow? I decided that this was a better use of my time than watching Dale and Minya struggle against the Golems in my depths again.

Barry looked up at the sky, which was almost entirely covered by the moon. There was a small filter of blue that could be seen through the varied shards, but it was obvious that time was nearly up. The S-ranked man looked around at the frozen abyss-scape below him, noticing that the monsters and creatures in the area were becoming agitated. They were even… fighting? They were fighting for dominance! Whatever had been keeping them in check had obviously begun to fail, and the power fluctuations were causing massive turbulence in the area.

"It seems that we are moving again, hmm? The dungeon must have caught on that things are getting worse here." Barry sat down and looked around, then pulled out a pendant and passed some energy into it. The jeweled surface darkened and warped, releasing a scream like a tortured soul. The air seemed to resonate, then the ground… then the sound vanished. Barry waited a moment, then looked around in annoyance. His eyes locked with a hypnotic pair of orbs that were inches from his own face, and he cursed and jumped back. Barry was *not* used to being snuck up on.

"Oh, well, it seems that you did as requested!" A body began to materialize around the eyes that had seemed to be hanging in the air. In a flash, Xenocide was standing before Barry in the flesh.

"It was simple after using the technique that you passed on to me, Master." Barry bowed to the man, but Xenocide had already pressed against a building and was fondling the door. "The Wisp never even knew that it was me forcing the impulse to turn to the northern lights."

That sneaky son of a–

"Such high-quality construction! Feel this wood. It's Inscribed so *beautifully*!" Xenocide moaned as he pressed himself against the frame of the door, which started to crackle and splinter from the pressure, Inscription or no. "Why? Why have people bound their power like this for a *door*? Why would they do this to themselves or force their *wants* on the world like this? Don't worry, little door… soon all shall be cleansed!"

"Master…?" Barry softly called, wanting to gain attention but not wrath. "Your teachings? The guiding technique worked just as you said it would! Placing a seed of Madness to guide the Wisp to her homeland was even easier than you had said it would be!"

Xenocide tore across the distance and hoisted Barry into the air by his neck. His breath hissed out as he demanded, "Are you calling me a *liar*?"

"N-no—*gack*—Master, I would never!" Barry didn't need to breathe, but the grip on his neck was tight enough to warp Orichalcum. "I was trying to pay my respects for your guidance!"

"Ah." Xenocide held up a finger and waved it in Barry's face. "Do you know the difference between a brown-noser and a feces face? *Depth* perception! Learn when you are going too far, Barry! That's always been your weakness!"

"Too far…?" Barry looked up at the falling moon. "Yes… master.

"You didn't capitalize my title that time!" Xenocide's eyes bulged. "Am I not worthy of the honor anymore?"

"I..." Barry was at a loss. Had he been less than respectful? "I don't understand."

"You wouldn't." Xenocide looked over the edge of the flying dungeon and stared at the melee of monsters mashing below. "After all these years, I have a chance of attaining what I have been working for! All that remains now is to make my way past all the guardians in my path! Good work, Barry. You exceeded my expectations, but my expectation was that you would exceed my expectations. Therefore, you have only *met* my expectations. Keep up the expected level of work! Also... feel free to go and collect *your* reward!"

Barry stared at the spot Xenocide had vacated; the insane SSS-rank man had swan-dived off of the cliff and was approaching the unstable dungeon below. All Barry could do at this time was shake his head and walk away, hoping that he had made the correct choice. He took a few steps and was crushed into the ground by The Master, who was now standing above him with shaking fists.

"You would work with *Xenocide*?" The Master punched Barry in the chest, forcing golden-red blood to dribble from his mouth. "You would work with the man who *killed us all*?"

"Where do you think you got the rarest of those materials from?" Barry sat up and glared at The Master. "Do you think that the S-rank rib bones just arrived *out of the blue*? Do you think that the knowledge we needed was *free*? That every nation joined together as one and worked to save more than themselves?"

"No!" Barry stood and punched The Master in the face, sending him reeling more in shock than in pain. "How naive are you? I made the *darkest* of deals to place the races in a position of strength, to bring them all together into one location, a place where they have a *chance* at surviving! I know that *I* can't go through that portal! I know that *you* can't either, and yet *you* still worked at it to place your people within! Why is it that I must let everyone die for no reason, just so that my hands stay clean? Don't you *dare* lecture me!"

The Master stared at Barry for a moment longer, then blinked out of existence. The leader of the Guild took a deep breath and walked away toward the entrance of the dungeon, muttering darkly to himself. He glanced around one last time before taking a step on to the first floor of the dungeon. "Almost, 'The Master'. You continue to weaken, and I'm *going* to end you before that moon destroys us. *I* want the satisfaction of being the one to finish you off after the humiliation that you've heaped upon me."

Frankly, I was shocked. This entire situation had not played out at all as expected. Now Barry was going through the dungeon to… what? Experience what I had to offer? Try to wrestle Raile? Maybe he was…

"No one is going to come through here, and even the dungeon is going to be gone soon," I heard Barry muttering. "No need to let all this go to waste!"

A moment later, a thick green fog roiled out of his mouth. In a matter of moments, the entire floor was covered. Then my vision of the area went dark. Son of the *abyss*! That *hurt*! That maniac was going to eat my dungeon because he was bored and no one else would be bothered by it? *I* was bothered by it!

<Listen up everyone, I need you all to retreat to the maintenance areas!> I sounded the alarm to all the sentient creatures in my depths. <Barry the Devourer is coming, and I think he is going to eat the majority of the dungeon! If you want to escape, get ready, and I'll have you all run to the surface! From there, I need you all to get through the black portal and into my Soul Space!>

I took manual control of the gyroscope, freeing Navigation Bob to run. I stopped the Mana and Essence sinks that were creating monsters and rewards, taking that all back into myself. No need to leave it behind for Barry to chew up. The only positive of this situation was that Barry didn't seem to be in a rush, or perhaps, he was digesting his meal.

Even as I had that thought, Barry arrived on the second

level and walked to the center, where his deadly fog arrived once more. Again, a floor vanished from my view, and I worked harder to pull back all power and influence from the area. <Hurry up, everyone! He's coming to floor three!>

CHAPTER FORTY-EIGHT

Dale and Minya were stunned as the words reached them. They were being told to *run*? Then the words sank in, and they realized the danger. Dale's eyes went wide, and he kicked the golem, destroying it and not even noticing that it had gone limp even before he had attacked. Without Cal's influence urging the automatons to fight, they tended to stay in a statue-like state.

"We need to run," Dale reaffirmed Cal's order. "Barry has been known to eat people that were in his way, and I don't think he would do anything but smile if he realized that he had the option to chew on my Mana."

"I'm with you, Dale." Minya pointed at a door that was sliding open for them nearby. "Let's run. I don't think Cal wants to keep that open any longer than needed."

Indeed, the door was already starting to slide down the wall. They raced along the pathways and dove in, letting the corrupted stone walls provide them with safety. Now in the maintenance area, Dale could feel Cal's mind brushing his again and knew that his influence remained here. "Cal, is he just eating the main things on each floor?"

<Just?> The reply was scathing. <Oh. Wait, I see what

you're asking. Yes, he doesn't seem to realize that there is more behind everything. Most people didn't know about it, so I'm not surprised. Plus, he would need to eat *so* much basic stone to get at these areas, and I don't think he's gonna bother. Run, you two. Get to the surface and find somewhere to hide. Xenocide is in the area, so… good luck on everything. I'm going to get out through my portal when he gets close, just to be on the safe side.>

Dale winced as the connection cut off and scrambled back as an *orb* of some kind rolled past him. It was throwing so much Mana off that Dale *knew* it was at least in the A-ranks. "What is *that*? Is that from the lower levels of the dungeon?"

"It sure is." Minya looked at the creature with great interest. "*Wow*. That's an Elemental! I had no idea that he had been able to create such advanced Mobs! Stabilizing Mana to the point that it forms a will of its own is *impressive*! Did you know that those can be naturally occurring under the correct circumstances? A lot of people theorize that they are actually just Cores that specialized too heavily with their affinities and lost the power to create influence. They *might* have been dungeon Cores at one point, but–"

"Minya, you have a lovely voice, but we really need to get moving," Dale informed her calmly, though he had been trying to pull her out of harm's way as another Elemental came rolling past. "I don't think those things are tame, and I can feel that Cal has his mind elsewhere. Please?"

"Right! Sorry, dungeons have always been my passion!" Minya blushed as they started moving again. "I just keep getting so caught up in the amazing things that I get to learn firsthand that I forget to be *safe*, you know?"

"I sure *do* understand," Dale wryly replied. "I've seen you examine the Manticore's stinger when he was *sleeping* just because you thought he was sick. Because he wasn't producing *enough* poison!"

"Oh, Manny is the *best*!" Minya didn't seem to be talking about the same murder-monster that Dale was, so he opened his mouth to correct her, but Minya spoke first, "He's just a bigger version of Snowball! He might be scaled and able to taunt people with words, but Manny is still just a big softie!"

"What, he just doesn't like all that many people?" Dale snorted as they chose a smaller side tunnel that the Elementals were avoiding. "I never *was* a cat person."

"Of course not!" Minya poked him in the nose. "You're a *human* person!"

Dale groaned, which only seemed to make her more pleased with herself. "Now I see why you get along so well with Cal; to think I had been attributing maliciousness where only terrible jokes could be found."

"Well, at least now you know better!" Minya danced ahead, showing off her powerful—yet graceful—body. "Terrible jokes are good for the soul!"

Dale couldn't think of a response to this non sequitur, so he pretended not to hear her and simply went quiet. They were approaching a group of people that Dale didn't recognize, and he wasn't sure what to think of the intermixing of Goblins and various races. They looked at him and nodded, keeping their eyes on him in preparation for trouble. Apparently, being with Minya was enough to allow them to get close enough to talk but not enough to guarantee safety.

"Hello, everyone!" Minya waved at the group and seemed to undergo a sudden personality shift. "We are gathered here because there is an S-classed disaster striking the dungeon currently. Our mission, granted to us by the Great Spirit himself, is to escape and go through the portal above us. This portal will allow us to truly become a part of the dungeon, no longer trapped on the outside as we have always been. Prepare yourselves. This will be an all-out sprint across open ground with a hostile force possibly awaiting us."

Dale looked at Minya, impressed by the pure force behind her words. She was *inspiring*! He felt aggrieved and embarrassed that he had never given her a chance for the simple reasoning that her allies had been distasteful. Ah, well. Nothing to do now but learn from his mistakes and move forward with his eyes open the possibilities in front of him. The group approached the surface and found that all the buildings were gone except the one protecting the entrance to the dungeon.

Since there were no other structures remaining, it was easy to see the destination—the black portal. The group was about to make a break for it when Dale called out, "Wait! Something is… wrong."

A few of the members looked at him condescendingly, but Dale was still able to feel that there was *something* out there. He reached out through the influence that Cal had in the area, latching on with his mind and *looking* for things out of the ordinary. His eyes snapped open. "We need Bashers—as many as possible and have them scatter as much as they can."

There were plenty of the bunny-Mobs in the area, but they were standing calmly and waiting for their Goblin overlords to give them the command to move. Annoyed by the human giving orders, the Goblins almost ignored the warning. Minya took command, putting her foot down and kicking a Basher out into the open. As it landed, creatures swarmed out of the air and started fighting for the succulent meat that the bunny offered. The Goblins looked at Dale with new respect and sent their creatures running ahead, knowingly sacrificing them so that the group of sentients would stand a fighting chance.

The flying creatures swooped and screeched, snapping up the fleeing creatures no matter how they worked to twist or avoid the conflict. A steady stream of Bashers sprinted out of the hole in Mountaindale, and soon, they were spreading out and drawing away attention. Dale kept a mystical eye out, and everyone was watching him with bated breath. His jaw popped open, and a word tore out, "Go!"

The group ran, the longer-legged humans and Elven attendants outpacing the shorter Goblins. Only Bob-type Goblins were Mages, so the majority of this group was under the Mage ranks. This made them comparatively slow, and without the distraction of the Bashers, they would have *assuredly* been annihilated. As it was, the group started taking losses not even a quarter of the way across what was now an open field.

Dale and Minya devoted their time to fighting off a few of the creatures that were attacking, but most of the flyers were upper C-rank at the lowest. The others were easily Mage ranks, and the best the humans could manage was to drive them away. If they took the time to kill each monster they came across, the others they were trying to protect would be slaughtered. All of the people present were fine with whatever fate awaited them, knowing that even if they didn't make it into the portal, they would only need to wait a short while to be returned to life. Still, they appreciated *not* being attacked.

The frontrunners started diving through the portal, and Dale found that they didn't cause pain in his system like any other had. He briefly wondered if the reason for that was the fact that they were dungeon born and therefore attuned to his soul. The only reason his pondering was brief was that as the last of this group ran through the portal, the shifting curtain of energy suddenly narrowed and sliced the man in half. Dale and Minya skidded to a stop, and Dale fell to his knees.

He started to scream, clutching at his chest and head so hard that blood began to pour from wherever his grip had landed.

CHAPTER FORTY-NINE

Barry stepped on to the third floor, and I watched him cautiously. Only a tiny tendril of my influence remained in the area, ready to be retracted at the first sign of the gaseous green fog that came out of him. The High-Elf looked around and began speaking to himself, “So much effort has gone into getting everyone to this point, and yet here I stand, alone. Everyone else is either dead, dying, or deserted, but what about me?”

The man seemed to be rambling, going on about various faction disputes he had been in, lamenting his time in the Guild. “But now I have a new trick! Ah, Xenocide, how did I not see this aspect of my power before now?”

The conversation was just getting interesting, but the green fog was rolling out once more. I pulled back and felt a huge swath of my power vanish once more. Ouch. <Dani, Grace, it's time to go!>

“Are you sure, Cal? Shouldn’t we just go through the portal down here and stay with you in the physical world?” Dani was fretting, and I knew where her nerves stemmed from.

<But this way you will be in the physi-*Cal* world!> I

chuckled at her exasperation. <This is why I tested things with Mu, Dregs, and Xan. A Core absorbs you, but going through the portal will let you be with me. Do you *really* want to be trapped in an Inscribed tungsten ball, surrounded by feces, for however long it takes for the world to settle? Even then, I'll need to rebuild my dungeon around myself! The boredom, Dani. Think of the *boredom*!>

"If you're sure about this..." She was still hesitating, so I sent along all my feelings in a stream of consciousness, then linked with her as they raced to the surface.

Barry had just entered the room with Manny and seemed to be having fun letting the Manticore try to kill him. Stinger? Broken against Barry's skin. Teeth? Ineffective. Body slam? Manny stopped like he had flown into the side of Mountaindale. Eventually, Barry seemed to grow sick of the game and slapped the Manticore into a paste that covered the rear wall. Then the green fog rolled out once more, and my view vanished with a painful *lurch*. Ugh.

Good, Dani was getting close to the surface. Now, I could drop through the portal below me and–

Boom!

<What in the *abyss*?> I looked at what was happening in the dungeon, and it seemed that Barry had taken a page out of Xenocide's book and decided to go through the floor instead of across it! What was happening? This made no sense! Barry came out from the ceiling of the Elemental Pit, dropping down the center of it and only taking note of the increased gravity as a method of falling faster. What did he hope to accomplish? I snuck a look at Dani and Grace; they were almost to the portal! Only a few more seconds!

Barry landed on my spider Boss, using it to break his fall and then blatantly ignoring it. He walked over to the first of the challenge areas and smashed through the wall. Then the second... third... fourth... Dani and Grace vanished through the portal above me just ahead of some fleeing Goblins, and I released the catch to drop into the emergency escape portal just below me. C'ya in a few eons, planet!

In the second and a half that I was in the air, Barry appeared above me and caught my falling Core. He was moving so far above Mage speed that it appeared to be instantaneous teleportation. I was in absolute shock, my carefully planned escape had just failed, and I was being held in the palm of the second-most-dangerous man in the world. My contingency plan…! I didn't have enough time to use it! Barry lifted me up and stared into the colors of *me*. He was still moving surreally swift, and I could just *barely* understand the words he was speaking.

"Three hundred seventy-four thousand, four hundred and seventy-three people have gone through the portal. I'm *so* glad we were able to save so many." Barry's smile was dark and filled with malicious intent. "After all, what sort of reward would my time with Xenocide have been if there were only a mere *handful* of delicious souls or such *varied* Mana types weren't included?"

"Well, little Core with pure Mana." Barry's lips were *twitching*, he was smiling so hard. "Thank you for being the filter that I use to siphon *all* the power of the multiple races into myself. And… goodbye to all of my faithful followers. Your sacrifice will not be in vain."

The S-ranker let a cloud of green gas pour out of his mouth, surround the Core in his hand, and began to *squeeze*. I could only force myself to get a single sentence out, and I directed it at Dani. <Get *out*! Barry–>

Then the pressure became too much, and my Core began to crumble. I watched from multiple facets as Barry squeezed harder and harder. Just as it became too much, I saw The Master appear beside Barry and beginning to swing at him. Too slow.

Crack!

Just like that, my Core shattered, and I died.

The Master's voice shook the ground, but at that point, I was past caring. "I *knew* it, you twisted–"

My soul and all the energy I had accrued began to float away from my demolished body but was stopped by the cloud of green that surrounded me. I could feel the energy trying to eat away at me, I could feel the end *trying* to come, but instead of either of those outcomes… I collapsed inward, into my Soul Space. The fear vanished, the green energy no longer surrounded me, and then I was suddenly elsewhere. I was suddenly suppressed, a *small* part of something much greater.

I started to scream, clutching at my chest and head so hard that blood began to pour from wherever my grip had landed.

"Ow, *ow*!" I shouted downward at where I knew Barry stood. "Barry, you traitorous *snake*!"

"Dale, what's the matter?" Minya was already on edge from the screaming; it was attracting attention from the creatures.

"I'm fine, it's… Barry just shattered Cal's… *my* Core and tried to absorb everyone that had gone through the portal already," I whimpered and tried to deal with what was happening to me right now. "I feel like I'm on fire. Who… *am* I?"

"Cal is… *dead*?" Minya gasped, her eyes flickering to the still-stable portal. "What… Dale, what's happening to you?"

I groaned and fell back to the ground as my body worked to contain and control the power roiling through it. "I'm *fully* me again. I was always only a half of a soul, if even that. I'm gaining new insight on myself right now—in the worst way I can imagine. Me, as Cal, was able to keep my mind separate when we rejoined. I, as Dale, couldn't do that. *Can't* do it. I am once more a single being and mind."

Spitting blood on to the ground and convulsing a few times forced me to stop speaking, but when I could manage it again, I continued, "Minya, when I died and went into Cal's Core, I could remain separate and distinct. A human *cannot* maintain that separation. I'm an A-ranked Mage, a dungeon, a human, and a B-ranked Mage right now. The power discrepancy, the irregular flow, is tearing me apart. I have… an *hour* at best until

I explode or burn out. My body is not *built* for this! I'm not *ready* for this!"

"What can I *do*, Dale?" Minya desperately fretted. She placed her hands on my body to help me up but yelped and pulled back as her skin began to blister.

"I need you to come with me to my Core room." I laughed as blood flecked out of my lips. "So strange to say. I have another Core there that I was using as a mimicry of *me*, built to be an absolute perfect match. It was a decoy, set higher in the area where I resided. It was *supposed* to be part of my defenses, but I don't think I could fool Barry. Well, obviously not."

Minya shrieked as I clutched at my head and the blood vessels in my eyes began to rupture. "We… we need to hurry. Brains are an imperfect storage device. I need to preserve as *much* as possible."

"Let's go, Dale!" Minya started running to the dungeon, and I did what I could to keep up. She smacked flyers away from me, and soon, we were at the entrance to the dungeon. I had never appreciated it like this before. Now, with both the eye of an outsider as well as the creator, I could really and truly appreciate the beauty of this place like never before.

"Just gotta get to the bottom…" I coughed a spray of blood, and I simply hoped that I could make it to the Core room in time. The actual *travel* wouldn't be an issue, but there were currently two *powerful* people slamming each other around. "Ready to go, Minya?"

"Always, Dale." Minya gave me a thumbs-up and smiled.

"Great!" I passed a command to the wall beside me, and it slid upward *just* high enough to let me duck in. I was *all* of me, and I had all the power, knowledge, and experience of *both* my selves. "Get to the portal, Minya. There's no way for you to help me against S-rankers."

Minya squawked indignantly, catching the stone as it sank and trying to force it upward. I shook my head and took a few steps. "Thank you, Minya. This time with you was… just get to the portal, and I'll see you again soon, okay?"

"Dale! *Dale*!" Minya shouted as I forced the stone to the ground. I crawled a few more feet and let myself slide into an air tunnel. This one connected to the large one, and that would bring me straight down to the Mage's Recluse.

My face was grim as I reached free-fall. I really… *really* hoped that the information Eternium had given me would prove itself. There was only one way to know for sure. I created a blast of air with my Mana and sped down into the deepest depths of my old self.

CHAPTER FIFTY

I looked at my internal self as I fell the last few feet, inspecting myself as only a dungeon could. Or a being with the mind of a dungeon, I guess. I was bleeding out from various locations, but with a directed burst of Mana, I healed those areas. Of course, the overabundance of Mana was the issue in the first place. Healing the vital areas disrupted smaller patches, which started to bleed as the flesh was shredded. I had to ignore that for now; there was only so much I could do when healing did an equal amount of damage.

I was approaching the bottom... Here we go! I dropped the last dozen feet with nothing around me, splashing into an ornamental pond by one of the villas. The water scattered as I landed, but the water that rushed to cover me hissed and popped. In moments, I had a huge cloud of steam forming around me, and I was actually feeling relief. Maybe what I needed was a coolant system to be in place around me? I checked over my cells and decided not to bother. Though I felt a slight respite, the damage to critical systems was slowed an insignificant amount.

I got out of the water and started jogging toward the next

floor. I was regretting *not* setting easy paths down, and… I paused and turned, altering my course to bring me to the dungeon portal system. Not having a keygem shouldn't be an issue for me! I held up my hand and let a lasso of Mana settle on to the portal, then wrangled the controls to bring me to the deepest portal—the Elemental pit. I stepped through, then looked at the trial that awaited me. I cursed my past self as I looked over the edge of the pit.

This area wasn't spawning monsters anymore, but there were still Elementals populating the ramps. They didn't listen to me when I was in control of the area, and I didn't expect much as a human. Then there were the massive gravity spikes, where the only way to deactivate the Runes was to be at the base of the pit. I had built that protection into the system to prevent *exactly* what I needed to do, never expecting that the only person who needed it—or even *could* do it—was me. Oh, paranoia… you really messed me up here.

I needed to make it through my own traps, and I was… *concerned* about my ability to do so. It had to happen. I took my first step on to the ramp and began descending, on the lookout for my traps. Most of them were triggered traps, but a few were on timers or could be set off by the Mobs in this area. The first really dangerous portion was the first curve. This armed all the moving traps, and there was simply no way to avoid setting them off unless I could survive jumping across the open area. Frankly, I had made this. I knew that wasn't going to happen.

That meant that the floor tinged a light red as I strolled across it, and I stopped a hairsbreadth before the end of the section. An instant later, I had a block of stone brush my nose as it passed. Woo. Never realized my nose was so large. Or did I lean forward as I walked? Hmm. The block retracted, and I dashed forward. Again, the arrangement moved, and I took a single step back. The benefits of knowing the design couldn't be overlooked, and I grinned as the space I had been in had an explosive Elemental pop out of the wall. The blocks shifted, and I booted the Elemental *hard*. It flew through the suddenly open space and down the ramp, exploding between the wall and another Elemental that was then knocked over the edge.

I ran, and the blocks started moving faster in response to my own speed. Gah! Why was I so amazing at trap design? A wall appeared on either side of me, and I pushed off the ground to hold my palms against the wall and my feet on the one behind me just as the floor dropped away. Whew! Almost got myself there! Luckily, I had been working with the Moon Elves to perfect my bodily motions for so long, and this was nearly second nature. The walls retracted, and I rolled forward and pushed up, fighting gravity to get me over the ledge. I passed the scorch mark on the wall where the Elemental had exploded and pressed myself against the floor.

There was a whining, grinding noise, and a blade of force whizzed along a long section of the wall at waist height. It was designed to knock people into the pit, as most of the traps were, but it would severely damage my body if I allowed it to touch me. Couldn't have that! In fact, since I needed to wait a full two seconds, I reinforced an artery that was getting close to rupturing and replaced some muscle that I had just torn with my acrobatics.

I had a moment of 'why didn't I just make a new Core and use it', but I had to shake that thought off. I *knew* that the Core below was a perfect replica of myself before my Core was demolished. Anything that I made on the fly would simply be subpar and likely to be destroyed by the forces I would need to bring to bear on it. I couldn't trust my shaky hands and human frailty to design a container for my mind and soul. Too dangerous, and I *really* wasn't trying to disparage myself.

The Core that I had in my body was good for when I was *just* a human, but it couldn't contain the massive surge in energy that I was bringing upon it. Already the Core was flaking, losing pieces that I needed it to have. I didn't want to need to remake myself because that went back to the prior issue of 'I can't maintain the power and focus as a human'.

I pulled myself forward, sliding down the ramp and using

my momentum to get to my feet at a running pace. I was past the first layer of traps and now just needed to get past the A-ranked creatures in my path. Fun! The only thing I could think to do was use their natural tendency of territorial war to distract them. I started focusing on the Mana that was pouring off of me and began guiding it into a ball in front of my hands. I couldn't *stop* losing Mana, but this would work for now. My experience with my Shaman and my own ability at directing power in the air really came into play here.

Now, I had no idea what monster I would find first. They changed positions *far* too frequently. What I *did* have was really pure Mana that could be used for nearly any purpose. As I moved forward, I found a corrupted mudman. It was a lump of mud that had tinges of infernal Mana throughout, and it *really* didn't like celestial fire. Guess what, buddy? Scorching flames burst forward from the ball of Mana, and I left it in the air as the mudman focused on it. When I was past the Elemental, I pulled the ball of Mana to me along a tether. The fire continued to rage for a long moment but ran out of power quickly when the power source was removed.

I was on to the next one, and I repeated my actions each time. I *could—possibly—*defeat these things, but avoidance was a much better plan for my deteriorating body. My plan worked a few times, but then it *suddenly* didn't. I was tempting an Elemental, and it seemed to be hooked, but as I skirted around it… the water-based Mob changed directions and lunged for me. In a panic, I converted the ball of Mana into a shaped explosion and *blasted* my attacker away and over the edge.

"Drat, I must have gotten to the point where their intelligence is reaching apex predators," I muttered aloud as I took a few extra breaths. "Okay, they are trying to set traps for me now—gotta be ready for that."

I looked over the edge and nodded approvingly. "Halfway… go me!"

I continued onward, working hard to keep my cool and counter every Elemental that I came across. On the plus side, since no more were spawning, all I needed to fight were the Elementals that had won in their individual territory disputes. Normally, this place was *crawling* with the Mobs. The next time I took a break was after I had to convert my Mana into Aqua Regalia, the most potent acid I could make. I had set the liquid spinning, surrounded it with a thin coat of ice, and used that to penetrate the outer layer and dissolve the meaty area around an Elemental's Core.

That had taken a *lot* of focus to pull off, and I was suffering for it. My control of Mana was beyond what a human could dream of achieving, but that single *spell* had nearly cost me the use of my arm. My flesh was blistered and bleeding, also slightly smoking. Time was running out.

I moved deeper along the ramp, and soon, I was staring down at the golden-Aura-infernal-spider. It seemed slightly damaged. How did that happen? I really doubted I could sneak past, but I would give this my best shot. I turned invisible, condensed my Mana around me, removed all scents, and took a single step on to the floor.

The eyes of the Elemental Boss snapped open.

CHAPTER FIFTY-ONE

The spider Elemental unfurled, and the golden water orbiting around it began to move at high speed. I knew I was in trouble, but I had a plan for this. Gathering my courage, I ran as fast as I could toward the exit to the room.

The spider scuttled after me, and I zigzagged so that the droplets mostly missed me. Whatever *did* hit me was slowed by my armor, but I had never taken my own advice and gotten solid coverings for what amounted to awesome chainmail. The water went right through the holes, tearing into my skin and opening small wounds that I couldn't afford to heal right now. I kept running, but the spider spun through the air and blocked my exit.

I spun up a spell and sent a near-crystal shard of Mana at the Beast. This thing had *every* basic type of Essence in it. Shooting a fireball would do nothing, and really, any Elemental spell was out of the running. While the shard was hitting and digging into the main body, I followed it up with a field of force that I projected on to the trailing end, then spun in the air and kicked as hard as I could. The force transferred perfectly, driving the shard deeper before it detonated. As the smoke cleared, the counterattack came *hard.*

The scythe-like end of the spider leg caught my waist and would have cut me in half if my armor hadn't slowed it. As it stood, the Mithril armor tore and left my now-bleeding midriff exposed. That alone was shocking; I had not known of anything that could so easily demolish the resistant metal. It made sense; this creature was far beyond the rules of mere mortals, and I had been relying on something that a seasoned adventurer would wear. Well, seasoned adventurers still got messed up all the time.

A wave of water pelted toward me, seeking the weak section for maximum damage. I created a barrier of air to divert the water, using the slight shift to dodge fully. The huge barrage should have been able to catch me no matter where I turned, but the spider hadn't waited to find out if it would succeed. Three more blades were coming at me as I spun, and the only option was *up*. I got into the air just long enough to move over the blades, but then I was caught by the gravity and *slammed* to the ground.

I had seen an option though, and I was going to make sure to use it. As the next attacks came swirling and swinging at me, I dove *toward* the Elemental and focused a massive rush of sword Aura. I powered my attack with Mana and drove my fist upward. I *might* have been able to get away from taking any damage, but my fighting style *demanded* that I attack vital areas and use devastating blows to end fights as fast as possible. An 'X'-shape of the sharpest Mana I had ever created raced upward, through the Elemental, continuing all the way up to the ceiling. Debris rained down, the enhanced gravity making every pebble have the force equivalent of a C-ranker's fist.

I rolled under the huge body and ran toward the door, looking back to see if my attack had the intended effect. The spider started racing after me, and I realized that all I had gained was a head start! I pumped my legs and got to the door just as I heard a loud *crack*. I fell to my knees, looking back just in time to see a soft pink jewel fall to the floor as four shards. I had been on target, it seemed.

As the Core fell out, the two *diametrically opposed* Elementals that had been a single floor Boss began to fight for dominance. Instead of focusing in on me, they wailed on each other, tearing out huge chunks of power that steamed away and into oblivion. I threw open the door, slamming it closed behind me and lay there for three seconds to catch my breath and heal the worst of the damage being done to my organs.

I stood and moved to the next trial—control of Mana. This would be difficult since I had Mana steaming off of me. I grasped at it, twisting and twining it into a pseudo-Aura that surrounded my *actual* Aura and ran to the first test. When I got there, I looked up and paused. Right. Barry had smashed his way through here, and without *me* fixing it, the area was still open. Happy coincidence. I went through the five rooms and looked into the mess that was the Core room.

The Silverwood tree was demolished, reduced to splinters of wood with only a single, sad leaf remaining on the stone floor. The walls had taken so much damage that light was peeking through, and there were odd shadows being cast, as though the world out there was being set ablaze. Not having any clue what that meant allowed me to be far more terrified about what was happening *in* the room.

"I *win*."

Barry crowed his victory over The Master, his eyes shining a bright and fiery green. "All these years of being defeated by you at every turn, all this *disparagement* from the rankers of the Guild, all the *agony* of not being able to find the capabilities of my own power… and now! *Now!* I have you at my mercy, I *am* the Guild, and Xenocide has taught me my true power!"

"All you are is another *pest* that is about to die with the rest of the planet," The Master responded tiredly. He was being held on his knees, surrounded by a pool of blood. "Not only that, but you killed the seed that we had designed to grow into a new civilization. There is no point to *anything* anymore. End this, Barry the *Devourer*."

"With *pleasure*." Barry opened his mouth, and a thin cloud of gas poured out and surrounded The Master. I could see The Master's form begin to flake away, his spirit somehow being dissolved and taken into Barry's. As The Master took more damage, Barry released more of his gas cloud until all of his green power was surrounding The Master and Barry's body stood slack.

It was time to intervene. I reached out with my Mana, and the room lit up with potent Runescript. Every floor had a section devoted to this process, as I never knew when or where I would get my chance to strike back against this madman. I *poured* out my power, and the tip of my infernal cannons poked out from hidden sections of the floor, ceiling, and walls. Some had been demolished, so I needed to hope that this was enough. Wards sprung up around the room, waiting to contain the terrible power I was about to unleash.

A dark wind seemed to blow through the area, and I converted all of the pure Mana into something *else*. Something dark, heavy, and infernal. With one last push, I collapsed and had to hope that I had given enough. Any more, and I would burn out. Already, the stone I fell on was melting from the heat of my body, and burning fissures ran alongside my veins as my blood literally boiled

The Infernal cannons reacted, and the built-in Cores powered them all with perfect control. The power I had given was evenly applied, and spinning circles of darkness appeared in front of each cannon. With the firing of the cannons, all sound stopped, and the world went silent. The blood flowing from my ears told me that it was due to my eardrums bursting, and that by itself let me know that the actual volume must have been on another level. After all, I was *still* a Mage. The cannons had released black *bars* of power, so condensed and destructive that I had never been able to properly test their capabilities on any material before.

These were cannons designed to knock a soul out of a body, and the weaker versions had done exactly that. *This* version was supposed to do the same, but it also turned anything in its path into particles smaller than water molecules. All of these bars of energy converged upon a single point—right where the green gas of Barry's soul left his physical body through his mouth.

I could see that there was an effect happening, but I wasn't sure what it was. I decided against waiting to see if the surging green triumphed, and I moved over to a compartment under the remains of the Silverwood tree. Thankfully, the S-rankers hadn't *dug* during their fight, or I wasn't sure *what* would have happened. I pulled out the perfect Core that would be my new body and started transferring *me* into it. All my time as a dungeon had done well for me. I debated—I *really* did—separating myself into two once more, but as my mind and power drained from my brain and into the Core, I knew that being only a *part* of me had made me weak in areas that I couldn't understand.

This process wasn't *fast*, however. As I stood there with my new Core in hand, I watched the black bars suddenly lance through the green energy, continuing onward to tear huge holes out of the dungeon around us. Barry fell backward, toppling to the floor and no longer moving. The green cloud started to condense, and the severed soul mindlessly drifted toward the prone body of Barry only to be intercepted by the black bars. The motion and power of the bar caught the adrift soul and whisked it down and away—out of my dungeon entirely.

"Looks like ghost type *is* weak to darkness!" As the power waned, I saw that The Master was also on the floor, his body mutilated almost beyond recognition. Then his eyes popped open, and I almost screamed.

"You're alive!" I called out. His eyes rested on me, and The Master raised a shaky hand and pointed it at me.

"Dale, I swear myself to your service and the rules you have in place." That was all he could manage before collapsing to the ground.

I opened my mouth and said 'I accept', but an *instant* before I did so, Barry's lips moved. He only said two words, but I felt horror as I realized what the phlegmy sounds were.

"*Me too.*"

CHAPTER FIFTY-TWO

Two swirls of power lifted into the air, and the bodies that had once been renowned and terrifying S-rankers or higher… withered into nothing. All that remained of the two were their souls, minds, and the barest modicum of their power.

The two streams vanished upward, and after a moment, Dale felt the portal into his Soul Space widen to the absolute limit and permit these two access. He collapsed to the floor and wrapped his frame around the Core in his hand. "Gotta get outta here."

Dale's mind was filtering into the Core *much* faster, and the world started to go dark right around the halfway mark. By then, half of his mind and soul was in the new Core, and the process was fighting him less. To his chagrin, this also meant that he no longer had control over his body and his Mana. The rampaging power started to dissolve his organs, and though he was no longer in control, he was still aware enough to feel all the pain. Luckily, he was vacating the body for a much better one, but until then he was trapped in agony.

The last quarter of his mind and soul was sucked into the Core as his body was fully destroyed, turning to ash around him and leaving behind a suit of clothes and two Cores. One was perfect in every detail, and one was falling apart by the second. <There we go.>

It was interesting to be integrated into my Core again, in perfect sync with my mental faculties. I was also *way* more powerful; I could feel it. As all the sympathetic links to my ley lines transferred to me once more, the power was far more easily captured and maintained. <And now all I need is a way to get back into my staging area and through my escape tunnel.>

I reconnected to the dungeon, surprised that we were somehow still in the air. The Bobs had been having me add in integrated backup systems; it seemed that they were far more effective than I had expected. I checked in on Dani—it seemed that she was in my Soul Space and doing just fine. Whew!

Dani hadn't been able to get out of the portal, it seemed, and she was steaming mad about the lack of communication. I'll handle that later. Heh. I'll never tell her that that was my first thought on the subject. I'd have to do some research on making that portal omnidirectional. For now, it was getting *real* bright out there, and I didn't think I was seeing sunlight. I had my influence extend rapidly, easily done through my creation, and swallowed the gate whole.

As the full design was implanted in my mind, the wound in my soul began to close. This meant that people started panicking of course, but their view had been showing giant chunks of flaming moon approaching, so I hoped they'd get over it soon. There was an odd phenomenon that occurred as the portal closed, something that I really hadn't expected. As the portal vanished, every single person at the Mage ranks that wasn't bound to me staggered at the same time. Strange. To the escape hatch!

I lifted the ground and had it roll me along to the hole. I tipped over and mentally smiled as I dropped to the portal.

So long world!

"Not so fast, you silly goose!" Fingers clamped around me

once more before I could make my escape, and I was pulled into the air to see Xenocide's mad smile. "Leaving without saying *goodbye*?"

<Oh, come on!> I shouted as loudly as possible. He couldn't hear… oh right, he *could* hear me somehow!

"Where would I go?" Xenocide queried happily. "No escape for such as me! I'm actually surprised that you got a good chunk of those A-rankers! Whoever came up with the idea of sealing them in glorified shipping crates was *brilliant*! Of course, they are trapped in stasis for who knows how long, but *smart*!"

<Right, thanks, big guy.> I tried to think of anything that I could say to have him release me. <Um. Goodbye? Good luck out there?>

"Now you're catching on!" Xenocide cackled madly. "I just wanted to say *thank* you for helping me get an empty SSS-ranked dungeon Core!"

Now that I was thinking about it, I could see that the man in front of me was *bleeding*. It wasn't actually blood but some kind of Soul Energy that flowed from his body instead of the liquid of life. <I'm happy that you got what you wanted, but I *really* need to get going…>

"Oh, well, of course." Xenocide nodded and started to put me down, only to yank me back at the last second. "*Hey*! Hey, now! I almost did it! Ha! You… oh, you're a sneaky one! Now, see, what I need is a power source that can fuel my transition into this Core, and as it turns out… you are a treasure trove of **Madness**! Thank you in advance, now hold still…"

Xenocide let a spark of something appear on his finger, and the energy turned into a golden chain that wrapped around me. As soon as the chain landed on me, I was trapped in one small spot. There was no more influence for me to see out of; there was no more *reach* to my grasp. I could only feel what was coming *to* me—I could no longer *grasp* it. <What did you do to me?>

There was no sign that the man had heard me, and he continued doing… whatever it was until he glanced at a small paper he had with him. "Got the Core, got the sacrifices, reached the pinnacle of SSS, wrapped the power source in chains of chaos… I guess we just start!"

He lifted me up, positioning the *much* larger Core on his chest, and began to chant. I didn't feel anything, but I was at least faintly concerned. I was wrapped in chains of chaos? Where had I seen that before…? Rose. She had used that to hold a monster in place. The effect… was… the target couldn't affect anything around them, move, but was still aware. The spell would last for… a chaos determined amount of time. It could be one second. It could be *forever*.

The chanting was reaching a crescendo, and Xenocide started to shift the muscles in his hand. Suddenly, I was falling. I bounced off the floor and rolled back and forth until I came to a stop just in time to see a strange scene playing out. "This chase has gone on long enough."

Xenocide was standing still, his hand cut off and a sword through his chest. Kere, The Slayer of Shades, stood behind his father. Xenocide smiled, looked down at the sword, and leaned back. "Oh, I have missed this father-son bonding time! Want to go play catch? There's a giant ball coming at us right now!"

Kere lifted his sword, attempting to take the blade up the body and through Xenocide's skull… and Xenocide didn't bother resisting. As the sword cleaved through his skull, the man simply reformed the damaged areas and calmly turned around. "You know what *really* hurts me about you stabbing me like this?"

"I cannot imagine," Kere replied, holding his sword aloft.

"Being *stabbed*, you little brat!" Xenocide was suddenly behind Kere and knocked him to the floor with a slap. "You just stay there and watch me ascend, twerp!"

"How do you plan to *ascend*?" Kere groaned in reply, trying to stand and failing thanks to his now-warped spine.

"I'm going to fuel my transition to an energy being by transferring my soul through a Core!" Xenocide obligingly informed him.

"Huh." Kere winced. "Seems like you're gonna need a lot of power for that."

"I already destabilized the continent below." Xenocide managed to speak around his wide grin. "*All* of the power of an SSS-rank dungeon is going to detonate upward, and the destruction of the falling moon will generate Essence on a scale unimagined in this world!"

"So… thanks to you the world is both *ending* and being *saved*." Kere shook his head. "So glad you didn't need this then. My quest is complete. I shall happily die to take you with me."

With a flick of Kere's fingers, my Core was tossed down the hole and through my little escape portal. I heard a scream of rage, then agony, just before the portal winked out of existence and left me floating in a huge sphere of liquid Essence. My… my safe sphere on the main continent! Thousands of miles away from Xenocide! My mind was buzzing, and as I tried to process everything that had happened… the world seemed to shudder. Huge streams of Essence raced along the ley lines as Xenocide's plans came to fruition, and all I could hope was that I was the only beneficiary.

Trapped by the chains of chaos, I could do nothing to affect the world around me, and so I turned my thoughts inward. This couldn't last forever, right? Or… could it? Could something last forever? An eternity? Was that where Dungeon Eternium got his name from?

Wait, in that case, did this make *me* Dungeon Eternium?

EPILOGUE

I had gathered all the leaders of the races and the people that had been my council. I hadn't put out a call or anything; I simply whisked them over and dropped them on the ground. Even the people that had been sealed away into the specially-prepared crates—like Madame Chandra—were able to project a semblance of themselves to interact with the world, which I thought was just nifty.

I created a body for myself and stepped onto the 'ground'. The first thing I did was pull Dani and Grace over and let them get used to my new form. Dani was understandably concerned but swiftly came to terms with the change. Grace was *delighted* to have her 'daddy' be able to play with her in person, and we took a few minutes to get to know each other again.

I might have blown Grace's mind when I chased her through the ground. For me, it was as easy as swimming, as I had far more control over this space than I had even in my old dungeon. When we were all finally comfortable, Grace landed on my head, and Dani started lazily orbiting me. It was time to get to work, time to sort out the mess that had been made by dropping everyone into the same space.

<Hello, everyone!> I projected into all of their minds, making them wince. I whisked the leaders of each group, as well as people I knew personally, over to where I was standing. A few of the people looked at my body, Dale, in confusion, not realizing who I was. I thought it would be easier to give them someone to talk to when I was speaking, but I also found that this form *really* restricted my sight of the surrounding area. Not something I would use often if possible. Dani suddenly zipped around, catching their attention and stopping the stares.

"As you all know, we are inside my soul right now," I, from my mouth as Dale, informed them. "I want to know what you all want to happen and what you would like to do about a little situation we find ourselves in."

"Hi, Dale!" Hans called from the crowd I had gathered. "Nice place, buddy! Sorry for looking at you so strangely when you told all of us that you wanted us inside you! *Ow*!"

"Why, Hans?" Rose scolded him, red-faced. "*Why*?"

"Dale, *please* continue," Queen Marie ordered, her arm around King Henry.

When I told them that the world was all messed up, they nodded, bu~u~ut when I told them that I had been wrapped in chaos and there was no escape, they got a little testy and tried to kill me. Obviously, *that* wouldn't work here. I simply locked them in position and let them struggle. "My house, my rules, folks. You all agreed to my terms when you came here. Your Mana lets me do whatever I want, and I *don't* have to do *anything* for you except bring you back after you die. Now, let's try again."

"I want you to let me hunt the Wolfmen," Odin demanded, glaring at Aiden Silverfang, who offered a rude gesture in return. "When I arrived, he was hunting and killing Amazonians! They have all made a commitment to me, to serve as my Valkyries until *both* our people are restored!"

"Brother… how could you?" Tom was staring at Aiden in total shock, his worldview shattered.

"The Dark Elves must *die*!" the High Elf elder demanded,

pointing at Princess Brianna. "They came here through trickery and deceit!"

"You tried to murder us all by not granting access to the portal!" Brianna scoffed, twirling her dagger. "It's *almost* like you don't like me or something."

I cut into the outbreak with a thunderous clap. "So instead of a paradise for *all* of you, you want to kill each other and hold ancient grudges so that only a *few* of you survive?"

The instant '*Yes*' still took me by surprise somehow. "Great, well… I guess I'll split you all up and let you get at it then."

I raised my hand to send them back from where they came when a voice cut me off, "Wait! I cannot seem to use my Mana properly!"

I looked around, and by all the nods, this seemed to be a common problem. I took a look at someone, gestured him forward, and had him cast a *spell.* I watched the Mana use, how it dispersed, and most importantly, how his Mana was *lessened.*

"Interesting." I followed his Mana back to its source, finding that being surrounded by my soul caused his link to the node in the tower of ascension to be cut off. "I guess… I'll need to create a method to get you Mana again. Good thing we have forever! Until then I guess… use your Mana conservatively? It isn't coming back."

The looks of horror were priceless. When they ran out of Mana, they would essentially be regular people again or possibly worse off than before. Perhaps they would suffer horrible mana deprivation pains, and die over and over and over as I brought them back?

Happy eternity!

A man stepped forward with a sunny smile and raised a hand in greeting. Artorian was a bundle of enthusiastic pleasantry as he spoke to me directly and with warm familiarity. The headmaster—unlike a good majority of the crowd—had no issue with the experience that his disciple and oath-holder were now truly one and the same.

"Hello there, Great Spirit, my boy! I'd love to help you

figure this mess out, maybe work off some of my debt to you right away? I fluffed around a bit to have a look and had a few ideas about improvements we could put in place!"

"Sounds good, Artorian. Welcome aboard!" Dale had done a few things right for Mountaindale, namely pushing for Artorian to be hired, and the acquisition of a good administrator was certainly going to be helpful.

The projection of Madame Chandra also spoke out. "I have no interest in fighting an unceasing war. Is there something I can do to help you spruce this place up?"

"I'm sure we could find something." I banished the rest of the crowd, then reached out into my soul and pulled The Master to us. "How about you, big guy? Want to help out?"

He looked around, then felt at his new body. "So… weak…"

"You sure are, The Master!"

"No, please, I am so *sick* of that title. Would you believe that it was given to me as an anagram of my real name? Can I leave it behind and take a new name?" When I nodded, he gave a sigh of relief and smiled. "Many thanks. I wanted to leave *all* of that life behind me. I have so much information to give, and I'm sure we will find more that was hidden or forbidden on our old plane of existence."

"Let's call you 'Occultatum', then," I offered easily. "It means 'holder of hidden and forbidden knowledge'. Work for you?"

"Perfectly," the newly-christened Occultatum replied. "Ah, that reminds me! We had been discussing what we would title you as when you reached a high enough rank, and I think that we settled on a proper homage to how you use your abilities."

"What do you mean?"

Madame Chandra chimed in, "You know how I am Madame Chandra? He was 'The Master', and Barry was 'The Devourer'?"

"Yes?" I smiled politely as she rambled.

"This might not be the best time for this, but we may as well do it now. Dale, Cal, we have settled on a title for *you* as well. No matter who you are or choose to be, Cal or Dale or some amalgamation of the two… from now on, you are…" Madame Chandra and Occultatum both rested a hand on my back and pulled me in for a combined hug. Chandra finished her statement, a tear dripping down her face.

"The savior of *all* of our peoples, you have truly earned the title:"

"*The Divine Dungeon.*"

ABOUT DAKOTA KROUT

Good. Clean. Fun.

Dakota Krout is a celebrated author known for infusing fantasy novels with fun, punny, and clean humor. With multiple best-selling series—including "Divine Dungeon", "Completionist Chronicles", "Cooking With Disaster", and "Full Murderhobo" —he brings joy and laughter to readers. Dakota's work, renowned for its wit and creativity, earned a place as one of Audible's top 5 fantasy picks in 2017, a top 5 bestseller rank featured on the New York Times, and was chosen by Audible as among "the top 100 fantasy books of all time" in 2024.

Dakota's journey in publishing has been filled with gratefulness, and a deep desire to continue bringing smiles and laughter to the readers. "I hope you Read Every Book With A Smile!" - Dakota Krout

Connect with Dakota:
MountaindalePress.com
Patreon.com/DakotaKrout
Facebook.com/DakotaKrout
Twitter.com/DakotaKrout
Discord.gg/mountaindalepress

ABOUT MOUNTAINDALE PRESS

Dakota and Danielle Krout, a husband and wife team, strive to create as well as publish excellent fantasy and science fiction novels. Self-publishing *The Divine Dungeon: Dungeon Born* in 2016 transformed their careers from Dakota's military and programming background and Danielle's Ph.D. in pharmacology to President and CEO, respectively, of a small press. Their goal is to share their success with other authors and provide captivating fiction to readers with the purpose of solidifying Mountaindale Press as the place 'Where Fantasy Transforms Reality.'

Connect with Mountaindale Press:
MountaindalePress.com
Facebook.com/MountaindalePress
Twitter.com/_Mountaindale
Instagram.com/MountaindalePress

MOUNTAINDALE PRESS TITLES

GameLit and LitRPG

The Completionist Chronicles,
Cooking with Disaster,
The Divine Dungeon, and
Full Murderhobo by Dakota Krout

A Touch of Power by Jay Boyce

Red Mage and
Farming Livia by Xander Boyce

Ether Collapse and
Ether Flows by Ryan DeBruyn

Unbound by Nicoli Gonnella

Threads of Fate by Michael Head

Lion's Lineage by Rohan Hublikar and Dakota Krout

Wolfman Warlock by James Hunter and Dakota Krout

Axe Druid,
Mephisto's Magic Online, and
High Table Hijinks by Christopher Johns

Dragon Core Chronicles by Lars Machmüller

Pixel Dust and
Necrotic Apocalypse by D. Petrie

Viceroy's Pride and
Tower of Somnus by Cale Plamann

Henchman by Carl Stubblefield

Artorian's Archives by Dennis Vanderkerken and Dakota Krout

APPENDIX

Adam – A mid-D-ranked cleric who joined Dale's group. He was corrupted by a massive influx of celestial Essence which may have given him powerful abilities.

Adventurers' Guild – A group from every non-hostile race that actively seeks treasure and cultivates to become stronger. They act as a mercenary group for Kingdoms that come under attack from monsters and other non-kingdom forces.

Affinity – A person's affinity denotes what element they need to cultivate Essence from. If they have multiple affinities, they need to cultivate all of those elements at the same time.

Affinity Channel – The pathway along the meridians that Essence flows through. Having multiple major affinities will open more pathways, allowing more Essence to flow into a person's center at one time.

Aiden Silverfang – The new leader of the Northmen, this Barbarian turned Wolfman has a deep grudge against Amazonians.

Amber – The Mage in charge of the portal-making group near the dungeon. She is in the upper A-rankings, which allows her to tap vast amounts of Mana.

Artorian – The new Headmaster of the Academy. He made a deal with the dungeon to swiftly advance to the Mage ranks.

Assassin – A stealthy killer who tries to make kills without being detected by his victim.

Assimilator – A cross between a jellyfish and a Wisp, the Assimilator can float around and collect vast amounts of Essence. It releases this Essence as powerful elemental bursts. A pseudo-Mage, if you will.

Aura – The flows of Essence generated by living creatures which surround them and hold their pattern.

Barry the Devourer – A powerful S-ranked High Elf with the ability to turn all matter within a certain range into pure Essence and absorb it.

Basher – An evolved rabbit that attacks by head-butting enemies. Each has a small horn on its head that it can use to "bash" enemies.

Beast Core – A small gem that contains the Essence of Beasts.

- Flawed: An extremely weak crystallization of Essence that barely allows a Beast to cultivate, comparable to low F-rank.
- Weak: A weak crystallization of Essence that allows a Beast to cultivate, comparable to an upper F-rank.
- Standard: A crystallization of Essence that allows a Beast to cultivate well, comparable to the D-rankings.
- Strong: A crystallization of Essence that allows a Beast to cultivate very well, comparable to the lower C-rankings.

- Beastly: A crystallization of Essence that allows a Beast to cultivate exceedingly well, comparable to the upper C-rankings.
- Immaculate: An amalgamation of crystallized of Essence and Mana that allows a Beast to cultivate exceedingly well. Any Beast in the B-rankings or A-rankings will have this Core.
- Luminous: A Core of pure spiritual Essence that is indestructible by normal means. A Beast with this core will be in at least the S-rankings, up to SSS-rank.
- Radiant: A Core of Heavenly or Godly energies. A Beast with this Core is able to adjust reality on a whim.

Brianna – A Dark Elf Queen that intends to build a city around the dungeon. She is a member of the council and knows that the dungeon is alive and sentient.

Cal – The heart of the Dungeon, Cal was a human murdered by necromancers. After being forced into a soul gem, his identity was stripped as time passed. Now accompanied by Dani, he works to become stronger without attracting too much attention to himself. Too late.

Cats, dungeon – There are several types:

- Snowball: A Boss Mob, Snowball uses steam Essence to fuel his devastating attacks.
- Cloud Cat: A Mob that glides along the air, attacking from positions of stealth.
- Coiled Cat: A heavy Cat that uses metal Essence. It has a reinforced skeleton and can launch itself forward at high speeds.
- Flesh Cat: This Cat uses flesh Essence to tear apart tissue from a short distance. The abilities of this Cat

only work on flesh and veins and will not affect bone or harder materials.

- Wither Cat: A Cat full of infernal Essence, the Wither Cat can induce a restriction of Essence flow with its attacks. Cutting off the flow of Essence or Mana will quickly leave the victim in a helpless state. The process is *quite* painful.

Celestial – The Essence of Heaven, the embodiment of life and *considered* the ultimate good.

Center – The very center of a person's soul. This is the area Essence accumulates (in creatures that do not have a Core) before it binds to the Life Force.

Chandra – Owner of an extremely well-appointed restaurant, this A-ranked Mage is the grandmother of Rose. She has an unknown history with The Master.

Chi spiral – A person's Chi spiral is a vast amount of intricately knotted Essence. The more complex and complete the pattern woven into it, the more Essence it can hold and the finer the Essence would be refined.

Cleric – A Cultivator of Celestial Essence, a cleric tends to be support for a group, rarely fighting directly. Their main purpose in the lower rankings is to heal and comfort others.

Corruption – Corruption is the remnant of the matter that pure Essence was formed into. It taints Essence but allows beings to absorb it through open affinity channels. This taint has been argued about for centuries; is it the source of life or a nasty side effect?

Craig – A powerful C-ranked monk, Craig has dedicated his life to finding the secrets of Essence and passing on knowledge.

Currency values:

- Copper: one hundred copper coins are worth a silver coin
- Silver: one hundred silver coins are worth a Gold coin
- Gold: one hundred Gold coins are worth a Platinum coin
- Platinum: the highest coin currency in the Human Kingdoms

Cultivate – Cultivating is the process of refining Essence by removing corruption then cycling the purified Essence into the center of the soul.

Cultivator – A cultivator is one who cultivates. See above. Seriously, it is the entry right before this one. I'm being all alphabetical here. Mostly.

Dale – Owner of the mountain the dungeon was found on, Dale is now a cultivator who attempts to not die on a regular basis. As a dungeon born person, he has a connection to the dungeon that he can never be rid of.

Dani – A *pink* dungeon Wisp – Is that important? – Dani is the soul bound companion of Cal and acts as his moral compass and helper.

Distortion Cat – An upper C-ranked Beast that can bend light and create artificial darkness. In its home territory, it is attacked and bound by tentacle like parasites that form a symbiotic relationship with it.

Dregs – A dungeon Core that has limited intelligence. It was installed into Cal's dungeon to control floors 1-4 so Cal could focus on other things.

Dungeon Born – Being dungeon born means that the dungeon did not create the creature but gave it life. This gives the creature the ability to function autonomously without fear that the dungeon will be able to take direct control of its mind.

Dwarves – Stocky humanoids that like to work with stone, metal, and alcohol. Good miners.

Egil Nolsen – Known to the world as 'Xenocide', this man is of unknown ranking and fully insane.

Elves – A race of willowy humanoids with pointy ears. There are five main types:

- High Elves: The largest nation of Elvenkind, they spend most of their time as merchants, artists, or thinkers. Rich beyond any need to actually work, their King is an S-ranked expert, and their cities shine with light and wealth. They like to think of themselves as 'above' other Elves, thus 'High' Elves.
- Wood Elves: Wood Elves live more simply than High Elves, but have greater connection to the earth and the elements. They are ruled by a counsel of S-ranked elders and rarely leave their woods. Though seen less often, they have great power. They grow and collect food and animal products for themselves and other Elven nations.
- Wild: Wild Elves are the outcasts of their societies, basically feral, they scorn society, civilization, and the rules of others. They have the worst reputation of any of the races of Elves, practicing dark arts and infernal summoning. They have no homeland, living only where they can get away with their dark deeds.
- Dark: The Drow are known as Dark Elves. No one knows where they live, only where they can go to get

in contact with them. Dark Elves also have a dark reputation as Assassins and mercenaries for the other races. The worst of their lot are 'Moon Elves', the best-known Assassins of any race. These are the Elves that Dale made a deal with for land and protection.

- Sea: The Sea Elves live on boats their entire lives. They facilitate trade between all the races of Elves and man, trying not to take sides in conflicts. They work for themselves and are considered rather mysterious.

Essence – Essence is the fundamental energy of the universe, the pure power of heavens and earth that is used by the basic elements to become all forms of matter.

Father Richard – An A-ranked Cleric that has made his living hunting demons and heretics. Tends to play fast and loose with rules and money.

Fighter – A generic archetype of a being that uses melee weapons to fight.

Frank – Was the Guild Leader of the Adventurers' Guild. He had his Mana bound to the concept of kinetic energy and could **stop** the use of it, slowing or stopping others in place.

Grace – A *purple* dungeon Wisp – Is that important? – Grace is the offspring of Dani and Cal.

Hans – A cheeky assassin that has been with Dale since he began cultivating. He was a thief in his youth but changed lifestyles after his street guild was wiped out. He is deadly with a knife and is Dale's best friend. Now Rose's husband.

Incantation – Essentially a spell, an incantation is created from words and gestures. It releases all of the power of an enchantment in a single burst.

Infected – A person or creature that has been infected with a rage-inducing mushroom growth. These people have no control of their bodies and attack any non-infected on sight.

Infernal – The Essence of death and demonic beings, *considered* to be always evil.

Inscription – A *permanent* pattern made of Essence that creates an effect on the universe. Try not to get the pattern wrong as it could have… unintended consequences. This is another name for an incomplete or unknown Rune.

Mages' Guild – A secretive sub-sect of the Adventurers' Guild only Mage level cultivators are allowed to join.

Mana – A higher stage of Essence only able to be cultivated by those who have broken into at least the B-rankings and found the true name of something in the universe.

Meridians – Meridians are energy channels that transport life energy (Chi/Essence) throughout the body.

Mob – A shortened version of "dungeon monster".

Necromancer – An Infernal Essence cultivator who can raise and control the dead and demons.

Noble rankings:

- King/Queen – Ruler of their country. (Addressed as 'Your Majesty')
- Crown Prince/Princess – Next in line to the throne,

has the same political power as a Grand Duke. (Addressed as 'Your Royal Highness')

- Prince/Princess – Child of the King/Queen, has the same political power as a Duke. (Addressed as 'Your Highness')
- Grand Duke – Ruler of a grand duchy and is senior to a Duke. (Addressed as 'Your Grace')
- Duke – Is senior to a Marquis or Marquess. (Addressed as 'Your Grace')
- Marquis/Marquess – Is senior to an Earl and has at least three Earls in their domain. (Addressed as 'Honorable')
- Earl – Is senior to a Baron. Each Earl has three barons under their power. (Addressed as 'My Lord/Lady')
- Baron – Senior to knights, they control a minimum of ten knights and therefore their land. (Addressed as 'My Lord/Lady')
- Knights – Sub rulers of plots of land and peasants. (Addressed as 'Sir')

Pattern – A pattern is the intricate design that makes everything in the universe. An inanimate object has a far less complex pattern that a living being.

Raile – A massive, granite covered Boss Basher that attacks by ramming and attempting to squish its opponents.

Ranger – Typically an adventurer archetype that is able to attack from long range, usually with a bow.

Ranking System – The ranking system is a way to classify how powerful a creature has become through fighting and cultivation.

- G – At the lowest ranking is mostly non-organic matter such as rocks and ash. Mid-G contains small plants such as moss and mushrooms while the upper ranks form most of the other flora in the world.
- F – The F-ranks are where beings are becoming actually sentient, able to gather their own food and make short-term plans. The mid-F ranks are where most humans reach before adulthood without cultivating. This is known as the fishy or "failure" rank.
- E – The E-rank is known as the "echo" rank and is used to prepare a body for intense cultivation.
- D – This is the rank where a cultivator starts to become actually dangerous. A D-ranked individual can usually fight off ten F-ranked beings without issue. They are characterized by a "fractal" in their Chi spiral.
- C – The highest-ranked Essence cultivators, those in the C-rank usually have opened all of their meridians. A C-ranked cultivator can usually fight off ten D-ranked and one hundred F-ranked beings without being overwhelmed.
- B – This is the first rank of Mana cultivators, known as Mages. They convert Essence into Mana through a nuanced refining process and release it through a true name of the universe.
- A – Usually several hundred years are needed to attain this rank, known as High-Mage or High-Magous. They are the most powerful rank of Mages.
- S – Very mysterious Spiritual Essence cultivators. Not much is known about the requirements for this rank or those above it.
- SS – Pronounced 'Double S'. Not much is known about the requirements for this rank or those above it.

- SSS – Pronounced 'Triple S'. Not much is known about the requirements for this rank or those above it.
- Heavenly – Not much is known about the requirements for this rank or those above it.
- Godly – Not much is known about the requirements for this rank or those above it.

Rose – A Half Elf ranger that joined Dale's team. She has opposing affinities for celestial and infernal Essence, making her a chaos cultivator.

Rune – A *permanent* pattern made of Essence that creates an effect on the universe. Try not to get the pattern wrong as it could have… unintended consequences. This is another name for a completed Inscription.

Silverwood tree – A mysterious tree that has silver wood and leaves. Some say that it helps cultivators move into the B-rankings.

Soul Stone – A *highly* refined Beast Core that is capable of containing a human soul.

Tank – An adventurer archetype that is built to defend his team from the worst of the attacks that come their way. Heavily armored and usually carrying a large shield, these powerful people are needed if a group plans on surviving more than one attack.

Tom – A huge red-haired barbarian prince from the northern wastes, he wields a powerful warhammer and has joined Dale's team. He is only half as handy to have around right now.

Xan – A *green* dungeon Wisp that Xan is the Wisp bonded to Dregs.

www.ingramcontent.com/pod-product-compliance
Lightning Source LLC
Chambersburg PA
CBHW020221260626
47156CB00002B/487
9781950914098